Games Traitors Play

Jon Stock is the author of four spy novels and a columnist with The Week magazine in India. He lives in Wiltshire with his wife and three children.

Also by Jon Stock

The Riot Act
The Cardamom Club
Dead Spy Running

JON STOCK

Games Traitors Play

blue door

Blue Door
An imprint of HarperCollins*Publishers*
77–85 Fulham Palace Road,
Hammersmith, London W6 8JB

www.harpercollins.co.uk

Published by Blue Door 2011
1

Copyright © Jon Stock 2011

Jon Stock asserts the moral right to
be identified as the author of this work

A catalogue record for this book is
available from the British Library

ISBN: 978-0-00-730072-3 (Hardback)
978-0-00- 730073-0 (Trade Paperback)

Typeset in Minion by Palimpsest Book Production Limited,
Falkirk, Stirlingshire

Printed and bound in Great Britain by
Clays Ltd, St Ives plc

FSC   © 1996 Forest Stewardship Council

FSC is a non-profit international organization established
to promote the responsible management of the world's forests.
Products carrying the FSC label are independently certified
to assure consumers that they come from forests that are managed
to meet the social, economic and ecological needs
of present and future generations.

Find out more about HarperCollins and the environment at
www.harpercollins.co.uk/green

*In memory of
my father Peter Stock*

'For while the treason I detest, the traitor still I love'

John Hoole

1

A hot afternoon in Marrakech, and the square was already full of people and promise. If the storyteller was aware of the crowd around him, he didn't show it. The old man sipped at his sweet mint tea and sat down on a plastic chair, first brushing something off it with his empty hand. Had he looked up, he would have seen men and women surge across the square like iron filings, drawn by the magnetism of his act. But he never raised his head, not until he was ready to begin his tale.

Daniel Marchant wondered if he prayed in these moments, or was just running a mental finger over the bookshelves, choosing his narrative. He had been watching this particular storyteller – or *halaka* – for a week now, convinced that he held the answer to a question that had occupied every waking hour and all of his dreams since he had arrived in Morocco three months earlier.

From his vantage point on the rooftop terrace of the Café Argana, Marchant was able to watch the half-dozen *halakas* who worked the northern end of Djemaâ el Fna square. None of the others drew a crowd like this one, with his cobalt-blue turban, untidy teeth and cheap pebble glasses that magnified his eyes. Locals came for the stories, tourists for the photos, unable to understand a word but swept along by the drama.

This *halaka* could tell a thousand and one different tales of dervishes and djinns, each one recounted as if, like Queen Scheherazade, his own life depended on it. Marchant had learned that storytelling had been in his Berber family for centuries, passed down from father to son. In his hands, the tradition was safe, despite the rival temptations of Egyptian television soap operas. And he knew just when to pause, leaving his story on a knife edge. Only when the money bowl had been passed around would he continue.

On a good day, he was even more of a draw than the Gnaoua musicians from the Sahara who somersaulted and swirled their way through the crowds down by the smoky food stalls. When he was talking, the square's snake charmers rested their cobras, fire-eaters paused for breath, even the travelling dentists put down their dentures and tools.

Marchant sat up in his chair, sensing that the time had almost come. He wasn't sure how the *halaka* judged when the crowd had reached critical mass. The man was a natural showman, milking the moment every afternoon when he finally lifted his sunbeaten face and surveyed his audience with a defiant stare. Marchant reached for his camera, focusing the lens on the top of the man's turban. The storyteller's head was still bent forward, concealing his face.

The lens was not the sort that could be bought in a camera shop, but anyone watching Marchant would not have suspected that it was many times more powerful than its innocuous length suggested. He appeared like just another tourist as he slid it through the ornate metal latticework of the restaurant railing and observed the scene below him. Except that a tourist might have taken a few photos, particularly when the *halaka* finally looked up to address his expectant crowd. But Marchant forgot he was watching through a camera, forgot his cover. He could see that the man in his lens was frightened.

Marchant had come to know the *halaka*'s assured mannerisms, the tricks of his trade. The street wisdom of yesterday had vanished, his stage presence replaced by fear. He should have been staring ahead, hypnotising his audience with a narrator's spell, but instead the man's eyes flitted to the back of the crowd, as if he were searching for someone. Pulling on the hem of his grey *djellaba*, the local head-to-toe garment, he rocked on his battered *baboush* slippers, shifting his weight from heel to toe. For perhaps the first time in his life, the storyteller appeared lost for words.

Marchant checked with his own eyes, as if the camera might be lying, and then looked again through the lens. He took some photos, cursing himself for his slackness, and scanned the back of the crowd. The man was here somewhere, he was sure of it, waiting to hear the *halaka*'s coded phrases that would send him off into the snow-tipped Atlas Mountains to the south of the city. And Marchant would follow, wherever the man went, however remote, knowing who the message was for.

For several weeks, Marchant had been convinced that someone was planning to make contact with Salim Dhar through the story-tellers of Marrakech. He had overheard something in the souks, a fleeting remark in amongst the chatter. Using the *halakas* was a primitive form of communication for the world's most wanted terrorist, but that was the point. Echelon, the West's intelligence-analysis network, was in meltdown, monitoring every email, phone call, text and Twitter for the faintest trace of Dhar. It had been ever since he had tried to assassinate the US President in Delhi the previous year. Every time the analysts at Fort Meade in Maryland thought they had found him, the information was relayed to the CIA's headquarters in Langley. Its drone strikes in Af-Pak, where most of the sightings were reported, were now running at thirty a month.

But Dhar was still free, on the run. And Marchant was certain that no amount of software would ever find him. Dhar was shunning technology, keeping one step ahead of the modern world by retreating into the old. Ancient oral traditions, such as the *halakas*, were beyond the range of the spy planes and stealth satellites that orbited the globe in ever more desperate circles.

It had worked for fugitives before. During the 1970s, when General Oufkir was Morocco's hardline interior minister, the *halakas* used code words to refer to him and alert the public to planned raids by his secret police. Snakes were more than serpents sliding through the narrative: they were warnings of time and place. It was a way of communicating without suspicion. Information could be passed anonymously, without one-to-one meetings: textbook tradecraft. And now the *halaka* was about to issue another message.

Marchant pushed his tea away, folded some *dirhams* under the silver pot, and went to the stairwell. He knew he didn't have long.

Down in the square, a man approached him from a narrow alley to one side of the café.

'Hashish? You want some hashish?'

Marchant managed a smile. His student cover must have been convincing. Officially, he was in Morocco for a PhD on Berber culture, and took his studies very seriously. His dirt-blond hair was cut short, and he was wearing a woollen *djellaba*.

'Thanks, no,' he said, walking on towards the crowd.

'Souk tour? Leather? Instruments? I show you Led Zeppelin photos. Mr Robert, he came to my friend's shop.'

Marchant ignored him and walked on. He could do without the attention. The tout was not giving up, though, trotting along beside him, pouring out a list of random words that he must have gleaned over the years, like a magpie, from visiting tourists.

'Which place are you from, Berber man? London? I know UK. Yorkshire pudding, 73 bus, Sheffield steel.'

4

But the tout was losing interest. He peeled away, calling half-heartedly after Marchant, 'M&S? A303?'

Marchant had almost joined the crowd now. He didn't want any trouble in future from this man, so he raised a hand in a friendly farewell, his back to him.

'Terrorist,' the tout said, loud enough for one or two people at the edge of the crowd to turn around. Marchant had been called a few things in Marrakech, but this was a first. The choice of that term of abuse was nothing more than an unfortunate coincidence, he told himself, but he scanned the square again. Most of the sellers had got to know him in the past few months, letting the diligent British student practise his Berber on them. This tout was new to the area. Marchant threw him another glance. He was now leading two female tourists into the medina, looking at their map. Was it a CIA cover? Did someone else share his suspicions of the *halaka*?

The Americans had kept an eye on Marchant when he had first arrived in Marrakech, but they had soon lost interest, believing that the British agent was barking up the wrong tree. Langley was sure that Salim Dhar wasn't in North Africa, but had headed north after attempting to assassinate the President, smuggling himself across the Kashmir border in a goods lorry. The trail had gone cold in Pakistan, as it so often did, and they assumed he was now in hiding on the north-west border with Afghanistan, along with many of America's other most wanteds.

Marchant joined the back of the crowd and listened, watching the people around him. They had already fallen under the spell of the *halaka*, who had regained his composure. As he listened to the story of Sindbad the sailor, Marchant wished his Berber was better. He was back lying on the floor of his childhood home in the Cotswolds. A recording of Sindbad was the first vinyl album his father had ever bought him. For weeks after playing it on the big old wooden-cased HMV player, Marchant had had nightmares about the Roc bird, terrified that the skies would darken with its enormous wings.

The *halaka* had paused. Marchant watched him closely, the droplets of sweat beading his brow. He had caught the eye of someone near the back of the crowd, holding his gaze for barely a second. Marchant had clocked the man earlier, a Berber, early twenties, calico skullcap. Marchant waited for the *halaka* to begin speaking again – of giant serpents and the Roc bird – and then glanced back at the man. But he was already gone, walking briskly across the square, trying not to break into a run.

2

The six US Marines had been travelling all night and most of the day, bound, gagged and blindfolded. But now the 4x4 had come to a stop, giving their bruised bodies a brief respite. The vehicle's suspension was shot through, and they had been driven over poor mountainous tracks. No one, though, was under any illusion about what lay ahead: if they had reached the end of their journey, they were close to the end of their lives.

They had expected to die the night before, when a group of Taleban insurgents had ambushed their radio reconnaissance unit on a notorious stretch of road near Gayan in Paktika, eastern Afghanistan. They should have been in Helmand with the rest of their Marine Expeditionary Force, but had been seconded to Paktika in a push to hunt down the local Pashtun warlord, Sirajuddin Haqqani. After a stand-off, waiting in vain for the air support they had called in, the Marines had stepped out from behind their disabled Hummer with their arms up, exhausted, expecting to be shot. But the Taleban had taken them prisoner. It was a high-risk strategy: the US response would be on an overwhelming scale. The AC-130 gunships, though, never showed, and the Taleban moved out quickly with their captives.

The rear and side doors of the 4x4 opened and two Taleban began to pull the Marines from the vehicle, grabbing the collars of their sweat-soaked fatigues. As their platoon commander, Lieutenant Randall Oaks knew he had to be strong, set an example for the others, but in truth he wished he had been shot the previous night. He thought of the videos of beheadings he had told himself not to watch before coming out to Afghanistan, the stories that had circulated in the camp when they had first flown in from North Carolina. It wasn't good to be a prisoner of the Taleban.

Oaks could tell through his blindfold that the daylight was dying. It was cooler, too, compared to Gayan, where they had been ambushed, and he had been aware of gaining height during the long drive. If they were being taken to the mountains, maybe they could hope to live for a few more days. They would become bargaining chips, a way to buy some advantage in a war that neither side was ever going to win. But now he sensed another agenda.

None of their Taleban captors said anything as they pushed the Marines along a track. Oaks could hear the others stumbling, like him, on the rocky terrain, but there was one noise that was different. The Taleban were dragging someone along, a Marine who was too weak to walk. Oaks knew it was Lance Corporal Troy Murray. They were a tight-knit unit, had been ever since they had arrived five months earlier, but Murray had stood out for all the wrong reasons from the start. It wasn't just the word 'INFIDEL' that he had had tattooed in big letters across his chest. He was physically the weakest and mentally a mess, unable to go out on patrol unless he had taken too many psychological meds. This was his fourth tour, and he should never have been sent.

One more month and they were due to return to Camp Lejeune. Their families' banners would soon be up on the fencing that ran along Route 24 outside the base, joining the mile upon mile of 'Missed you' and 'Welcome home' messages that had become a part of the North Carolina landscape. It was a public patchwork of loss, each banner telling a private story, of missed births, heart-ache, lonely nights, enforced chastity.

Oaks remembered the first time he saw them, returning from his inaugural tour of Iraq. Envious cheers had gone up on the bus when Murray, in happier days, had seen his: 'Get ready for a long de-briefing, stud muffin.' And then he had seen his own, written in bright purple felt-tip on a big bedsheet, near the main gate: 'Welcome Home Lieutenant Daddy. Just in time for the terrible twos.' He was a family man now.

In recent days, the platoon had begun to brag about what they would do when they got home. Visit the clubs in Wilmington: The Whiskey, The Rox; shoot the breeze on Onslow Beach, listen out for the bell of the man selling snowballs. But there was only one thing now on Oaks's list: to become a more loving husband, a less absent father. He would attend church every Sunday, every day if necessary. As an adult, he had never been religious, but in the past twenty-four hours he had prayed with a desperate intensity, trying in vain to remember the brief period in his childhood when he had fallen asleep in prayer, risen early to read the Bible at the kitchen table. Within the last hour, as his own elusive faith had slipped through his hands like desert sand, he had even attempted to address other people's gods, too, explaining, apologising, beseeching.

The group was being herded into what felt like a small farm outbuilding. The few outdoor sounds – faint wind, distant birdsong – were partly muffled, but not entirely. It was as if they were surrounded by walls, but were still outside. Above their heads, Oaks thought he could hear the sound of a canopy flapping. Before he could think any more about their location, he was pushed down to the dry floor, his back up against an uneven wall. The gag in his mouth was peeled up and a bottle of water put to his chafed lips. He drank deeply until the bottle was pulled away, his gag replaced. It was not as tight as it had been, though, and Oaks began at once to work his jaw, keeping it moving.

The removal of his sight had heightened his other senses. He knew there were two Taleban with them. One was administering the water, but what was the other doing? He listened above the delirious moaning of Murray, who sounded barely conscious. There was the click of a case and the sound of something metallic being placed high up on a wall, on a windowsill perhaps. Was it an Improvised Explosive Device, set to be triggered by their movement? There was silence again. The two Taleban were leaving them. There were more muffled moans from the men, sounds of primitive despair as they dug their boot heels deep into the mud.

Oaks heard the 4x4 start up outside. He was expecting some wheelspin, a triumphant circling of the prisoners before it roared off. But the vehicle just drove back down the track, as casually as his father's station wagon when he used to leave for work, until the sound of its engine was lost in the stillness of the night. That slowness terrified him. It was too calm, too rehearsed, indicative of a bigger plan.

Ten, maybe fifteen minutes later, his thoughts were interrupted by the sound of someone speaking Urdu, coming from close by. Oaks's tired brain struggled to work out what was happening, whether he was hallucinating. He tried to focus on the name the man had given when he first spoke. It hung in the air above them like a paper kite, nagging at Oaks's mind as it bobbed in the evening breeze: Salim.

3

This was the moment Omar Rashid had been trained for, but he had never actually expected it to happen, not to him. But there it was, an unambiguous flashing light on his console. He knew his life would never be the same again. He was just a junior analyst on the SIGINT graveyard shift, always had been, ever since he'd signed up to the National Security Agency at Fort Meade in Maryland. And that was exactly how he liked it. Success happened to the ambitious, to the hungry. Rashid was more than happy to draw his modest salary and listen through the night to the regional traffic, before heading home to his basement apartment in Baltimore. He enjoyed his work, but it wasn't loyalty to the NSA that drove him.

A few hours earlier, he had tuned in to a pro-Western Pakistani politician and his wife arguing on a phone in Lahore. Later, when the husband had returned to his home in a wealthy suburb, he had listened to them making love, too, thanks to a wire installed in the bedroom by the ISI, Pakistan's main intelligence agency. The ISI was unaware that its heavily encrypted surveillance frequencies had been breached, but Rashid didn't concern himself about that. Just as he tried not to dwell on the pleasure he derived from such interceptions, known as 'vinegar strokes' among the nightshift analysts. He had feigned indifference when he handed in his transcript to the line manager, but it was a gift, and he hoped she would enjoy it later. Didn't everyone at SIGINT City?

This, though, was different. The flashing light was an Echelon Level Five alert, triggered by a keyword integral to one of Fort Meade's biggest-ever manhunts. Rashid's able mind worked fast. Despite Echelon's best efforts, it was impossible for the West to monitor more than a fraction of the world's phone calls and emails in real time. Most of the daily 'take' was recorded and crunched later by NSA's data miners, who drilled down through the traffic, searching for suspicious patterns. They worked out in Utah, where a vast data silo had been built in the desert. Rashid was one of a handful of Urdu analysts who worked in the now. He cast his net each day on the Af-Pak waters and waited.

Real-time analysts knew where to listen, but the odds of catching anyone were still stacked against them. As a result, Rashid was left alone. Anything he could bring to the table was a bonus. But if this latest intercept was what the flashing light suggested it was, he would be fêted, hailed as a hero. His work would suddenly be the centre of attention. A manager would study his previous reports, discover a pattern, the unnaturally high number of bedroom intercepts. Someone would sniff the vinegar.

The keyword and a set of coordinates in North Waziristan were triggering alarms all over the system. Rashid adjusted his headphones. He was listening to one half of a mobile-phone conversation in Urdu: the other person must have been speaking on an encrypted handset. COMINT would track it down later, unpick its rudimentary ciphers. The voiceprint-recognition software had already kicked in, analysing the speaker's vocal cavities and articulator patterns: the interplay of lips, teeth, tongue. Rashid didn't need a computer to tell him whose voice it was. The whole of Fort Meade knew it. It had been played over the building's intercom in the months after the attempt on the President's life.

Photos of the would-be assassin were on every noticeboard, along with details of the bonus for any employee who helped bring about his capture.

In a few seconds, Rashid would have details of the mobile number's provenance and history. Occasionally, this yielded something, but ninety-nine times out of a hundred it was a clean pay-as-you-go phone, bought over the counter in a backstreet booth in Karachi. Rashid's supervisor arrived at his shoulder just as the screen started to blink.

'You got something for me, Omar?' she said, more in hope than expectation.

Rashid nodded at his computer, feeling his mouth go dry. Two lights were now flashing. The number had been used once before, in south India, days before the assassination attempt on the President in Delhi. It was the last time Salim Dhar had made a call on a mobile phone.

'Sweet holy mother of Jesus, you've been fishing,' the supervisor whispered, one hand on his shoulder. With the other, she picked up Rashid's phone, still staring at his screen. 'Get me James Spiro at Langley. Tell him it's a real-time Level Five.'

4

Marchant had nearly lost the man several times in the network of narrow lanes off Djemaâ el Fna. He appeared to be heading south, walking fast down the rue de Bab Agnaou, occasionally looking behind him, but only at junctions, where he could pass off the glances as normal behaviour. The man knew what he was doing. Marchant kept as much distance as he dared between them, but he was on his own. In normal circumstances, a surveillance team of six would be moving through the streets with him, ahead of and behind the target like an invisible cocoon, covering every possibility. Marchant had no such luxury.

He kept one eye out for a taxi as the street widened. It was a less popular part of town for foreigners, and he needed to work harder to blend in. Instead of shoe shops selling yellow *baboush* and stalls piled high with pyramids of dates and almonds, there were noisy industrial units, larger and less welcoming than the tourist-friendly workshops in the medina. Marchant would follow the man like-for-like. It helped the pursuer to think like his target, to try to anticipate his choices. If he had a car parked somewhere, Marchant would find a car. If he got onto a bicycle, Marchant would find a bicycle.

The man had stopped outside what seemed to be a small carpet factory. Marchant hung back in the shadow of an empty doorway, fifty yards down the street. He could hear the sound of looms weaving, shuttles shooting. Bundles of wool hung from an upstairs window, the rich cupreous dyes drying in the low sun. A woman came to the factory entrance. She chatted briefly with the man, looking up and down the street as she spoke, and pressed a key into his hand.

Without hesitating, the man walked around the corner, started up an old motorised bike and drove off slowly, blue smoke belching from the two-stroke engine. For a moment, Marchant wondered if it would be easier to pursue him on foot, but he checked himself: like-for-like. Despite being in a hurry, the man had specifically chosen low-key transport. He was trying not to draw attention to himself, which suggested he was worried about being followed or watched.

Marchant crossed the road to a row of parked mopeds. Marrakech was overrun with Mobylettes and other Parisian-style motorised bikes, a legacy of when Morocco was a French protect-orate. They weaved in and out of the tourists and shoppers in the souks, taking priority like the cows in the markets of old Delhi, which he used to visit on his ayah's shoulders as a child.

He glanced at the selection. There was an old blue Motobecane 50V Mobylette, top speed 30 mph, and a couple of more modern Peugeot Vogues. The Mobylette was slower, but it would be easier to start, and the man was already out of sight, the noise of his engine fading fast. It also held a certain appeal for Marchant. For years, the Mobylette was made under licence in India. A few months before his father finished his second posting in Delhi, the family had presented Chandar, their cook, with one, to replace his old Hero bicycle. Chandar used to maintain it lovingly, showing Marchant, then eight years old, how to start it, both of them laughing as Chandar pedalled furiously in his chef's whites until the engine coughed into life.

Marchant checked that the Mobylette's wheel forks weren't locked. Nothing he had done since his arrival in Marrakech had aroused any attention from the authorities. That was part of the deal, one of the conditions he had agreed with MI6 in return for being sent to Morocco and allowed to operate on his own. He hadn't wanted back-up or support. It was, after all, a very personal quest: family business, as his father would have called it. Marcus Fielding, the professorial Chief of MI6, had agreed, knowing that if anyone could find Salim Dhar, it was Marchant. But Fielding had warned him: no drinking, no brawls, no break-ins, nothing illegal. He had caused enough trouble already in his short career.

Marchant had kept his side of the bargain. For three months, he had stayed off the sauce, savouring life outside Legoland, MI6's headquarters in Vauxhall. The CIA had prevented him from leaving Britain in the aftermath of the assassination attempt, but after a frustrating year, Fielding had finally prevailed, much to Marchant's relief. London was no place for a field agent.

He had studied hard in Marrakech's libraries, researching the history of the Berbers and taking the opportunity to reread the Koran. It had been required reading during his time at Fort Monckton, MI6's training base on the end of the Gosport peninsula. But he read it now with renewed interest, searching for anything that might help him to understand Salim Dhar's world.

In the cool of the early mornings, he had gone running through the deserted medina. The first run had been the hardest, not because his body was out of shape, but because of the memories it brought back: the London Marathon, Leila, their time together. He had returned after two miles, in need of a stiff drink, but he managed to keep his promise to Fielding. After two weeks, he no longer missed the Scotch. In a Muslim country, abstinence was easier than he had feared it would be. And he realised that he no longer missed Leila. It felt as if life was starting anew.

In the year following Leila's death, he had been unable to go running. He had missed her every day, seen her face wherever he went in London. The coldness that had encased his heart since he arrived in Morocco had shocked him at first, but he knew it had to be if he was to survive in the Service. His trained eye had spotted one suicide bomber amongst 35,000 participants, but he had failed to identify the traitor running at his own side, the woman he had loved.

Now, though, he was about to cross a line, and for a moment he felt the buzz he'd been missing. It was hardly a big breach, but if someone reported a foreigner stealing a Mobylette, there was a small chance that the local police would become involved. A report might be filed. He would show up on the grid, however faintly, and he couldn't afford to do that. London would recall him. He would be back behind a desk in Legoland, analysing embellished CX reports from ambitious field agents, drinking too much at the Morpeth Arms after work. But he couldn't afford to lose his man.

He glanced up and down the street. No one was around. He sat on the Mobylette, which was still on its stand. He checked the fuel switch, then began pedalling, thinking of Chandar as he worked the choke and the compressor with his thumbs. The engine started up, and he rocked the bike forward, throttled back and set off down the road. It wasn't exactly a wheelspin start.

As the Mobylette struggled to reach 25 mph, the only thing on Marchant's mind was where the man could be heading on a motorised pedal bike. Marchant had assumed all along that if he was right about the *halaka*, the contact would carry his message south into the High Atlas mountains, to Asni and beyond to the Tizi'n'Test pass, where the Moroccan Islamic Combatant Group (GICM) was known to run remote training camps (it had others in the Rif mountains, too).

The GICM had its roots in the war against the former Soviet Union in Afghanistan, and had forged close ties with al Q'aeda, providing logistical support to operatives passing through Morocco. After 9/11, it had become more proactive, and a number of sleeper cells were activated. The synchronised bombings in Casablanca in 2003, which had killed forty-four people, bore all the hallmarks of GICM, and the leadership had helped with the recruitment of *jihadis* for the war in Iraq. Marchant was convinced, after three months in Marrakech, that the organisation was now shielding Salim Dhar in the mountains. But the smoking bike ahead of him would struggle to reach the edge of town, let alone make it up the steep climb to Asni.

5

Lieutenant Oaks had worked the wet gag loose enough to speak. It was still in his mouth, but the tension had gone and he was able to make himself heard.

'Everyone OK?' he asked, breathing heavily. He could tell from the grunted responses that the others had been propped against the wall on either side of him, two to the left, two to the right. Only one of them hadn't replied.

'Where's Murray?' Oaks asked. There was a faint reply from across the room. At least he was still alive. Outside, the noises of an Afghanistan night offered little comfort: the distant cries of a pack of wild dogs. The Urdu had stopped a few minutes earlier, and Oaks was now certain whose voice it had been.

'We don't have long,' he said, edging himself across the floor to what he hoped was the centre of the hut. Movement was difficult, painful. His legs were bound tight at the ankles, and his wrists had been shackled together high up behind his back, his arms bent awkwardly. No one moved, and he wondered if any of them had understood his distorted words.

'We've got to get into the centre, right here,' he continued, falling on his side. He lay there for a few seconds, his cheek on the mud floor. It smelt vaguely of animals, of the stables he had visited in West Virginia for a childhood birthday. They had minutes to live,

19

and he only had one shot at saving them. 'Get your asses over here!' he shouted, his voice choking with the effort of trying to right himself. 'Jesus, guys, don't you get it?'

He heard the shuffle of fatigues across the floor. 'Is that you, Jimmy? Leroy? Bunch up tight, all of you.' Slowly, the Marines dragged themselves into the centre of the room, even Murray, who was the last to arrive, rolling himself over on the dry mud. He lay at Oaks's feet, listening to his leader, breathing irregularly.

'That voice,' Oaks said, composing himself, frustrated by his distorted words. He was sounding like the deaf boy in his class at high school. 'It was Salim Dhar's.' He worked his jaw again, trying to shake off the sodden gag. No one said anything. They still hadn't realised the implications. 'A UAV will be on its way, you understand that? A drone. The fucking Reaper's coming.'

Murray let out a louder moan. Oaks tried not to think about the two Hellfire missiles he had once seen being loaded under an MQ-1 Predator at Balad airbase in Iraq. The kill chain had been shortened since then. There was no longer the same delay. And the MQ-1 Predator had become the MQ-9 Reaper, a purpose-built hunter/killer with five-hundred-pound bombs as well as Hellfires.

America had learned its lessons after it had once seen Mullah Omar, the one-eyed leader of the Taleban, in the crosswires of an armed Predator. It was in October 2001, a few weeks after 9/11, and the CIA had wanted to fire at Omar's convoy of 4x4s, but the decision was referred upwards to top brass in the Pentagon, who consulted lawyers and withheld the order while Omar stopped to pray at a mosque. The moment passed, and the story, true or false, entered military folklore. Americans had been trying to make amends ever since, taking out hundreds of Taleban and al Q'aeda targets with pilotless drones, or UAVs, but Oaks knew that the military had never quite got over the Omar incident. Now the Taleban was taunting them again.

'We'll show up on the UAV's thermal imaging,' Oaks said. 'This lousy cowshed's just got a sheet for a roof.' He had little confidence in his plan, but he had to try something. He owed it to his daughter. 'Do exactly as I say, and pray to your God.'

6

Marchant knew as soon as the man pulled into the petrol station that he was going in for an upgrade. The bike had made it five miles out of Marrakech on the R203, across the dry plains south of the city, but it was now starting to struggle. His own Mobylette was suffering too, and the frosted mountains were looming, floating on the horizon in the evening light. But it wasn't the scenery that interested Marchant: it was the group of touring motorbikes that had stopped to refuel at the station. His mind was beginning to think like a thief's. He pulled up two hundred yards short of the garage, bought a bottle of mineral water from a roadside stall, and drank deeply, watching the dusty forecourt.

There were at least ten bikes, powerful tourers laden down with carriers covered in ferry stickers and English flags. Marchant knew from his three months in Marrakech that Morocco was a popular 'raid' for British bikers. He had seen them rumbling into town on their way to the Atlas Mountains, where the roads were good and the passes were among the highest in Africa.

The riders, bulked out in their padded leathers, had crowded around one bike. It was set apart from the others, next to a support Land Rover Defender. A man was lying on the ground beside the back wheel. The bike seemed to have a mechanical problem of some sort, and the group was deep in discussion, talking animatedly with two local guides. The other bikes were unattended. If the keys were in the ignition, it would be easy for the man to set off on one of them. But he drove past the bikes, past the petrol pumps, and parked his moped on the far side of the forecourt shop. He then walked around the back of the building, out of sight.

What was he doing? Marchant kept watching as he slipped the lid back onto the plastic bottle of water. Moments later, the man reappeared, helmeted and riding a powerful touring bike. As if making a token check for traffic, he looked back down the dusty road in Marchant's direction – was he taunting him? – and was gone, roaring off towards Asni and the mountains.

Marchant felt sick. He was about to lose his man. He also knew that he was right, that Salim Dhar was up there somewhere in the High Atlas. And that made his stomach tighten so much that he wanted to throw up. The only good thing was that none of the bikers had clocked the man as he had driven off. In Marchant's experience, bikers usually checked out each other's hardware, but they were too preoccupied with their own broken machine.

Marchant remounted his Mobylette and rode up to the garage. He switched the engine off before he turned into the forecourt, and freewheeled silently for the last twenty yards. He passed the first two bikes, checking the ignitions. Neither had a key. But the third, a BMW GS Adventure, did. Marchant parked up beyond it and glanced once in the direction of the group. It was then that he realised that the man on the ground was not trying to mend the bike. He was the focus of the group's attention, and he was lying very still. The bikers were too far away for Marchant to hear what they were saying, but he thought he heard someone mention a doctor.

Ignoring an instinctive urge to go over and help, Marchant switched quickly from his moped to the tourer, turned the ignition and felt the 1150cc engine rumble into life beneath him. Without looking up, he moved off the forecourt, joined the main road, and accelerated slowly away from the garage, heading for Mount Toubkal, the highest peak on the horizon.

7

James Spiro had not enjoyed his job with the CIA since he had been moved to Head of Clandestine, Europe. It was a promotion, and should have been rewarding, a few comfortable years in London before he returned to Virginia for greater things. But he hadn't counted on Salim Dhar proving so elusive. Ever since he had slipped through the net in India, Dhar had been Spiro's biggest headache. He would wake at night, sheets drenched in sweat, seeing his President take the bullet that had somehow missed him in Delhi. His in-tray was full of daily requests from the Pentagon, the White House, the media, all wanting to know where Dhar was and why he hadn't been eliminated. And in his darkest moments, he couldn't stop thinking of Leila, the woman who had died instead of the President, the woman he had slept with only hours before.

Spiro knew his career hung in the balance, which was why he was now back on home soil, coordinating the Agency's biggest manhunt since the search for Osama bin Laden after 9/11. There had been dozens of credible sightings of Dhar around the world, each one proving false, each one ratcheting up the pressure on Spiro to find him. The collateral damage from drone strikes hadn't helped his cause. The last one, in Pakistan, based on an ISI tip-off, had killed thirty civilians, mostly women and children.

And what were America's greatest allies doing to help? Diddly shit. London's relationship with Dhar was 'delicate', according to Marcus Fielding. Dubious, more like. Daniel Marchant, the one person who might be able to find Dhar, was on vacation in North Africa, if such a thing was possible, eating too much couscous in Marrakech. If it had been up to Spiro, Marchant would have been strapped back onto the waterboard, telling them all he knew about Dhar, rather than being allowed to wander around Morocco's souks as if nothing had happened.

Now, though, the end seemed finally in sight. It was always going to be only a matter of time until Dhar made a mistake.

'Run me those coordinates again,' he said to the operator next to him. He was standing in the 'cockpit', a hot and crowded trailer, also known as a mobile Ground Control Station, in a quiet corner of Creech US Air Force Base, Nevada. In front of him, two operatives were seated in high-backed chairs, each monitoring a bank of screens. One was a pilot with 42 Attack Squadron, a seasoned officer in his forties who used to fly F-16 fighter jets but was now directing MQ-9 Reapers, the most advanced hunter/killer drones in the world. The other was his sensor operator, a woman no older than twenty-five who controlled the Reaper's multi-spectral targeting suite.

Spiro had spent a lot of his time at Creech in recent weeks, too much for his liking. And he had eaten too many Taco Bells in Las Vegas, thirty-five miles south-east. Creech used to be a bare-bones facility, a rocky outpost in the desert, but now it resembled a building site. New hangars were going up all the time around the main airstrip, which had once been used for landing practice by pilots from the nearby Nellis Air Force Base. Spiro found it hard to believe that such a bleak, uninhabited place represented the future of aerial combat. But he guessed that was the point: the USAF's first squadron of Reapers was unmanned.

The pilot in front of him read out the coordinates. Dhar's voice had been traced to a remote location in North Waziristan, on the borders of Pakistan and Afghanistan. Fort Meade had done a good job for once. Someone had been listening in real time, and not just to Pakistani generals having sex. This was the big one, and there was a palpable sense of excitement in the cockpit, even from the base commander. He had stepped into the trailer when news spread across the base that Salim Dhar might be about to be taken down. It would be a big moment for the commander. His unit, 432 Air Expeditionary Wing, had stood up at Creech in 2007 to spearhead the global war on terror, and he needed a result. Spiro knew the commander blamed the CIA for the recent spate of bad publicity. The last strike in Pakistan had brought relations between the Agency and the USAF to a new low.

'I think we have our man,' Spiro said, turning to the commander.

'We need to do this by the book,' he replied. 'You know that.'

'Of course. And the book says we take Dhar out. We have an 80-per-cent confidence threshold.'

'Are there any legals?' the commander asked, turning to an officer next to him.

'Negative, sir. Potential for civilian collateral is zero. The building is remote, nearest population cluster five miles south. And this is a Level Five.'

'Colonel, we're locked onto the target,' the pilot said, turning to the sensor operator. 'Can you put thermal up on screen one?'

Spiro watched as blotches of bright colour appeared on the screen between the two seated operators. The surrounding screens were relaying live video streams from electro-optical and image-intensified night cameras mounted under the nose of the Reaper, and stills from a synthetic aperture radar. Spiro still hadn't quite got his head round the fact that these images were streaming live, give or take a one-to-two-second delay, from 30,000 feet above Afghanistan, 7,500 miles away.

'Fuse thermal with intensified,' the pilot said. The image on the main screen sharpened a little, but it was still no more than a series of yellow, red and purple shapes.

It was at this point that the young female analyst first began to worry about their target. She wasn't meant to be on duty now. The 24/7 rota they worked to had lost its shape in the previous few hours, and she should have been back in her room, getting some sleep and reading the bible before her next shift. (A lot of the analysts headed off to Vegas after work, but she found the contrast too great: one moment looking at magnified images of a destroyed Taleban target, the next shooting craps.) But the next analyst on duty had phoned in sick, and she had agreed to work on until cover showed up. That was two hours ago. She didn't like bending the rules. She tried to leave a quiet, disciplined life. All she could hope for was that the base commander didn't glance at the rota sheet on the wall behind them.

'Sir, we have multiple personnel in the target zone,' she said, looking closely at the screen. 'And what looks like a pack of wild dogs forty yards to the east.'

Night-time image analysis was a skill that not everyone on the base appreciated. The pilots did, but she resented the disdain with which the CIA officers appeared to view her profession. Spiro was the worst, but that was also because he kept trying to look down her blouse. He hadn't the first idea about the subtleties of either women or her job.

During the day, with clear visibility, it was easy enough to distinguish man from woman, cat from dog, even from 30,000 feet. The images were pin sharp. But at night you had to rely on the digitally enhanced imagery of the infra-red spectrum. Interpreting the ghostly monochrome of the mid-IR wavelengths required intuition and training to flesh out the shapes. You had to impose upon them known patterns of human behaviour. Two years earlier, she had averted a friendly-fire attack when she realised that the four targets on an Afghanistan hillside, thought to be insurgents, were doing press-ups. She had never seen the Taleban working out, and assumed, rightly, that they were US soldiers.

The shapes in front of her now, clustered together inside a hut on a mountainside in North Waziristan, were not normal, even allowing for the local atmospheric conditions, which were making the images less clear than she would have liked. She isolated the feed from the thermal infra-red camera, which detected heat emitted from objects, and then fused it again with the image-intensified images. She had seen Taleban leaders talking many times before, and they never stood so close. When they sat, they formed circles. These people had created something else: a glowing crucifix to warn off the Reaper.

8

Marchant pulled off the dusty track and parked the BMW behind a cluster of coarse bushes, out of sight. It was almost dark and he could see the headlights of a lorry coming down over the Tizi'n'Test pass in the far distance. He wished he had been able to steal a scrambler rather than a tourer, as the BMW had struggled with the rough terrain. They had left the main road, and followed an increasingly remote and bumpy track for the past half-hour, Marchant keeping at least a mile between them. The man he was pursuing had stopped here a few minutes earlier and parked his bike on the other side of the track, without bothering to hide it. He was in a hurry, and had already disappeared on foot, following a steep path that zigzagged up through windblown juniper-berry trees that clung to the hillside.

Marchant set off up the path, confident that he had left enough time between them not to be seen. He thought he was fit from his running and his abstemious life in Marrakech, but the mountains were soon sucking the thin air from his lungs. Occasionally, as he crested another false ridge, he saw his man in front of him, at least five hundred yards ahead, covering the ground with the ease of a mountain goat. Whenever he turned, Marchant pressed himself flat against the dry earth, feeling his chest rise and fall as he tried to keep his breathing quiet.

It was after forty minutes of climbing that he heard the first cries on the wind. The mountains around here were farmed by Berber goatherds, who called out to each other across the valleys as they followed their animals. Sometimes they sang bitter songs about arrogant Berbers who had travelled abroad and returned with enough money to build ugly modern houses on the hillside. But tonight they seemed to be singing of something else. Marchant struggled with the dialect, but he could pick up enough to detect the agitation and fear in their voices. Had his man come up here to give his coded message to the goatherds, who would pass it on from man to man across the mountains, until eventually it reached Dhar? It would be in keeping with the primitive means of communication used so far.

Marchant listened again to the Berbers' agitated calls as a goat stumbled out of the gloaming next to him and moved off down the hillside. Something had disturbed the peace of the mountains. The man he had been following had stopped now. His hands were cupped around his mouth and he was calling out into the dying light. The wind was in the wrong direction for Marchant to hear, but the man's body language said enough. He had sunk to his knees with exhaustion. Had he come with a warning? Was it that he was too late? Then he heard him cry out again. The swirling wind carried the sound down the hillside to Marchant. There was panic in his voice, and they weren't Berber words this time.

'*Nye strelai!*' he shouted. '*Nye strelai!*'

Moments later, a short burst of automatic gunfire rang out, echoing through the mountains, and the man slumped over. Marchant pressed himself closer to the earth, breathing hard, searching around for better cover, calculating where the shots had come from. He slid across to a bush, keeping his eyes on the horizon. And then he saw it, hovering up over the crest of the hill. *The Roc bird rose into the sky.*

He knew at once that it was Russian-built, an Mi-8, its distinctive profile silhouetted in the dusk light. It was white, but there were no UN markings. The shots had come from the machine-gun mounted beneath the cockpit. Marchant was dead if the pilot had seen him, but the helicopter turned, nose down, and rose into the star-studded sky, heading towards the Algerian border.

9

The doubt that had been sown in the young sensor operator's mind grew stronger with each passing second. She had tried to tell herself that she was just seeing things, that she was suffering from exhaustion, too many late nights reading God's word, but there was no escaping the yellow shape that the heat of the bodies had formed. Although the hut only had a canvas roof of some kind, it was impossible to tell precisely how many people there were inside, as the bodies were bunched so closely together – too close for Taleban.

'Sir, there's something abnormal about the target imagery,' she said, turning to her pilot.

'Would you care to elaborate?' Spiro said, before the pilot had time to reply.

The analyst paused, struggling to conceal her dislike of Spiro. 'They're too close together.'

'Perhaps they're praying. What's the local time anyhow? I'll put money on it being the Mecca hour. If we have no other objections, I say we shoot.'

Spiro directed his last comment at the base commander, who was on the phone to the Pentagon. Spiro knew the commander needed the break just as much as he did.

'We're green-lit,' the commander said, replacing the phone.

Spiro could tell he was concealing his excitement. He just had to make sure the USAF didn't get to take any credit.

'Then let's engage, people,' Spiro said, putting a hand on the pilot's shoulder. The pilot flinched, and Spiro withdrew it. He knew at once that it had been an inappropriate gesture. These pilots were under pressure, too. There was talk on the base of combat stress, despite their distance from the battlefield. Unlike a fighter pilot, who pulled away from the target after dropping his payload, the Reaper pilots stayed on site, watching the bloody aftermath in high magnification.

'Sir, given the subject is static, I'd appreciate a second opinion,' the pilot said, catching his colleague's eye. 'If she's not happy, neither am I.'

'Are you not happy?' Spiro asked the analyst. No one in the room missed his sarcasm. 'The Pentagon's happy, I'm happy, your commander here is goddamn cock-a-hoop. Salim Dhar, the world's most wanted terrorist, just spoke on a cell from the target zone, and you're not happy. As far as we know, nobody has gone in or out of that lousy shack apart from a pack of crazy Afghani dogs. This is paytime, honey. And we'll all get a share, don't you worry your tight little ass. I'll see to it personally.'

As Spiro's words hung in the air, a phone began to ring. The commander picked it up and listened for a few moments, nodding at the pilot. 'Could you stream it through now? I'd appreciate that. Channel nine.'

The pilot leaned forward and flicked a switch. Moments later, Salim Dhar's voice filled the stuffy room. It was only a few words, a short burst from someone who seemed to know the risk he was running by speaking on a cell phone, but no one was in any doubt. They had all heard his voice too many times in the last year, seen his face on too many posters.

'Fort Meade picked it up a few seconds ago,' the commander

34

said. 'Same coordinates, same cell, 100 per cent voiceprint match, confidence threshold now at 95 per cent. Gentlemen, ladies, I hope 432 Air Expeditionary Wing will be remembered for many things, but as of this moment, we'll be known for ever as the people who took down Salim Dhar. Engage the target.'

Lieutenant Oaks spent the last minutes of his life in frustration as much as fear. He had managed to corral everyone into the middle of the hut, including Murray, and persuaded them of the merits of his plan. The cross was as good as he could make it in the circumstances: four men lying in a line, hands still tied behind their backs, heads below the next man's shackled ankles, and then two lying perpendicular to them, one either side of Oaks, who was second in the upright. Even if it didn't show up as a cross, Oaks figured it would look pretty damn weird on a thermal-imaging screen.

But then, as they lay there, each praying to his own God, Salim Dhar was suddenly amongst them for a second time. It was only a few words, spoken on his cell phone, but it was enough to make Oaks realise what was happening. When he heard him, he screamed, hoping that his voice would be picked up by someone at Fort Meade, but he was too late. Dhar had stopped talking by the time he was railing at the sky.

He started to sob now, lying in the mud on his imaginary cross, the smell of urine filling the air. There was nothing left to do. For a moment he stopped, trying to hear the sound of the drone above the murmurings of his colleagues. A Reaper's turboprop engine at altitude purred like a buzzing insect – that's what they said, wasn't it? – but he heard nothing. Just the noise of the dogs, which whined and ran in all directions when the first Hellfire exploded deep in the Afghan mud beside him.

10

Marchant had to call London, tell them what he'd seen, but his mobile phone had no signal. Satisfied that the helicopter had been operating on its own, he broke cover and ran back down the path to the motorbike, stumbling and falling as he went. The mountains were quiet now, the Berber goatherds stunned into silence by whatever had just happened. He started up the engine and headed back down the track to the main road and on towards Marrakech.

He couldn't decide if it was safer to dump the bike and get back to his apartment before he called Fielding, or to ring as soon as he was in range. His mobile phone was encrypted, but the events he had just witnessed made him nervous of talking in the open. The sight of the man being shot had heightened his senses, stirred a primitive survival instinct.

He also felt an irrational sense of loss. He had never met the man, but they had been joined in some way, had listened to the same story in the square, ridden the same route out of town, first on Mobylettes then on more powerful machines. It could have been him in the line of fire. All he wanted to do now was get as far away as possible from the mountains, and the haunting Berber goatherds' calls that had warned of danger.

It was as he throttled back the engine that he began to rethink his plans. A line of single headlights had appeared a thousand yards ahead, coming up the straight road towards him, fanned across both lanes. He knew at once that it was the group of British bikers, one of whose machines he had stolen. Should he stop, try to explain? They had clearly seen him at the petrol station, and would immediately identify the bike as theirs. It was out of the question. He could never play his employer's card. It was a last resort, reserved for tight spots with foreign governments. He would have been allowed to tell his immediate family who he worked for, too, except that he didn't have any. Not any more. Not unless he counted Dhar.

His priority was to get a message to Fielding, tell him he had been right, that someone had taken Dhar away by helicopter. He was convinced that the *halaka* had relayed a message to Dhar, tried to warn him of a Roc bird rising into the sky. It would explain the recent increased level of chatter about Dhar in the souks. But had time run out? Had the warning come too late?

There was only one option. It had been a few years since he had ridden a motorbike at speed, but he had felt comfortable on the journey out of Marrakech. In his first months at Legoland in Vauxhall, working as a junior reports officer, a few of the new recruits used to take bikes out for test rides at lunchtime. There was a motorcycle dealer opposite the main entrance to Legoland, and the staff there were always obliging – one eye on a government contract, perhaps – without ever acknowledging which building Marchant and his colleagues left and entered each day. Marchant would sometimes play it up, hinting that he lived life in the international fast lane, when the truth of his head-office existence was much more mundane. That was one of the reasons he wanted to stay in Morocco.

He watched the needle move across the dial and adjusted his position in the saddle, wishing he was wearing a helmet. If he approached the bikers fast enough, he reckoned they wouldn't hold the line. Five hundred yards from them, he turned off his headlight and took the machine up to 90 mph, riding in darkness, his face cooling in the night wind. Not for the first time in his life, he felt liberated rather than scared as death drew near, sensing as he had done before in such moments that he was closer to those he had lost: his father, his brother.

Still the bikers were fanned across the road, no gaps between them. An image of the London Marathon came and went: the police roadblock, trying to find a way through. Then, as the needle nudged passed a hundred, a gap started to appear at one end of the line, in the opposite lane. He headed for it, feeling the surface change beneath him as he crossed the middle of the road. For a moment he thought he had lost control, but the BMW handled well and he accelerated again, touching 110 mph. Fifty yards from the line, all the bikes began to peel away, and then he was through them, the sound of their anger fading in his ears.

He liked the bike, but he didn't want to steal it. Turning the headlight back on, he glanced in the mirror and saw that no one had decided to give chase. A madman had clearly stolen their bike, and he would be dead quicker than they could catch him. When he looked ahead again, he saw the oncoming lorry's headlights, but there was no time to think. Instinctively, he swerved inside the vehicle and was almost thrown by the draft as it passed him, horn blaring in the darkness.

He moved back onto the correct side of the road. The petrol station where he had picked up the bike was shut, but he parked it there, flashing the headlight on and off once. A mile back up the road, one of the bikers broke away from the group and started to ride towards him. But Marchant was long gone by the time he had arrived, heading into the heart of Marrakech across rough ground, talking on his mobile to London.

11

Marcus Fielding, Chief of MI6, looked out of his fourth-floor window at the commuters walking home across Vauxhall Bridge beneath him. Two of them had stopped, jackets slung over their shoulders, to take in the evening sun as it set over a hot summer London. The Thames was out, the muddy shores busy with sand-pipers. On the far bank, below the Morpeth Arms, a woman weighed down with plastic bags was searching through the flotsam and jetsam.

Beside Legoland, one of the Yellow Duck amphibious vehicles that took tourists around London was parked up on the slipway, waiting while its captain briefed passengers on what to do if it sank. Sometimes, Fielding wished it would. Its proximity to Legoland had long made him uneasy, the guided tours attracting too much publicity, too many fingers pointing up in his direction. Still, Fielding couldn't deny that he had enjoyed the time he had taken the Duck with Daniel Marchant. They were happier days then, full of hope. Marchant had received a text while they were on board together, and the Morocco plan had been born. But that was over now.

Fielding was supposed to be going to the opera tonight, but he needed to wait for Marchant to ring in again from Marrakech. The call had come through earlier on Marchant's mobile, but the line had dropped, the encryption software unhappy with the integrity of the local network. He knew Marchant wouldn't make contact unless it was urgent, but it all seemed irrelevant now. He wondered how best to break the news about Salim Dhar to Marchant.

There was a chance, of course, that James Spiro was mistaken. He had been wrong before, most famously about Marchant's late father, Stephen, Fielding's predecessor as Chief of MI6. According to Spiro, Stephen and Daniel Marchant were both infidels, worshiping at the altar of a very different god to the rest of the West. Spiro had tried to bring down the entire house of Marchant, and MI6 by implication, until the son had cleared the father's name.

But the evidence coming out of North Waziristan suggested that this time Spiro was right. The CIA had finally nailed their man. Two intercepted phone calls, a red-hot handset last used in south India: it was hard to disagree with them. GCHQ was running its own tests on the voice, but the match was perfect, as Spiro had repeatedly told him a few minutes earlier on the video link.

There were few people Fielding despised more than Spiro. He should have been cleared out with the old guard when the new President was sworn in, hung out to dry with the attorneys who had sanctioned torture, but somehow he had survived, thanks to the President himself, of all people. The White House's attitude to the Agency had changed overnight after the assassination attempt in Delhi. Briefly a champion of noble values, it was now an admirer of muscle, and in particular of Spiro, who had taken all the credit for protecting his leader. The clenched fist had replaced the hand of friendship. Now, God help them all, there was no stopping him. Spiro's star was in the ascendant again. Not only were his enhanced methods back in fashion, but the CIA had been given permission to resume playing hardball with its allies.

40

Salim Dhar's elimination was a particularly sweet victory for Spiro. The Agency had never seen Dhar in the same way as the British, struggling to countenance the possibility that he might one day represent an opportunity rather than a threat. For them, Dhar was the problem, not a potential solution, a man who had come close to heaping the ultimate shame on them. From where Fielding stood, it was all deeply frustrating: the President had promised an era of more nuanced attitudes to intelligence, but it appeared to be over before it had begun.

Fielding turned away from the reinforced window and walked across to the cabinet behind his desk. The collection of books reflected his Arabist tastes, charting his career through the Gulf and North Africa. He envied Marchant his time in Morocco, operating on his own, without the bureaucracy of Legoland. It was how he had worked best when he was Marchant's age, drifting through the medinas, talking to the traders, listening, watching.

He took out a volume of *The Book of the Thousand Nights and a Night*, presented to him years ago by Muammar al-Gadaffi after he had helped to persuade the Libyan leader to abandon his nuclear ambitions. It was Sir Richard Francis Burton's ten-volume 1885 limited edition, for subscribers only, and he had never enquired too closely about its provenance. Fielding had been obliged to declare the gift to Whitehall, but it was his counter-intelligence colleagues across the Thames who were most interested, subjecting the volumes to weeks of unnecessary analysis.

The rivalry between the Services had bordered on war in those days, and Fielding had assumed that MI5 would do all it could to embarrass the Vicar, as he knew they called him. Gifts from foreign governments were a favourite cover for listening devices. No one had forgotten the electric samovar presented to the Queen at Balmoral by the Russian Knights aerobatics team, later suspected of being a mantelpiece transmitter, or the infinity bug hidden inside a wooden replica of the Great Seal of the United States, given by Russian schoolchildren to the US ambassador to Moscow at the end of the Second World War.

But the sweepers at Thames House found nothing, and resisted the temptation to insert something of their own. The volumes were reluctantly passed back over the river to Legoland. There was talk of donating them to the British Library, but the Vicar was eventually allowed to keep his unholy gift.

As he began to read about Shahryar and Scheherazade, there was a knock on the door and Ann Norman, his formidable personal assistant, appeared. She was wearing her usual red tights and intimidating frown, both of which had protected four Chiefs from Whitehall's meddling mandarins for more than twenty years.

'It's Daniel Marchant. Shall I put him through?'

'Line three.'

Fielding went over to his desk and sat down, placing the open book in front of him, next to the comms console that linked him to colleagues around the world as well as to his political masters. The book's presence made him feel more connected, less detached from Marchant's world. He let him talk for a while, about a *halaka*, and his trip out into the High Atlas. Fielding stopped him as he began to talk of helicopters.

'Daniel, I think you should know we've just had a call from Langley. NSA picked up a mobile intercept late this afternoon, from Salim Dhar in North Waziristan. One hundred per cent voice match.'

Marchant fell quiet, the hum of a Marrakech medina suddenly audible in the background.

'Have they killed him?'

'They think so. A UAV was in the area, eliminated the target within fifteen minutes of the intercept. I'm sorry.'

'Without even checking? Without talking to us?'

42

'The Americans aren't really in the mood right now for cooperating on Dhar. You know that.'

'But Dhar was here, I'm sure of it. In Morocco. Barely an hour ago, up near the Tizi'n'Test pass. The *halaka* spoke of a Roc bird.'

Fielding absently turned the pages of *The Arabian Nights*, hearing a younger version of himself in Marchant's voice. Fielding had been less hot-headed, but he rated Marchant more highly than anyone of his generation. A part of him wondered again if Spiro had made a mistake, but it was hard to dispute the CIA's evidence, at least those elements of it that they had pooled with Britain. The Joint Intelligence Committee was convening first thing in the morning, by which time Britain's own voice analysis from Cheltenham would be in. GCHQ was running tests through the night, but Fielding didn't expect a different result.

'And how do I present your evidence to the JIC tomorrow?' Fielding said, knowing it was an unfair question. Unlike police work, intelligence-gathering was seldom just about evidence, as he had explained to MI6's latest intake of IONEC graduates earlier that day. Agents had to be thorough but also counter-intuitive; 'Cutting the red wire when the manual said blue,' as one over-excited graduate had put it.

'Someone took him away. Whoever owns the helicopter has Dhar.'

'And who does own it?'

'It was white, UN, but no markings.'

'White?' Fielding's interest was pricked. He knew that the Mi-8 was used by the UN, knew too that the government in Sudan wasn't averse to flying unmarked white military aircraft to attack villages in Darfur.

'I was about to tell you that when you interrupted me.'

Fielding could hear Marchant's anger mounting. He had always preferred field agents who were passionate about the CX they filed to London. It made for better product.

'Suppose it was just an exercise,' he said, testing him.

'An exercise? They shot someone, the man I'd been following from Marrakech, the same man who'd been listening to the story-teller.' Marchant fell silent again. 'Remember when Dhar sent me the text, after Delhi?' he continued, trying to restore his Chief's belief.

Fielding stood up, his lower spine beginning to ache. It always played up when he was tired, and he suddenly felt world-weary, as if he had been asked to live his entire life over again, fight all his old Whitehall battles, relive the fears of raised threat levels, the waking moments in the middle of the night.

'Daniel, we've been over this many times,' he said, thinking back to their journey down the river. They had both thought the text was from Dhar. GCHQ was less sure.

'The words were taken from a song. *Leysh Nat'arak.*'

'And that text was one of the reasons I gave you time in Morocco. I would have let you go earlier if I could. You were no good to anyone in London. Langley thought otherwise. We all hoped that you'd find Dhar, that he'd make contact. But that's not going to happen now. I'm sorry. It's time to come home.'

'You really believe the Americans have killed him, don't you?'

Fielding hesitated, one hand on the small of his back. 'I'm not sure. But whatever happened in Morocco, I want you away from it. For your own sake. If someone was killed, and you saw it, we have a problem, and that wasn't part of the deal. I also sent you to Morocco to keep out of trouble.'

'*Yalla natsaalh ehna akhwaan.* That was the lyric. *Let's make good for we are brothers.*' Marchant paused. 'Dhar was out there, up in the mountains. I'm sure of it. And he wanted to come in. But someone took him, before he could.'

'Someone? Who, exactly?'

Marchant tried to ignore the scepticism that had returned to Fielding's voice. He had thought about this question on the way back to his apartment, wrestled with the possibilities, the implications, knowing how it would sound. But it was quite clear in his own mind, as clear as the Russian words he had heard on the mountainside: *Nye strelai. Don't shoot.*

'Moscow.'

12

Marchant swilled the Scotch around his mouth for a few seconds before swallowing it. He had hoped the alcohol would taste toxic, that his body would reject it in some violent way, but it was sweeter than he had ever remembered.

He was sitting under a palm tree in the courtyard of the Chesterfield Pub, a *bar anglais* at the Hotel Nassil on avenue Mohammed V. It was not a place he was particularly proud to be, but there was a limited choice of public venues serving alcohol in Marrakech. The Scotch was decent enough, though, and there were fewer tourists than he had feared. His only worry was if the group of British bikers had decided to turn back to Marrakech for the night and came here for a drink.

He had learned to trust his gut instinct since signing up with MI6, and at the moment it didn't feel as if Salim Dhar was dead. The Americans had claimed to have killed a number of terrorists with UAVs in recent years and later proved to have been wrong. Only time would tell if they were right about Dhar. It would be too risky to send in anyone on the ground to collect DNA. Later perhaps. For now, the CIA would look for other evidence, listen to the chatter, assess *jihadi* morale.

Marchant knew, though, that Fielding was right: his Morocco days were over. He had already booked himself onto the early-morning flight back to London. In India, when he was a child, his father had once told him to live in each country as if for ever, but always to be ready to leave at dawn. At the time, his father was a middle-ranking MI6 officer who had served in Moscow before Delhi. He was used to the threat of his diplomatic cover being blown, of tit-for-tat expulsions.

Marchant wasn't being expelled, but there had been an incident of some sort in the mountains and he had witnessed it. Whether anyone had seen him, he wasn't sure, but he knew MI6 couldn't afford for him to be caught up in another controversy, not after the events in India. And if he was right about Moscow's involvement, an international row might be imminent.

After finishing his Scotch he ordered another. He had swapped his *djellaba* for jeans and a collarless shirt before coming to the pub, and guessed the waiter had marked him down as just another drunken Western tourist, tanking up before a night at the clubs. So be it. He needed to cut a different figure from the one who had ridden out to Tizi a few hours earlier.

It was after an hour and too much Scotch that Marchant saw the dark-haired woman walk up to the bar. He recognised her at once as Lakshmi Meena, the local Operations Officer the CIA had sent to keep an eye on him when he had first arrived in Marrakech. London had briefed him about her. She was a beneficiary of the CIA's ongoing programme to recruit more people from what it called America's 'heritage communities', particularly those who spoke 'mission critical' languages. MI6 had always recruited linguists, unlike the CIA, which had been found wanting after 9/11. Even in its National Clandestine Service, only 30 per cent of CIA staff were fluent in a second language. Meena spoke Hindi, some Urdu and, most importantly, the Dravidian languages of southern India, which had been upgraded to critical in the ongoing hunt for Salim Dhar, whose parents were originally from Kerala.

Marchant had also been told that she was a breath of fresh air, one of the recent intake who had joined the Agency on the back of the new President's promises of change. He had yet to see any difference, at least in the CIA's attitude to him.

Meena was young, late twenties, dressed in jeans and a maroon Indian top with mirrorwork that caught the light around her neckline. Officially, she was in Morocco teaching English as a foreign language, working at the American Language Center up in Rabat. Marchant had to admit that she looked the part, one up from his own student cover. He wished he'd thought of it for himself.

Meena walked over to Marchant's table in the courtyard, checking her mobile phone before putting it away in her shoulder-bag. Marchant was momentarily wrongfooted by the direct approach. They had met face to face only once before, shortly after Marchant had arrived: a cold exchange in the foyer of a hotel.

'Do what you have to do,' Marchant had said, trying not to see Leila in Meena's limpid eyes, her dark olive skin. 'Just don't expect any answers from me.'

'You flatter yourself,' she had replied. 'We ask questions later, remember?'

It hadn't been the beginning of a beautiful friendship. He knew afterwards that he had played it too cool, that she was only doing her job, but he wasn't in the mood to mix with female field agents, particularly ones who reminded him of a woman who had betrayed him. Meena was taller, her manner more hardened, but there was unquestionably something of Leila in her: an attitude, sexual poise. And Marchant knew that any likeness was no coincidence, that it was a cruel joke by Spiro. Frustrated that he wasn't allowed to lock Marchant up and torture him again, Spiro had sent someone to remind him of his past. But Marchant ignored the ploy, ignored Meena. For the following few weeks, they had played cat and mouse on the streets of Marrakech, before Meena had finally backed off to Rabat.

'Mind if I join you?' she asked, taking a seat.

'Go ahead,' Marchant said, concealing his surprise. A waiter was standing beside them. For a moment, he was back in a pub in Portsmouth, chatting up strangers as part of a training exercise. All new recruits at the Fort, MI6's training base in Gosport, were dispatched to the city's bars and pubs to chat up unsuspecting locals and solicit private information: bank-card details, National Insurance and passport numbers.

'Bourbon and Coke, thanks. Daniel?'

Marchant knew Meena was taking in the scene, measuring the milligrams of alcohol in Marchant's blood, whether his defences were down. The only consolation was that she wasn't the sort to flirt. He didn't think he could handle that right now. Leila had used her sexual charms shamelessly, in the office and in the field, but he sensed that Meena did things differently.

'A Scotch, thanks,' Marchant replied, nodding at the waiter.

'I thought you'd given all that up,' she said, fingering her Indian necklace. 'Gone native.'

'Celebrating. I didn't think you drank either.' He had read her files: vegetarian, non-drinker, decaffeinated coffee, herbal tea.

'Celebrating, too.'

Marchant thought her necklace was from south India, similar to one his mother had once worn. He raised his glass, trying to run his own check on himself, calculate the damage. A drinking session after three months' abstinence wasn't a good idea, but he was sober enough to extract some leverage from the situation, fool Meena into thinking he was drunker than he was. At least, that was the plan. His dulled brain could think of two reasons why she had stepped out of the shadows tonight. To say goodbye, having heard that Dhar was dead; or to find out if he knew anything about the helicopter in the mountains. He had a problem if it was the latter.

'You heard the news then,' she said, glancing around the bar before looking at Marchant, his already empty glass.

'I heard,' he said, thinking it could still be either.

'Mixed feelings, I guess.'

He sat back, relieved that she had come to talk about Dhar.

'To be honest, I don't really know what to say,' she continued, brushing some crumbs off the table. 'Langley's kind of over the moon, as you'd expect. But it's a little more complicated for you guys.'

'Is it? He tried to kill your President. Now you've killed him. End of story.'

'But, you know, the whole half-brother thing.' Meena leaned in towards Marchant. 'I realise you didn't exactly grow up together, but that could have been new territory, for all of us –'

'Why did you come here tonight?' Marchant was suddenly irritated by Meena's appearance on his last evening in Morocco, riled by how much she knew, her after-work pub manner. He had been about to leave, take one last walk around Djemaâ el Fna. Now he was in an English bar, having a drink with someone he had avoided for the past three months.

'I figured you'd be pulling out of town,' Meena said. 'Thought it would be civil to tie this whole thing off, say goodbye.'

Marchant allowed the awkwardness to linger for a few seconds, in case there was anything else to flush out. But there was nothing. The Americans thought they had killed Dhar, and he was happy to let them. Marchant wasn't sure if it was the alcohol or sudden empathy for a fellow field officer, but something made him change tack and end the awkwardness, drop his guard.

'Thanks,' he said, watching the waiter place their order on the table. 'You know, for coming. We should have had this drink three months ago.'

She wasn't so bad, he told himself. He was the one who had been stubborn, too angry with the way he had been treated by the Americans. Meena was younger than him, still believed that she was making a difference. And she could have made his life a lot more difficult.

'I wasn't really getting the right vibes,' she said, smiling, putting her hands up in mock defence. 'Hey, look, I don't blame you for not trusting us. Not at all.'

'I gave up trusting people when I signed up.'

'We're not all like Spiro,' Meena said, sitting back.

'I wasn't thinking of Spiro.' For a moment, Marchant wondered if she would take the bait, begin to talk of Leila, but she didn't, and he was shocked by his own disappointment.

'I don't know about you, but I joined the Agency in search of some light and shade. It's why I'm here in Morocco and not in some sweaty UAV trailer in Nevada. I can't pretend I'm sorry Dhar's dead, but I was open to other ways of winning this war.'

'I'm sure you were,' said Marchant. He looked again at Meena, wondering whether he could confide in her, open up, reveal what he had seen in the mountains. But he knew he couldn't. Despite the unexpected entente, they were working to different agendas.

'What made you choose the Agency anyway?' Marchant asked. 'You don't strike me as –'

'– the right colour?' She laughed.

'Christ no, I wasn't going to say that.'

'The right sex?' She laughed again, and then they both paused, her words hanging between them. Marchant thought he saw a sadness in her eyes, or maybe he was confused by his own nostalgia.

'My father wanted me to train as a doctor. Failing that, he

51

wanted me to marry one. I was studying medicine at Georgetown University, but then, after 9/11, everything changed.'

'Did you lose someone?'

'Not directly. Friends of friends, you know.'

'But it felt personal.'

'Yeah. And the CIA had always been a part of my life.'

'Really?'

'We grew up in Reston, Virginia, not far from Langley. My father used to talk so proudly of the Agency, said it was there to protect all Americans, including ones who had come from India. To prove it, we drove up there one day to take a look, when I was seventeen, maybe eighteen. There's a public sign on the main highway, next right for the George Bush Center for Intelligence. So we took the exit and drove up through the woods, Mom and Dad in the front, my younger brother and me in the back. We were nearly shot by the guards. I think they thought we were a family of suicide bombers.'

'What did they do?'

'Waved their machine-guns at us and shouted at us to leave. I thought they were going to shoot the tyres out.'

'And your father?'

'He was mortified. He couldn't understand why we hadn't been welcomed with open arms. He'd been naïve to go there, but I hated seeing him so upset.'

'And that's why you joined?'

'One reason. I wanted to prove to him – to me – that we're welcome in America. That the Agency is there to defend my family as much as anyone else's. When the Towers came down, they were suddenly looking to recruit from the subcontinent.'

'Why did it take you so long to sign up?'

'It took a new President.'

'And is it everything you hoped?'

'I'm seeing the world.'

'But not changing it.'

'I'm not sure tailing a renegade British agent on compassionate leave through the streets of Marrakech is quite what I had in mind.'

'You weren't very committed.' Marchant matched her smile, thinking back to the first time he had seen her, watching her from across Djemaâ el Fna before giving her the runaround.

'OK, so you lost me a couple of times in the medina. I salute your superior British tradecraft. But come on, Daniel' – she was leaning forward now, voice lowered – 'you didn't really think Dhar would show up in this place, did you? Maybe I missed him. Maybe he was that guy selling dentures in the main square, the one being photographed day and night by thousands of American tourists.'

'No, that wasn't him.'

Marchant thought back to the *halaka*. Again he wanted to confide in Meena, ask her opinion, but he knew he was drunk. He hadn't discussed Salim Dhar with anyone since he had arrived in Marrakech. The text he had received on the Thames had haunted him for the first few weeks. He had checked his phone repeatedly, in case Dhar made contact again, but he never had.

Marchant had begged Fielding to let him go to Morocco, but the Americans had insisted he stay in London. After a year of frustration and too much alcohol, he had finally arrived in Marrakech, expecting the trail to have gone cold. But as he settled into his sober new life, working the souks, listening to the storytellers, he had begun to pick up chatter here and there that gave him hope he was still on the right track.

'Did you listen to any of those guys, the *halakas*?' Meena asked.

'One or two.' Meena's interest in the storyteller triggered a distant alarm, like a police siren a few streets away.

'Terrific tales, although some of the Berber street talk threw me.'

53

The alarm faded. Marchant was impressed by Meena's local knowledge. He hadn't given her enough credit, and chided himself for judging her too swiftly. Again, he wondered whether she had been a missed opportunity, someone he should have nurtured rather than avoided. But he knew why he had kept his distance.

'Where next for you, then? When I'm gone?' he asked.

Meena paused. Marchant thought that she too seemed to be weighing up how much to confide, thrown perhaps by how well they were getting on. Up until now, she had hidden behind her words, preferring to spar rather than open up. She sat back, glancing half-heartedly around the bar.

'I want out, if I'm honest. I thought I'd joined a different Agency, a new one working for a new President.'

'But you haven't.'

'No. I haven't.'

'Spiro?'

She paused again. 'For the record, he wanted me to make your life here not worth living.'

'But you chose not to.'

'What did you *do* to him?'

'We go back a bit. He thought my father was a traitor. Then he accused me.'

Meena stood up with his empty glass, ready to head to the bar. 'Must have been that terrorist brother of yours.'

The remark annoyed Marchant, cut through the fog of Scotch. It was a reminder of their differences, confirmation that a junior CIA officer had seen his file. He had hoped that his kinship would remain known only to a few people in Langley and Legoland, but he realised that was wishful thinking. Meena would have been fully briefed before arriving in Morocco, given the full, shocking picture.

He thought again about the text. *Let's make good for we are brothers.* The lyrics were by an Arabic singer, Natacha Atlas. Had Dhar known that she was one of Leila's favourite artists? Marchant was getting sentimental. He couldn't afford to dwell on Leila, not in his present state. And he couldn't afford to talk any more with Meena.

By the time she returned to the table with another Scotch, Marchant had gone.

13

Paul Myers wouldn't have bothered to listen to the audio one more time if it hadn't been for Daniel Marchant. He knew his old friend had spent the past three months in Marrakech largely because of him. His line manager at GCHQ had dismissed the theory that Dhar had texted Marchant from Morocco, but Myers had thought otherwise. Like Marchant, he didn't believe Dhar would hang around the Af-Pak region after the assassination attempt. It was too obvious, despite the mountainous terrain and the volatile political climate, both of which made it difficult for the West to search. He could never prove that Marchant's text had been sent by Dhar, but he had run his own checks on some dodgy proxy networks, and would gladly bet his (unused) gym membership that it had originated in Morocco. And if it was a coincidence that the lyric in the text was by a singer who shared her surname with a North African mountain range, he found it a reassuring one.

So it was guilt more than anything that made him put his headphones back on, adjust the fluorescent band at the base of his ponytail and play the US audio file again. He owed it to Marchant to prove that the Americans were wrong about Dhar. He sat back and yawned, scratching at his slack stomach through his fleece jacket as he looked around the empty office.

His desk, littered with chocolate-bar wrappers and filled-in sudokus from various broadsheet newspapers, was in the inner ring of the GCHQ complex, dubbed the Doughnut because of its circular shape. The Street, a glass-roofed circular corridor, ran around the entire building, separating the inner from the outer circles. Its purpose was to encourage separate departments to share their data. No one on the building's three floors was more than five minutes' walk from anyone else, and face-to-face meetings in softly furnished break-out areas were the way forward.

At least, that was the idea. In truth, people kept to themselves. Myers used the Street solely for walking to the Ritazza cafés and deli bars that dotted its orbital route. The workforce at GCHQ, with its mathematicians, cryptanalysts, linguists, librarians and IT engineers, was the most intelligent in the Civil Service, but it was also the most socially dysfunctional, steeped in a long tradition of strictly-need-to-know that dated back to Bletchley Park and its campus of separate huts. Myers wouldn't have had it any other way.

He looked out onto the secure landscaped gardens in the middle of the building, hidden below which was GCHQ's vast computer hall. It was down there, in the depths of the basement, that the mathematicians worked, and that the 'Cheltenham express', an electric train, shuttled back and forth day and night, carrying files along a track beneath the Street. To the right of Myers' window was a decked area, where people could walk out from the canteen. Beyond it was a large expanse of lawn that had been nicknamed 'the grassy knoll' and was meant for blue-sky meetings. Myers liked to sit there in the summer and take his lunch.

The garden was dark and empty now, its edges bathed in a pale, energy-efficient light spilling out from the offices around it. Myers used to work as an intelligence analyst in the Gulf Region, on the opposite side of the Doughnut, his desk looking out at one of the two pagodas that had been built in the garden for smokers, but he had asked for a transfer to the subcontinent after

Leila had died. He had carried a hopeless torch for her, and still hadn't come to terms with her betrayal, let alone her death. Listening to intercepts in Farsi had proved too painful.

The voice in the headphones was definitely Dhar's. His American colleagues had run every test there was, subjecting it to a level of spectrographic analysis that had even met with Myers' jaundiced approval. But what had caught his attention was the lack of data about the background noise. All ears had been tuned to the voice.

Myers listened to the Urdu, noting instinctively that it was a second, possibly third, language, but his eyes were on the computer screen in front of him and the digital sound waves that were rolling across it to the rhythm of Dhar's speech. When the Urdu stopped, Myers eased forward in his seat and scrutinised the data, watching the waves moving along the bottom of his screen until the segment ended. He moved the cursor back to where the Urdu had stopped and played the final part again, his tired eyes blinking. This time he magnified the wave imagery, boosting the background noise. At the end of the clip, he did the same again, except that he only replayed the final eighth of a second, slowing it down to a deep, haunting drawl.

After repeating the process several more times, he was listening to fragments of sound, microseconds inaudible to the human ear. And then he found it. Moving more quickly now, he copied and pasted the clip and dragged it across to an adjacent screen, where he had loaded his own spectrographic software, much to his IT supervisor's annoyance. He played the clip and sat back, taking off his headphones, cracking the joints of his sweaty fingers. The 'spectral waterfall' on the screen in front of him was beautiful, a series of rippling columns of colour; but the acoustic structure was one of intense pain. At the very end of the second call made by Salim Dhar, there was a sound that Myers had not expected to hear: the opening notes of a human scream.

14

Lakshmi Meena didn't know what to expect as her car pulled up short of the police cordon on the side of the mountain. She parked beside two army lorries and a Jeep and stepped out into the cool night, pulling a scarf over her head. The area beyond the cordon was swarming with uniformed men, one of whom Meena recognised as Dr Abdul Aziz, a senior intelligence officer from Rabat who had left a message on her cell phone half an hour earlier. She had been leaving the *bar anglais* at the time, wondering what she had said to so upset Marchant. She didn't like Aziz, disapproved of his methods, his unctuous manner, but he had been the first person on her list of people to meet when she had arrived in Morocco.

Two floodlights had been rigged up on stands, illuminating a patch of rugged terrain where a handful of personnel in forensic boilersuits were searching the ground. Meena talked to a policeman on the edge of the cordon, nodding in the direction of Aziz, who saw her and came over.

'I got your message,' she said.

'Lakshmi, our goddess of wealth,' Aziz said, smiling. 'Morocco needs your help.' He lit a local cigarette as he steered her away from the lights, his hand hovering above her shoulders.

Meena was always surprised by Aziz's displays of warmth and

charm, so at odds with his professional reputation. He had run a black site in Morocco in the aftermath of 9/11, interviewing a steady stream of America's enemy combatants on behalf of James Spiro, who had dubbed him the Dentist. It was before Meena's time in the Agency, but she knew enough about Aziz to show respect to a man whose interrogation techniques made the tooth-extractors in Djemaâ el Fna look humane. And Meena hated herself for it, the cheap expedience of her chosen profession.

'What happened here?' she asked. 'The Moroccan Islamic Combatant Group? Last I heard, you had them on the back foot.'

Aziz laughed. His teeth were a brilliant white. 'Since when did they fly Mi-8s?'

'Who said anything about helicopters?'

'The Berbers.' Aziz nodded to a group of goatherds sitting on the ground in a circle, smoking, *djellaba* hoods up.

'Oh really?'

'Our national airspace was violated tonight, and we'd like to know who by.'

'Forgive me, but isn't that what your air force is for?'

'The country's radar defences were knocked out. It was a sophis-ticated system. At least that's what your sales people told us when we bought it from America last year. Our Algerian brothers don't have the ability to do that.'

'Not many people do.'

'The Berbers are saying the helicopter was white.'

'Any markings?'

'None.'

Meena had been down in Darfur the previous year, and had seen the same trick pulled with a white Antonov used for a military raid. But the Sudanese government had gone one step further, painting it in UN markings.

She looked at Aziz, who was lost in thought, drawing hard on his cigarette. She remembered the cocktail party in Rabat when he had enquired about her health. A month earlier, she had checked in to hospital for a small operation, something she had kept from even her closest colleagues. Perhaps his question had been a coincidence, but it had disquieted her.

'Is that why you called me?'

'There's something else. An Englishman was seen heading up here this evening.'

Aziz handed Meena a grainy photograph taken from a CCTV camera. It was of the gas-station forecourt on the road out of Marrakech. Someone who could have been Daniel Marchant was in the foreground, arriving on a moped. The date and time was wrong, but otherwise Meena thought the image looked authentic. It was too much of a coincidence, an odd place to be heading on a bike. Marchant had gone off-piste, and Meena should have known about it. No wonder he had left the bar early. He hadn't been honest with her.

'Marchant's booked on the first flight to London tomorrow,' Aziz said.

'I know.' Meena looked at him. Neither of them wanted to say anything, but each knew the other was thinking the same. The only reason Marchant would have gone to the mountains was if it had something to do with Salim Dhar. And Dhar was meant to be dead.

'What do you think he was up to?' Aziz asked.

'I thought you were watching him.'

'Both our jobs might be on the line, Lakshmi. Please tell me if you want Marchant delayed.'

Aziz smiled, his teeth glinting in the beam of a passing flashlight.

15

Marchant stepped aside as a donkey cart was led past him by an old man, his face hidden by the pointed hood of his *djellaba*, his cart stacked high with crates of salted sardines. Marchant headed across the square to the food trestles and benches, where a few butane lamps were still burning, but the crowds and the cooks had long gone, the smoke cleared. The only people in the square now were a handful of beggars, some sweepers in front of the mosque and a woman taking dough to a communal oven in one of the souks.

It was not quite dawn and the High Atlas were barely visible, no more than a reddish smudge on the horizon. Marchant had been walking around the medina since he left the *bar anglais*, taking a last look at his old haunts, drinking strong coffee at his favourite cafés. Now, as he sat down on a bench in a pool of light, he felt ready to return to Britain. He was more confident of his past, clearer about his relationship with Dhar.

For almost all of his thirty years, Marchant had thought that he only had one brother, his twin, Sebastian, who had been killed in a car crash in Delhi when they were eight. Then, fifteen months ago, on the run and trying to clear his family name, he had met Salim Dhar under a hot south Indian sun and asked why his late father, Stephen Marchant, Chief of MI6, had once visited Dhar, a rising *jihadi*, at a black site outside Cochin. 'He was my father, too,' Dhar had said, changing Marchant's life for ever.

After the initial shock, the grief of a surviving twin had been replaced by the comfort of a stranger. Marchant was no longer alone in the world. He was less troubled by the discovery of a *jihadi* half-brother than by the thought of what might have been. There had been a bond when they met in India, an unspoken pact that came with kinship. They were both the same age, shared the same father.

Their lives, though, had run in wildly different directions, one graduating from Cambridge, the other from a training camp in Afghanistan. Marchant knew that Dhar would never spy for the US, but he might work for Britain. It was why Marchant had been so keen to travel to Morocco: to establish where his half-brother's loyalties lay, and then try to turn him. Dhar was not, after all, a regular *jihadi*. How could he be, with a British father who had risen to become Chief of MI6? Tonight, though, he had accepted that his plan had failed. Dhar had not come forward, as he had hoped, and agreed to work for the land of his father.

The butane lamp above Marchant flickered and died. Dawn was spreading fast across the city from the east, where the mountains were now bathed in warm, newborn sunlight. Marchant stood up, his aching brain holding on to two things: Dhar was still alive, and he could still be turned. But there was something else. Whether Dhar had chosen to leave Morocco without making contact, or someone had taken him, Marchant couldn't deny that he felt rejected. When it had come to it, Dhar's family calling hadn't been strong enough.

Perhaps that was why, as he left the square, he didn't at first see Lakshmi Meena standing in the doorway of the mosque, watching him with the same intensity as the hawk that had begun to circle high above the waking city. But then he spotted her, turned off into the medina and ran through its narrow alleys as fast as he could.

16

James Spiro took the call 35,000 feet above the Atlantic, sitting near the front of the Gulfstream V. He had a soft spot for the plane, which he had used regularly in the rendition years. The line wasn't good, but he knew immediately that it was Lakshmi Meena. He made a mental note not to call her babe.

'Lakshmi. What have you got for me?'

Meena explained about the unmarked white helicopter that had been seen in the mountains, then took a deep breath – another one – and told him about his old friend Dr Abdul Aziz, the Dentist, and what he had said about the GICM and their hideout in the Atlas mountains.

'Where are we running with this?' Spiro asked, cutting her short. 'I'm on the red-eye here.'

Meena sensed that their conversation would be over almost before it had started. Spiro was too full of Dhar's death to listen to a junior officer phoning in with a hunch. 'Aziz thinks Daniel Marchant was in the mountains,' she continued, feeling that she had nothing to lose. 'Stole a bike, took a ride up there at the same time the helicopter was seen.'

'Tell me you were with him.'

'I'd backed off, as instructed. The guy's done nothing but go jogging and read the Koran for three months.'

Spiro thought for a moment. Reluctantly, Langley had agreed with London to leave Marchant alone after Delhi, but he wasn't allowed to travel abroad. After a year, Spiro had acceded to Fielding's demands and let Marchant fly to Morocco. There was no doubt in Spiro's mind that the kid should have been locked up, just as his father should have been. The subsequent revelation that he was related to Salim Dhar only confirmed his worst fears. Now might be the time to take him out of the equation, particularly if everyone was distracted by news of Dhar's death. Besides, what the hell was his so-called vacation in Morocco all about? The Vicar had called it a sabbatical. As far as Spiro was concerned, if someone needed some R&R, they headed for Honolulu, not North Africa.

'Check him in for some root-canal work,' Spiro said. 'Aziz could do with the practice.'

'That would be a breach of existing protocol, sir,' Meena said.

'I think you misheard me, Lakshmi.'

'No, sir, I didn't.'

There was a pause, a calculation. Spiro knew she was right, but he wasn't going to let anyone ruin his visit to London, least of all Daniel Marchant. He cut her off.

It had been a good day in Washington, one of the best of his career. He had personally briefed the President about the drone strike on Salim Dhar. Although it was still too early to go public, the signs were good: no collateral for once, just a clean hit on the world's most wanted. It didn't get much sweeter. Now he was on his way to Fairford, and would shortly be making Marcus Fielding's life a misery, something he always enjoyed.

The CIA was already all over MI5, running its own large network of agents and informers in Britain. As Spiro had discussed with the President, a Pakistani entering the US from 'Londonistan' on a visa-waiver programme now represented the biggest threat to America. As a result, 25 per cent of the Agency's resources dedicated to preventing another 9/11 were being directed at Britain. MI5 wasn't up to the job, and the CIA had recruited half of Yorkshire in the past few years. Immigration security at all major British airports was being coordinated by the Agency, too. Now he was about to rub the Vicar's nose in it.

His phone rang again. This time he hesitated before answering it. His boss, the DCIA, only called him in the middle of the night if there was a problem.

17

It was two o'clock in the morning, and Marcus Fielding was still in his Legoland office, playing his flute: Telemann's Suite in A-Minor. It was something of a tradition in MI6. Colin McColl, one of his predecessors, had filled the night air at the old head office in Southwark with his playing. Fielding rarely drank, but tonight was an exception. A bottle of Château Musar from the Bekaa Valley stood on his desk, half empty. He knew Spiro had come to gloat in London and he was determined to deny him the pleasure.

He stood up, arched his stiff back and went over to Oleg, the Service's newest recruit, a two-year-old border terrier. Fielding had adopted him from Battersea Dogs' Home the previous month and named him after two great Russian servants of MI6. There had been a few raised eyebrows the first time he brought Oleg into Legoland, but he only accompanied the Chief to work when he had to stay late, like tonight. His driver had brought him across the Thames from his flat in Dolphin Square, Pimlico, walking him along the towpath before handing him over to security at a side gate.

Oleg had undoubtedly made life more tolerable, absorbed some of the stress. His presence broke up the neatness of Fielding's existence, which he was aware had become an obsession since his return from India. He had almost lost his job helping Daniel Marchant in Delhi. For a few dark days, the Americans had taken over the asylum. Legoland had been raided and he had been on the run, just like Marchant. He was too old for that game, too tired, which was why he had tried to restore some order to his life, a protection against the chaos of the raging world outside.

Tonight, though, that chaos threatened to return, and it had nothing to do with Oleg or the Lebanese wine. His mind had been racing ever since he had spoken with Marchant in Morocco. Normally, he would have dismissed his talk of Moscow as wild speculation from a field agent under pressure. But earlier in the day, a routine memo from MI5 had landed in his in-tray that made Marchant's words – *Nye strelai* – hang in the air long after the encrypted line from Marrakech had dropped.

Harriet Armstrong, Fielding's opposite number at Thames House, had come over the river to talk about it in person. She was no longer on crutches, but she still had a slight limp, the only legacy of her car crash in Delhi. One of her officers in D4, the counter-intelligence branch that monitored the Soviet Embassy in Kensington Palace Gardens, had intercepted a routine diplomatic communication. A man called Nikolai Ivanovich Primakov was about to be posted to London under cultural attaché cover. The young duty officer had run the normal checks, calling up Primakov's file from the library and cross-referring it with known SVR and GRU agents operating under diplomatic cover.

To the duty officer's surprise, he found that Primakov had once enjoyed a high-flying intelligence career, but his prospects had suffered when Boris Yeltsin set about disbanding the KGB in 1991. After a three-year stint in the private security business, protecting banks in Moscow, Primakov returned to the SVR, as the KGB's First Chief Directorate had become, where he continued to rise through the ranks until he suffered a series of sideways moves.

His imminent arrival in London was a promotion, prompting the duty officer to conclude in his daily report that it was significant.

At no point did he realise quite how significant it was, but behind the scenes his routine inquiry had triggered a flagged message to drop into Armstrong's in-box. As Director General of MI5, she was one of only a handful of people who knew that Primakov had once been MI6's most senior asset in the KGB and later the SVR, on a par with Penkovsky and Gordievsky.

Fielding and Armstrong were allies now, thick as Baghdad thieves, united in their resentment of America's growing influence in Whitehall. And Fielding sensed the makings of a mutually beneficial plan, a shoring up of defences against Spiro, something that might buy both their Services a little respect again after a torrid year.

He gave Oleg a scratch behind the ears and walked back to his desk. One of Primakov's restricted MI6 files from the 1980s, known as a 'no-trace' because any database search for it would yield nothing, lay in front of the framed photos of Fielding's favourite godchildren, Maya and Freddie. Beside it was a neat grid of Post-it notes he had been writing all evening.

The file was open on a page that showed a tourist-style photo of Primakov taken in Agra in 1980, standing in front of the Taj Mahal. Beside him was Stephen Marchant, smiling back at the camera. He had good reason to be happy, and not just because his wife had recently given birth to twins, Daniel and Sebastian. It was eight years before disaster would strike, when Sebastian was so cruelly taken from him. Stephen Marchant was already a rising star in MI6, but his recruitment of Primakov, then attached to the Soviet Embassy in Delhi, would propel him all the way to the top of the Service.

Primakov rose swiftly through the KGB, too, on his return to Moscow, specialising in counter-intelligence, much to the satisfaction of Marchant and his MI6 superiors. But his relationship with the West was built on personal friendship. He would only agree to be handled by Stephen Marchant, which created problems for everyone. Not for the first time, Primakov began to arouse the suspicion of Moscow Centre, his career stalled and the RX eventually dried up. Primakov's posting to London marked a return to the fold. And Fielding sensed that it was in some way linked to whatever had happened in Morocco. Patterns again.

A line from the switchboard was flickering on Fielding's comms console. He had been about to look at another file on Primakov that not even Armstrong knew about. It told a very different story about his friendship with Marchant, but that would have to wait. He took the call, wondering who would be ringing him so late at night.

'I have a Paul Myers from GCHQ for you, sir,' the woman on reception said.

The last time he had spoken to Myers had also been in the middle of the night, when he had rung to talk about Leila. It was partly because of Myers that she had been exposed as a traitor, something that Fielding had never forgotten.

'I assume this is important,' Fielding began, sounding harsher than he meant. He liked Myers.

'Sorry for ringing so late, but I thought you should know,' Myers began. At least he wasn't drunk this time.

'Go on.'

'I've been working on the Salim Dhar intercept, in advance of the JIC meeting tomorrow.'

'And?'

'There was someone else in the farm building with him.'

'Quite a few people, I gather.' Perhaps Myers had been drinking after all.

'There's a voice at the end of the intercept, sort of screaming.'

Fielding instinctively peeled off a fresh Post-it note and began to write, trying to contain any implications within the boundaries of his neat hand.

' "Sort of" screaming? Either it was screaming or it wasn't.'

'I've been running it through filter analysis, comparing it with thousands of other screams. It's an American voice.'

Myers paused. The nib of Fielding's green-ink fountain pen hovered.

'There's something else. I ran a few spectrographic checks. There wasn't much to go on, but the voiceprint appears to match one of the US Marines who was taken by the Taleban.'

'Are you sure?' There had been a news blackout when six US Marines had been seized two days earlier, but the Americans had told a few of their closest allies, which still included Britain.

'Fort Meade patched over some voice profiles of the Marines to Cheltenham, told our Af-Pak desks to listen out for them. I think Salim Dhar might have been with them, maybe part of the team holding them hostage.'

There was a long silence. Oleg raised his head, as if sensing the missed beat.

'Sir?'

But Fielding had already hung up.

18

Spiro looked in the mirror and straightened his tie. The Joint Intelligence Committee was already assembling down the corridor, but there was still time. Entering and locking a cubicle behind him, he marshalled two lines of cocaine on the porcelain surface of the cistern, using his Whitehall security card. Then he stopped, held his breath. Someone had come into the room, humming. It sounded like Fielding. Did the Vicar know more than he did? Cheltenham would have picked up the *jihadi* website before Langley had shut it down.

Spiro waited for him to leave, listening to the crisp discipline of the Vicar's unhurried ablutions, the way he dispensed the soap with two short stabs, turned the taps, tore the paper towels. A man in control of his life, unhurried. Spiro envied him, but he knew that he too would have that feeling in a few seconds. When the Vicar was gone, he leaned over the powder, a rolled ten-dollar bill shaking in his hand. The next moment he was flushing the cistern, the tumbling water masking his snorts. Steady, he told himself. He had to hold it together.

Spiro unlocked the cubicle door and rinsed his hands, glancing again at himself in the smoked mirror. At moments like this he could take reassurance in his ageing face, find comfort in the lines of experience, each one a reminder of a hardship survived, one of life's obstacles overcome: brought up in Over-the-Rhine, then a rough quarter in downtown Cincinnati; an abusive father; the first Gulf War; his cheating wife; their disabled son and his desire to make the world a better place for him.

Few people saw him that way. The British had him down as an ex-Marine who had forgotten to leave his battle fatigues at the door, which was fine by him. He hadn't been hired to be nice. Christ, he hadn't been *born* to be nice. One of his first jobs at Langley had been to oversee the freelance deniables the Agency regularly hired to do its heavy lifting. They were all ex-military, like him, and they got along with him fine, respecting his distinguished career in the Marine Corps.

He knew, though, that he had been lucky to hold on to his job. The end of the rendition programme and the fall-out from the so-called 'torture memos' had led a number of staff to leave, sapping the morale of those left behind. Spiro had thought about jumping into the private sector before he was pushed, but he had stayed on, never doubting that his approach to intelligence would be in demand again in the future. He just hadn't figured it would be so soon. Salim Dhar was to thank for that. The jumped-up *jihadi*'s long-range shot at the President had changed everything, including Spiro's career prospects.

'Thank God, I didn't fire you,' the new DCIA, a moderate, had joked after promoting Spiro to head of the National Clandestine Service's European operations. 'The bad-ass guys are back in town.'

But his job now looked to be in doubt again. Dark clouds were rolling in from Afghanistan. The tone of the DCIA's voice on the phone in the Gulfstream V had reminded him of the consultant who had broken the news about their disabled child. Mom and baby were doing fine. They just needed to run some tests. Euphoria qualified.

According to the DCIA, a *jihadi* website was claiming that six kidnapped US Marines had been killed in a drone strike. The website had been flooded immediately by Fort Meade, temporarily shutting it down, but the signs weren't good, and the news, true or false, would soon come out elsewhere. The thought made Spiro want to throw up. He had served in the Gulf alongside one of the soldiers, Lieutenant Randall Oaks, knew his wife, heard they had a young daughter.

'Don't beat our drum too loud in London,' the DCIA had said. 'We might need our friends in the days ahead.' So it was with a deep breath that Spiro splashed water on his weathered face, dried himself with a paper towel and hoped that the Vicar might offer a prayer for the dead.

19

Marchant had a contingency plan for leaving Morocco, the first part of which he had already put in place. The ticket he had booked on the morning flight out of Marrakech was in his own name. But the passport he now held in his hand as he sat in the back of the speeding taxi was in the name of Dirk McLennan, a 'snap cover' stitched together by Legoland's cobblers before he had left. The biography was not as detailed as an operational legend, but it was good enough to get him out of Morocco. And the airport he was heading for was Agadir, not Marrakech.

Marchant didn't miss his previous cover identity, the back-packing student who had done such an efficient job of getting him to India when the CIA had been on his case in Poland. He had enjoyed winding back the clock, smoking weed and getting laid by Monika, the hostel receptionist, but it had been compli-cated, raised too many issues. His new identity was far more straightforward: a libidinous snapper who ran residential photo-graphy courses in Marrakech, mainly for parties of single British women of a certain age.

And this time there was none of the cobblers' bitterness that had characterised his last legend, no biographical flaws echoing the tragedies of his own life. Dirk McLennan was a good-time cover, full of *joie de vivre*: girlfriends aplenty, all-night benders and an interesting sideline in glamour photography. In short, Marchant saw it as a gift, his bonus from Legoland for a difficult year.

He checked the passport, his business card and the Billingham bag of cameras and lenses that he had kept in his flat, then caught a glimpse of himself in the driver's mirror and adjusted the sunglasses that were perched on the top of his head. McLennan's hair was slightly darker than his own, which was dirt-blond, but he had had no time to dye it. After spotting Meena, he had collected a small overnight bag from his flat and jumped in a taxi, ordered by a man he could trust in the medina.

Now, as the taxi drove down the highway to Agadir, Marchant thought back three months to when Fielding had called him into his office on the morning he had left for Marrakech. The Vicar had reminded him of his responsibilities, the need to keep his head down. They had both survived a challenging time together in India, and their relationship was close, at times almost like father and son. Fielding had risked his own career to support him, something Marchant would never forget. The ensuing year in London had not been easy for either of them. Confined to Legoland by the Americans, Marchant had drunk too much and caused trouble in the office. Fielding had grown tired of having to bail him out. They both knew that Marchant was the only person who could find Dhar, and he wasn't going to do it chained to a desk in London.

'The Americans have retreated, lifted the travel ban, but they insist that you remain a legitimate target for observation,' the Vicar had said, sipping at a glass of the sweet mint tea he had asked Otto, his Eastern European butler, to prepare for the two of them. 'We've protested, of course, but there's no movement.'

'And our rules of engagement, have they changed?'

'Despite everything that happened, to you, to me, to Harriet

Armstrong, America remains our closest ally,' Fielding said. 'Remember that. The appalling truth is that we can't live for long without them or the intel they share with us.' He paused. 'Langley is on record as having cleared you and your father of any wrongdoing. That counts for something. Salim Dhar is the enemy combatant here, not you. But we both know that your relationship with Dhar presents the CIA with a problem. If they ever cross the line again, hold you against your will, interrogate –'

'Waterboard,' Marchant interrupted.

'Yes, well – you may have to cross the line, too.'

'And the real reason for my presence in Marrakech remains deniable,' Marchant said.

'Utterly. As far as the Americans are concerned, you are in Morocco on sabbatical. Marrakech is a natural place for you, an Arabist, to sort your life out. HR have signed off on it, citing ill-health and low office morale. Given the disruption you've caused in Legoland over the past year, they are only too pleased to see the back of you.'

Marchant reckoned that the circumstances he found himself in now satisfied Fielding's conditions. Lakshmi Meena had crossed the line. The woman Langley had sent to keep an eye on him was suddenly on his case after weeks of inactivity. He might be wrong, of course, but it was odd that Meena had come back to watch him late in the night after their meeting at the *bar anglais*. The only explanation was that she must have heard about the helicopter incident and Marchant's presence in the mountains. But who had seen him? He assumed it was a local informer. The CIA was closer to the Moroccan intelligence services than MI6, particularly after the courts in London had revealed details of torture at a Moroccan black site.

By the time he reached Agadir airport, Marchant was confident that nobody had followed him by road from Marrakech. His worry was that a reception committee might be waiting for him in the departures hall. If Meena meant business, she would be watching all the country's exits, particularly when Daniel Marchant didn't show up for his flight from Marrakech. But security at the airport was no more rigorous than usual.

After checking in one piece of luggage, Marchant was about to make his way to passport control when he heard a commotion behind him. He turned to see a man in shades being escorted into the departures hall by three policemen, an air stewardess and a posse of screaming middle-aged women. Behind them were half a dozen paparazzi, cameras flashing as they jostled for position.

'Who's the celeb?' Marchant asked the attractive woman behind the check-in desk.

'Hussein Farmi,' she said, a faint blush colouring her face.

Marchant nodded knowingly, but the woman wasn't convinced.

'Star of more than a hundred films,' she explained. '*Khali Balak Min Zouzou*? With Soad Hosny?'

'Of course.'

'He's one of the Middle East's most popular actors. And he has been married five times.' She stifled a giggle.

'I'd better get a few shots of him then,' Marchant said, nodding at the canvas bag slung over his shoulder. Without thinking, he pulled out a camera, snapped the check-in woman and gave her a wink as he walked off in pursuit of Farmi. Photographers could get away with murder, he thought.

20

Fielding couldn't remember such a tense meeting of the Joint Intelligence Committee. Even the ones that had been hastily called in the hours after 9/11 and 7/7 had been characterised by unity rather than discord. Everyone had been pulling together then. There were no divisions, no conflicting agendas. The Americans had needed Britain's help after 9/11, and the British had needed their help after 7/7.

This time the Cabinet Room in Downing Street was crackling with resentment and rivalry as Spiro addressed the London heads of the Canadian, Australian and New Zealand intelligence services, Harriet Armstrong, Director General of MI5, the head of GCHQ, accompanied by an awkward Paul Myers, a raft of faceless Whitehall mandarins, and the clammy-cheeked Sir David Chadwick, still chairman of the JIC despite the Americans' best efforts to unseat him in a cooked-up child-porn sting.

'I had hoped to bring better news to you all today,' Spiro said, studiously avoiding any eye contact with Fielding. 'As you know, we believe we have eliminated Salim Dhar in a Reaper strike in Afghanistan. We still maintain the target was destroyed, but there are rumours this morning that Dhar might have been with the six US Marines who were taken at the weekend by Taleban forces. In terms of potential collateral, that particular scenario couldn't be worse.'

Six US Marines struck Fielding as a result, compared to the normal quota of innocent women and children who were destroyed by drone strikes, but he kept his peace, preferring to make his point with a short dry cough. Spiro looked across at him for the first time.

'They are all fine soldiers. One of them, Lieutenant Randall Oaks, served alongside me in Iraq. As things stand right now, the picture is a little confused. A *jihadi* website posted images this morning of the strike zone, one of which I can show you now.'

He pressed at a remote in his hand and a grab from a website appeared on a flat screen behind Spiro. It showed a group of local Afghanis waving at the camera. One was holding a damaged Marine's helmet, its US markings just visible.

'NSA managed to crash the site by overloading the server, but it's fair to assume the images will soon appear elsewhere. We happen to believe they're fake, but clearly it's an unhelpful story. Right now, the President, whom I personally briefed yesterday, is holding back on an announcement about Dhar. He wants DNA, but that could be tricky, given the hostile location of the strike zone.'

Chadwick cleared his throat loudly enough for Spiro to pause. 'Just supposing Dhar is still alive, is he likely to address his followers, make a video to prove he's not dead?'

'First up, we don't believe Dhar's alive. Our position remains that he was killed in the Reaper strike. Personally, I also think the Marines story is a red herring, put out to distract attention from Dhar's death. No way would Salim Dhar, the world's most wanted terrorist, risk being with the Marines, knowing our ongoing military efforts to find and retrieve them. But if Dhar is still alive – and that's a mighty big if – it's not his style to show himself.'

'So should we be putting out rumours that he's dead?'

'Absolutely. Fort Meade's already posting to that effect in

jihadi chatrooms. We'd be grateful if Cheltenham coordinates the European side of things. I don't want a repeat of Rashid Rauf. His supporters were claiming he was alive and well within minutes of the Reaper strike. It's imperative we move quickly.'

Fielding caught Armstrong's eye. He wondered what she was feeling as she sat there, watching the humiliation of Spiro, a man she had once so foolishly admired. She glanced away and looked at Myers. The three of them had talked earlier about the audio evidence. The head of GCHQ was not happy – Cheltenham had better relations with the Americans than MI5 and MI6 – but Fielding had reassured him that he would take the heat.

Just as Spiro was about to speak again, Fielding began, his languid body language – long legs out to one side, head bent forward like a concert pianist's – at odds with the devastating intelligence he was about to pool.

'Some product crossed my desk this morning that I think should be shared.'

'That's very good of you,' Spiro said, managing a thin smile. Fielding savoured his rival's fluster, the nervousness that everyone in the room would have detected in the American's voice. 'Go ahead. After all, sharing product is what this meeting's all about, isn't it?'

'Your position, as I understand it, is that Dhar was not with the Marines at the time of the strike.'

'No, that's not my position. The Marines were not with Dhar when we eliminated him.'

Spiro's voice was wavering more now, a top-end tremolo that was music to Fielding's ears.

'Let's just suppose for a moment that we could prove that the Marines and Dhar were together when the Reaper struck.'

'I hope that this evidence, whatever it is, came in to your

possession after and not before we launched our attack. Because that would frickin' upset me if you weren't sharing intel.'

'I can understand that. For the record' – a nod at Chadwick, the chairman – 'we learned about it late last night.'

'And what exactly is this intel?'

'Paul?' Fielding turned to Myers, who was sitting next to him, looking more uncomfortable than usual. 'Paul Myers has been on attachment with us from Cheltenham' – a glance at the Chief of GCHQ, who turned away as if Fielding had just thrown up over him – 'and last night he ran some further tests on the Dhar audio intercept.'

Fielding looked again at Myers, who appeared too nervous to take up the story, biting at what was left of his nails.

'Some tests,' Spiro said, not trying to disguise his disdain. 'In addition to Fort Meade's thorough spectrographic analysis?'

'That's right. And he found a fragment of sound at the end of the second intercept that I think we should all hear.'

Myers stood up and walked over to an audio console beneath the main screen. He had suddenly grown in confidence, evidently more at ease with technology than people. After checking the levels, he half turned towards the room, instinctively crouching down at the height of the console when he saw all the faces.

'I was looking for something else when I found it,' he said, to no one in particular. 'Often the way.' A nervous laugh, immediately regretted. 'It's only a few milliseconds, but I've slowed it down so you can hear.' He pressed a button, and there was silence. Then a deep, distorted, drawn-out call, like a wounded animal's, filled the room.

'And what in God's name was that?' Spiro said, suddenly more confident. He had seen his enemy's best shot, and he could live with it. He stood up, as if to defend himself better, knuckles pressed into the oak table.

Myers stood up, too, and looked across at Fielding for guidance. Fielding nodded.

'It's a scream,' Myers began. 'An American scream.'

Fielding watched as the ensuing silence sapped Spiro of all his bravura, his large frame collapsing like a punctured tyre.

'An American scream,' Spiro managed to repeat, more as a statement than a question. Fielding had to give him credit. He was trying to put on a brave face.

'I've compared it with the audio IDs sent over by Fort Meade.' Myers paused, fiddling with his ponytail. 'It's a perfect match with one of the Marines.' He paused again. 'Lieutenant Randall Oaks.'

21

It was as Marchant was taking his seat in the departure lounge that he first sensed security at the airport had been raised a level. Two men in charcoal suits had appeared at the gate and were standing by the entrance to the airbridge that led down to the plane, a twin-turboprop ATR 42. Marchant knew that the aircraft was used by courier firms, but it also flew short-haul passenger flights.

The two men, badges on their jackets, scrutinised the group of people waiting for the flight, then glanced down the list of passengers with a member of the ground crew. One of the officers caught Marchant's eye, checked the list, and then looked at another passenger. They didn't appear to be interested in him, but he was on edge now, searching for anything that might suggest he was a target.

Earlier, after he had taken a few photos of Hussein Farmi and joked with the other photographers, he had passed through passport control without a problem. Not even a second glance at his photo. He hadn't been worried that the cobblers' work wouldn't be up to scratch; he was more concerned that Meena might have called in a favour, asked Moroccan intelligence to keep a lookout for him.

There were no more than twenty passengers in total, and they started to form an orderly line when their flight was finally called.

Marchant was about to get up from his seat when one of the suited men came over to him, smiling.

'Mr McLennan?'

'That's me,' Marchant said, keeping it upbeat. He followed up with what he hoped was a cheeky smile. 'Is there a problem?' He wouldn't have asked if he had been Daniel Marchant, but he felt Dirk McLennan was the sort of man who liked to put his cards on the table.

'Not at all. The flight is less than half full, and we are upgrading today. Please, follow me.'

'Great, sounds a blast,' Marchant said, assessing the risk. He was instinctively worried. The badge on the man's suit indicated that he worked for the local airline, but Marchant didn't believe it for a second. 'Terrific, in fact. But what about these good people here?' He glanced at the other passengers.

'I should say it is because you are a guest of our country and we have a long and honourable tradition of hospitality, but I would be lying.' He paused. Marchant thought for a moment about running, but he returned the man's steady gaze as a bead of sweat rolled down his back. 'We upgrade randomly from the passenger list, and providing the individual is what we call SFU – suitable for upgrade – we invite them to enjoy their flight in the comfort of business class. Come.'

Marchant shrugged at the other passengers and walked to the front of the queue, sprinkling apologies as he went. He showed his boarding card to a member of the airline crew and tried to flirt with her, but she was having none of it. He mustered a swagger as he walked down the airbridge towards the aircraft. It was tempting to look back, but he knew it would be inappropriate. Dirk McLennan was a chancer, and would be loving every minute of this. If only he felt the same. Something was very wrong, but how could he protest about an upgrade?

'Please, enjoy your flight, Mr McLennan,' the man said, ushering him on board the plane.

Marchant nodded at the two cabin crew who greeted him at the door. They steered him left into the small business-class area, where there were eight seats in total. He eased across to a window and sat down with his camera bag on his lap, his limbs heavy with adrenaline. Trying to control his breathing, he considered his options, but the sense of imminent danger was overwhelming. The plane would have been claustrophobic even if he hadn't felt out of control of the situation. The only exit point was the door he had just entered, and his last opportunity to escape was now. But how far would he get? The boarding gate, if he was lucky.

Again he ran through the situation in which he found himself: Lakshmi Meena was on his tail, turning up at dawn on the streets of Marrakech. Booking a flight as Daniel Marchant from the city's airport had given him a head start, but Meena had friends in the Moroccan intelligence service, and someone might have recognised him here at Agadir. No one had stopped him at passport control, but then he was given an upgrade. Perhaps he was over-reacting, and Meena was just making sure he left town. It was too easy to see threats where none existed. But he knew he was right, particularly when another passenger was shown into business class and sat down in the seat beside him.

'Mind if I join you?' the man asked. He was Moroccan, and looked faintly familiar.

'Sure,' Marchant said, glancing at the empty seats on the other side of the aisle.

'You're a photographer?' he asked, nodding at Marchant's camera bag.

'For my sins,' Marchant said, struggling to stay in character. 'And you?'

'Me?' He paused. 'I'm a dentist.'

22

'There's something else,' Myers said, after Spiro had sat down. It was more of a slump, but Spiro somehow managed to make it look controlled. For a moment, Fielding wished he felt sorry for Spiro, a pang of pity. But there was nothing but cold contempt, the sort he normally reserved for Russians. 'Work for the Foreign Office if you want to be liked,' he had been told by the don who had tapped him up at Oxford. What Fielding didn't know was that another blow to Spiro's self-esteem, his career, his whole *raison d'être*, was about to come from Myers, who was still standing in front of the audio.

This time, Myers didn't look to Fielding for guidance. He was on his own now, score abandoned, improvising. 'Actually, I agree with the American analysis that Dhar would not risk being with the captured US Marines.'

Spiro seemed to take heart from this, and sat up to listen.

'I didn't at first, but I do now. Using this assumption as my starting point, I went back to the audio this morning and asked myself, in the light of the American scream, how it was possible for Salim Dhar and Lieutenant Oaks to be in the same place.'

'And?' Chadwick said, glancing at Spiro. Like Fielding, he was intrigued to see what this awkward analyst from Cheltenham was going to say next. Spiro was staring out of the window, lost in his own thoughts. The head of GCHQ didn't know where to look.

Myers picked nervously at the back of a front tooth and then stopped himself, as if being chided by a parent. 'The only explanation is that Dhar's voice was recorded.'

Spiro looked from the window to Myers, suddenly encouraged.

'Don't you think that scenario might just have been checked out by the NSA?'

'Of course. And I've looked into it, too. But the quality of the intercept is too poor to be able to establish if Dhar's voice is a recording. There's also no audio trace of a recorder activating before or after Dhar speaks.'

'So?'

'For once, the answer doesn't lie in technology.'

Fielding was enjoying this, watching Myers grow in confidence, trying to guess where it would lead. This was what intelligence work was all about: intuition.

'You're an analyst, right?' Spiro heckled. 'Stick to IT and leave the couch work to others.'

Myers ignored him, more out of dysfunctional shyness than defiance.

'Why did Lieutenant Oaks scream?' Myers asked, addressing the whole room now.

'Why?' Spiro echoed. 'He was about to be incinerated by a Hellfire missile, that's why.'

'About to be. Exactly. It's not my area, of course –'

'Too right.'

'– but my understanding of munitions is that such things are pretty instant. Like, no time to scream. Oaks had worked out what was going on. It was the second time Dhar had spoken. He wouldn't have known what was happening the first time he heard his voice. But when he spoke again, Oaks would have realised that there was nobody else in that hut apart from the six Marines. He was trying to give Fort Meade a message, tell them it was a mistake, that there was a tape recorder strapped to Dhar's phone. Just like this one.'

With uncharacteristic panache, Myers reached into his fleece pocket and pulled out a small mobile phone strapped with masking tape to an equally thin tape recorder. Myers was turning out to be a natural showman, Fielding thought, despite the phone catching awkwardly on his pocket. Next up, he'd be pulling rabbits from a hat, sawing Harriet Armstrong in half, performing the Indian rope trick. Armstrong would like that. She wasn't afraid to play to the gallery. At Cambridge, she had played the fairy godmother in a university production of *Cinderella*.

The two units were linked by a small audio lead, which might have looked like a detonator to an inexperienced eye. The room didn't exactly gasp – those present were too versed in the modern tools of terror to be surprised – but there was a shuffling of papers that Fielding had come to recognise over the years as civil servants' applause.

'As soon as Lieutenant Oaks heard the voice a second time,' Myers said, brandishing the phone, 'the penny dropped and he screamed, but it was too late. The phone had already disconnected. Except that it wasn't too late. We heard him, and we know Dhar's still alive.'

Spiro knew as soon as Myers had spoken that he was right. He thought back to the UAV trailer at Creech, to the sensor operator who had cast doubt on the target. For a moment, Spiro had imagined he had seen what looked like a crucifix, but the image was blurred and he had shut it out of his mind. Just as he had removed the operator's suspicions from his official report afterwards.

It took almost a minute for someone to speak after Myers

had shuffled back to his seat. Chadwick was the one who broke the silence, and his comments were addressed to Spiro.

'I think I speak for all of the British agencies when I say that we offer you our unconditional sympathy. It's at times like this that allies must pull together and help one other.'

Whitehall shorthand for *Thank Christ the mistake wasn't ours*, Fielding thought.

'That's good of you,' Spiro said quietly. America wasn't used to needing its allies. 'I must make some calls.'

Fielding thought that Spiro looked a genuinely broken man as he stood up to leave. But again there was no sympathy, just the thought of what could be leveraged from the situation.

'Before you go,' Chadwick said, 'I want you to know that there's no reason why our official position should change: Dhar is thought to have been killed, but it is believed, with great regret, that six US Marines whom he had taken were killed too. Adopting such a line carries a political risk, and the Prime Minister will make no official statement on the incident, but our experience of Dhar is that he's not the sort of *jihadi* who will turn up on a website telling the world he's alive and well. It suits him better that the world thinks he's dead. Clearly, we need to qualify any statement we make to give us sufficient slack if he does show up, but for the time being, Dhar is dead.'

23

'Please, have a rinse,' Abdul Aziz said.

Marchant sucked at the straw that was put to his bruised lips, swilled the liquid round his mouth and then spat out a mixture of blood and fragments of his lower right molar. Aziz held a kidney-shaped stainless-steel dish up to his mouth, resting it on his lower lip, and caught the debris.

The moment Aziz had introduced himself as a dentist, two men had appeared from behind the economy-class curtain. Aziz had stood up to let them through to Marchant, who had put up a fight, taking one of them out, but it was still two against one, although Aziz had held back, limiting himself to a gratuitous kick to Marchant's groin. Eventually, he was forced down into an aisle seat, his wrists bound to the armrests with plasticuffs and his legs secured to the footrest.

The two men left the plane before it took off, one helping the other, leaving only Aziz and a pilot on board. Lakshmi Meena never showed, but Marchant assumed she was the one who had set him up with Aziz. He regretted opening up to her in their chat the previous night, knew he should have listened to his instinct, not trusted anyone. The sole grain of comfort was his right hand. In the struggle to secure him to his seat, he had been cut in the soft flesh of his wrist. It wasn't a deep incision, but it was painful enough to give him hope, because it meant that somewhere there was a sharp edge.

Marchant had heard of Aziz, knew the enhanced techniques he had used on enemy combatants as they had passed through black sites in Morocco on their way to Guantanamo; but what was it with the polite small talk? Had he once trained as a real dentist? He'd be offering him an old copy of *Punch* next, something to read while he waited for his teeth to be extracted without anaesthetic. He wondered if Aziz knew about Marchant's long and painful relationship with dentists, or whether he just assumed that dentistry would always touch a raw nerve in his detainees.

'We don't have to do this, Daniel,' Aziz said, adjusting the settings on the steel brace that held Marchant's head in position. Marchant couldn't reply. His mouth had been wedged open with a metal clamp that tasted of linseed oil. He was also barely conscious. At least his business-class seat was upright. Up until now it had been fully reclined, reminding him of an actual dentist's chair, which was no doubt the point. Aziz's entire approach – the perverse offer of mouthwash, his authentic tools of the trade – seemed designed to remind him of the real thing. Except that there was no soothing classical music, no funny posters on the ceiling. Just the hum of the aircraft and a silence behind the curtain that confirmed Marchant's worst fears. He was the only passenger who had proceeded to boarding.

'All I need to know is what you saw in the mountains and if it had anything to do with Salim Dhar,' Aziz said. He was standing in the aisle, examining an ultrasonic scaler that was buzzing in his hand. The reverberating whine began to shake down memories from the walls of Marchant's skull.

'Unfortunately, this instrument is a bit faulty,' Aziz apologised, lowering the scaler into Marchant's mouth. 'I borrowed it from a horse vet who didn't seem to care so much about maintenance.

The problem is the sharp tip at the end – it isn't being cooled by water, so it becomes red hot. Normally, a dentist moves quickly from one tooth to the next to prevent overheating, but I am not a normal dentist.'

Marchant screamed as Aziz pressed down with the instrument, scorching into the soft pulp of his molar. The surrounding gum seemed to explode into flames, the heat spreading through his head, licking down into his neck and shoulders until it felt as if his whole upper body was being blowtorched.

'Please try to remember the mountains, Daniel. Because if what you saw did involve Salim Dhar and I didn't know about it, the Americans will remove my teeth after I've finished pulling yours.'

Aziz unfastened the clamp and put down the scaler. He then picked up a steel dental drill and tested it. More whining, as if the drill was suffering pain rather than about to inflict it.

'Tungsten carbide,' Aziz said, inspecting the drill's burr. 'You see, I'm meant to hear about everything that happens in Morocco, or as our friend James Spiro put it so politely, "every fucking fart from Fes to Safi". I know it's not fair, but that's the way it goes. The Americans, they expect a lot from us, and I would hate to let them down.'

'I didn't see anything unusual,' Marchant repeated, his voice thick with blood. He thought back to what he had said a few minutes earlier, knowing that if he repeated it verbatim, it would be a clear indication that he was lying. He remembered the instructor – army moustache, tight-fitting T-shirt – who had taught him at RAF St Mawgan in Cornwall, where all new MI6 recruits were sent for basic SERE (Survival, Evasion, Rescue and Escape) training. Small errors and variations were more convincing than perfect recall, which suggested a fake story that had been well rehearsed.

'It was my last night in Marrakech,' Marchant continued. 'I wanted to go up into the mountains one last time, so I borrowed a friend's motorbike, went for a ride.'

'Sometimes I think you British believe Moroccans are a genuinely inferior people,' Aziz said. Marchant braced himself for more pain. 'It's the only explanation for the way your courts of justice betray us. We interrogate terrorists on your behalf, in confidence, beyond your jurisdiction so nobody in your country breaks the law, then you release details of our work because of so-called freedom of information, and suddenly the whole world knows about it and treats us like pariahs. Never mind that it was your questions we were asking.'

'We objected to the publication of the information,' Marchant said. 'Unfortunately, the courts overruled us.'

Aziz laughed. 'What sort of secret service is it that gets pushed around by a judge?'

One that operates in a democracy, Marchant thought, but he held his swollen tongue.

'Tell me one thing, my friend: who is going to remember it was Britain's dirty work we were doing? No, all anyone remembers is that someone got tortured in Morocco. Happily, we're not in Moroccan airspace any more, so please answer my questions. Was Salim Dhar in the High Atlas?'

Marchant hesitated a moment too long. Aziz pulled his mouth open and inserted the clamp again, tightening it until his top and bottom jaw were so far apart that he thought his mouth would split at the corners. It was a repeat of what Aziz had done earlier, but he was angry now, curiosity replaced by irritation. Once again, Marchant couldn't talk, move his head or his jaw, but the sense of vulnerability was nothing compared to the next wave of pain that he knew was about to break over him.

'We have a choice, Daniel. Either you tell me what you saw, or I will have to remove the molar – it will be no good to you now.'

Marchant instinctively checked the bloodied tooth with his tongue, working it around the edge of the cavity. At the same moment, he flexed his right wrist, trying to find the sharp edge. He felt rough metal cut into his skin again. It was the lid of the ashtray in his armrest, flipped half open. Suddenly his predicament was bearable. He moved his wrist and felt the plastic of his cuffs rub against the edge of the ashtray. It would take time, but at least there was hope.

'All right, then. I think it's better we take it out,' Aziz said, just as turbulence rocked the plane enough for him to steady himself on Marchant's arm. He hadn't noticed Marchant working his right hand. 'I can see it's clearly causing you some discomfort.'

Again, Marchant wondered if Aziz had ever tried to go into dentistry. When it suited him, he had an excellent bedside manner, a soothing tone of authority that was utterly at odds with his work.

'Unfortunately, Morocco can be a very backward country at times, as tourists from Britain often remind us, and I'm afraid we have no anaesthetic with us today.'

Marchant thought for a moment that he saw genuine remorse pass across his face.

'But I do have these. Extraction forceps. The ones for molars have these beak-like ends, do you see?'

He didn't look at the steel pliers Aziz was holding up in front of him. They were in a medically sealed plastic bag, which seemed an unnecessary precaution in the circumstances. Aziz ripped it open and removed the pristine tool. Marchant guessed he had reached the point of Aziz's interrogation process that broke his victims. It used to be scalpel cuts to the genitals, but clearly things had moved on.

'First, though, we have a problem. Your molar is too big, even for these forceps. Maybe I got the wrong ones. Maybe they are for children's teeth. But it's OK. We have this.'

He put down the forceps and picked up the drill again, testing it one last time.

'Perhaps I will drill down through the molar, deep into the nerve, and split the tooth clean in two.'

Marchant could feel his legs shaking. His body was already in shock. He inhaled deeply, letting his diaphragm rise as high as it could, and breathed out slowly, trying to block the pain, focus on the only way out.

'It's funny, you know,' Aziz continued, resting the drill on Marchant's bottom lip. 'I was going to say "Open wide," the way they do, but I was forgetting.'

Fucking hilarious, Marchant thought, tasting the metal of the drill. His right wrist wasn't free yet, and he was beginning to wonder if it ever would be. The one thing he still had control over was his eyes. The point about torture, the SERE instructor had told him, was that the victim must feel totally out of control in order for it to be successful. He must not believe that he can influence anything in his immediate environment except through compliance.

When the CIA had waterboarded him in Poland, he had managed a soaked, defiant laugh, but he couldn't even muster that with his mouth levered open like Jonah's whale. He desperately wanted to shut his eyes, but he kept them open, fixing Aziz with a stare that momentarily unsettled his torturer as he began to drill.

24

'I'm sorry,' Myers said, cracking a knuckle so loudly it made Harriet Armstrong jump. The American, Australian and Canadian representatives had all left the Cabinet Room for the second half of the Joint Intelligence Committee, which was traditionally for UK agencies only. 'I know I should have briefed you all before, and I know it wasn't my business, but –'

'I think, in the light of your initial analysis, we can overlook the histrionics of the second act,' Fielding said, turning to Chadwick for formal approval.

'Of course, it was a significant breach of JIC protocol,' Chadwick said. 'But I agree, an exception can be made.'

'Does that unit actually work?' Armstrong asked, nodding at the handset in front of Myers. She was back to wearing her familiar severe suit jackets. Apart from her crocked knee, the only other visible legacy of her Indian adventure was a silver necklace, which had a hint of tribal art about it. She had also confided in Fielding that her mornings now began with half an hour of Vipassana yoga, something she wholly recommended as a way of getting through tedious meetings at the Home Office.

Myers picked up the handset.

'I tested it this morning. With the direct audio input between the two units, it sounds just like a phone call is being made.'

'So what now?' Chadwick said. 'Dhar is clearly not only alive, but several steps ahead of the Americans.'

'It might not have been Dhar's doing,' Armstrong said. 'All that was needed was a recording of his voice and his old SIM card, both of which could have easily been procured by Iran, his previous sponsors.'

'Our view remains that Dhar's too hot for Tehran,' Fielding said.

'So where is he?' Chadwick asked.

'Daniel Marchant is on his way back from Morocco,' Fielding replied.

'No surprise there. I don't think anyone seriously expected that avenue to yield anything, did we, Marcus?' Chadwick had been opposed to Marchant's trip to Morocco from the start, fearing that it would only aggravate Britain's already fragile relationship with America.

'I know you didn't,' Fielding said. He had never had much time for Chadwick, and often wondered if the Americans had been on to something when they had tried to frame him. 'As you all know, we had hoped Dhar would make contact with his half-brother, but he never did. However, something has come up in the last twenty-four hours which suggests that Marchant might have been right about Dhar seeking refuge in North Africa.'

The assembled chiefs looked up, but before Fielding could tell them about the unmarked helicopter in the Atlas mountains, there was a knock on the door and Ian Denton, now Fielding's Assistant Chief, put his lean face around the door.

'Marcus, sorry to interrupt, but I'm afraid Daniel Marchant's dropped off the grid.' Denton's voice, laced with a hint of a Hull accent, had become even more *sotto voce* since his promotion, Fielding thought, but he liked the fact that his trained ear was alone in hearing every word. It was almost as if Denton was speaking in a code known only to his Chief. 'He was meant to have boarded a flight from Marrakech this morning, but he flew out using his snap cover from Agadir.'

'And?' Fielding asked, wondering whether Spiro had already left the building. If Marchant had been taken, it could only be on the CIA's orders. They had done it once before, smuggling him out of Britain on a rendition flight to Poland. Spiro had given assurances that it would never happen again, but he had evidently hoped the death of Dhar would serve as a distraction.

'The local airline filed a false flightplan,' Denton said. 'All we know is that the plane has a very limited range.'

'Find Spiro and bring him back here. And if he complains, tell him we've decided to go public about Dhar.'

25

Marchant felt a new pulse of pain overload his nervous system as the drill began to work its way deep into his molar. He remembered the power surges they used to have in Delhi. Every room in the house would suddenly become unnaturally bright, then there would be the sound of popping lightbulbs, followed by the tinkle of glass. Bright lights were flashing across his vision now, and it felt as if synapses, rather than bulbs, were exploding in his brain, their sharp-edged debris falling across raw pathways.

He should have been unconscious, but Aziz would kill him if he passed out. Besides, the sustained eye contact had started to get to the Moroccan, breaking up his routine, causing his hands to shake. The turbulence didn't help either. Occasionally, the drill would slip away from the tooth and cut into Marchant's gum. He tried to focus on his teeth, their impregnability, the fact that they were the only body parts that survived intense fires. They were stronger than bones, weren't they? His molar wasn't going to split. It was too strong, too durable. He thought back to biology classes at school, labelled drawings of teeth: enamel, dentine, pulp, gum. Weren't strontium isotopes found in enamel?

Marchant was screaming now, deep guttural roars. Aziz covered Marchant's eyes with a scarf, but for some reason that interrupted his stride even more. Perhaps he needed to see his victim's eyes, open or shut. Would Meena have looked him in the eye if she were here? For a few brief moments, he had liked her at the *bar anglais*. He should have known better.

But amongst all the pain and anger, a crude plan had crystallised, forged from a visceral survival instinct. As far as Marchant could tell, the pilot had made no contact with Aziz since they had taken off. Marchant presumed he had been told by Meena to circle until he was ordered to land again. No questions, no reassuring chit-chat over the intercom. Which meant that it was just Aziz and him. When the clamp was in his mouth, Marchant was powerless, but Aziz would be removing it again in a moment to ask more questions. At least, he hoped he would. That had been the routine so far: questions, answers, clamp in, clamp out, more questions, more answers, clamp in . . . His only chance was at the point when the clamp was being unscrewed. Aziz was vulnerable then, leaning in close, inches from Marchant's face.

The plastic tie on his right wrist was still not broken, and it would take time before his hand was free. He also knew that he would need something to attack Aziz with. As he sat there strapped into a dentist's chair, only one course of action presented itself. The thought appalled him, but he was beyond caring now. Aziz was the one behaving like an animal. Marchant was simply responding in kind: a tooth for a tooth . . . It didn't get much more primitive, but Marchant had run out of options.

Aziz stepped away from him into the aisle and shook his head like a disappointed school teacher. He hadn't been able to get a clean run at the molar with his drill. He looked at Marchant for a moment, and then leaned across to unscrew the clamp in his mouth. His left hand was just above Marchant's open lips as his fingers loosened the screws on his right jaw. Marchant closed his eyes and inhaled deeply through his nose, trying to acquaint himself with the scent of Aziz's skin: the sweet musk of his aftershave. Then, as

Aziz lifted the clamp out of his jaw, Marchant opened his eyes and stared at his torturer, holding his gaze. It was enough to distract Aziz. Marchant's right hand broke free.

His arm flew upwards in a sweeping arc, clubbing the back of Aziz's head. Grabbing at his hair, Marchant pulled him down onto the brace that was holding his own head in position. Aziz grunted as his face crumpled against the steel frame. But the pain of the impact was nothing compared to the agony that started to shock-wave out from his right cheek. Marchant tried to put the taste of warm salt out of his mind as his front teeth closed, locking their two heads together.

With his right hand Marchant thrashed around for one of the tools on the fold-down table in front of him. He found one, and slashed at the tie holding his left hand, cutting his own wrist as he did so. Aziz's body made it hard to see what he was doing. When both hands were free, he held Aziz's head on either side as if he was kissing him, removed his teeth from the Moroccan's cheek and pulled him down hard into the steel frame again, bracing himself against the impact that shuddered through his spine. This time Aziz slumped to the floor in the aisle.

Marchant spat out whatever was in his mouth. It seemed to halt his rising nausea, so he spat again, and then again, purging his body of Aziz, expressing his disgust, at Aziz, at himself, at Meena. He knew that he was about to collapse. The adrenaline was draining away from his body like bath water, leaving his raw pain exposed. He unscrewed the steel head brace, then freed his legs. Next he lifted Aziz into the chair and secured his legs and arms, using the remains of the ties. He didn't bother with the brace, but he put the clamp in Aziz's bloodied mouth and jacked it open as far as it would go. At least he would be able to breathe.

26

Spiro was in no rush to call off the dogs, but he phoned Meena as he crossed Horse Guards Road and walked into St James's Park. He needed to take some air after the meeting.

'What do you mean you can't contact him?' he said, drawing hard on a cigarette as a gaggle of Japanese tourists cycled past him on hired bikes.

'He's with Aziz, as you ordered.'

'And where's Aziz?'

'Twenty-five thousand feet above the Mediterranean.'

'Christ, can't you get ATC to contact the pilot?'

There was a pause. Spiro knew it would take time. Meena had refused to contact Aziz earlier, but he guessed she would be more cooperative now that he was calling time on the dentist.

'Has something happened, sir?'

Spiro drew hard on his cigarette again, watching the flamingos. His hand was shaking.

'Dhar's not dead. He set us up, fooled Fort Meade, fooled fucking all of us, including six dead US Marines.'

He had been looking forward to disciplining Meena for her insubordination, but that would have to wait now. He was no longer in a position of strength. All he could ask of her was to clean up the mess.

'And you think Marchant knows where Dhar is?' she asked.

'Don't go dumb on me, Lakshmi. Of course not. But the British are holding all the cards right now, and if they find out Aziz is pulling Marchant's molars, we'll all have toothache. Get him off the plane, away from Aziz. And dump him somewhere nice, where he can recover. We might need him.'

He hung up just as Ian Denton appeared out of nowhere next to him. Spiro didn't know where to place Denton. The Vicar was easy: he was an upper-class, suspiciously unmarried academic with a bad back and too much sympathy for Arabia. Denton was more complicated. In theory, he should have been an ally: a grammar-school kid from Hull who had risen through the ranks because of hard graft and dirty tricks in the SovBloc, rather than old-school favours and fair play in London. But Spiro remained wary of him. There was something reptilian about Denton's body, lean and sinewy like a long-distance runner's. He also had an unnerving ability to be present in a room without appearing to have entered it. And that quiet voice.

'Daniel Marchant's missing,' Denton said, cutting straight to the chase.

'It's OK. He's fine. A little misunderstanding with our station in Rabat.'

'We had an agreement,' Denton said, surprising Spiro with the suddenness of his attack. Denton usually stayed in the long grass.

'Did we?'

'We go public about Dhar if anything happens to Marchant, is that clear?'

Spiro paused, looking at Denton, listening to his accent, its roughness softened by the quiet delivery. Denton's eyes were soulless, unblinking behind small oval glasses. It had been a smart move by Fielding to make him his deputy. Every Chief needed a troubleshooter, a hard man to sort out the messy stuff. Fielding liked to refer to Denton as his gallowglass. Spiro had played a similar role himself for the previous DCIA. But Denton was different, less muscular, more serpentine. Apparently, he had once saved Fielding's life in a tight spot in Yemen. Now it was payback time.

'Congratulations on your promotion, by the way. I never got the chance to say.'

Denton refused to rise to the bait. Instead, he just looked at him with his lifeless eyes.

'Marchant's doing fine, Ian,' Spiro continued, turning to head off into the park. 'The tooth fairy's watching over him.'

27

Lakshmi Meena took a deep breath before the member of the ground-crew staff opened the plane's heavy door. Her life seemed to be punctuated by deep-breath moments, she thought: informing her father that she wasn't going to pursue a career in medicine; telling Spiro that she wasn't prepared to sleep with him or with anyone else at Langley to further her career.

Now her lungs were full again, her chest tight. Did other people have to summon composure in the same way, make such a conscious choice to square up to the world each day? Her father, a structural engineer, had always stressed the importance of blending in, but when she looked at him now, designing bridges in Reston, West Virginia, she sometimes struggled to see anyone at all.

She bunched her right hand tightly around a silk handkerchief and nodded at the two ground crew. The three of them were standing at the top of a set of steps, bringing them even closer to the hot Moroccan sun. There was no shade on the runway, but at least the twin-turboprop had taxied to a quiet corner of Agadir airport, away from the restless tourists queuing to return home to Britain. Beyond the plane, a military ambulance stood waiting, two medics idling by its open doors, smoking and talking to an armed policeman and a couple of Aziz's intelligence colleagues.

One of the men put a hand up unnecessarily to keep the door open as Meena stepped into the plane. She had learned to command authority since joining the Agency, but it still felt like an act, not something that came naturally. She hoped Marchant hadn't suffered too much. Despite their differences, she liked him, envied his equanimity. He seemed to possess an inner calmness that she would never know. And although she had refused to help Spiro set Marchant up with Aziz, she knew she could have done more, protested formally to Langley.

It had also taken too long for her to be patched through to the pilot. As she had suspected, he had been given orders to circle for two hours and then return to Agadir. He had had no contact with Aziz during the flight. The cockpit door was locked, and Meena sensed that the pilot preferred it that way. It clearly wasn't the first time Aziz had taken a passenger on a tour of the Med.

Meena saw Aziz first, head back and to one side, his mouth wide open, as if he was singing grotesquely in his sleep. But there was no sound, and for a second she thought he was dead. She moved forward, trying to process the scene: the clamp in Aziz's mouth, the dark, congealed stain on his cheek, the faint rise and fall of his chest, the tools littered across the floor. Her orders were to get Marchant away from Aziz, but where the hell was he?

She glanced around at the two rows of seats in business class. Aziz was in an aisle seat, its upholstery stained and torn. The seats around were also flecked with blood, the crisp paper headrests ripped or missing. Then Meena saw him, slumped on the floor, his back against the open door of the lavatory, hands by his side. Marchant's eyes were open, but he was barely conscious. The bottom half of his face was badly bruised, his lips bloodied and swollen like slices of overripe peach.

'Daniel,' she said, putting the handkerchief to her mouth, as much to reassure herself about her own lips as to cut out the stale smell of burnt flesh, which was suddenly overpowering. She rushed over, but by the time she was kneeling down beside him, Marchant's eyes had closed.

28

Giuseppe Demuro was good at recognising guests. It was part of his job, one of the reasons they came back to his resort year after year. Guests liked to be remembered. Some of his colleagues kept notes on the high rollers, hoping that a personal aside on arrival – namechecking the children, asking after a relative – would secure a more generous tip. But Demuro was in no need of any props. He also had a unique manner, honed over the years into what he hoped was a self-respecting obsequiousness, somewhere between a butler and the boss. But it was his memory for faces that had helped him rise to become manager of one of the most luxurious resorts in Sardinia. It was also why he was in the employ of several of the world's intelligence agencies, who provided more reliable revenue streams than gratuities.

These organisations weren't after state secrets or sexual scandal. (A friend of his at a nearby resort made even more money by tipping off the newspapers whenever politicians came to stay with unsuitable companions, but that was beneath Demuro.) All they wanted to know about was unusual combinations of visitors: patterns. In recent years, the resort had become popular with Russians, from oligarchs who moored their yachts offshore to extended families who paid in cash, stayed mostly in their rooms (always sea-facing), lifted weights in the gym and consumed vast quantities of watermelon and cucumber. If an oligarch's holiday overlapped with a prominent politician's, Demuro would ring the relevant contact.

He liked working for the British the most. There was something glamorous – almost Italian – about the MI6 officers he had met, particularly the man they called the Vicar. He would have preferred working for a priest, of course, but he didn't complain, provided his monthly retainer was in euros.

Demuro had no hesitation, then, in dialling a secure London number after the young American woman checked in to a sea-facing room with a recuperating guest. It wasn't that he recognised her as CIA. Nor that she had a sick companion. The Americans had brought injured people before. It was the fact that a young Russian couple had arrived shortly after them, asking to be near the sea, too.

Normally, he would have greeted the couple in fluent Russian. The previous winter, in the off-season, he had been sent to study at a language school in St Petersburg for three months. There were now more Russian than Italian guests at the resort during July and August. But something made Demuro hold back, and speak in broken English. As he walked with the couple to their room, pointing out the tennis courts, pool and restaurant, he overheard a brief exchange between them. It was only a few Russian words, but when he repeated them on the phone, the Vicar hinted at a bonus and Demuro offered a quiet prayer of thanks.

29

Marchant awoke to the sound of a chipping noise. It took him a few seconds to realise that it wasn't coming from inside his mouth. He put his hand up to his jaw, which felt disfigured and swollen. His gums were throbbing, but the pain was less than it had been on the plane. Where was he? He was lying on white cotton sheets, in a whitewashed room. The ceiling was high and latticed with cream-coloured wooden beams. On one wall there was a large mirror, framed in pearl mosaic. A twenty-four-inch television screen perched on a chest of drawers, and fruit – peaches and apricots – had been left in a bowl in front of it. Beside his bed, on a writing table, there were several bottles of pills next to an orchid and some mineral water. He leaned across and picked up one of the bottles: it was amoxicillin, an antibiotic. The other was diamorphine.

He sat up with some effort. His neck muscles were sore and his head throbbed more when he moved. A net curtain had been drawn across an open window, its white shutters pushed partly open. The branches of a weeping fig stopped them from opening fully. Beyond its leaves, he could see pine trees against a brilliant blue sky. The sun was too bright for Britain, the birdsong too exuberant. As he listened to the chorus, a small bird hovered outside the window for a few moments and disappeared.

He reached over and examined the bottle of mineral water, reading its label: Frizzante – sparkling – and made by Smeraldina, a 'product of Sardinia'. Twisting open the metal cap, he drank deeply, resting the bottle gently on his swollen lips. His mind was still too muddled to think clearly. At least he was out of Morocco. It was only when he put the bottle down that he noticed a figure sitting outside on the terrace, beyond the double doors on the far side of the room. He couldn't see any more than their profile through the net curtains, which moved gently in the breeze. The doors were open a few inches, and the person must have heard him opening the bottle of water, because she stood up and put her head in the room.

'How you feeling?' It was Lakshmi Meena.

Marchant tried to speak, but his tongue failed to respond. Instead, he grunted and sank back into the deep pillows, closing his eyes. What sort of a question was that? He had that top-of-the-world feeling that usually followed a trip to a dentist with an aversion to using anaesthetic. Aziz should go into full-time practice when he retired, set himself up in the square in Marrakech. Tourists would be queuing around the block for his gentle touch.

He heard Meena walk across the marble floor and draw up a cane chair beside the bed. He remembered that she worked directly for Spiro. Someone must have had a change of heart.

'I'm sorry, really. It shouldn't have happened. I should have done more, protested louder.'

Marchant wasn't going to make this any easier for her as he lay still, listening to the chipping noise that had started up again. He realised now that it was workmen, the rhythm of their hammers slowed by the day's heat. His brain had established some distance between the outside world and the inside of his skull, but the sound was still too familiar for comfort.

'They're fixing the path outside,' Meena continued, her manner more businesslike than bedside. Marchant assumed that it was her way of dealing with the situation, which was fine by him. He didn't want her sympathy. 'One of the tiles was cracked, so they dug it up and are putting in a new one. Relax if you never made it to Jackson's Neverland, because it's right here, in Sardinia. No litter, no crime, sidewalks buffed up at night. I'm not kidding, I've smelt the floor polish.'

The less Marchant acknowledged Meena, the more she talked. He didn't have enough energy to interrupt, ask her to leave, tell her she was as bad as the rest of them, despite her protests.

'We flew in to Cagliari yesterday morning. You've been asleep ever since. The drugs aren't going to replace your molars, I'm afraid, but they should stop any infection spreading to the bone, brain and lungs, reduce the chance of systemic sepsis. And take the morphine in moderation, only when it's really hurting.'

He recalled that Meena had once trained to be a doctor. He opened his eyes, tracing the patterns in the plaster on the ceiling.

'We didn't get Salim Dhar.' Marchant looked across at Meena, who was standing now. 'Killed six of our own Marines instead. Spiro's butt's on the line, mine too. I don't know what you saw up in the mountains, but come to me, not him, if you ever want to talk. I might just listen.'

Meena turned away when Marchant caught her eye. She had found it difficult enough to look at him when he was sleeping, his bruised mouth distorted as if in accusation. Now that he was awake, she saw in his eyes everything that was wrong with the Agency, everything that was wrong with the decisions she had made in her life. This wasn't why she had signed up. She also saw something else, but buried the thought as soon as it surfaced.

The military ambulance had taken Aziz away from the airport, but not before two of his colleagues had threatened to inflict further injuries on Marchant. Meena had talked them out of it, pulling rank, acting the part, then arranged for another ambulance. They wouldn't allow him to travel in the military one. At the Hassan II Hospital, on route de Marrakech, a doctor had patched Marchant up and prescribed painkillers and antibiotics. He knew better than to ask how the British man had come to lose two teeth. He knew, too, that there could be consequences for helping him, but the American woman had given him a bulging envelope of *dirhams* as well as reassurances.

By the time Meena took Marchant out to the airport, a Gulfstream V had arrived to fly them to Sardinia, where the CIA had a discreet account with a luxury resort on the south of the island. It had the use of a villa away from the thoroughfare of restaurants and tennis courts. Senior officers checked themselves in for some R&R after tough tours of duty in the Gulf. NSA officers visiting the listening base in Cyprus also dropped by for a few days to clear their heads from intercepts. And there was always the possible bonus of picking something up from the Russians. Meena hadn't hesitated to book Marchant in. It was the least she could do. Besides, Spiro had told her to look after him and to send Langley the bill.

'London knows you're here,' she said, standing at the double doors now. 'You're on a flight back to Gatwick in a week. Relax, recover. It's on us.' She paused. 'I've got to go. Pacify the Moroccans. You nearly killed Aziz.' She paused again, fighting an urge to go over to him. 'You'll be safe here. And, you know, I'm sorry, truly. It was my fault. Should never have happened.'

Marchant stared at her blankly, then drifted back to sleep.

30

'I think someone should be with Marchant,' Denton said, wondering if Fielding had heard him. His Chief was standing at the window of his fourth-floor office, lost in thought, watching a pair of Chinooks fly up the Thames towards a setting sun. The Union flag outside the window was rippling in the evening breeze. Sometimes Fielding's apparent indifference to his own staff frightened Denton, but he told himself it was just his manner.

'Do we know what happened?' Fielding asked, turning around suddenly, as if trying to make up for his previous inattention.

'The Americans handed him over to Abdul Aziz. Marchant proved a difficult patient.'

'You think we should have protected him more, don't you?'

'I just –'

'Don't go soft on me, Ian. It doesn't suit you. Daniel Marchant knows how to look after himself. Besides, we had an agreement with Langley.'

'For what it was worth,' Denton said. He liked Marchant, and feared for his health if he was subjected to more trauma at the hands of the CIA.

'Spiro saw his chance. He thought the world would be looking the other way, watching the death of Salim Dhar on YouTube. Who's out in Morocco for them? Still Lakshmi Meena?'

'Yes.'

'Young enough to be my granddaughter.'

Except that you don't have one, Denton thought. No grandchildren at all, in fact. No children, wife or lover of any description. Just a dog called Oleg and an extended tribe of godchildren. There had been talk once of an elderly mother, somewhere on the south coast – Brighton, or was it Eastbourne? – but that was long ago. Denton used to have a wife. A shared love of jazz and canal boats had brought them together, the Service had driven them apart, as it eventually did with most of its married employees. She still worked as a librarian in the House of Commons, down the river, but they no longer saw each other. There were no children, just a few Miles Davis albums still to be returned. Perhaps Fielding's chosen path of apparent chastity was the only way to arrive at the top of MI6 without any baggage.

'She said the Agency was putting Marchant up for a few days – Sardinia – but she had to get back to Morocco,' Denton said.

'Send Hugo Prentice. Marchant helped him out in Poland. And he knew his father.'

Denton had never liked Prentice, but now wasn't the time to object. There would come a time, in his new role, when he could set the record straight, not just question Prentice's expenses, but his very worth. They had both worked the SovBloc beat, in very different styles, Denton's discretion in marked contrast to Prentice's public-school flamboyance. Both had done long spells in Poland. Everyone knew Prentice gambled, drank too much, but for as long as he continued to come up with good product, Fielding turned a blind eye. Denton knew a part of him envied Prentice. He was still out there in the field, where agents belonged, while he himself had chosen to climb Legoland's greasy pole.

He walked to the door, leaving Fielding in preoccupied silence. Not for the first time in his career, Denton felt that he had merely confirmed information already known to his Chief rather than told him something new. It was in such moments that he felt destined to be a deputy, one of life's permanent number twos. He glanced back at Fielding, pacing his spacious office, and closed the door with more force than was necessary.

Fielding didn't like to exclude Denton from anything, but sometimes it was unavoidable. The thoughts in his head were forming too fast to share even with his loyal deputy, the implications backing up like a restless queue. He went back to his desk, opened a drawer and removed a file on Nikolai Primakov.

31

The next time Marchant woke, it was to the sound of a Russian voice, talking on a mobile phone on the terrace outside his room. Marchant's Russian was rusty, but good enough to understand what was being said.

'Yes, he's here.' A woman's voice, not Meena's. 'Still sleeping.' He could see her outline through the net curtain, turning towards him, holding something in her hand, a photo perhaps. 'The American woman's gone, left yesterday . . . He's a little under the weather, but it's incredible, he looks just like his father.'

Marchant tried to rouse himself, but he couldn't even turn over. It was as if he was lying in thick treacle, the sort his father used to pour over sponge puddings on those rare occasions when they spent Christmas in Britain, at the family home in the Cotswolds. It was his father's only contribution in the kitchen. He stared at the lace curtain, billowing gently in the breeze, and tried to work out where he was, who the woman might be, why he didn't care. His mouth wasn't hurting any more, but he couldn't distinguish one part of his body from another. A numbness had cocooned him. *He looks just like his father* – the words floated around his medicated head until he drifted back to sleep again.

*   *   *

'Marchant's got a babysitter,' Prentice said, grinding a cigarette into the dusty ground outside the roadside bar with his heel. The pine trees were shading him from the hot Sardinian sun, their roots pushing up through the dry soil, moulding it like a plasticine map of mountainous terrain. He had taken a walk out of the resort's gates and down to a collection of shops eight hundred yards along the straight main road. The only shop that was open was a deserted supermarket, where he had bought two bottles of chilled Prosecco, a packet of Marlboro cigarettes and too many Lotto tickets. Next door was a closed fishmongers and an empty bar, run by a woman in a short skirt whose red-lined eyes and swollen stomach suggested she drank more beer than she served.

'She's called Lakshmi Meena,' Fielding said, getting up from his desk in Legoland.

'Not unless she's dyed her fanny hair.'

Fielding knew Prentice was trying to shock him. He had a habit of being crude at inappropriate moments. Perhaps it was a reaction against his own proper background, or frustration at never having taken to the stage. Like so many agents Fielding knew, Prentice was a natural actor, the office joker who could mimic everyone in authority. (Fielding had once overheard Prentice's impression of his own voice: a combination of camp archbishop and repressed Eton housemaster.) Give or take a few venial sins, he was also one of the best agents he had in the field.

'Oh yes, and she's speaking Russian.' Prentice winked at a small boy who had appeared at the end of the bar, legs crossed, one hand in his mouth, the other tugging at his mother's nylon skirt. Prentice turned his back and walked away from the bar, cutting across the scrubland that lay between the shops and the main highway to Cagliari. He stepped carefully over the pine roots as he went. Despite the dust, his polished yard boots glistened in the high sun.

'Is she on her own?' Fielding asked, surprised at the speed of events in Sardinia.

'She checked in to a double room, near Marchant's. On the beach. Two sets of flipflops outside the door, couple of towels. Husband-and-wife cover.'

'But you haven't seen the husband yet?'

'I only reached here last night. What do you want me to do? Get him out of here? She's a swallow, sent to seduce him.'

'And Meena's definitely gone?'

'Checked out yesterday.'

'A little too hasty, no?'

'We met at the airport. She was embarrassed. Told me Marchant's room number, the medication he was on, then buggered off. Marchant's a sitting duck if the Russians want to compromise him.'

'They probably have already.'

32

The woman made no effort to cover herself as she stepped from the shower, walked across the bathroom and removed a towel from the radiator. She tilted her head, drying her blonde, shoulder-length hair as she looked over at the bed and smiled. Marchant wondered if she had been waiting for him to open his eyes. Her actions had a rehearsed choreography about them, more subtle than a porn star's but no less calculated.

He knew before she began to speak that it was the same woman who had been sitting on the terrace earlier, whenever that might have been. Bells were ringing so loudly in his head that he thought, for a moment, that they were the reason he had woken. He hoped that something visceral in his sleeping state had raised the alarm. An uninvited Russian woman in his hotel room was about as bad as it could get for an MI6 field agent, the sort of scenario they taught on day one at the Fort.

If the implications weren't so serious, his situation was almost funny. Textbook honeytrap, perfected in the 1960s, fell out of fashion after the Cold War, seemingly back with a vengeance. A British diplomat had recently been fired after he was filmed by the FSB with a couple of Russian tarts in a hotel room.

His head was clearer now, but he couldn't be sure how long he had been lying in bed. Several days, at least. Where was Lakshmi

Meena? Why had no one from London been to visit him? Hadn't she said that MI6 knew where he was? And what was a naked woman doing in his bathroom?

He propped himself up in bed and took in his surroundings, tried to order random memories. He was in Sardinia, brought here by Meena after the Americans had handed him over to Abdul Aziz. He touched his mouth again, which was less swollen. *He looks just like his father.*

'You've been sleeping for three days,' the woman said. Her English was good, but there was no disguising the Russian mother tongue that thickened her cadences. She was standing in the doorway now, between the bathroom and the bedroom. Her shoulders were broad, like a swimmer's, her breasts high and firm. Marchant estimated she was in her early thirties. Despite himself, he began to stir. Her pubic hair was tidy, trimmed rather than shaved, its soft brownness framed by tanned thighs.

'I tell you this because I know how much the British men like to be in control,' she smiled, glancing at the sheet covering Marchant. 'On top of things.'

For a moment, Marchant felt pity for her, the wooden lines spoken with all the conviction of a hard-up lap dancer. But something about the way she moved across the hotel room and picked up a hair dryer made Marchant's hands begin to sweat. And it wasn't because of any desire she might have roused. Despite the air of a performance, her manner had a lover's familiarity, an easiness born of intimacy. Instinctively, he felt about on the sheet next to him, trying to be discreet. It was damp.

'Please, put something on,' he said. More memories, scent, taste. 'A dressing gown, clothes, anything.'

'Clothes? It's 40 degrees outside and you want me to put something on? Relax. You're on holiday.' She was sitting now, one leg tucked under her, head tilted, hair dryer in hand.

'Where's Lakshmi Meena?'

'You ask too many questions. Please, try some of this.'

She picked up a plate piled high with watermelon and walked over to him, placing it beside the bed. Then she slid a piece into her mouth, holding it carefully between thumb and finger. A small trickle of juice escaped from her lips as she crushed the fruit. She gathered it in with her tongue, which lingered a moment longer than was necessary.

'Do you know why Russian men like watermelon so much?' she asked. Marchant had sat up now, careful to cover himself with a sheet.

'I need you to leave,' he said, strength returning to his voice, his body. More memories: Morocco, the mountains, *Nye strelai*. The woman might have some information on Dhar, but he wasn't in control. He needed time to think, rid his head of the drugs he must have been given with his morphine, work out how to play the hand in front of him, but she held all the cards. 'Ten minutes. Some time to wash, freshen up. Recharge.' He managed to garnish the last word with a twist of innuendo.

'Of course. I'll go to the beach. Join me in the restaurant when you're ready. I'm Nadia, by the way.'

He watched her walk over to a wardrobe and put on a black bikini. The bottom was decent enough at the front, but hardly covered her buttocks. Again, she knew she was being observed, which annoyed Marchant, who turned away when she catwalked towards the sliding glass doors. As she started to close them behind her, she leaned back into the room.

'Watermelon juice is a natural Viagra, at least that's what our men believe. Yes, it's sweet too, and we love sweet things in Russia, but this is not the main reason. Enjoy.'

She slid the door shut, the click of the catch cutting into Marchant's thoughts. Once he was sure she had gone, he lifted the receiver on the hotel phone, but the line was dead, as he expected. He stood up, unsteady on his feet, and went over to the wardrobe, where he had seen some of his clothes. His wallet was there, complete with some Moroccan *dirhams* and the 'litter' he had put in it for his photographer's cover (Dirk McLennan's business card, some studio receipts), but his phone was missing. He looked around the room. Had they slept together? He kept seeing them on the bed, caught in the reflection of the mosaic mirror. How could he have allowed himself to get into such a vulnerable situation?

After taking a shower, washing off any traces of what might have been, he put on a pair of shorts, a T-shirt, sunglasses and some flipflops that someone – Meena? Nadia? – must have bought from the resort shop for him. They all fitted well enough. He glanced in the mirror, put a hand to his bruised jaw, and stepped outside into the midday sun, watched discreetly by a gym-toned man lying on a sunbed outside the adjacent villa.

33

'I want you to hold back,' Fielding said, standing up to rub his lower back. No one had fixed the grandfather clock that stood against the far wall of his office. It had been built by Sir Mansfield Cumming, the first Chief, and had worked well enough until the Service's move from Southwark, since when it had kept stopping. Fielding meant to do something about it, but there was never enough time.

'It's too late anyway. She's all over him.' Prentice was back in the resort now, standing in some shade beside a rack of red bikes for hire. Behind him he could hear children playing football on an Astroturf pitch: German, English, Italian and Russian voices. He had taken a look earlier. The football facilities were provided by Chelsea, the club he'd followed since childhood, and there were huge posters of all the top players on the fencing around the ground.

'Has he met the man yet, or just the woman?'

'He's sharing a pizza with them both now. Down by the sea.'

'And no one's seen you?'

'Not yet.' Prentice glanced at a nearby CCTV camera, hidden in the bushes. He doubted the guests knew that every inch of the resort was being filmed, day and night, low and high season. The cameras were very discreet, he had to give them that. He had already checked out the control centre, behind the main reception building, where a bank of screens captured most things that went on at the resort. As far as he could tell, it was also from there that the master satellite TV signal was distributed to all the villas.

'Get him on your own after lunch and try to limit the damage.'

Prentice hung up, surprised by the Vicar's calmness.

'We want you to meet someone in London,' Nadia said. 'An old friend.'

'A friend of your family,' her partner, Valentin, added. He had joined them from the sunbed a couple of minutes after their arrival at the beachside restaurant. Marchant assumed that he had followed him from his room, in case he tried to leave the resort. But Marchant didn't have the strength to escape. Not yet. Valentin was tall, muscular, wearing a T-shirt as tight as his skin. Marchant was struck by his small, Prussian-blue eyes.

'I don't have any family,' Marchant replied.

He was sitting in the shade of their table's brightly coloured umbrella. It reminded him of the parasols that kept the *mahouts* cool when they were riding ceremonial elephants in India. The two Russians were in the sunshine. Valentin had just come back from a cigarette on the beach, ten yards away. The restaurant was open-air but there was still a no-smoking policy. Valentin turned the packet of Parliament cigarettes over and over on the table, looking out to sea. Then he looked straight at Marchant, his eyes even smaller.

'Our friend knew your father. He always speaks very highly of him, and would like to meet you. Talk about old times.'

'Which friend?' Marchant asked, his mind racing. The only Russian he could recall was someone his father had known in Delhi, but Marchant had been a child at the time, and the memories were distant. He knew there must have been many

127

others, his father's illustrious career in MI6 being built on successes behind the Iron Curtain. Some he was aware of: the ones who had been blown and were dead now, executed by Moscow Centre after Aldrich Ames had exposed them. He would never know about the others who were still alive, still betraying their motherland, their files known only to a select few in Legoland.

'All we ask is that you meet him once,' Valentin said, ignoring Marchant's question. 'One meeting, nothing more. In London.'

Marchant wanted a name, someone to run past Fielding, who had known his father better than anyone, but they weren't playing. More important, he told himself, was the approach itself. The Russians' interest in him gave him hope that he could be right about Dhar, the mountains, the helicopter. And that thought banished any lingering effects of the medication, his brain suddenly as fresh as a forest after rain.

'He will attend an exhibition opening,' Valentin said, passing Marchant an embossed invitation card. 'In Cork Street. The artist is from the Caucasus, South Ossetia. He is very accomplished, but not as well known outside Russia as he should be. Picture number 14, a nude sketch, has been reserved with a half-dot on the price label. It's a very beautiful work. You may recognise the model.' He looked across at Nadia and smiled. 'Your contact will confirm the purchase on the night, towards the end of the evening. If it already has a full red dot beside it when you arrive, the meeting has been cancelled.'

Standard SVR tradecraft, Marchant thought. The plan was a little elaborate, but it implied intent. They meant business. A crowded place had been chosen, a venue where contact could be accidental, ambiguous, denied.

Marchant glanced around at the restaurant, trying to spot any watchers. It was one of his best skills as a field agent, the thing that had most impressed his instructors at the Fort. But this time he was struggling. More than half the diners were Russian. A senescent man with an eighteen-year-old escort in a short skirt; another, younger Russian businessman more interested in his BlackBerry than his gorgeous wife. She was wearing diamante jeans, listlessly following their young son as he tottered around the tables with a beach ball almost as big as him. Maybe Nadia and Valentin were operating on their own.

'And if he's not my kind of artist?' Marchant asked, knowing the answer. As far as they were concerned, he had already been compromised enough to guarantee his cooperation.

'Our friend will be very disappointed,' Valentin said.

'We all will,' Nadia added, smiling at him with a coyness that made Marchant's palms moisten again.

'You and your father, you both seem to share a dislike of America.'

'I wouldn't put words into my mouth,' Marchant said, touching his jaw. 'It's not a nice place to be at the moment.' Despite the bravura, Valentin's comment unsettled him. The Americans had long accused his father of disloyalty, eventually driving him from office.

'But they didn't treat you very well.'

'That wasn't the Americans.'

'Of course not. And they couldn't have cancelled your appointment with Dr Aziz.'

Marchant looked at him.

'Our friend is eager to see you again,' Valentin said. 'Your father once gave him a photo of all his children. He still treasures it.'

'All?'

'You, Sebastian . . .' Valentin paused, looking hard at Marchant, as if he hadn't finished.

'And?'

'And your father.'

Marchant didn't buy it. 'All his children' was an odd phrase for two sons, even allowing for some loss in translation. The Russians knew about Salim Dhar.

34

Fielding had told him he was coming. It was courtesy, but it was also a matter of security. Giles Cordingley lived at the top of Raginnis Hill, overlooking the Cornish fishing village of Mousehole, ten miles from Land's End, and visitors to his granite farmhouse were rare. He was too old for surprises. A security camera was positioned discreetly to the left of the high oak gates, and it took a while for them to swing open and let Fielding's Range Rover pass through into the gravel courtyard. His driver parked in front of an old stable block and took a look around, taking in other security cameras, the high walls that enclosed a forgotten orchard. Then he made a call on his mobile and returned to the car, leaving Fielding to approach the house on his own.

Cordingley had been Chief of MI6 in the 1990s, serving for three years before becoming master of an Oxford College and then retiring to Cornwall. He was the last of the Cold War Chiefs, the end of an era. Well into his sixties by the time he reached the top, he had enjoyed a long career that had begun with a role in Oleg Penkovsky's recruitment. He had managed the defection of Vladimir Kuzichkin when he was head of station in Tehran, over-seen the handling of Oleg Gordievsky, and lost agents at the hands of Aldrich Ames. Most importantly, he was one of the few people who knew about Nikolai Primakov, having personally authorised his recruitment.

There was no answer when Fielding rang the doorbell and he eventually found Cordingley behind the house, tending to a row of beehives in what must have been the old vegetable garden. Fielding thought his face looked fleshier than he remembered, like pale putty, big heavy-rimmed glasses making it seem rounder, more vulnerable. Despite the dramatic clifftop setting, there was no sense of a man enjoying his retirement in the great outdoors, no ruddy, windblown cheeks or healthy complexion. He looked like a man unused to daylight. For a moment, Fielding wondered if he was ill, if that was why he had moved to Cornwall.

'Good of you to see me, Giles,' Fielding began, knowing that it would be futile to wait for him to stop tending his bees. Cordingley was wearing a protective veil but no gloves or suit. His hands looked feminine, unthreatening. Fielding assumed he had operated the main gates with the device that was hanging around his neck. His hospitality didn't seem to extend beyond allowing entry, and he hadn't bothered to come round and greet his visitor. It was a reminder that Cordingley's relationship with the Service was complicated, that he had left under a cloud of homophobia, been denied a KCMG, the usual gong for a Chief.

'Duty rather than goodness,' Cordingley said, putting a lid back on one of the hives. Fielding kept his distance, knowing that angry bees were all part of the welcome. The garden, he thought, looked tatty and tired. Only the hives were well tended. A gentle wind was blowing in off the sea far below. On the far side of the bay, St Michael's Mount rose out of the water like a fairytale castle. A brace of beam trawlers were returning home to nearby Newlyn under a high mackerel sky, their nets hung out on either side for a final trawl of the bay. If it wasn't for the *froideur* of his host, Fielding thought that the idyllic scene was almost heart-warming, reason enough for him to have dedicated his life to the Service.

Cordingley walked past him towards the back door of the house, a slow amble that still drew a cloud of bees in his slipstream. Fielding swatted one away as nonchalantly as he could. He felt a sharp pain on the back of his hand.

'They only sting when they sense fear,' Cordingley said, entering the house. He was almost eighty, but he hadn't missed Fielding's flinch.

35

Marchant knew that there was something wrong with his room twenty yards before he reached it. The sliding doors were open, and he could hear a couple inside, the unmistakeable soundtrack of sexual pleasure. At least, he could hear a woman; the man sounded more subdued, set upon. The Russian couple had told him to rest, agreed to meet for a drink before dinner, talking as if he had the liberty to do as he pleased. But he knew it was a pretence, that he had no freedom. They were already back at the villa next door, watching, waiting. Marchant wasn't a guest at the resort, he was a prisoner.

As he approached the sliding glass doors, he could see the blue flicker of a TV screen reflecting off his apartment's white walls. Had he got the wrong number? The layout of the sprawling resort, each house set back from the smooth-tiled paths that meandered through them, was confusing, but the number by his apartment matched the key in his hand.

He stepped into the small garden, careful not to touch the half-open iron gate, and edged towards the glass doors. He knew what was going on now, but he still kept his approach silent, in case he was wrong, in case there really were people in his room. But he knew there weren't. Not in the flesh.

He looked at the large TV screen for a second, distracted by the rhythmic movement of Nadia's taut buttocks, the winking recesses. Then he realised that it was his body beneath them, and felt sick. He stepped into the room and grabbed the remote, which was on the table beside a replenished bowl of watermelon. It was only as he turned away that he saw Hugo Prentice standing by the bathroom door, arms folded, watching the screen with a smirk on his fifty-something face.

'It's showing in my room, too,' Prentice said, careful to remain out of sight from the window. 'On a loop. Every room in the resort, nationwide release. It's the most exciting thing I've seen on an in-house hotel channel in years.'

'You took your time,' Marchant said, turning off the TV and dropping the remote onto the bed, which had been freshly made. 'Fielding send you by boat?'

'Take off your shirt and close the curtains. You're tired, remember? Sent to your room for a sleep.'

Marchant looked at Prentice for a moment, then pulled off his shirt, threw it on the bed and walked to the glass doors. Nadia was sitting outside her villa now, sunbathing topless, waiting to see how he would react to the video. She gave him a coy wave. He didn't wave back, but drew the thick curtains.

Prentice remained by the bathroom door as Marchant went over to the pedestal sink and splashed water on his face. He didn't want to dwell on the video, the fact that Prentice had just witnessed him having sex. Strangely, he found that more troubling than the implications for his career, the consequences of being compromised by a textbook honeytrap. Perhaps it was because Prentice had been a good friend of his father, who had perfected the knack during Marchant's teenage years of striding into the sitting room whenever he was watching a sex scene on television.

'It's OK, I looked away for the money shot,' Prentice said, trying to lighten the mood. 'Fielding sends big love and kisses.'

Marchant wasn't sure if he was pleased that London had sent Prentice. On balance, he thought he was. To look at, Prentice was smoothness personified, from the swept-back hair to the cut of his safari suit: old-school spy. Just the sort Marchant needed to help him out of the old-school fix he found himself in. Prentice had recently returned from a three-year tour of Poland, where he had helped Marchant escape from a black site, but he was too old for regular deskwork in Legoland, too much of a troublemaker for a management role. Human Resources had branded him a 'negative sneezer', spreading dissent rather than 'flu. Fielding had ignored the warning memos, as he usually did with anything sent from HR, and deployed him as a firefighter, ready to be dispatched to global trouble spots at the drop of a panama.

'They want me to meet someone,' Marchant said. 'A friend of my father's.'

'That narrows it down,' Prentice replied. 'Your old man was a popular Chief. Any other clues?'

'The meeting's in London.' He decided not to tell Prentice about the private view. In his current situation, it helped him to feel in control if he knew at least something that others around him didn't. 'I presume it's with one of theirs, given the need to persuade me,' Marchant continued, glancing at the television.

'Moscow still rules. Christ, it's a while since I've seen Eva Shirtov in action. Makes me feel almost nostalgic.'

'I need to sort it.' Marchant wasn't in the mood for flippancy. He was embarrassed.

'It's already taken care of.' Prentice walked over to the TV and ejected a disc from the player in the cabinet below it. 'Master copy,' he said, throwing it onto the bed next to the remote.

'I thought you said it was being broadcast around the resort.'

'That was their plan. I retrieved the disc while you were having lunch.'

Marchant felt a wave of relief, but he was also irritated. He hated being indebted to anyone.

'Aren't they going to notice?' He knew it was a pointless question, that Prentice would have tied off any loose ends. He had more experience of the Russians than anyone in the Service. Marchant remembered listening to him at the Fort, which he visited every year to address the new IONEC recruits. They had sat in rapt silence as he spoke of brush passes in Berlin, dangles, and how, as a young officer, he had played Sibelius's *Finlandia* on the car stereo to let a defecting KGB officer called Oleg Gordievsky, who was hidden in the boot, know that they had safely crossed into Finland. 'And you know what actually got us past the border guard? A nappy full of crap. My colleague's wife started to change her baby on the car boot when the guard asked to see inside. One whiff and he changed his mind.'

Sure enough, Prentice didn't reply to Marchant's question, letting its foolishness grow in the silence. Instead, he went to the window and peered through the curtain at the Russians' villa. Marchant joined him.

'When the Russians cross the line, you have to respond with interest,' Prentice said, watching as a suited man approached the villa with a posse of local Italian police behind him. 'Remind them where the line is. Otherwise it moves. They'll respect you more, too. They don't like weak enemies.'

'Who's that with the police?'

'Giuseppe Demuro, manager of the resort, old friend of the family. He received an anonymous tip-off half an hour ago that the occupants of villa 29 were trying to broadcast pornographic videos across the resort.'

'But we've got the disc.'

'I swapped it for a different one.'

Prentice turned and picked up the remote from the bed, then

clicked onto the resort's in-house channel. The footage was grainy, but it was possible to see an older man with a younger woman, lying on a bed. It was also possible to see that the man was the Prime Minister of Russia and the young woman wasn't his wife.

'The oligarch currently staying in the penthouse by the sea is a close friend of the Kremlin. He won't be amused. Come, we must go.'

36

'Nikolai Primakov was an unusual case,' Cordingley said, stopping at a disused coastguard hut to take in the view of the bay. 'Once in a lifetime.' They were walking west along the cliffs towards Lamorna. Cordingley was too old to go far now, but he had insisted that they should talk in the open, away from his house. His former hostility had passed, but there was no warmth, no offer of tea. 'The initial approach was made by Stephen,' he continued. 'Never forget that. He'd met Primakov a few times at cultural events in Delhi, liked him on a personal level, singled him out for company. He also sensed a deep unhappiness behind all the smiles.' Cordingley paused. 'Primakov wasn't the dangle, we dangled Stephen Marchant.'

'And you're still sure of that?' Fielding asked.

'More so than ever. And I think back over it often. Once Stephen had recruited him, Primakov's true value became apparent to us. Dynamite. K Branch, First Chief Directorate. You couldn't get better than that. And he knew much more than his rank should have allowed, particularly about KGB operations in Britain. The problem was, he kept talking about defecting, which would have been no good to us at all. To keep him useful, he needed to be promoted, not exfiltrated, so Stephen and I devised a plan for him, something to impress his superiors in Moscow Centre.'

'You let Stephen be recruited by Primakov.'

Another pause as they watched the seagulls circling below. 'It was actually Stephen's idea. Brilliant, even now. Moscow thought they'd turned a rising MI6 agent, giving Primakov an excuse to meet regularly with Stephen. There was just one problem: the intel we had to give Primakov to keep Stephen credible as a Soviet asset.'

They both knew what Cordingley meant by this, but neither wanted to speak about it. Not yet. The moment demanded a respectful pause, a lacuna. Instinctively, they looked around to see if anyone might be within earshot, then walked on. On one side the coast path was overshadowed by a steeply rising hillside of gorse, pricked with yellow flowers. On the other was the Atlantic, swelling over flat black rocks far beneath them. It would have been difficult for anyone to listen in on their conversation, except perhaps if they were on a well-equipped trawler, which both men knew was not beyond the realms of Russian tradecraft. But the last boat had now slipped past them towards Newlyn, and the bay was empty, the coast clear.

Cordingley spoke first. He had stopped again and was facing the Atlantic, his thin white hair teased by the sea breeze. 'We couldn't give Moscow chickenfeed. They would have been immediately suspicious. The decision to pass them high-grade American intel was never approved by anyone, never formally acknowledged. I assume it remained that way, even when the Yanks went after Stephen.'

'Cs' eyes only.'

Fielding thought back to his first week as Chief of MI6, the evening he had spent sifting through the files in the safe in his office. It contained the most classified documents in Legoland, unseen by anyone other than successive Chiefs. They were even more invisible than 'no trace' files, short, unaccountable

140

documents that read like briefing notes from one head to the next, outlining the Service's deniable operations, the ones that had never crossed Whitehall desks. It had reminded Fielding of the day he had become head of his house at school, more than forty years earlier. A book was passed on from one head to the next, never seen by anyone else. It identified the troublemakers and bullies, in between tips on how to deal with the housemaster's drink problem.

'There's no doubt someone in Langley got enough of a sniff to distrust Stephen, but I'm confident that Primakov's still known only to the British.'

'So why have you come here today?'

'He's back.'

'In London?' It was the first time Cordingley had seemed surprised.

Fielding nodded. 'Next week. I need to know if we can still trust him.'

'Primakov only dealt with Stephen. Refused to be handled by anyone else. He must have been frightened when the Americans removed Stephen from office, and upset when he died. It's whether he's bitter that counts. For almost twenty years, we kept promising him a new life in the West.'

'I think Primakov's about to approach Stephen's son.'

37

Marchant and Prentice waited until the police had led the Russian couple away to reception before they stepped out of the villa. Giuseppe Demuro had sent a small golf buggy to pick them up, and the driver was waiting patiently in the shade, trying not to show any interest in the police activity. Discretion at all times, Giuseppe had told him. That was why, perhaps, he didn't spot the two suited men moving fast and silently along the tiled path that cut behind the villa, only their heads and chests visible above the privet hedge. But Marchant saw them, and wondered how they could be travelling so fast with their upper bodies remaining still. They weren't on bikes, their posture was too upright. Then he recognised one of them, and didn't care about the laws of physics any more. It was the man who had ushered him onto the plane at Agadir.

'We need to go,' Marchant said to Prentice, nodding towards the two men, who were closing in on them quickly. Marchant jumped onto the back of the buggy with Prentice, who had a small hold-all with him. Marchant had nothing other than his phone, which Prentice had managed to retrieve from the Russians' villa.

'Giuseppe's arranged a taxi, back entrance, where the staff live,' Prentice said, looking at the two men, who were now less than fifty yards away and arcing around towards them. 'Friends of yours?' He had fixed the Russians, but hadn't anticipated another threat.

'Let's move,' Marchant said to the driver, ignoring Prentice, taking control. 'Pronto.'

The driver sensed the urgency in Marchant's voice and accelerated away across the smooth tiles, glancing back at the two men, who were looking across the hedgerows, their speed still a mystery.

'They work for Abdul Aziz,' Marchant said, holding on to the side of the buggy as it rounded a corner. 'Gave me a free upgrade in Morocco.'

'And they appear to have perfected the art of low-level flying,' Prentice said. It was then that the path the Moroccans were on joined the main thoroughfare, revealing their means of transport. They were riding on Segway Personal Transporters, their big rubber wheels rippling across the tiles. Marchant had seen a member of the resort's staff passing the pizza restaurant on one during lunch, thinking at the time that it was travelling faster than normal. They were meant to have a top speed of 12.5 mph, but the two Moroccans were travelling at least twice as quickly as that, leaning on the T-bars to propel themselves forward. The resort's machines must have been customised, making them much quicker than Marchant and Prentice's electric-powered golf buggy. Marchant had heard that the police in Britain had made similar changes to their own fleet of Segways.

'Turn left up here, to the beach,' Marchant said. The Moroccans were thirty yards from them now, and closing. 'Pick me up in the car, further down the coast. I can outrun the Segways on sand.'

Before Prentice could say anything, Marchant had jumped off the buggy and was sprinting down to the beach, kicking off his flipflops. Prentice turned around just in time to see the two men passing him. Without pausing, he swung his hold-all up and out

143

of the buggy, knocking the nearest Moroccan off his Segway. He hit his head hard on the tiles and rolled over. The other man stopped, pulling hard on the T-bar, looked down at his colleague and then across to the beach, down which Marchant was running away from them. For a sickening moment, Prentice thought the Moroccan was going to pull a gun on him, but he just cursed and accelerated off on his Segway, staying on the smooth path that ran parallel to the coast.

38

'The beauty of their relationship was that it was seemingly out in the open, beyond reproach,' Cordingley continued.

They were walking back to the farmhouse now, pursued by charcoal clouds tumbling in over Land's End. Cordingley had become increasingly animated as he recalled the past, almost breathless, and Fielding was starting to worry about his health. 'It was no secret that they were good friends. People expected to see them together at embassy parties, first nights at the theatre. Primakov reported back to Moscow Centre that Stephen had tried to recruit him and that he had refused. Stephen did exactly the same. At first, Moscow was suspicious of their closeness, even ordered him to stop seeing Stephen, but Primakov had always believed in friendship rather than blackmail as the best way to recruit someone, and for a while Moscow let him do things his way.'

'Did you ever doubt Stephen? Personally?'

'You knew him better than most. You were his protégé, his biggest fan.'

'I was. I still am. I was wondering where you stood.'

Fielding remembered how Cordingley had been the only Chief not to turn up at Stephen Marchant's funeral.

'If you're asking me whether Stephen sometimes passed on US

intel to the Russians a little too enthusiastically, with too much relish, then the answer is yes.'

'But that only made him more credible, reassured the Russians he was the genuine article.'

'Of course. Everyone knew Stephen was more wary of Langley than the rest of us, so we built on that for his cover story, turned a healthy scepticism of America into deep-rooted loathing. There were times, it's true, when I looked at the books and worried about the flow of information, the net balance of betrayal. We were getting the most extraordinary insight into KGB activities in the UK, but in return we were of course betraying our closest ally.'

'Would you run Primakov again?'

'Tomorrow. And if you're right and he's about to approach Stephen's son, then maybe there's a way. From what I've heard, Daniel shares many of his father's traits, not least a troubled relationship with our cousins across the pond.'

'I think it's fair to say that Daniel Marchant more or less ended the special relationship single-handedly.'

'The Russians will like what they see in him – a chip off the old Marchant block. But could you run the risk of giving them American intel again?'

Fielding paused. 'I think they're after something else this time.' He didn't want to mention Salim Dhar, the possibility that the Russians might have recruited him, too.

Cordingley was too seasoned to miss Fielding's reticence, knew he was holding something back. In his younger days he would have protested, but he didn't care any more. He was too old, too tired. Besides, they were at the house now, and he had done his duty.

'Just remember one thing, Marcus: Primakov had a cause, a genuine reason to betray his country. When his only child fell ill in Delhi, he asked Moscow if he could fly her to London. They refused. What was wrong with Russia's hospitals? She died on an overcrowded ward in Moscow. I don't think we ever upset Stephen that much, do you?'

Marchant didn't know how long he could keep running across the hot sand. The resort's private beach had already come to an end, and he was now amongst hordes of ordinary Sardinians on holiday: extended families gathered under umbrellas, toddlers paddling in the surf, teenage girls flirting, boys in shades keeping footballs in the air. Women of all ages were in bikinis, as if one-piece costumes were banned.

He glanced behind him to see if he was still being followed, and saw one of the Moroccans gliding along the path through the pine trees, set thirty yards back from the beach. He was momentarily hidden behind the wooden shacks serving espressos and ice cream, then he appeared again, looking across at him. If the man was armed, Marchant thought, he wouldn't attempt a shot while the beach was so crowded. And Aziz probably wanted to take him alive, book him in for a follow-up appointment.

He looked at the beach curving around the bay ahead of him. A fine spray hung above the surf in the late-afternoon sun. His body was no longer aching. The medication had cleared, and he felt the way he had on his morning runs through the souks of Marrakech, his body purged of alcohol, his mind disciplined by trips to the library. With each stride he felt stronger, dodging toddlers, jumping over towels. But he knew the real reason for the extra spring in his step, and it wasn't the glances from Italian women in shades. The Segway's electric battery was fading fast.

39

'You must forgive me if I seem a little underwhelmed by the prospect,' Fielding said, walking between the flowerbeds. Lakshmi Meena was at his side, glancing at the plants, reading labels: *Catharanthus roseus* (Madagascar Periwinkle), *Filipendula ulmaria* (Meadowsweet). 'This one here,' Fielding said, stopping in front of a bed, 'is *Hordeum vulgare*. Barley to you and me. It led to the synthesis of lignocaine.'

'A local anaesthetic,' Meena said.

'Correct.' Fielding walked on, leaving her to look at the plant. She drew level with him again, like a schoolchild catching up with her teacher.

Fielding stopped at the junction of two paths. He was tired after his journey back from Penzance the previous night, and had hoped the peaceful surroundings of the Chelsea Physic Garden would offer comfort and solace. He had become a member soon after joining the Service, but the garden had grown too popular in recent years to be of any use as a regular meeting place. In the past, he had used it when he met players from foreign intelligence agencies who wanted an encounter on neutral ground. Tonight, a warm July evening, the director had opened it especially for him. Half an hour on his own, the garden empty except for him and Meena, a chance to reacquaint himself with its pharmaceutical beds.

'Listen, we've hardly endeared ourselves over the past year or so, I'm the first to admit that,' Meena said. 'All I can say is that I think Daniel Marchant is a guy I can work with. And right now he's the only one who's gotten close to Dhar.'

Fielding turned to face her. He was struck again by how similar to Leila she looked in the soft evening sun. Perhaps that was why he had been wary of inviting her to Legoland. She brought back too many bad memories. They had all been fooled by Leila. So had the CIA, which had been out of favour with the British ever since it had renditioned Daniel Marchant.

The Agency had done little to improve its reputation in the subsequent year, wielding too much power in Whitehall. Marchant's treatment in Morocco at the hands of Aziz had tarnished its name even further. Now, following the very public death of six US Marines at the hands of a CIA Reaper, the Agency was a full-blown international pariah. Any trust that had started to come back between it and MI6 had turned to dust. But there had been something about Meena's call to his office earlier in the day that had made him agree to see her. A candidness that he feared he wouldn't be able to reciprocate.

'Do you think that Daniel was right about Dhar and the High Atlas?' Fielding asked.

'More right than we were about Af-Pak.'

'A shame that the Agency didn't let him travel earlier. Did you believe he was right when Spiro sent you to Marrakech?' Fielding knew it was an unfair question.

'Spiro was my superior. I did as he told me.'

'That's not what I've heard.'

Fielding had done some research since her call, walked down to the North American Controllerate and asked around. Meena had an impressive reputation for standing up to Spiro, which took courage, particularly for a woman. She had graduated from the

Farm with honours, impressing with her language skills but also her integrity, which must have been a novelty for the CIA examiners. In normal circumstances, her posting to Morocco would have been a sideways career move, but her brief was to keep an eye on Daniel Marchant, which reflected her importance.

Fielding had then spoken to his opposite number in Langley, the DCIA who had famously promised his President – and Britain – to end the bad old ways and then promptly promoted James Spiro to head of Clandestine, Europe. He had been phoning London repeatedly, presumably to try to patch things up, but Fielding had let him sweat. The last time he rang, Fielding had taken the call.

Spiro, the DCIA explained, had been suspended following the drone strike, and the Agency would be apologising formally for the treatment of Daniel Marchant in Morocco, even though it was at the hands of a foreign intelligence service over which the CIA had little control. 'And the British know all about that,' he had added caustically. (The British courts' decision to make public the torture of a detainee in Morocco hadn't played well in Langley.) As a gesture of goodwill, the Agency was transferring Lakshmi Meena to London and offering her services as a liaison officer.

'She represents the Agency's future, Marcus,' the DCIA had added. 'And this time she's above board.'

'Did you ever meet Leila?' Fielding asked Meena, sitting down on a bench in front of a bed of *Digitalis lanata*, a plant that he knew better as Dead Man's Bells.

'No, sir.' Meena glanced around briefly and then sat down beside him.

'She was a liaison officer for the Agency, too, only nobody ever bothered to tell us. We thought she was working for Six. In the end, it turned out she wasn't working for either of us.'

'But she saved our President's life.'

'Did she?' Fielding realised that Meena would not know about Leila's ties with Iran. That information was too classified. But had national loyalties really meant anything to Leila? Fielding couldn't deny that at the final reckoning in Delhi, she had stepped forward and taken a bullet meant for the US President.

'I appreciate that Leila's case was not straightforward,' Meena said. 'The Agency should have declared her to London as an asset. It was wrong, but those were different times. All I can say is that I'm not Leila.'

No, but you look like her, Fielding thought. Has anyone ever told you? That in a certain light, your hair falls over your eyes in a way that would have confused even your mothers.

'How did you get on with Daniel Marchant in Morocco?'

'Getting along might be stretching it. I don't blame him. I should have done more to stop Abdul Aziz.'

'Daniel's coming back to London today. Quite a toothache, I gather. With respect, can you give me one good reason why he would want to work with you?'

'Listen, we were wrong about Salim Dhar, and we've got six dead Marines to prove it. I don't know what happened in the High Atlas, but I think the DCIA now accepts that the only person who might be capable of finding Dhar is Daniel Marchant. And to that end, I'm here to help him, to help you.'

'I suppose we don't really see your arrival in London in terms of international aid. From where we stand, all the help would seem to be coming from our side. I'm not quite clear what you can give us in return.'

'I think our Delhi station has just found Dhar's mother.'

'Where?' Fielding struggled not to let his interest show. Dhar had always been very close to his mother, who had been identified by MI6's profilers as a possible weakness. Once it became clear that it was her son who had tried to assassinate the US President

151

in Delhi, she had gone into hiding, unlike her husband, who had very publicly disowned his wife and son, and reiterated his love of all things American.

'They've traced her to a temple in south India. Madurai. Given your progress with Dhar and our own catastrophic failure, Langley would like it to be a joint operation. They're closing in on her now.'

40

Marchant walked through arrivals, instinctively checking for cameras, scanning the Heathrow crowds. Prentice was a few yards behind. He had insisted on staying with him after he had picked him up from the far end of the beach, three miles from the resort. He had driven him to Cagliari airport, sat next to him on the plane, made sure no one was offering upgrades. Fielding's orders. Prentice wasn't to leave him on his own until he was safely in his Pimlico flat. Marchant couldn't complain. He'd messed up in Morocco, failed to leave the country under snap cover.

Marchant spotted Monika a moment before she began waving in his direction. There was little that gave her away as the Polish intelligence officer who had helped him to flee Warsaw more than a year ago, sharing joints and her bed with him, all in the line of duty. The gipsy skirt had been replaced by a jacket and jeans, the braided hair disciplined by a tight bun, but she still had the same carefree gait. Marchant had been travelling under the name of David Marlowe at the time, and he knew that she wasn't really called Monika, but he would always remember her as that, the woman in the hippy hostel with a flower in her hair.

He was about to wave back, surprised by the sudden quickening of his pulse, but then he realised that she wasn't looking at him.

'Recognise her?' Prentice asked, coming up on Marchant's

shoulder with a grin. The next moment, Prentice and Monika were kissing each other across the barrier. Marchant couldn't believe it was jealousy that made him turn away. He and Monika had both been operating under cover stories when they had met in Poland. He had been on the run from the CIA, she was helping him escape: each living a lie, doing their job.

'Hello, Daniel,' Monika said, breaking away from Prentice to give him a kiss on both cheeks. He remembered her smell as their skin brushed, and he wondered for a second if it had been more than duty in Warsaw. 'I'm sorry about Leila,' she added more quietly.

'Do I still call you Monika?'

'Hey, why not?'

Because that's not your name, Marchant thought, but he kept silent. Her English was almost perfect, better than when they had met in Poland. And her smile was still too big, her full lips out of proportion with her petite body. She was no more than twenty-five, young enough to be Prentice's daughter. Marchant should have been pleased for him, an old family friend. But he wasn't. Something wasn't right.

'Did I tell you?' Prentice asked him when they were a few yards from the main exit. Monika had fallen behind a crowd of arrivals and was out of earshot.

'What's there to tell?' Marchant said, trying to play things down.

'That I'm sleeping with the enemy.'

'Were you in Warsaw?'

'You know me better than that.'

Marchant didn't miss the sarcasm. Relationships within MI6 weren't unusual, but they weren't encouraged, and they seldom ended happily. 'Don't poke the payroll' – it had been one of Prentice's first bits of advice to Marchant when he had arrived at Legoland. Seeing someone from another intelligence agency was more complicated, but clearly not impossible, particularly for an agent as experienced as Prentice.

'Last time I checked, Poland was an ally,' Marchant said.

'Let's just say it's easier now I'm back in London. Listen, sorry to be neckie, but can you get yourself to Pimlico on your own? It will buy me some time with the office. You know how it is. She's only over here for a few days.'

Monika was standing beside Prentice now, an arm through his, tugging him away. She was playing the sexually outgoing coquette, just as she had with him.

'Of course I bloody can.' Marchant had had enough of being chaperoned. And he needed a drink.

'Is everything OK?' Monika asked him. He searched her eyes, but he no longer knew what he was looking for, or why he even cared. Was this the real Monika? Screwing an old rake like Prentice? She had never once been herself with him in Poland, not even at the airport, when he hoped their masks might have finally slipped. For a moment, Marchant wondered if he would ever know anyone properly.

'Everything's fine,' he said. 'I never got the chance to thank you.'

And with that he lost himself in the crowds. He was happy to have left Prentice behind, but by the time he reached the escalator down to the Underground ticket hall he was aware that someone else was following him. When he reached the bottom, he looked at his watch and took the elevator back up again, scanning the faces of the people coming down. Most were looking ahead, but a tall man in a beaten leather jacket had his face turned away, taking too much interest in the electronic advertising posters. If it wasn't Valentin from Sardinia, he had a twin in London. Hit back hard, Prentice had said.

The thought of Valentin following him to Britain was irritating. Marchant had expected him to have been arrested at the resort in Sardinia and flown back to Russia in disgrace for exposing his leader's sexual preferences to the world, but here he was, about to follow him home to Pimlico.

Marchant turned and took the elevator back down again. The Russian was now at platform level, peeling off left to the westbound platform. Marchant just had time to clock his shoes: fashionably long with narrowed, flat toes. 'Look at the footwear,' his father had always told him. It was something he had never forgotten, whether it was colleagues in Legoland or targets in the field. Often it was the one thing that they failed to change when outfits were swapped, snap covers adopted in a hurry.

By the time Marchant had reached the bottom of the escalator, there was no sign of the Russian. He tried to turn left, but the crowds were almost spilling onto the tracks. He had lost him. He pushed his way to the platform edge. First, he looked left down the long line of people waiting for a train, then to the right. Twenty yards away, a pair of shoes was sticking out beyond everyone else's. He had found his man.

Marchant moved as quickly as he could through the crowds, feeling the warm wind of an approaching train on his face. Thirty seconds later, he was positioned behind the Russian. It was definitely Valentin. He must have decided to drop off his tail, suspecting that he had been spotted, and was now standing with his legs apart on the platform edge, trying to steady himself against the crush of people swarming in different directions.

A member of the station staff asked over the Tannoy for people to move to the far end of the platform. He was unable to disguise his concern. The station was overcrowding. Marchant glanced at the tourists around him, holding anxiously to their suitcases, and then looked again at Valentin, who was only inches away. His hairline was edged with a thin strip of pale skin, suggesting that he had had his hair cut between leaving Sardinia and arriving in London.

It would be very easy to make it look like an accident, Marchant thought as the train approached, sounding its horn. For a moment, he pictured Valentin rolling onto the live rail, looking back up at him. His father had seen a jumper once, said it was the rancid smoke that had shocked him the most. The image of Valentin's burnt body wasn't as unsettling as it should have been. Which friend of his father's did they want him to meet? And why did they talk about him in that familiar way? He realised now how angry he was, how humiliated he felt by the events in Sardinia. Uncle Hugo had been sent to rescue him. Christ, he wasn't a new recruit any more. He was thirty, with five years' experience under his belt, a promising career ahead of him.

A couple of seconds before the train reached the point where they were standing, Marchant looked over his shoulder. 'Hey, stop pushing,' he shouted, and grabbed Valentin's arms as if to steady himself. Then he shoved the Russian forward as hard as he could.

41

'Betrayal requires a great leap of faith,' Fielding said, looking out of the window of his office. Marchant was standing beside him, watching the Tate-to-Tate ferry head down the river, trying to understand what Fielding had just told him.

'You're sure it's Primakov who wants to see me?' he asked.

'Who else would it be? A good friend of your father suddenly turns up in London after years out in the cold. It's hard to imagine that they'd want you to meet anyone else.'

Marchant didn't reply. Before the approach in Sardinia, he had forgotten all about Primakov, but the mention of his name began to sharpen blurred memories. The Russian had been a regular visitor to their house in India, a short man always arriving laden down with gifts for the children, peering over the top of them. It was so long ago. There had been an Indian toy, a mechanical wind-up train that went round a tiny metal track. His mother had taken it away because of its jagged edges.

'There's something I need to show you,' Fielding continued. 'A document that you would never normally see, not unless you become Chief – an appointment that would first require North America to sink beneath the sea.'

The CIA hadn't stopped his father becoming Chief, Marchant thought, ignoring Fielding's attempt at humour. Instead, they had waited until he was in office before humiliating him. Fielding stepped out of the room and told Ann Norman and his private secretary that he didn't want to be disturbed, then closed the door and went over to his desk. But he didn't sit down. Instead, he turned to the big safe in the corner behind him.

'Give me a moment,' he said, and bent down in front of the combination lock. Marchant instinctively looked away, out of apparent politeness, then watched in the window reflection as Fielding punched in some numbers – 4-9-3-7 – into a digital display and turned a large, well-oiled dial beneath it. His brain processed the movements in reverse: one and a half turns clockwise, two complete opposite turns, a final quarter-turn clockwise. Everyone who had ever been in the Chief's office had wondered what secrets the safe held, which British Prime Ministers had been working for Moscow, which trade union leaders had been Russian plants.

'Let's sit over there,' Fielding said a moment later, like a don about to discuss a dissertation. In his hand he held a brown Whitehall A4 envelope. He gestured towards two sofas and a glass table at the far end of his office, below the grandfather clock that Marchant had yet to hear ticking. Before he sat down, he placed the envelope on the table and put both hands on the small of his back. 'The combination changes twice a day, by the way,' he said, stretching, 'should you ever think of opening it.'

'I'd expect nothing less,' Marchant said, trying to hide his embarrassment. He sat down on the edge of the sofa, watching Fielding unpick the quaint brown string that kept the envelope closed at one end. In addition to the normal security stamps on the front, Marchant saw another one, in faded green, that read 'For C's eyes only.'

'I don't need to stress the classified nature of what I am about to show you,' Fielding said.

'God's access?' Marchant asked. Fielding nodded. Product didn't come more secret.

'Your father was one of the most gifted officers of his or any other generation. We both know that. He recruited more valuable assets behind the Iron Curtain than anyone else. But the most prized of them all was Nikolai Primakov.'

'I remember him from Delhi. At least, I remember he used to bring us presents.' Marchant could also recall big smiles and warm laughter, but he couldn't trust his memory. Why hadn't there been the normal household caveats about Primakov, given that he was from a hostile country? After the family had left India for the final time, he had never seen the Russian again, although his father talked of him often.

'The two of them were well known on the South Asia circuit, celebrated sparring partners who were also close friends.'

'How did that work?'

'Such overt friendships were more common in the Cold War. Vasilenko and Jack Platt in Washington, Smith and Krasilnokov in Beirut.' Fielding paused. 'Only a handful of people know that Primakov eventually succumbed to your father's overtures and became one of ours. This is a brief summary of the case.'

He handed Marchant an A4 document that had been typed rather than printed out from a computer, an indication that it was an only copy. Marchant tried to hold it between his hands, but realised they were shaking, so he put the sheet of paper onto the glass table and read. It was a series of bullet points, explaining how his father had recruited Primakov in Delhi and how the Russian had returned to Moscow and eventually risen to become head of K Branch (counter-intelligence) in the KGB's First Chief Directorate. It made impressive reading, but something didn't stack up. Officers other than Chiefs would have been involved in the running of Primakov, heads of stations, Controllerates back in London.

'The version in front of you is for general reading,' Fielding said. 'It's the copy new Prime Ministers see when they come to office. This one is a bit more confidential. South of the river only.'

He slid another sheet of paper across the glass table. Marchant recognised his father's handwriting at once, the green ink faded but legible. He read fast, taking in as much as he could, trying to ignore his hands, which were still trembling. It soon became clear why no one other than fellow Chiefs had read the document. In it was an admission by his father that made Marchant swallow hard.

In order to keep the information flowing from Primakov, Stephen Marchant had let himself be recruited by the Russian. It was the highest stake an agent could play for. Marchant read on, and realised that his father had crossed the sacred line. To keep his enemy handlers happy, he had passed over classified Western documents to Moscow. As far as Marchant could tell, the CX seemed to have been about America, mainly Cuba. He could see nothing that might have directly damaged Britain. He hoped to God he was right.

'Is this why the CIA went after him?' he asked.

'Not unless I'm working for Langley.' Fielding smiled. 'No, the Americans never knew. No one knows. But it is why the Russians are going after the son. They've seen a pattern, a family gene. Some call it "the treachery inheritance". In their eyes, your father betrayed America. As for you, they look at the last year and conclude that the CIA is probably not your favourite intelligence agency either.'

Marchant felt a range of emotions, but in amongst them the thought of his father handing over US intel was strangely re-assuring. It made his own visceral distrust of the CIA seem more understandable.

'Cordingley? Has he seen it?' He was the only previous Chief who was still alive.

'Yes, but his issues were never with America.'

'Someone in Moscow might have told the Americans that an MI6 agent was betraying them.'

'There's always that chance. But not in this case. Moscow thought they had the crown jewels, and the operation would have been known only to a very few people. Your father went on to be Chief, after all.'

'But Primakov was working for us.'

'And we hope he will again.' Fielding paused. 'No one in Moscow Centre knows that he was once loyal to London. He's approaching you as a seasoned Russian intelligence officer with instructions to recruit an unhappy British agent with family form. And you must close your eyes and jump, let yourself be recruited by him.'

'Just like that?' Marchant liked to think of himself offering some resistance.

'See how he plays it. One or two senior people in the SVR still have reservations about Primakov's past, his relationship with your father. He knows that. They suspected your father might have been a worthless *podstava*, and will be quick to dismiss you as a dangle, too. Fight the rod a bit. As I said, betrayal requires faith. Don't expect the smallest sign that Primakov is one of ours. He'll give you nothing. When you meet him at the gallery in Cork Street, he'll be wired. Moscow Centre will be listening. And all you can do, deep down, beneath the cover, is hold on to what you believe to be true: that Nikolai Ivanovich Primakov once worked for your father, and is now hoping to work for you.'

'And what do we hand Moscow in return?'

Fielding paused. 'We give them Daniel Marchant, of course.'

Marchant looked at him and then turned away to the window, pressing his nails deep into his palms.

'No one other than me knows that we're encouraging Primakov to recruit you. As far as everyone else is concerned, you're trying to recruit him. It's important you understand that. Prentice, Armstrong, even Denton – they'll all think you're hoping to turn Primakov. No one must suspect the reverse is true.'

'And the Russians?' Not for the first time, Marchant was struck by the loneliness of being Chief, the solitude of the spymaster's lot, unable to trust anyone, even his own deputy.

'Moscow Centre must believe that you've been landed, not presented to them on a plate.'

Marchant nodded. It was unsettling to think that the Russians had believed for so long that his father was theirs.

'I'm sorry, you were right about the Russian-speaking Berbers,' Fielding continued. 'We're now certain that the SVR is protecting Dhar.'

Marchant had never doubted who had taken Salim Dhar from the High Atlas, but it was still reassuring to hear someone else spell it out.

'The approach in Sardinia confirmed it,' Fielding added. 'We know the SVR are not averse to using Islamic militants when it suits them. Roubles and rifles continue to flow freely into Iran and Syria. Moscow controls mosques in Russia that preach *jihad* against America.'

'And do the Russians know we're related?'

'It would seem so. We're back to the treachery inheritance again: the anti-American family gene. If you had to identify the one single thing that defines Dhar, it would be his hatred of the US. Moscow Centre is demonstrating an ambition we haven't seen from them for a very long time. If they're successful, they'll have two brothers on their payroll. One, the world's most wanted terrorist; the other, the Western intelligence officer charged with finding him. And they share a father who once worked for Moscow, too. A lethal combination, wouldn't you say? The house of Marchant could do a lot of damage.'

163

'Which is why they've recalled Primakov.'

'He's the only person in the world who could recruit both of you. He knew your father. Moscow Centre is still wary of Primakov, but they had no choice but to trust him, bring him back in from the cold.'

'And what do you expect Primakov to give us?'

'Advance warning, I hope, of whatever act of proxy terrorism the Russians and Dhar are planning. And given they're counting on your help, we must assume that this time Dhar's target will be mainland Britain.'

42

It was the incessant rain that Salim Dhar couldn't bear. He could put up with the canteen food, and the training, morning, noon and night. Even the lack of sunshine was something he felt he could get used to. But the interminable drizzle was like nothing he had ever experienced before. The rain of his childhood had been joyful, thick drops that drenched the dusty streets of Delhi within minutes. He had danced with friends in the downpours, celebrating the monsoon's long-awaited arrival, washing himself as the warm water cleansed the land all around. This rain penetrated the soul with its leaden persistence.

The surrounding countryside, deep in the Arkhangelsk oblast of northern Russia, offered little comfort from the misery of the weather: dense dark forests of pine and spruce as far as the eye could see. There was something about pine trees that he found particularly depressing, as if they had been sapped of the very will to live.

Dhar wondered if he would have been happier in the cold. It had been freezing at night in the mountains of Afghanistan, where he had gone after the attack in Delhi. But he had been there many times before, attending and then teaching at training camps, and his familiarity with the terrain seemed to reduce the chill. And winter was also over. It had been much warmer in Morocco's High Atlas. Mount Toubkal was still tipped with white when he had first arrived more than a year ago, but he had kept below the snowline, moving on every night, holding on to the latent warmth of the previous day, encouraged by the promise of morning.

There was no respite where he was now, no prospect of a break in the slate-grey skies. His veins felt like roof gutters, flowing with rainwater. The guards said it wasn't usually so wet. Early July could be beautiful. Some mornings, when he first woke up in his hangar, he wondered if he had travelled back fifty years and been sent to work at the nearby logging Gulag in the forests rather than to Kotlas air base. But as he rolled out his prayer mat on the concrete floor and heard the twin jet engines of a MiG-31 firing up in the damp dawn outside, he knew where he was and what lay ahead.

Kotlas, better known as Savatiya, was a small military airfield, headquarters of the 458th Interceptor Aviation Regiment. Security was already tight, but it had been discreetly increased around the perimeter fence to protect the airfield's anonymous guest. Dhar was being kept in a draughty hangar at the northern end of the 2.5-kilometre-long runway, close to a parking sector deep within a wooded enclosure. There was only one other building in the area, a smaller maintenance hut where he carried out most of his training. On the far side of the runway was an alert ramp where two MiG-31s were positioned on permanent standby. The base was also home to MiG-25s and, as one of his guards had told him, was the 'target of opportunity' that was destroyed by an American B52 bomber in Stanley Kubrick's film *Dr Strangelove*.

Dhar had been told that today would be different. Not the weather, which showed little sign of lifting, but the daily training: less theory. His personal routine, though, would remain unchanged. Self-discipline was how he had kept his life together, the only constant in his world. It was something that his mother had taught him from an early age, when they were living in the American Embassy compound in Chanakyapuri in Delhi, although in those days it had meant helping with her early-morning *pooja* rather than praying towards Mecca. He had been born Jaishanka Menon, a Hindu, but by the time he was eighteen he had converted to Islam and was reading the Koran in Arabic. At first, his conversion was about spiting the man he thought was his father, an infidel who had tyrannised his childhood with his demeaning obsession with all things American, but he had soon grown into his new life, first in Kashmir then in Afghanistan.

His guards knew not to disturb Dhar until he had finished his prayers and ablutions. Sometimes, as he lay awake at night, he heard the stamping of their feet outside, the strike of a match, the rubbing of thick gloves. He felt no sympathy for them. They were part of the FSB, the domestic arm of the former KGB, and had been instrumental in the slaughter of thousands of his Muslim brothers in Chechnya.

He knocked on the side door of the hangar and waited for the guards to unlock it from the outside. He moved his toes in his oversized flying boots, trying to force warmth into them. In winter, he had been told, there was a place in Siberia called Oymyakon where spit froze before it reached the ground, birds froze in mid-flight. He shivered, glad it was summer.

By the time the door was opened, Dhar had wrapped a scarf around his face so that only his eyes were visible, and then put on an old pair of mirrored sunglasses. Without even a glance, he walked past the two guards, who stepped back and followed him across the runway towards the training hut.

To his right, a jet fighter was being prepared in the secluded parking area surrounded by trees. Dhar knew at once what it was: a Sukhoi-25, rugged workhorse of the Soviet air force, the plane he had first seen in Afghanistan as a nineteen-year-old *jihadi*. That one had been a rusting wreck, a legacy of the Soviet invasion almost thirty years earlier. More than twenty had been brought

167

down by Stinger missiles supplied to the Mujahadeen by the CIA. The pilot had been shot after he ejected, and the remains of the plane covered in camouflage netting, deceiving the Soviet search-and-rescue helicopters that had flown over later.

For years afterwards, Taleb children had sat and played in its titanium bathtub of a cockpit, until the wingless fuselage was eventually moved to a training camp. When Dhar had first set eyes on it, he too had sat at its controls, transfixed by the possibilities. It was eighteen months before 9/11. Planes and their potential role in the *jihadi* struggle had always fascinated him. One of the camp leaders had noticed his interest, and encouraged him to start playing flight-simulator games.

Gaming was widespread amongst *jihadis* at the time, a way to stave off boredom during the endless hours of concealment. (The only problem was the pirated software, which crashed continually.) There were a few consoles in Dhar's camp, run off car batteries, and there was talk of a real role for those who excelled at virtual flying.

Dhar had been one of the best, and he knew his planes. He looked again at the jet on the runway and saw that it was in fact an SU-25UB, similar to the model he had been flying on the simulator for the past week, except that it was a two-seater trainer. It must have flown in overnight, as there had been no plane there before. A mechanic was by the far wing, looking up at the underside. Dhar turned away when one of the guards gestured at him.

He felt a thrill ripple through his body as he looked ahead again. He pushed his gloved hand into his coat pocket and felt for the letter, which was still there, a little crumpled. But before he could pull it out and read it again, a voice was calling from the training hut in front of him.

'Today, I watch you fly the *Grach*, our little rook,' the man said, using the SU-25's Russian nickname. 'Then I must leave for London.' It was Nikolai Primakov.

43

Marchant had been surprised to get a call from Monika. She had wanted them to meet alone for a drink, and they were sitting now in the roof terrace restaurant at Tate Modern, after a whirlwind tour of the galleries. He had thought her interest in art at the Polish guesthouse more than a year earlier had been purely cover, but like all good legends, it was based on fact. Her knowledge was considerable.

'You know what Picasso once said?' she asked, sipping a glass of rosé. The London skyline was spread out below them, St Paul's immediately across the river. ' "Art is a lie that makes us realise truth." In our work, you and I lie every day, but somehow the truth gets lost along the way.'

'Were you lying in Warsaw?'

'Of course.'

'And there was no truth in what happened?'

She held his gaze as she put an olive to her full lips. Then she turned away.

'I lost my brother last month. He was with the Agencja Wywiadu, too. A more senior officer than me, always more professional. I tried to do a good job, make sure you had your freedom.'

'And you did.'

'I enjoyed being with you,' she said, keen to change the subject. 'You were very gentle.'

Marchant recalled the brief time they had spent together, making love, smoking joints, each playing out their legends: he the tie-dyed gap-year student, she the hippy hostel receptionist. He had thought about her often since then, her confident sexuality worn so close to her skin.

'But not as gentle as Hugo.'

She laughed, throaty and heartfelt, then lit a cigarette.

'You're not jealous, are you, Mr Englishman?'

Marchant looked away.

'You are.' She laughed again and prodded him in the ribs. 'Daniel.'

It wasn't what he had expected. For a moment, he wondered if he really was jealous. He had been with Monika for twenty-four hours in Poland, most of it spent in bed. But he knew it was something else – suspicion rather than jealousy – that made him keep probing.

'Of course I'm not jealous.'

Her smile faded. 'Hugo's been a good friend. Lifted my gloom.'

Marchant felt a pang of guilt. Prentice had helped him through difficult times, too, particularly when his father had died. He could be a generous colleague, a man who lived life for the moment and wanted others to share in his luck.

'I'm sorry about your brother.' Marchant sensed that Monika wanted to return to the subject, talk about him some more.

'He was shot by the SVR. Four of our agents have been killed in the past year. Another one was murdered last week.'

'All by the Russians?'

'We think so. Someone's betraying them. An entire network's been taken down. The WA's in turmoil, searching for a mole.'

'Is that why you're here in London?'

She paused. 'No. Hugo wanted to show me off to his friends.'

'I lost a brother once. He was called Sebastian. Sebbie. We were twins. He died when I was eight.'

'I'm sorry.' She rested a hand on Marchant's forearm. 'I had no idea.'

'He died in a car crash. His turn to sit in the front seat. We were living in Delhi at the time.'

'You must miss him. They say the bond of a twin is unbreakable.'

'Every day. I wish I could say it gets easier with time, but it doesn't. I'm sorry.'

They sat in silence for a while, her hand resting on his. For once there were no legends, no cover stories. Their grief was real, their own.

'I must go,' Monika said eventually, 'otherwise another Englishman will be getting jealous.'

She stood up from the table, gave Marchant a light kiss on the lips and was gone.

44

Prentice and Marchant were standing well back from the first-floor window of the Georgian townhouse, but they could see people walking up and down Savile Row beneath them in the summer-evening sun. Marchant hadn't been aware that the tailor's had a connection with the intelligence services, but it was an old arrangement brokered by Prentice, which made sense. He never bought his suits from anywhere else.

'The gallery will be crawling with SVR,' Prentice said. 'Armstrong's fixers tried to get a wire in there last night, but security's been like a convent's dormitory for the past three days.'

'So I'll be on my own,' Marchant said.

'I'll be wired, but it's too risky for you,' Prentice replied, glancing behind him. Two technicians with headphones were sitting at a table, fine-tuning a bank of audio units. 'The whole area will be flooded with jammers, but we must expect them to be able to communicate with each other. And to hear us, despite the best efforts of Five,' Prentice added, glancing again at the technicians. 'Primakov has been given the codename "Bacchus".'

Two minutes later, Marchant was turning into Cork Street. It was easy to see which gallery was hosting the opening. People were spilling onto the pavement outside the Redfern, glasses of wine in one hand, catalogues in the other. He checked the street – Harriet

Armstrong had provided a team of watchers at Fielding's request – and recognised an agent sitting at the wheel of a black cab with its light off, thirty yards down the road. He wasn't reassured. The Russians would not make contact if they saw he had company.

Inside the gallery, Marchant nudged through the crowds, declining a glass of wine. A tray of sushi canapés looked more tempting, but there was always a risk with the Russians that it might come with a side order of polonium-210. He headed downstairs, where there were fewer people. He was familiar with the gallery's layout, having studied the floor plans, but something told him that the artist would be lurking in the basement, and he wanted to see him. Sure enough, he was holding court with a couple of younger men, both of whom had notepads. Marchant assumed they were journalists, and tucked in behind them to hear what was being said.

The artist must have been in his seventies, short with a full but close-cropped head of dyed-black hair that had been wetted down in jagged edges. He was wearing a bright pink open-necked shirt and socks with sandals. His face was angular, chiselled like a rough-hewn bust, and he had a fidgety, eccentric manner, massaging the top of his head with both hands as he explained his art.

'This is one of my favourites,' he said in a thick Russian accent, gesturing towards an abstract nude, all spatchcocked limbs and vibrant colours. His hands moved back up to his head. 'Lots of cunt.'

Both journalists visibly flinched. Marchant glanced at the painting, the patch of cross-scratched charcoal. Even he was startled by the word, still hanging awkwardly in the air. Then everyone remembered that artists were meant to shock and the mood settled, more questions were asked. Besides, he was from South Ossetia, and might not even know what he had just said. Marchant doubted it. The old man's moist eyes were dancing.

Upstairs, Marchant looked at some paintings (more nudes, more scratching), making his way around in reverse order towards number 14. He recognised the nude model as Nadia and felt a flicker of unease, particularly as the naked figure next to her bore a striking resemblance to himself. He glanced around instinctively, wondering for a moment if someone might recognise him. The Russians sometimes had a warped sense of humour.

A half-sticker had been stuck next to the price, indicating that the picture had been reserved – and that his meeting with Primakov was still on. But he hadn't spotted anyone at the opening who matched the latest photos Fielding had shown him of the Russian. He looked around the crowded room again, and then he saw Valentin through the main window, smoking on the pavement outside.

Hidden by the surging crowds on the tube platform, Marchant had pulled Valentin back a moment after pushing him towards the oncoming train. He hadn't caught the Russian's curse, but he saw his blood-drained face as he turned around.

'So sorry,' Marchant had said. 'Everyone was pushing from behind.'

To his credit, Valentin had maintained his composure. 'In that case, I must thank you for saving my life.' There was no acknowledgement that they had met before, just the same shiftiness in the Russian's small blue eyes.

'London's a dangerous city,' Marchant had said as the train doors opened. 'I'll catch the next one. Less crowded.'

Valentin squeezed into the crowded carriage, and Marchant waved to him as the train pulled out, the Russian's pale face pressed close to the glass. A warning had been served. Next time, Marchant would push him under.

Valentin still seemed anxious now, glancing up and down Cork Street in expectation. Marchant wondered where Prentice was.

He had points to prove, and he wished he was operating on his own. Besides, Prentice had not been given the full picture about Primakov. According to Fielding, all he had been told was that the Russian had expressed an interest in making contact with Marchant. Primakov had known his father, and Marchant would use the meeting to sound him out for possible recruitment. Prentice knew nothing about Primakov's past role as a British asset.

Marchant looked across at the picture again, and was about to walk over and stand in front of it when he heard a commotion at the entrance. A loud group of Russians strode in: dyed-blonde women weighed down with make-up and designer labels, middle-aged businessmen in blue jeans and chalk-striped jackets. A few steps behind them was a short, overweight man in his late fifties whose gnomic smile and wine-flushed cheeks exuded bonhomie. He was dressed differently from the others. The cord jacket, open shirt and silk scarf suggested a man of culture rather than commerce. Primakov, no question.

Hugo Prentice slipped into the gallery a few moments after Primakov. A Russian waitress greeted him with an offer of wine. Instinctively, Prentice checked himself. He didn't drink on duty, but he needed to blend in, and there was only one glass of orange juice on offer. He took a red wine from the middle of the tray and smiled at the waitress.

'*Za vashe zdorov'e*,' he said, raising his glass and moving into the crowded room.

He recognised a couple of Primakov's babysitters, but the sight of Primakov in the flesh caught him off guard. Despite his experience, he struggled not to look at him twice. It was like seeing a reclusive celebrity come out of hiding for the first time in years. Prentice had read the files, watched film footage of him and studied various photos, but for some reason their paths had never crossed, which was unusual, given their respective Cold War careers.

He knew all about him, of course. Stephen Marchant used to talk to him of their public sparring, how he had tried in vain for many years to recruit the Russian. Everyone in Legoland had heard about his spats with Britain and America in the 1980s. Primakov seemed to love and despise the West in equal measure, teasing with his friendships, annoying his own superiors. And now he wanted to meet Daniel Marchant, the son of his oldest adversary, who was going to try where his father had failed.

'Bacchus has arrived,' Prentice said into his concealed lapel wire, moving towards the bar at the back of the gallery, where the crowds offered more cover.

Before Marchant could do anything, Primakov had placed both hands on his shoulders and was admiring him as if he was one of the canvases on the walls.

'It's so true, you look just like your father,' he beamed, standing in the middle of the gallery and making no effort at discretion. His accent was almost completely Westernised, more American than English, with only a hint of Russian. 'I can't believe it. Can you believe it?' He turned towards one of his babysitters, who shuffled awkwardly. 'This boy's father was my very dear friend,' Primakov said, 'and a lifelong enemy.'

The group's entrance had silenced the gallery. Still smiling, Primakov leaned in towards Marchant and kissed him on both cheeks before hugging him. Marchant caught the strong smell of garlic, and for a moment he was back in Delhi. Just before Primakov pulled back, he whispered into Marchant's ear. 'Goodman's, Maddox Street, ten minutes. I've a letter from your father. We'll take care of the Graham Greene joker.'

Marchant glanced across at Prentice standing by the bar, chatting up one of the waitresses, who topped up his glass as they flirted. He then turned to the group of Russians, who were now being introduced to the artist. *A letter from his father?* The room suddenly felt very hot as Marchant headed for the door. He had no time to warn Prentice. Not much inclination either.

Outside in the street, he hailed the parked taxi he had seen earlier. Its light came on as it drove towards him. Marchant met it halfway and climbed in.

'A friend of mine in there needs a cab, too,' he said, nodding at the gallery window. 'Now.'

'He's left the gallery,' Prentice said, walking down a side corridor and back into the main gallery.

'Get yourself out of there,' Fielding ordered, glancing at Armstrong. They were in his fourth-floor office in Legoland, watching a bank of CCTV screens relaying images from the West End. In one of them, a black taxi was making its way down Conduit Street.

'Repeat please,' Prentice said. His voice was being broadcast in the office, but it was barely audible, breaking up.

'Marchant's flagged a code red alert,' Armstrong said. She had never liked Prentice, but the message had been given to one of her officers, so she felt obliged to pass it on. 'You need to move now.'

Prentice hadn't heard Armstrong's words, but he caught her tone of anxiety just before his comms dropped. He had also noticed Valentin, the tall Russian from Sardinia, who had peeled away from the group around Primakov and was coming towards him, blocking his exit from the gallery.

'You caused me a lot of embarrassment with your little home movie,' Valentin said, his body language at odds with his thin smile. 'It was a fake, of course.'

'Of course. But a good one, no? An Oscar, surely, for best foreign film.'

'Our politicians don't like to be ridiculed.'

'And Her Majesty's agents don't like to be compromised.'

'The boy seemed to be enjoying himself. At least, that's what Nadia said. Where is he now? I thought I saw him earlier.'

'No idea. I must go, though. It's been a pleasure.'

But Prentice knew already that he was going nowhere. With a taut smile, Valentin took the glass of wine from him and handed it back to the waitress, just as the gallery began to spin and blur.

45

Marchant was shown by the female *maître d'* to a back room of Goodman's, separated from the main restaurant by a screen.

'A drink while you're waiting?' the woman asked, ushering him to a table that had been made up for two. She let her hand linger on his shoulder a moment longer than was appropriate. There were four other tables in the room, but they were empty. 'Nikolai will be here in a few minutes.'

'A whisky, thanks,' Marchant said. 'Malt.' He had drunk a glass of wine at the gallery once he had seen others being served from the same tray, but he had declined a top-up, despite the persuasive charms of the waitresses. He wouldn't drink his malt until he had heard what Primakov had to say.

The taxi from MI5 had dropped him off in Maddox Street, outside the restaurant, where the parked cars were a wealthy mix of Porsches and Bentleys. He needed to talk to Primakov on his own, but it was no bad thing if Armstrong's people knew where he was. He thought for a moment about Prentice. He had looked tired tonight, too old for street work.

Goodman's served American steaks, but it was owned by a Russian who ran a chain of similar restaurants in Moscow. To judge from the main room, at least half the clientèle was Russian too.

Marchant had seen few female diners when he was shown through to the back room.

He glanced at the starters on the menu – sweet herring with hot mustard – and listened to the subdued hubbub of conversation on the other side of the panel, which must have been more solid than it appeared.

Then suddenly Primakov was in the room, quieter now, taking a seat opposite him, leaning back to whisper something to the *maître d'*, who had reappeared with two crystal glasses of whisky. Marchant thought how at home he looked in a restaurant, his natural habitat. The waitress put the glasses down on the table then left the room, closing the sliding door firmly. They were alone.

'I presume you've had the "big talk" with the Vicar,' Primakov began, burying the corner of a linen napkin under his chins and spreading the rest out across his chest as if he was hanging out the washing. His breathing was thickened by a slight wheeze. 'Let MI6 believe what they want. Your father and I were very close, it is true – unnaturally so, I suppose. But I never once considered working for him. Please remember that.'

Marchant tried not to blink at the Russian's bold opening gambit. If Primakov was lying for the sake of Moscow Centre's ears, he was making a good job of it. For a split second, Marchant doubted everything – his father's judgement, his own, Fielding's. Maybe the Americans had been right to suspect the house of Marchant. Then he recalled the Vicar's words. *Betrayal requires faith. Don't expect the smallest sign that Primakov is one of ours. He'll give you nothing.* Marchant's immediate task, he told himself, was to be recruited by Primakov.

'So why do you want to see me?' Marchant asked. 'I don't really have the time or the desire to sit around discussing old times.'

'You share a family look, and the same taste in whisky.' Primakov took a sip from his glass, ignoring Marchant's insolence. 'Your father liked Bruichladdich, too. I ordered it in specially. It takes me back, just sitting here across the table from you. We shared many happinesses together, your father and me. They were good times.'

'Different times. The world's moved on.'

'Has it?' Primakov paused, raising a silver lighter to his cigarette.

Marchant wondered if his father might have been friends with the cultured Russian even if there hadn't been an ulterior motive. In Delhi, they had both enjoyed going to the theatre, visiting galleries, attending concerts, which had made meetings easier. And Primakov had an undoubted warmth about him: a camaraderie that drew people in with the promise of stories and wine, the stamina to see in the dawn.

'When we were both first posted to Delhi, we used to argue late into the night over local whisky – Bagpiper in those days – about the Great Game, what our countries were doing there. Your father was an admirer of William Moorcroft, an early-nineteenth-century East India Company official who was convinced Russia had designs on British India.'

Marchant knew the name well. 'He wanted to publish a book about Moorcroft,' he said. 'It was going to be his retirement project. Unfortunately, he found himself retired earlier than expected, and wasn't ready to write it.'

'No.' Primakov paused, lost in thought. 'Moorcroft was also dismissed earlier than he intended. He took it badly, felt betrayed by his own country, just like your father, but he continued on his great quest to buy horses in Bokhara. Turkomans. He was a vet by training. He tried to reach Bokhara through Chinese Turkestan, but was held up in Ladakh, where he discovered he had a rival.'

'A Russian?'

'Persian-Jewish, a trader called Aga Mehdi. But he impressed our Tsar so much with his shawls that he was given an honorary Russian name, Mehkti Rafailov, and was sent to talk with Ranjit Singh, ruler of the Punjab kingdom, on behalf of Russia.'

'So Moorcroft was right.'

'Rafailov's orders were to open up trade routes, nothing more.'

'Of course.'

'What intrigued your father was the relationship between Moorcroft and Rafailov, who was due to arrive in Ladakh while Moorcroft was there. The British spy was keen to meet his Russian enemy, but Rafailov died in the Karakoram pass before he reached Ladakh.'

'So they never met.'

'No, but Moorcroft made sure that Rafailov's orphaned son was provided for and educated. He was an honourable man, respected his adversaries.'

'Maybe that's why my father wanted to write about him. He respected you.'

'And he had a son whom I promised to look after.' Primakov hesitated, but not long enough for Marchant to decide if he meant him or Salim Dhar. 'I'm sure there would have been a market for the book,' he continued. 'Maybe you should write it?'

'I don't think you came here tonight to offer me a publishing deal.'

Primakov sat back, looked around and finished his whisky. 'We are free to talk in here. The room was swept before we arrived. So tell me. How much did the Vicar explain to you? About your father?'

'Nothing,' Fielding said, removing his headphones. The live feed had deteriorated until he could hear little more than white noise. He had heard enough, though. Marchant was being swept out of his depth.

'The entire area's been jammed,' Armstrong said, putting one hand over her mobile. 'Our best people are on it.'

That was what worried Fielding, but he didn't say anything. He wished MI6 was running the show, but London was Armstrong's patch and he needed her support, particularly as his own man, Prentice, had uncharacteristically messed up.

'What about your officer in the restaurant?' he asked.

'Shown the door after his starter.'

Fielding turned away and looked out onto the river, glowing in the evening sun. The encrypted feed from the restaurant was being relayed to his office and to no one else, given the extreme sensitivity of Primakov's case. Armstrong was one of the few who knew that Primakov had once been a British asset, and Fielding trusted her. It was Marchant who was starting to worry him.

46

Marchant glanced at Primakov, trying to read his face for more. His nose was big, slightly hooked. It was a strange question to ask. *How much did the Vicar explain to you?* What did the Russian want him to say? *He told me everything, that you betrayed Mother Russia and worked for my father?* The room might have been purged of British bugs, but Moscow would be listening in on their conversation.

'He told me that there were doubts about my father's loyalty to the West. Fielding didn't personally believe them, but he said the Americans had harboured suspicions about my father for many years. But that was the nature of his job, the risk he took – when he agreed to run you.'

'Run me?' Primakov managed a dry, falsetto laugh, shifting in his seat as it dissolved into a wheezy cough. Somewhere in Moscow Centre, Marchant thought, an audio analyst would be adjusting his headphones, calling over a superior. Had he overplayed it?

'Fielding showed me some of the intelligence you supplied to him,' Marchant continued.

'It is true, we gave your father some product once in a while, to keep his superiors happy, but it was nothing important.'

'Chickenfeed?'

'Organic. Nice writing on the label, but overpriced.'

Primakov paused, as if to reassess the rules of their engagement. Marchant wondered again in the ensuing silence if he had said too much. Then the Russian leaned forward, his voice suddenly quieter, like a doctor with news of cancer. Marchant smelt the garlic again as he traced a delta of broken blood vessels across Primakov's cheeks.

'It was the least we could do, given the nature of the product your father was supplying us.' Primakov drew on his cigarette and sat back, watching Marchant, his barrel of a body turned sideways as he blew the smoke away into the middle of the room. 'I think you already knew, deep down.'

Now it was Marchant's turn to shift in his seat. Primakov's words weren't a surprise, but they still shocked him. Up until this moment, he had tried to convince himself that the knowledge of his father's betrayal of America could be kept inside Fielding's safe, confined to an A4 piece of paper covered with green ink. Hearing a third party confirm it brought it out into the open, made it tangible.

'You seem troubled,' Primakov said. 'Hurt, perhaps.' His voice was even softer now, almost tender in tone. 'Please understand why he never told you himself. It was not because he didn't trust you. He wanted you to come to it yourself, to reach your own, similar conclusions. And I don't think you are so far from the place that your father occupied.'

'No.' It was time to give Primakov some encouragement, to tire on the line, but Marchant was struggling to sound convincing. Too many thoughts were chasing through his mind. What if his father had been happy to give more than he received?

'Not everyone can boast of being waterboarded by the CIA, after all. And they accuse us of being animals. Understandably, you share a similar distrust of all things American, which is to be applauded. Apart from their grain-fed steaks from

185

Nebraska, of course, which your father loved, just as I do. Come, we must eat.'

Marchant laughed. It was detached, out-of-kilter laughter. Then he laughed again, like the last man standing at a late-night bar.

'What's so amusing?'

'I came here tonight with orders to sound you out for recruitment, but now here you are trying to recruit me.'

'I don't blame you for the confusion. Sometimes I find the Vicar's faith in his flock almost moving.'

Marchant looked hard at the Russian in the silence that followed. *Don't expect the smallest sign that Primakov is one of ours.* For the second time, as Primakov's words lingered in the twisting cigarette smoke, he wondered if the Russian was telling the truth and Fielding was wrong. *He'll give you nothing.* Perhaps there was nothing to give.

'I'm not trying to recruit you, Daniel. I just want you to meet someone. Another son who has discovered he has much in common with his father. Family business.'

Marchant paused. Had he fought hard enough against the rod?

'And if I don't want to meet him?' The words stuck in his throat. He realised how much he wanted to see Salim Dhar.

'Moscow will have no option but to go public on your father, expose him for the traitor he was. Your government would no doubt respond in kind, accusing me of treachery, but then we would tell the world about Salim Dhar, that his biological father was the former head of MI6. I think the world would make up its own mind, don't you?' He paused. 'Please, read this. It's a letter from Stephen, which I have kept with me until this day. I hope it will make things easier for you.'

Marchant looked at the folded letter before taking it, as much to steady his hand as wonder about its contents. He knew already that it was genuine, that the writing was his father's. He began to read, resting his hand on the edge of the table:

My dear Daniel,

If you are reading this, it must mean that you have finally met Nikolai Ivanovich Primakov. I will not try to guess at what path led you to him, only to offer reassurance that I have trodden a similar one before you. You are old enough, of course, to make your own judgements in life, but in the case of Nikolai, I merely wish to assist you, because other influences will be in play. He is, first and foremost, a friend, and . . .

47

'. . . *you can trust him as if he was a member of our family.*'

Salim Dhar rested the letter on his lap, tears stinging his eyes, and looked out of the cockpit at the slanting rain. It was only his second flight in the two-seater SU-25UB, but already he felt at home in the confined titanium-alloy space. It would take longer to adjust to the colossal G-forces that blurred his vision as the aircraft banked and climbed into the sky, but he was determined not to show any weakness.

Sergei, his Russian instructor, also known as the Bird, was sitting behind him, putting the plane through another roll, the Archangel countryside spinning around to settle above his head. There was something about Sergei that Dhar liked. He became a different person in the air, less lugubrious, as if all his worries had been left on the ground. And Sergei had plenty to worry about. According to Primakov, he had been one of Russia's best pilots until he had crashed a MiG-29 into the crowd at an air show, killing twenty-three people and ending his career. The crash still haunted him day and night.

'I don't trust him,' Sergei said over the intercom, spinning the jet back over and pulling into a steep climb.

'Who?' Dhar managed to say, his jaw heavy with G-force. He could feel himself being pressed down into his seat, the blood rushing to his legs and feet. In training, Sergei had taught him how to squeeze his abdominal muscles to prevent blood flowing to the lower body. He tried to squeeze, but his vision was already greying at the edges.

'Primakov,' Sergei said calmly.

'Why not?' Dhar harboured similar suspicions, but he was struggling to speak, unable to see anything now except blackness. He was close to losing consciousness as Sergei banked hard left.

'Just a feeling. Are you ready to fly?' According to the dials swimming in front of Dhar, the plane was levelling out at 15,000 feet.

'I'm ready,' Dhar said, his vision returning. Euphoria swept through him as he looked around, blood flowing freely to his brain. He had waited a long time for this moment. *Inshallah*, his new life was coming together. He could do this. What lay ahead suddenly seemed possible. More importantly, his past had shifted too, on a tectonic scale, giant plates of data slipping into place beneath the surface.

Primakov had left him twenty-four hours earlier, and in that time Dhar had read and reread the letter the Russian had given him, thinking back to the only time he had met his father, when he was being held prisoner at a black site facility in Kerala. *To Salim, the son I never knew.* South Indian *jihadis* were suspected of being behind a series of bomb attacks in Britain at the time, and Stephen Marchant, then Britain's head of MI6, had travelled all the way to Kerala to ask Dhar if he knew anything about the campaign. Dhar couldn't help him.

It was then, as the monsoon rain beat down outside, that Marchant had detonated a bomb of his own: Dhar was his own son.

'If it's any consolation, I loved your mother,' Marchant had continued, walking around Dhar's dank cell. A solitary lightbulb hung from the ceiling. 'I still do.'

Dhar had been too tired, tortured too many times, to feel anything at first. Instead, he just stared at the betel-nut juice stains that streaked down his cell walls. There was blood mixed in with the red marks; his own blood. Eventually, he looked up from the threadbare *charpoy* on which he was lying. Any anger he felt towards Marchant was tempered by relief that the man he had thought for so long was his father, a man he despised above all others, was no such thing. After a long pause, during which the rain outside increased to a deafening downpour, Dhar sat up with difficulty, and spoke.

'How did you meet her?' he asked, rubbing his bruised and swollen wrists together. They were shackled and chained to a steel ring on the wall.

'She worked as an ayah at the British High Commission when I was stationed in Delhi. 1980. She was there for a year, I think. Before she switched to the American Embassy.'

Dhar had cast his eyes down at the mention of America.

'She asked me never to make contact with her or with you again. I agreed, with reluctance, but I always provided for you both, sending money once a month.'

Dhar wondered why the British spymaster had broken his promise. He could have sent a colleague to interrogate him. The south Indian rendezvous was a risk in itself, but the news Marchant had brought was far more dangerous, more compromising – for both of them. Western spy chief fathers *jihadi*. Then, as Marchant had talked on into the monsoon night, peppering his conversation with anti-American asides, Dhar had begun to understand. His world, far from being fractured by the revelation, had in some way become more complete.

'The West is not as simple as your people sometimes like to think,' Marchant had said – the last words Dhar was ever to hear his father speak.

Now, here in his hands, 15,000 feet above the Archangel countryside, was written confirmation of what Dhar had barely dared to hope: a father who had the same enemies as him. If Primakov was to be believed, Stephen Marchant, Chief of MI6, had spent more than twenty years spying for the Russians, inspired by a mutual distrust of America.

'Your father was a true hero of Russia,' Primakov had said. 'It was an honour to work with him.'

Dhar knew it wasn't important, that, *inshallah*, he would answer to a higher calling, but it mattered. He was being asked to follow in his father's footsteps. And for a son who had never known paternal love, never been shown the way, the feeling of comfort was almost overwhelming.

He took one last look at the letter, then folded it into one of the clear plastic pockets of his flying suit. *I will not try to guess at what path led you to him, only to offer reassurance that I have trodden a similar one before you.*

'The *Grach* is yours,' Dhar heard Sergei say over the intercom. And for a brief moment, as his hands tightened on the stick and endless pine forests passed in a blur far beneath him, it felt as if life had a coherence that had so far evaded him.

48

'Call me if you need to talk,' Harriet Armstrong said, moving towards the door. Fielding nodded. He was grateful for Armstrong's support, but he needed time on his own. Inevitable cracks were beginning to show in their new-found friendship. Fielding had no choice but to keep her in the dark about some of the more sensitive aspects of the Dhar case, and she resented her exclusion. The encrypted audio file on his computer, procured by her officers, was for his ears only.

He didn't blame Armstrong, but he could never tell her that his real intention was for Daniel Marchant to be recruited by Primakov, or that his biggest concern was Marchant's seeming inability to play the traitor. Nor could he ever reveal the Faustian pact that Stephen Marchant had once signed with Primakov: the flow of American intel from London to Moscow in return for Russian product. He couldn't tell anyone.

Fielding waited for Armstrong to close the door before playing the audio file. Five's eavesdroppers had finally managed to get a live feed from the restaurant, but Daniel Marchant had already left. As soon as he heard it, Fielding recognised the voice: Vasilli Grushko, head of the SVR's London *rezidentura*. The Russian's cold tones still made his pulse quicken, even though he was familiar with it from countless intercepts. Perhaps it was because he hadn't heard the anger before. Grushko was reprimanding Primakov, and he could almost hear the sweat dripping from his brow.

'Give me one good reason why we should trust him,' Grushko said. He then used a word that Fielding had dreaded to hear in connection with Daniel Marchant: '*podstava*', a dangle. Grushko wasn't buying Daniel Marchant.

'His loyalties are no longer with the West,' Primakov protested. 'The apple never falls far from the tree. He is his father's son.'

'That's what worries me,' Grushko said. Fielding was well aware that Grushko was one of those SVR officers who believed that Stephen Marchant had been a *podstava*, too.

'What harm will it do if he meets Salim Dhar?' Primakov said. 'The Muslim has asked to see Marchant.'

'We already have someone in London who could help. Why can't you persuade Dhar to work with them?'

We already have someone in London who could help. Was Grushko bluffing, or had the SVR been on a recruitment drive? Fielding would run it by Ian Denton afterwards.

'Because I doubt that they can claim to be Salim Dhar's brother,' Primakov said.

'Half-brother.' Grushko paused. 'I am sorry, Nikolai, but I have not heard enough tonight to be persuaded that Daniel Marchant is no longer loyal to his country.'

'How much do you need? Here is a man who has been waterboarded by the CIA. And now he has been tortured in Morocco. If past experience is any guide, British intelligence must have been aware of what was happening to him. What more do you want?'

'So why does he keep returning to his job after being so poorly treated?'

'Because he wants to meet his brother, and he knows his best chance is with MI6.'

There was a pause, long enough for Fielding to wonder if the feed had dropped.

'Maybe you are right,' Grushko continued, his voice fainter now. 'I'm not so sure. It is clear that Marchant dislikes America with commendable passion, but that is not the same as being ready to break the bond with your own mother country.'

Fielding listened as Primakov showed his boss out, then took off his headphones and walked to his desk, mulling over what Grushko had said. Moscow Centre clearly didn't believe that Marchant was ripe for recruitment. He was too damn loyal. It was understandable, given the implications. Marchant was being asked to act as if his father had been a traitor, an accusation he had fought long and hard to disprove.

It would have been so much easier if Primakov had slipped up at the restaurant and given Marchant a sign, but the Russian had been too professional. Now Primakov's superiors were growing restless. Grushko wanted proof of Marchant's willingness to betray, evidence of his treachery inheritance. It was time to cut Marchant loose.

'Can you get me Lakshmi Meena on the line?' Fielding asked Ann Norman over the intercom. The American might be useful after all.

He then replayed Grushko's words for a second time. *We already have someone in London who could help.* Fielding moved to call Denton, but then he paused. If Moscow Centre really had penetrated Six, he knew what lay ahead. He had watched Stephen Marchant go through a similar molehunt when he had been Chief. There would be a top-down investigation. Morale in Legoland would plummet. Everyone would be under suspicion, especially people like Denton, whose reputation had been made in Russia. He couldn't tell anyone what Grushko had said, not yet.

49

Marchant walked up the iron steps, trying to get his bearings. Primakov had offered him a circuitous back exit from the restaurant, through the cellar into the basement of an adjoining wine bar, which he had gladly accepted. He wasn't in the mood for small talk in the back of a black cab with one of Armstrong's watchers. According to Primakov, Maddox Street was crawling with them, which had annoyed him. Fielding and Armstrong had promised him he would be left alone. One officer had even tried to get inside Goodman's, posing as a diner.

'It's the footwear that gives them away,' Primakov had joked. 'Only your policemen and MI5 wear such ridiculous rubber soles.' No wonder the Russian had got on so well with his father. Marchant resisted mentioning Valentin's tell-tale shoes.

He knew that Fielding would be expecting him back at Legoland for a debrief, but he needed to clear his head, walk the summer-evening pavements. He stepped out onto Pollen Street, a narrow, dog-legged lane that ran down between Maddox Street and Hanover Street. Opposite him was the Sunflower Café, closed for the day. He glanced right and then headed away towards Hanover Street, turning into the square. No one had seen him.

It was only as he was heading west down Brook Street that he became aware of a tail, and it didn't feel like MI5. At the junction with New Bond Street, he waited to cross the road, giving himself an opportunity to glance back down Brook Street. He spotted two of them, on either side of the road, a hundred yards away. The first man kept walking, head down, not letting Marchant get a look at his face. The second, further back, peeled away into a pub. Marchant guessed there would be at least two more. They didn't look Russian either. Or American.

He had two choices. Keep walking to see how good – and who – they were, or call in and get picked up by MI5. He opted for the former, and increased his pace, continuing west down Brook Street towards Grosvenor Square. The American Embassy was not his favourite building in London, but the armed policemen that guarded it night and day might unsettle whoever was following him. If his tail pursued him for two brisk circuits of the embassy building, there was a good chance that they would be stopped by the police on the third. But before he could give them the run-around, a car drew up next to him.

'You're a guy in a hurry.' It was Lakshmi Meena, sitting at the wheel of an Audi TT convertible. Its roof was down.

'Working off dinner,' Marchant said, continuing to walk.

'Fielding said I might find you around here. He wants us to talk.'

'Well, now you can tell him we have.'

Marchant stopped, glancing back down the road, scanning the pedestrians for signs, shoes. He could see four of them in total. They had broken cover, making no attempt to conceal themselves. Their body language was more lynch mob than watcher. Marchant recognised the one at the back from Sardinia. He opened the door of Meena's car and climbed in.

'Aziz is dead. Last night in the military hospital in Rabat,' Meena said, looking in the rear-view mirror as they drove off. 'Complications unrelated to his original injuries, but clearly he wouldn't have been in there if you hadn't ripped half his mouth off.'

'Are they lodging an official protest?'

'Not their style. They don't want to draw attention to what they did to you first.'

'On your orders.'

'Spiro's.'

'And you do whatever he says.'

Meena pulled up at a red light and glanced again in the mirror, her knuckles whitening on the steering wheel. 'Look, I'm sorry for what happened. Truly.'

Marchant felt the gap in his gum with his tongue, but decided not to say anything. 'Where are we going?'

'Your flat, then Heathrow.'

'Heathrow?'

'Fielding wants us to go to India. Our flight's tonight, and you need to pack.'

'Our flight? Not so fast. I'm not going anywhere until I've spoken to him.'

Marchant shifted in his seat. He hadn't been back to India since the US President's trip, Leila's death.

'Fielding's meeting us at Heathrow. He'll explain everything. How was Primakov, by the way?'

Marchant hesitated. A new arrival at the Russian Embassy in London would arouse even the doziest CIA desk officer, but her question still surprised him.

'The sous-chef at Goodman's is one of ours,' she continued by way of explanation. 'It's one of the most popular Russian restaurants in town. You showed up on our grid before you'd even ordered your herring with mustard. How can you eat that stuff?'

'You're not from Calcutta then?'

'Reston, Virginia, actually. Why?'

'Bengalis like their mustard.'

'I meant the fish.'

'They like that too. Primakov was fine. Fatter than I remember him. He was an old friend of my father.'

'Friend?'

'Sparring partner.' He paused. 'So who showed up first on your grid? Me or Primakov?'

Meena hesitated. 'OK, I'll admit, we don't have a great deal on Primakov. Cultural attaché, brought out of retirement, medium-ranking KGB officer before the fall.'

'But you have a bulging dossier on me. Says it all, doesn't it? So where in India are we heading?'

'The south, Tamil Nadu. Where my parents are from.'

'Great. Meet the in-laws time. A bit premature, isn't it? We haven't even slept together.'

Meena drove on in silence, glancing in the rear-view mirror.

'I'm sorry,' Marchant said, more quietly now. It had been a crass thing to say. Sometimes it was easy to forget Meena's Indian heritage. She talked like a ballsy, confident American, trading coarse comments with colleagues, but there was an inner dignity about her that he recognised as uniquely subcontinental.

'Actually, we're going to find your father's lover.'

He looked across at her for more.

'Our Chennai sub-station is closing in on Salim Dhar's mother. Fielding thought you should be there when we bring her in.'

50

Salim Dhar turned the navigation lights on as the canopy closed, and took a deep breath. Then, after running through the cockpit checks he had practised so often on his ancient PC, he leaned forward and flicked the switch to start the right engine. The RPM dial in front of him spooled up to 65 per cent, and the exhaust-gas temperature rose to 300 degrees. He did the same with the left engine, lowered one stage of flap and used his thumb to reset the trim to neutral.

For a moment, he was back in Afghanistan, sitting in the cockpit of the crashed SU-25. He remembered a solitary poppy pushing up through a broken dial. It was the first time in his adult life that he had been happy. The camaraderie at the training camp had made him realise how little friendship he had found until then. The darkest days of his childhood had been at the American school in Delhi, where his father had insisted on sending him. There were a few Indian pupils, sons of New Delhi's business elite, but he was not like them, nor was he like the diplomats' children, who made no effort to talk unless it was to taunt him – *Allah yel'an abo el amrikaan'ala elli'awez yet'alem henaak* (God damn the fathers of those Americans and whoever wants to study there!).

He turned the landing lights on, requested taxi clearance from the control tower, and again flicked the trim switch, setting it for take-off. Then he tested the wheelbrakes as he ran the throttle up to 70 then 80 per cent.

'Brakes holding, airbrake closed,' he said to himself as he felt for the switch on the side of the throttle. As jets went, the SU-25 wasn't a demanding plane to fly. Unlike its more recent successors, it didn't have a modern avionic suite, but it was a reliable ground-pounder, which was why it had been in Russia's air force for so long. According to Sergei, his instructor, the SU-25 could operate at very low speeds without 'flaming out'. Nor did it stall easily. 'It can take a real beating and still bring you home,' Sergei had said. But Dhar knew there would be no return flight.

After taxi-ing to the runway threshold and running through his pre-take-off checks, he waited for his clearance from control. At last it came. He took his position on the runway's centreline, gazing at the white ribbon that stretched away as far as he could see. Engaging the wheelbrakes, he ran the power up to 90 per cent and checked that all the gauges were still in the green. Then he released the brakes and applied full military power, watching the air speed build quickly to 260 kmh.

Something was wrong.

'Sometimes you need to add a little right rudder as you firewall the throttles,' Sergei had said, but Dhar remembered too late. His fingers fumbled to deploy the twin drogue chutes, but it was hopeless. There was too little tarmac left. 'Eject, eject!' said a voice in his head. But as he overcompensated for the yaw, the plane lurching right, left, right again, the right wingtip hit the ground, breaking off in a shower of sparks and fire. He thought of his mother, closed his eyes and prayed.

51

Fielding took the call in the back of his chauffeur-driven Range Rover on the way to Heathrow. Cars didn't particularly interest him, but he couldn't deny that he had been impressed with the latest security upgrades to his official vehicle. Most of them were to do with jamming opportunist electronic eavesdroppers, but the car had also benefited from lessons learned in Afghanistan, where IEDs had caused such havoc. Its floor was now protected by hard steel armour blast plates, and the sides had been reinforced with composite ballistic protection panels.

'Thank you for ringing back,' he said, trying to picture his opposite number in America, his Langley office, the bland Virginia countryside. Fielding's relationship with the DCIA had been at rock bottom during the past year, but he knew that things had to improve sooner or later. Much as it would like to, Britain couldn't survive indefinitely without America's intel.

'What can I do for you, Marcus? No problems with Lakshmi Meena, I hope?'

'No, she's fine.'

'Treat her as yours, Marcus. A shared asset. She's good.'

Better than the last one, you mean, Fielding thought, but he said nothing. 'Thank you. She's briefed me fully about Dhar's mother.'

'That's what she's there for. Keeping our allies in the loop.'

Like hell, Fielding thought. He looked out of the window at the grey scenery either side of the Westway: tatty tower blocks, car showrooms, digital clocks, vast hoardings. It was such a drab part of London, a depressing first impression of Britain for anyone driving in from the airport.

'How's Jim Spiro these days?' Fielding asked.

'I never knew you cared. He'll be touched, truly.'

'Is he still suspended?'

'To all intents and purposes. He's the subject of an ongoing internal inquiry, based largely on evidence provided by MI6.'

'I need to talk to him.'

52

Daniel Marchant moved quickly around his one-bedroom basement flat in Pimlico, removing a suitcase from underneath the
bed that was already packed with three sets of clothes and a wash
bag containing a razor, toothbrush and two passports. The
cobblers had given him a new spare one after Morocco. He had
asked for two, but they had talked about budgets and come back
to him a few days later saying that the passport in Dirk McLennan's
name, the snap cover he had used to get out of Morocco, had
not been compromised.

Out of habit, he checked the issue date, making sure it was
still valid, and then he saw an old Islamabad visa stamp on one
of the pages. A trip to the Islamic Republic of Pakistan had been
fine for Morocco, but it might cause problems in India. He
cursed the cobblers and put the passport on his desk. He paused
for a moment, looking at the photo of Leila that he had tried
so often to throw out. She was smiling back at him, the bright
lights of a carousel blurred behind her. He had taken the photo
at the funfair in Gosport, across the water from the Fort, a few
hours before they had slept together for the first time. The
instructors had given them a rare day off after two weeks of
intense training.

He knew it was a weakness to keep the photo, but something

about her expression made it impossible to get rid of it. For a few heady months, he had thought it was love in her eyes. It was still hard to accept that he had been deceived. Wasn't it his job to be vigilant while deceiving others? Perhaps he kept the photo as a reminder, a warning.

'I guess you still miss her, right?' He turned to see Lakshmi Meena standing in the doorway. She had dropped him off outside on Denbigh Street. He put the photo back on the desk, annoyed that he hadn't heard her walk down the iron steps to his flat. Leila could still make him drop his guard, even now.

'Have you ever had to sleep with someone as part of the job?' he asked, unnecessarily adjusting the photo frame on his desk.

'Spiro once tried it on. Said it was all part of the promotion process.' She could still recall the approach: first month at Langley, fresh from the Farm. Spiro liked to call all the new female recruits into his office for a friendly one-to-one.

'I don't mean with our side.'

'I know we're not always the good guys, but we're not the enemy.'

'Leila wasn't just working for you. Read the files.'

'I tried. Hey, way beyond my security clearance. All I know is that she saved our President's life.'

'That's one way of looking at it.'

'And another way?'

'She betrayed me.' Spiro had used similar words when she played him back an audio recording of his advances. A colleague had tipped her off, and she had gone into his office wired, claiming later that she was testing out new equipment and had forgotten to turn it off. It had been a colossal career risk, but Spiro had never bothered her again. If anything, he respected her more.

'And you can't forgive her that?' she asked.

'Not yet.'

'Is that why you won't trust anyone?'

'Anyone?'

'Women.'

'It was a calculated act of betrayal.'

And now, like King Shahryar's virgin wives, we all stand accused, Meena thought, but she didn't have time to say anything. They heard a car slow down on the road above them. Marchant glanced up through the basement window at the pavement.

'Where did you park?' he asked.

'Around the corner, Lupus Street. I drove round the block twice first. No tail.'

'Come, quickly,' Marchant said, locking the front door to the flat, where Meena was standing, and going through to the bedroom. A pair of french windows looked out onto a small patio garden. He opened them and ushered her outside, glancing back at the front of the flat. Someone was coming down the metal stairs. How had they got his home address? He went into the small adjoining bathroom, turned on the light and the shower and returned to the bedroom. Then he took the key from the inside of the french windows, joined Meena on the patio and locked them from the outside.

'Spiro's orders again?' he asked.

'No,' Meena said. 'The Moroccans are upset Aziz is dead. Very upset.'

Marchant walked across to the back wall, which was about twelve feet high and covered in a wooden lattice for climbers he had never planted. In the corner, there was a rockery. Soon after he had bought the flat, he had built up the rocks at the back to help him climb up the wall, should he ever need to. He had cemented in three bricks above the highest rock, at eighteen-inch intervals up the wall, that stuck out by half a brick and acted as steps, but he had never got round to trying them.

'Up there, quick,' he said, pointing at the corner as if it was the obvious way out of the garden. When Meena reached the top of the wall, she looked back down at him.

'You forgot to build any steps on the other side,' she said before jumping. He heard a groan as she landed in the mews below. Then he followed her, glancing back at his flat as he reached the top of the wall. Two men had broken in, and one of them was looking at the passport he'd left on his desk. The other was moving towards the bathroom, gesturing to his colleague. For a moment, Marchant wanted to go back inside and confront them, show them his broken teeth, knock out theirs, but he resisted.

As he jumped from the top of the wall, a car turned into the quiet mews, driving too fast for a resident. Marchant got to his feet and rushed at its sweeping headlights, ignoring a shooting pain in his ankle. He knew he had to move fast. Without hesitating, he opened the driver's door and grabbed the driver, pulling him out onto the road. He was aware of Meena doing the same on the other side. It was only as he pinned the man up against the wall, holding him by his throat, that he realised it was one of Armstrong's watchers.

He held the man for a moment, then released him.

'They're Five,' Marchant called across to Meena, who had wrestled the passenger to the ground and was holding both his arms behind his back. He made a mental note that she was no slouch when it came to unarmed combat. Marchant's man dropped to his knees, one hand massaging his throat.

'Christ,' he said, out of breath. 'Armstrong sent us.'

'I'm sorry. I thought –' But he suddenly felt too tired to finish.

'Two men are in Daniel's flat,' Meena said, taking over, reluctantly releasing her man. She made no apology for the mistake. 'Moroccan intelligence.'

'That's why we're here,' the other man said, getting up off the road. 'They showed up on the grid this evening.'

A bit late, Marchant thought, recalling the trouble he'd had earlier in Grosvenor Square.

'Delay them, will you?' he said. 'We need to get to the airport.'

53

Salim Dhar sat back and stared at the screen, watching his plane spin in a sickening cartwheel of flames.

'You forgot to add some right rudder,' Sergei said, coming over to the simulator with a cigarette hanging limply from the corner of his mouth. He was tall and loose-limbed, wearing a flying suit and holding a helmet in one hand. His face was awkward and angular, almost avian in its features. Dhar assumed that was why comrades called him the Bird.

After the air-show crash, Sergei had been stripped of his wings, tried and sent to prison, where he would have remained for the rest of his life if it hadn't been for the unusual summons to train up a surly Muslim for an SVR black op. He knew enough not to ask any questions, that he was expendable if he played up. 'They will shoot me after I have served my purpose,' he had once said, only half jokingly, to Dhar.

The daily training sessions took place in an airless hut across from the hangar where Dhar was living at Kotlas airbase. Dhar didn't know where the Bird roosted at night. They didn't do small talk. No one else was in the hut, and there were two armed guards positioned outside the door.

'How will you ever learn to deploy your missiles if you're always crashing on take-off?' Sergei continued. 'We've one week left and you've only got the *Grach* airborne twice.'

Dhar sat in silence, his hands resting on his legs. He tried to filter out the instructor's tone of voice and focus on the content. He was right. Just then a jet roared low over the hut, mocking Dhar with its menacing ease.

'Let's do it again,' Dhar said calmly. 'In formation this time.'

Sergei looked at him for a moment and smiled.

'OK,' he replied, tossing away his cigarette as he walked over to the other simulator. 'So the Bird is your wingman.'

54

The lights were off in St George's Chapel, but Marchant could make out the tall figure of Marcus Fielding sitting quietly at the back of the airless room, in front of the font. It was Heathrow's only chapel, built into the basement like a vaulted crypt. Marchant had found it quickly. Its location between Terminals 1 and 3 was well signposted. He was sure he had been here before, a long time ago, coming from or going to India. His father had sat outside with him in the memorial garden, where he could picture a large wooden cross. It must have been not long after the death of his twin brother, Sebastian.

Fielding didn't look up as he entered the room, and for a moment Marchant wondered if the Vicar was praying. His eyes were closed. Marchant hesitated by the door, looking at a plaque that commemorated the crew of Pan Am Flight 103, who had died 31,000 feet above Lockerbie. Then he walked over and sat down on the brown padded seat next to Fielding. Still the Vicar said nothing, his eyes closed behind his rimless glasses. Finally, he spoke.

'Did he give you anything?'

'Nothing. He told me he'd passed information to my father, low-grade product, but that it was the least he could do in return for the quality of RX my father was giving to the Russians.'

Fielding's face creased into a smile as he opened his eyes.

'And did you begin to doubt him?'

'Who? My father?'

'Yes.'

Marchant didn't say anything. Instead, he tried to read the words on another plaque, by the font, which had been put up by Dr Jim Swire, whose daughter had died over Lockerbie, too.

'Moscow was all ears,' Fielding said. 'I told you he'd give you nothing.'

'Were you able to listen?'

'I heard enough to be worried.'

'About Primakov?'

'About you. Perhaps it was asking too much. No one likes to hear his own father being branded a traitor.'

Marchant bridled at the implied criticism. Did Fielding think he wasn't up to the job? 'Can I ask you something?'

'Please.'

'Did you ever doubt him?'

Fielding paused, long enough for Marchant to look up, for more thoughts to ferment.

'Your father always talked about this country as an island, our sceptred isle. It wasn't shared democratic values with America that made him go to work in the morning. It was the mist rising from fields at dawn in the Cotswolds.'

'I take it that's a "no", then.'

Fielding didn't answer, closing his eyes instead. For a moment, Marchant wondered if he hadn't heard. He hated it when Fielding did this. The ensuing silence unnerved him enough to keep talking, just as Fielding intended. It was how he got people to reveal more than they wanted to.

'I still thought Primakov might give me something – a look in his eye, a scribbled note on a napkin, the smallest hint that we both knew. But nothing. Just a letter.'

Fielding opened his eyes. 'From whom?'

'My father. It told me to trust Primakov as if he was family.'

'Well, there's your sign. If you trust your father, then you must trust Primakov, too.'

'And if I don't trust Primakov? If I don't believe he's one of ours?'

Then you must accept that your father was a traitor. It didn't bear thinking about. Fielding clearly thought the same, as he chose to ignore Marchant's question.

'Did Primakov mention Dhar?' Fielding asked.

'He wants me to meet him.'

'That's good. But you mustn't appear too keen. Not yet.'

'Which is why you're sending me to India with Lakshmi Meena, the delightful dental assistant.' Fielding had met Meena in the chapel before Marchant. She was now waiting in departures.

'Our new Leila. At least this time we know she's working for the CIA.'

'And for anyone else?'

'She's different, Daniel. You can trust her.'

'Thanks for the advice.' The Vicar as agony aunt, Marchant thought. God help us all.

'I want Dhar's mother brought back to the UK. It won't be straightforward. The Russians have got wind of her too, and will try to bring her in.'

'What about the Americans?'

'I've spoken to the DCIA. Provided we pool everything, he's happy for her to be brought here for questioning, given their recent track record with Dhar. But they want Meena to run the operation. That's the deal.'

'Is that wise?'

'They won't try anything with you on board. They need you.'

'That didn't stop them in the past.'

212

'That was before they killed six of their own Marines in a drone strike. The truth is, it's too dangerous for us. We can't jeopardise London's relationship with Delhi. An unauthorised flight into Indian airspace is a risk the Americans can afford to take. We can't.'

Fielding stood up and walked towards the door, stopping to read the names of the Pan-Am crew. Marchant followed him.

'Tell me, Daniel, do you think Salim Dhar still wants to make contact with you?' Fielding asked.

'Yes, I do.'

'Why?'

It was a question Marchant had been wrestling with ever since Dhar had failed to make contact in Morocco. In the early days, he had genuinely believed that Dhar might be turned, persuaded to work for Britain, the country his real father had served. But now he was less sure.

'Why does Dhar want to see me? Because we're lonely half-brothers? I doubt it. I think he wants to meet up because he believes I'm a traitor, just as he believes our father was.'

'At the moment it's more a case of hope than belief. Primakov will have told Dhar exactly what he told you about your father: that he was a Soviet mole at war with the West. And he will also have told Dhar about your treatment by the CIA, your growing disaffection with the West. Dhar sees you as a potential ally, which is a good start.'

'Is it?'

'Primakov can only do so much. He can bring two brothers together with tales of their father's treachery, but it's up to you to persuade Dhar that you're a traitor too.'

And if you don't, Fielding thought, Dhar will kill you. But he said nothing as he walked out of the chapel into the harsh neon lighting of the airport.

213

55

The Hotel Supreme was not Madurai's finest, but their room did apparently have a view of the temples, which was what Marchant and Meena had asked for when they checked in unannounced at the wood-panelled reception desk. Too many staff were standing around, some in dark suits behind the desk, others in baggy brown bellboy uniforms waiting by the lift, hands behind their backs. Guests seemed to be a mixture of businessmen and Indian tourists. Meena had made an advance booking at another place across town, but switching hotels reduced the chance of their room being bugged.

'The view is there, but it is only partial,' the manager explained, at the same time indicating to two staff to carry their suitcases to the lift. He picked a brass key off a row of hooks behind him and handed it to Marchant.

'Meaning?' Meena asked, raising her eyebrows at Marchant.

'They are painting the temples at this time. You will see.' The manager wobbled his head from side to side, smiling like a child with a secret.

'But we've come a long way to be here. A view of them at sunrise would be nice,' Meena said, sticking to her legend. As she had explained to passport control at the airport, she and Marchant were a couple. They were visiting India for a traditional wedding in a village near Karaikudi, about eighty miles east of Madurai, where one of Meena's distant cousins was marrying an accountant from Chennai. First, they were doing some sight-seeing in Madurai, where the main tourist attraction was the Sri Meenakshi temple, with its brightly painted towers, or *gopurams*, and ornate carvings.

As soon as they looked out of the window of their top-floor room, the view of the temple became clear. At least, the manager's explanation did. As he had promised, it was possible to see the tallest *gopuram* from the room's balcony, if you leaned over the side of the crumbling wall. But every inch of it was covered with scaffolding and organic sheeting made out of matted palm fronds. From a distance, it looked like a giant *papier-mâché* structure.

'I think that's what he meant by partial,' Marchant said. Meena was walking around the double bed, checking the light switches and wall hangings for audio devices.

'I was hoping for twin beds,' she said.

'We're married, remember?'

'I know. I'll sleep over there, on the sofa.'

'It's OK. I will.'

There was silence for a few seconds as Marchant watched her go through her suitcase. She was wearing white trousers and a cream-coloured shirt with long sleeves. On the plane, she had been in tight jeans, but she had changed in the lavatory, explaining about temple etiquette. Marchant had reminded her that he used to live in India, promising he wouldn't wear shorts and a T-shirt, however hot it was.

'Thanks for not making all this any harder than it is already,' she said quietly, her back to him as they stood on either side of the bed. 'Blame my strict upbringing.'

Ever since they had boarded their flight to Chennai in London, Marchant had done only the bare minimum that was required for them to appear as a couple. In his experience, intelligence officers the world over usually took husband-and-wife cover as an opportunity to flirt with colleagues, a brief and unconditional escape that often led to more, but he could see how much Meena struggled with it. She seemed troubled, not her usual sparring, confident self. Her sexual poise had disappeared. She hadn't spent long with Fielding on her own, but whatever the Vicar said had left her even quieter. Marchant suspected he had laid down a few ground rules, reminded her about Leila.

'Come on. Let's go and be ignorant Western tourists together,' Marchant offered, trying to lighten the mood.

Meena seemed to rally at the thought of the task that lay ahead of them. She found the map she had been looking for in her suitcase and spread it out on the glass coffee table in front of the windows.

'We think Dhar's mother is working in the centre of the temple complex, near the main shrine to Shiva,' she said, pointing at the map. 'We've got two of our people inside, posing as temple staff, and two more outside.'

'Indian origin?'

Meena gave him a sarcastic smile. 'Yeah. It kind of helps them to blend in.'

'I didn't know Langley was so enlightened.'

'We're getting there. And there's someone from our Chennai sub-station – OK, white guy, redneck – who's hanging around Madurai as a tourist. Have you been inside a temple like this before?'

'Not since my gap year.'

'Believe me, it's one big crazy city in there. Shops, animals, ponds, people, food. Worship is just a part of it.'

'Did you used to come here when you were younger?'

'As a little girl, yes. We moved to the States when I was seven.

I grew up near Karaikudai, where we're meant to be going for my cousin's wedding.'

'So this was your local big temple.'

'I guess so. I don't remember a lot about it. Just that it was very full-on inside. Let's go,' she said, hooking her arm through Marchant's and heading for the door.

56

Salim Dhar looked at the photo of Daniel Marchant on his wall as another jet took off outside. Kotlas airbase was busy today, more activity than usual. He was meant to be flying with Sergei, but they had been grounded on account of the increased air traffic. More classroom theory, more work on the simulator.

He tried to think back to the time he had met Marchant in India. The Britisher's appearance had been different then, a crude cover identity. His hair had been shorter, his clothes more dishevelled, like those worn by the Westerners he had seen and despised in Goa. He reached out for the photo, gently prised it from the wall, and studied it more closely. According to Primakov, it had been taken by a young SVR agent from the top of a number 36 bus in London. Marchant was in a suit, looking through the window of a motorcycle showroom, across the road from MI6's headquarters in Vauxhall.

Dhar had never been to London, but he felt he knew the city well. Although he had studied at the American school in Delhi, his education had been heavily influenced by Britain. He didn't know why at the time, but his mother used to bring home books about London, talk to him about the country in a way that he realised now expressed a heartfelt affection. She had only been employed briefly at the British High Commission in Delhi, before he was born, but she had loved the place and its values. Dhar remembered playing Monopoly with her under a lazy fan, wondering at the names on the board: Old Kent Road; The Angel, Islington; Marylebone Station.

He had thought about the game again when the London Underground was attacked on 7 July 2005: Liverpool Street, King's Cross. For some reason, his mother had always liked to buy up the stations.

'Mama, but the maximum rent is only £200,' he used to tease her.

'I know,' his mother had said, smiling, with a knowing tilt of the head. 'But there are four stations, and only two or three of everything else.'

Dhar was in Afghanistan at the time of the London attack, fighting American troops, but he hadn't joined in the cheering when news reached his camp of the bombings.

'Why do you not salute our brothers in Britain, Salim?' the commander of the camp had asked.

Dhar had walked off. Such methods had never been his style. His approach had always been to target the West's troops and political leaders rather than its people. It was why he preferred to operate alone whenever he could, outside al Q'aeda's indiscriminate umbrella. But he knew it was something else, too. In his mind, it was his mother's world that the 7/7 bombers had desecrated; a board-game fantasy, but still her world. It was only later that he had understood why: it was his father's, too.

It would have been easy for Dhar to dismiss Marchant's bond of half-brotherhood as worthless. In his childhood he had had countless 'cousin brothers', distant relatives who played up family connections whenever it was convenient. It was acutely compromising, too, for a *jihadi* to be related to a Western spy Chief. But now that Dhar understood his father's loyalties, he knew that he had to see Marchant again. The Britisher had been a potential ally when they had met in India. He was a man on the run from the CIA, but who had returned to a job at the infidel's castle on the shores of the Thames, ignoring his coded text to join him in Morocco. Now, according to Primakov, he was finally ready to betray his country, to follow in their father's footsteps.

Dhar pinned the photo of Marchant back on the wall. He knew there was another in London who could help him, but he had insisted to the Russians that it should be Marchant, telling them that the mission was off if it was anyone else. It wasn't ideology. It was curiosity. There were too many questions he wanted to ask him. How had he coped with being waterboarded by the Americans? Who was the beautiful woman in Delhi he had shot instead of the President, the woman whose *meenakshi* eyes had haunted him ever since? And, most of all, what was their father like, the man who had hoodwinked the West for so long?

57

There was a queue of people waiting to enter the Meenakshi temple by the east gate. A female police officer checked the women, frisking their saris with a lollipop-shaped metal detector, while a male officer did the same with the men. No one was wearing any shoes, not even the police. Marchant and Meena had left theirs around the corner at a stall with thousands of others, not expecting to see them again.

Marchant approached the policeman and stood with his arms out and legs apart. Security seemed to be tight today, he sensed – thorough rather than a gesture – and he wondered if the temple was on a heightened state of alert. It wouldn't have anything to do with Salim Dhar's mother, but it might make things more difficult when they lifted her. They had already had to abandon their plan of using their wires in the temple, as they would have been picked up by the police detectors.

He smiled at the policeman once he was done and walked on, waiting for Meena at the bottom of the stone steps. He couldn't be certain, but he thought he detected a slight hostility towards her from the female officer, who glanced over at him as she frisked her. Meena had daubed her hair parting with vermilion, a sign of marriage, but she couldn't do much about the colour of Marchant's skin. Perhaps mixed-race marriages didn't play well in Madurai.

'Sometimes I remember why we left this country,' Meena said as she joined him. They walked down a colourful colonnade of pillars, leaving the sunlight behind them. Marchant thought he heard the sound of hesitant *slokas* being recited in a distant class-room. In front of them he could make out the profile of an elephant, its head almost touching the ornate roof, from which carved lions looked down. A queue of worshippers was waiting to be blessed by the animal. In return for a banana, bought from the elephant's *mahout*, it would raise its trunk and touch their heads.

Before they had entered the temple complex, the CIA officer from Chennai had given Meena an update, in between shooting a tourist video of devotees queuing up to smash coconuts before entering the temple.

'It's kind of quaint, isn't it?' he had said. 'Signifies leaving one's identity behind.'

Marchant wasn't sure if the American was playing his legend or being himself. He showed them a video he had shot earlier of a Russian behaving erratically outside the east entrance. Marchant recognised the tall figure as Valentin.

They walked further inside the temple complex, the light fading until all Marchant could see were pillared halls and corridors disappearing off into the darkness in all directions. In every corner there seemed to be small shrines to Hindu deities, like tiny puppet theatres, the gods visible deep within dark recesses, their bright colours lit by flickering oil candles. Stone sculptures of animals with lions' bodies and elephants' heads reared out of the shadows. A man wearing only a *lunghi* around his waist was lying prostrate, hands in prayer above his head, in front of a statue of Ganesh. They stepped around him and walked on, passing briefly through a courtyard where three camels were tethered. All around them, Hindu prayers were being chanted over a loudspeaker system, the priests' voices distorting at full volume.

'I told you it's another world,' Meena said, stopping beside a pillar encrusted with what seemed like centuries of crumbling red turmeric powder and candle wax. 'This is Lakshmi, my goddess,' she added, looking at an idol of a benign woman with four arms. Its surface was also streaked with yellows and reds, and weathered by generations of worship. 'The goddess of wealth and fortune, courage and wisdom.'

'And beauty,' Marchant added, looking at the lotus flower the goddess was sitting on. He thought back to the Lotus Temple in Delhi, where Leila had been killed. Her lips had still been warm as she had lain lifeless in his arms, her hair sticky with blood. He watched Meena daub some red on her forehead and bow in front of the statue. For a moment, she seemed genuinely at peace. Then she turned to a man standing behind a trestle table beside the idol. On it were tumbling garlands of white jasmine, coconuts and pyramids of turmeric. She gave him a few rupees and picked up a garland. At the same time, they exchanged a few words, too quietly for Marchant or anyone else to hear. Then she placed the fragrant flowers around Lakshmi's neck, turned back to the table and dabbed her finger in the turmeric.

'Come on, Indian boy,' she said, smudging a *tilak* on Marchant's forehead and walking on. 'She's here.'

A moment later, she pulled him back from the main thorough-fare, just as a white cow came running out of the shadows, draped in a gold-embroidered cloak and accompanied by two breathless temple priests. The tips of the cow's horns had been painted red and green, and two drums had been strapped to its back, one on either side. The priests, chests bare and glistening with oil, were beating the drums, accompanied by the jangling silver bells that swung from the cow's neck.

After the cow had gone, Marchant and Meena headed towards Shiva's shrine, walking through a thriving market of brightly lit shops selling souvenirs and incense that hung heavily in the air. Further on, they passed the Golden Lotus Pond, a bathing pool on the stepped sides of which pilgrims and worshippers washed and chatted. Marchant was alert now, his senses heightened, on the lookout for other agencies. Because Meena was leading the operation to find Dhar's mother, he had been momentarily entranced by the temple's sights and sounds, let them carry him back to his childhood in Delhi.

Their plan was a simple one. If Meena's colleagues were right, Dhar's mother, Shushma, was selling devotional candles in the hall outside the Shrine of Lord Sundareswarar, Shiva himself. She had been there for the past two days, making the small clay pots at night and filling them with *ghee*, or clarified butter, and wicks during the day. The CIA had not wanted to alert the Indian authorities to her whereabouts, preferring to interview her in the West, so Meena could not call on local police support. And the temple surrounds made it impossible to seize her against her will, even if she was sedated. Instead, the operation would be low-key and discreet, not words Langley was familiar with; but this was Meena's job, and she had insisted on it.

Marchant would strike up a conversation with Shushma in his rusty Hindi, explaining who he was and that she was in danger. Better to come with him back to Britain, where waterboarding was still off the menu, than be seized by the CIA. After he had walked her out of the temple complex, they would drive her to a disused airfield east of Madurai where Meena had arranged for a plane to take her to the UK.

It was a risk, but there weren't many options. Legoland's profilers had given Marchant a brief psychological assessment of Shushma, which he'd read on the plane. Their conclusion was that she was on her own, abandoned by her husband and wanted by the authorities, and that the thought of being protected by

Daniel Marchant, son of the man whom she had once loved and who had financially supported her, would prove sufficiently comforting for her to cooperate.

Marchant wasn't so sure as he passed a small statue of Hanuman the monkey god – covered in *ghee* and worn smooth with endless touching – and then turned into the hall that led to Shiva's shrine. Ahead of him was an imposing icon of Nandi, Shiva's bull. As a non-Hindu, this was as far as he was allowed to go. Several foreign tourists had entered the hall at the same time as him, one of them peering into the shrine to try to get a glimpse of the holy *shivalingam* that lay within. Out of the corner of his eye he spotted another foreigner moving away in the darkness, disappearing beyond a statue that he recognised as Nataraja, Shiva as lord of the dance. His father had always kept a small bronze one beside his bed.

Marchant looked again at where the foreigner had been standing, and saw that Meena had clocked him too. She nodded in the direction of the shrine entrance and then moved towards Nataraja. The deal was that he would focus on Shushma while she dealt with any outside interest. He joined a queue of people waiting to collect their *ghee* candles and enter the shrine. It wasn't easy in the darkness, but he caught a glimpse of the woman who was handing out the candles to the devotees. She had shaved her head and was wearing a threadbare *kurta*. Outside the temple complex she could have been mistaken for a beggar.

As he drew near to the front of the queue, Marchant glanced behind him, but he couldn't see Meena. He was on his own, just how he preferred it. As far as he could tell, the people around him needn't give him any cause for alarm. His only worry was the priest up ahead at the shrine entrance. The chatty couple in front had travelled from Bangalore, and the extended family immediately behind him were from Chennai. Both had expressed their friendly concern that he wouldn't be permitted to enter the shrine for *darshan*.

'The priests, they are very strict about this sort of thing, you know,' the man from Bangalore had said. But Marchant had reassured them, explaining that he was just there for the atmosphere. In the darkness, he had calculated that he wouldn't be turned away before he reached Shushma.

Suddenly he was at the front of the queue, standing before her. They exchanged eye contact, and he could already see surprise in Shushma's eyes, which was just what he wanted. She glanced across at the priest, who was wearing a white *lunghi* bordered with green and gold, and a sacred thread slung diagonally across his bare chest. He was too busy with a big party of devotees to have noticed a foreigner apparently trying to talk his way into the shrine.

'Sorry, Hindus only,' Shushma said, in surprisingly good English. He remembered that she had worked at the British High Commission for a year. He studied her for a moment, tracing her features, thinking that his father had once looked into the same big eyes. She was undeniably beautiful. Marchant's mother had never been a big influence in his life. If she had, he imagined he would feel some hostility towards the woman who had slept with his father and was standing before him now. Instead, he felt only warmth. And pity. Her small features had a filigree fragility about them.

'You need to come with me, now,' he said quietly. 'Your life is in danger.' Shushma dropped the candle she was holding. The yellow *ghee* spread out across the table. 'Don't be alarmed, please. I'm here to help you. Look at me.'

She fumbled with the spilt candle and slowly raised her eyes.

'Who are you?' she asked. Was there a flicker of recognition? Marchant detected a growing restlessness in the queue behind him.

'I'm not with the police,' he said quietly. 'I'm Daniel, Stephen Marchant's son.'

58

Meena moved quickly back through the hall, following the foreigner at a safe distance. He looked Russian to her. Something about his manner, the tan socks on his shoeless feet. When he passed the Golden Lotus Pond, he broke into the open and pulled out a mobile phone. Meena dropped back and did the same, calling her CIA colleague who was still stationed outside the east gate.

'We're bringing her out in five,' she said.

'Your taxi's waiting,' he replied.

'And we've got company,' she added.

She hung up and rang her colleague at the Lakshmi idol. The signal was faint, but he heard enough to make his way quickly towards the Golden Lotus Pond, picking up another colleague, who was posing as a market-stall seller, along the way. They knew what to do. Delay the Russian for as long as possible, accuse him of taking photos without a camera ticket. Anything. Just play up the paperwork, Meena had told them.

'How can I trust you?' Shushma asked, glancing around her again, but Marchant sensed that she already believed he was who he said he was.

'My father used to keep a Nataraja on his bedside table in Delhi,' he said. She looked at the icon across the hall, and then back at Marchant. It was a gamble. He didn't know where his father and Shushma had made love, where they had conceived Dhar, but there was a chance it had been in his parents' bedroom in Delhi.

Shushma stared at him, this time tracing his features, recognising in them the man she had once loved.

'I have been in danger most of my life.'

'The Americans want to ask you some questions. We'd rather you talk to us, in London.'

'I don't know where my son is,' she said. 'If that's what you want.'

'I'm sure you have no idea. But the Americans won't believe you. Trust me, I know. Please, we have to go. The east entrance.'

Shushma paused for a moment and then went over to talk to another female temple worker, who was lifting candles out of boxes in the shadows. After a brief exchange, the woman came up to the table and began to hand out candles to the devotees who had grown increasingly agitated in the queue. Shushma said something to her in Hindi, touched her forearm and then made her way out of the hall, followed a few yards behind by Marchant.

59

Marchant saw Meena up ahead and drew alongside Shushma, who was walking swiftly, her small feet barely lifting off the ground.

'This is Lakshmi, she's with us,' he told her as Meena approached. 'You can trust her.'

Meena stopped, expecting them to slow up. But Shushma kept moving, head down, as if she was trying to shut out the world, an approach to life that Marchant reckoned didn't look too out of place in a temple.

'A car's waiting for us outside,' Meena said, catching up with them. She turned to Marchant with raised eyebrows. Hadn't she expected him to close the deal, to appear with Shushma?

'She's American,' Shushma said quietly, still walking fast.

'Don't worry,' Marchant said. 'We're going to London. I promise.'

'Please, relax,' Meena said, speaking in fluent Hindi and slipping an arm through Shushma's. For a moment, she resisted, but after glancing at Marchant, who managed a smile, she let Meena's arm stay interlocked with hers. 'We're here to help you,' Meena added.

Satisfied that Shushma was in safe hands, Marchant looked back down the crowded colonnade. Again he thought he saw someone slipping away, disappearing behind the pillars. He was certain it was Valentin.

'I thought your people were taking care of the Russian,' he said.

'They were. Why?'

'He's behind us. I'll catch you up.'

'Daniel, we need to get her out,' Meena said, a sudden urgency in her voice.

'You don't know this man. Get her into the car. I'll find you.'

Before Meena could protest further, Marchant had peeled away and was heading back down the colonnade. He knew it wasn't part of the plan – Meena was meant to neutralise any threats – but Valentin wasn't going away. He should have pushed him under the train.

60

The tall Russian was moving fast through the devotees now, walking towards the Hall of a Thousand Pillars in the west corner of the complex. It was one of the temple's main tourist attractions, a sixteenth-century architectural marvel, according to Meena. She had talked about it on the flight, explaining with a smile that there were in fact only 985 pillars. It reminded Marchant of a round of golf his father had told him he once played at the Bolgatty Palace in Kochi harbour, southern India: nine holes, but only six tees.

Marchant hung back behind a pillar to watch Valentin, trying to establish what he was doing. The Russian showed a ticket and entered the hall, glancing in his direction before he disappeared out of sight. Marchant was confident that he hadn't been seen. Was he meeting someone? Hoping to draw him away from the others? Marchant knew he should have stayed with Meena and Shushma, but it wasn't tradecraft that was driving him now. The Russians – Valentin, Primakov – were too closely associated in his mind with something he never wanted to accept. They represented all that he despised about himself, about his father: the potential in everyone to betray.

He paid for a ticket and entered. Ahead of him was a low-ceilinged hall supported by row upon row of carved pillars. It was about to close for the day and was almost deserted, but there was no sign of Valentin. He walked forward, keeping close to the pillars and looking down the lines as they stretched away from him. He thought he saw a movement to his right, in the far corner, and headed towards it. But by the time he reached it there was no one there.

Then he spotted him, at the end of another row of pillars. The hall was also a gallery, and Valentin seemed to be studying a glass display cabinet of some kind. Marchant moved quickly, his bare feet silent on the cold floor. He stopped behind a pillar, four feet from Valentin, who still had his back to him. Marchant watched for a moment, wondering whether to strike from behind or get him to turn first. It seemed less cowardly. But then Valentin glanced at his watch and looked around, making up Marchant's mind for him.

He hit out hard and instantly, knocking the Russian to the ground. *His father was no traitor.* Without hesitating, Marchant fell on him and struck again and again, ignoring the voices, Valentin's, his own, others'.

'Stop, please,' someone was repeating behind him.

Marchant stood up, wiping his mouth, and backed away from Valentin, who lay bloodied and unconscious on the floor. It had felt good, too good.

61

The sun was setting, but it was still bright outside compared to the gloom they had left behind in the temple complex. Meena was surprised by Marchant's behaviour. He had been disciplined in Marrakech, which had impressed her. She was also concerned about her two colleagues inside the temple. They were meant to have delayed the Russian, kept him away from the exits. She knew mobile reception was patchy inside the complex, but neither was answering his phone.

Cars weren't allowed up to the east gate, so Meena had agreed to bring Shushma to the end of the closed-off street immediately opposite the entrance. It was a walk of about two hundred yards. She glanced up and down the road. A parked car had already caught her eye. Someone was sitting in the driver's seat, but she couldn't see their face. There was no time to collect her shoes.

She kept walking, her arm still linked through Shushma's. The older woman had remained silent since Marchant had left them. Meena thought again about her conversation with Fielding at Heathrow. She trusted him, but it didn't make what was about to happen any easier, particularly after her chat with Marchant at his London flat. King Shahryar would continue to distrust his wives.

At the end of the road, beyond a barrier, a white Ambassador had pulled up. Meena and Shushma climbed into the back. Meena glanced again at the car down the street.

'Where's your British friend?' the driver asked, dropping his tourist manner.

'We must leave without him. Let's go, *challo*.' Shushma looked up and felt Meena's arm tighten around her own.

62

Marchant brushed off the member of the temple staff who was attempting to hold him. He glanced down at the Russian. His eyes were closed and swollen, but he was trying to open them. Marchant turned and fled the hall, pushing away another temple worker who had heard the disturbance.

He thought he was heading straight for the east exit, but found himself in an open courtyard. A group of elderly priests, naked to the waist, were sitting on the ground in a circle, talking quietly as they ate food from stainless-steel tiffin boxes. One of them – bushy grey chest hair, forehead streaked with vermilion – was speaking on a mobile phone. He glanced up at Marchant and then looked away. Marchant asked one of the other priests for directions to the east gate and then set off again, walking fast.

He knew the authorities would soon be looking for him, and his heart sank as he turned the corner and saw a group of four policemen running down the corridor. But something about their manner made him hold his nerve. They hadn't reacted when he came into view, and were now turning off the main corridor. He glanced after them and saw a crowd gathered around the edge of the Golden Lotus Pond. Two bodies were lying still on the stone floor, surrounded by devotees. Marchant couldn't be sure, but one of them looked like the CIA officer Meena had met at the Lakshmi idol. Clearly, Valentin had been busy.

It took him longer to get out of the labyrinthine temple than he had intended, so he wasn't surprised when he didn't see Meena or a car in the street outside. He looked up and down the road and then walked over to the barrier, where Meena had arranged for them to be picked up by her redneck tourist friend. No one was about. He went to retrieve his footwear, watching the man take his ticket and turn to a row of hundreds of shoes. A moment later, he was holding two pairs, his and Meena's. He hesitated and then took both, slipping into his own and walking away with Meena's in his hand.

Meena had had no time to collect her shoes. Someone other than Valentin must have been outside. He glanced up and down the street, looking for a taxi, and then his mobile phone rang.

'It's me. Sorry,' Meena said. 'Where are you?'

'Waiting for you to pick me up outside the temple, as agreed.'

'We had to go. Head for the airfield. Call me when you get near.'

She had briefed him earlier. The airfield was near Karaikudi, outside a small village called Kanadukathan, and had fallen into disrepair. In the Second World War, the Allies had used it as a base for Flying Fortresses targeting Malaya and Singapore. It was also the place where Meena's legend was meant to be heading for her family wedding. She was thorough, Marchant couldn't fault her on that.

Half an hour later, he was out of Madurai and heading east through remote countryside in a taxi with a dodgy horn. To begin with, he had assumed that his driver was simply more eager than usual in his use of it, knowing that in India the horn was like a friendly nod of the head, but it was definitely broken, staying jammed on for ten seconds every time he deployed it.

'Sir, I will manage it, don't worry.' The driver grinned in the rear-view mirror.

Not using the horn would be a good start, Marchant thought,

but he knew that would be impossible. He tried to cut out the noise and take in the scenery. The reddish earth was barren and unfarmed, flat and dotted with sparse bushes. In the distance, he could see an outcrop of rock that had had its top sliced off. Earlier, he had passed rainbow-painted trucks carrying quarried rocks back to Madurai.

'Sir, are you knowing about the tourism business?' the driver asked, in between sustained blasts of the horn, which was beginning to grow hoarse. 'I have a good friend –'

'No, I'm afraid not,' Marchant interrupted.

'Cement sector?'

'No. Can we go a bit quicker? Faster?' It was not something he had ever thought he would ask on Indian roads, but he was worried that Meena hadn't rung again. He had tried to call but her phone was switched off.

'No problem. Isuzu engine.'

The taxi might have had Japanese technology under the bonnet, but its Indian suspension had long since gone. Marchant found the discomfort oddly reassuring, taking him back to his childhood, driving out of Delhi on a Friday night, the bright lights of the lorries roaring past, waking up at a remote Rajasthani fort. Then he thought of Sebbie and felt a ball tighten in his stomach. It shocked him how much he still missed his twin brother. He stared out of the window at the scenes of rural-roadside life: a woman shaking the coals out of her iron, a threshing machine, school-children cycling home on oversized bikes, their long legs languid in the heat.

'Sir, am I boring you?' the taxi driver asked, his face in the mirror now long with concern.

'Not at all. I'm sorry,' Marchant said, feeling guilty. 'Please, tell me about the cement sector.'

63

Meena's car turned off the dusty road into what at first looked like scrubland. The area was completely flat, covered in green bushes. Peacocks were strutting about, picking at the dry ground, the green sheen of their feathers glinting in the dying light of the day. She knew the airfield was disused, but she had expected a little more infrastructure. In the distance there were a few low buildings, derelict and overgrown. The control tower had long since been demolished. Towards the far perimeter, near a group of trees, a team of local women were loading long logs into stacks and covering them with tarpaulins. Beside the piles of wood someone had laid out cow dung to dry.

Meena left Shushma in the car and walked out into the open expanse. Beneath the vegetation the ground was concrete, but it had broken up over the years, and she wondered if a plane would still be able to land there. As she walked out across the wide expanse, she could see where the main runway had been. It was in better condition than the rest of the airfield's surface. She had been told that a local flying club had been campaigning for years for it to be reopened, and it looked as if volunteers had cleared away some of the vegetation.

She glanced at her watch and stared up into the dusk sky. There was no sign of a plane. If it didn't come before nightfall, the operation would be abandoned. A night-time landing was out of the question without any airport lights. She didn't know whether Delhi was onside or not about the flight, but that wasn't her problem. She looked again at her watch. A part of her hoped that Marchant would turn up after they had gone, but she owed him an explanation. She turned on her phone and dialled.

'Where are you?' she asked.

'Ten minutes away,' Marchant said. 'I've been trying to call.'

'There's a change of plan.'

'What sort of change?'

'I'll explain when you get here.'

She hung up and walked over towards the car, fighting back a tear.

Marchant saw the plane coming in low over the scrubland. He was still two minutes away, and urged his driver to hurry up. Events were spiralling out of his control. Meena's tone worried him. Nobody was being straight with anyone. He cursed himself again for going after Valentin, but he had felt better for it.

Marchant asked the driver to drop him off at the edge of the airfield. He ran across the broken surface, watching the plane turn slowly on the old runway, scattering peacocks. It was a Gulfstream V, the CIA's preferred choice for renditions after 9/11, the plane Spiro had used to fly him out of Britain the previous year. It had taken him to an old Russian airfield outside Syzmany in northern Poland, where they had waterboarded him. He shut out the thought as he approached Meena. Shushma was standing beside her, their arms too close.

'Glad you made it,' Meena said, glancing at the plane, which had now drawn up a few feet behind them. The noise of the jet engines made it necessary to speak loudly to be heard. Shushma was not happy, staring at the ground, trying to cut out the world again, or just in shock.

'Are you?' Marchant asked.

'It was your call to go after the Russian,' Meena said. 'The operation was compromised. I had no choice.'

'And if I hadn't?'

'There was another Russian on our tail, but we lost him. I know how to look after myself, Dan.'

'And her, I see,' he said, nodding at Shushma's wrist. It was joined to Meena's with handcuffs. 'Comforting.'

'They're a precaution.'

'I gave my word we'd take care of her, not treat her as an enemy combatant.'

They both heard the noise of the plane's door opening behind them. Meena turned around to look, and then faced Marchant again.

'Daniel, I told you, there's been a change.'

He detected something dancing in her eyes, but he couldn't be certain what it was any more: loyalty and deceit had begun to look the same in recent months. Then he glanced up at the open door behind her and saw James Spiro filling the frame, a gun in his hand.

'We need to get out of this hellhole,' he drawled.

'I'm sorry,' Meena whispered, still looking at Marchant.

'You knew?' Marchant said, glancing at Spiro again, trying to process the implications.

'Ask Fielding,' she replied, turning towards the plane. Shushma followed, pulled along by her wrist. Then she stopped and faced Marchant. For a moment, he thought she was going to say something, but instead she spat in his face and walked on.

'Fielding?' Marchant said, wiping the saliva off his cheek. He couldn't blame her.

'Send my love to the Vicar,' Spiro called out. 'And hey, thanks. We couldn't have got our hands on this piece of brown shit without you.'

Marchant wanted to run at the plane, pull Spiro down onto the Indian dirt, but there was nothing he could do, not while the American was armed. He thought about Fielding, who had sanctioned the change of plan without telling him, and wanted to drag him into the dirt too. Dhar's mother was meant to be flown back to the UK. Now she was heading to Bagram, or worse, with Spiro. A deal had been done. He knew he should never have believed in Meena, but this had been brokered far above her head. She was irrelevant. Why would his own Chief let Salim Dhar's mother – the only lead the West had – fall into Spiro's heavy hands? It didn't make any sense.

He watched helplessly as the plane taxied down the decrepit runway, shimmering in the heat as peacocks ran in all directions. It turned and then accelerated, lifting up into the evening sky. As it passed him, he picked up a rock and hurled it at the fuselage. On the far side of the airfield, the female workers were watching too, one of them transfixed by the mad *ghora*, a load of logs still balanced on her head. Marchant started to walk back towards his car, kicking at the dust, thinking fast what he could do, who he should ring. Fielding wouldn't take his call, but he wanted to challenge him, make sure his anger was logged by the duty officer in Legoland.

He started to dial London, and then stopped. Up ahead, a black car turned off the dusty road and drove towards him, bumping across the concrete. Marchant stood back as it drew up beside him, a darkened rear window lowering.

'Your American friends were in a hurry to leave,' a voice said. It was Nikolai Primakov.

64

Monika had always been relaxed about sex, ever since her first encounter, as a sixteen-year-old, with an English tutor who was five years her senior. It was something that came easily to her, which was a relief, as she was struggling at the time with other areas of her life. Her mother, a teacher, was desperate for her to achieve academic success and study at the University of Warsaw. Her father, a lecturer, had died when she was younger. She was bright, top of her class in languages, but she had no siblings, and life at home as a teenager with her mother could be claustrophobic, until she discovered sex and the freedom it gave her.

But she hadn't enjoyed sleeping with Hugo Prentice, who was lying next to her now. It wasn't his habit of smoking before they made love – she wasn't averse to kicking things off with a joint. And she wasn't upset that she was doing it for work rather than pleasure. She knew when she signed up to the AW that her job would occasionally require it, and in this case there had been a redeeming motive. What had cast a shadow over the sex was an encrypted text message that had come through from General Borowski. She had ignored her phone beside the bed, even though the unique alert tone indicated that it was her boss in Warsaw.

'Work can wait,' she had said, easing herself on top of him.

It hadn't been easy – Borowski only made contact when it was serious – but she didn't want to arouse Prentice's suspicions.

Now that he was asleep, she peeled away from his heavy limbs and dressed. Watching him all the time, she went to his bathroom, where evidence of Prentice's single life was everywhere. The small room wasn't unhygienic, but it wasn't clean either. The old iron bath had greenish stains where the brass taps dripped, and the sink hadn't been cleaned after his morning ablutions. A wooden-handled shaving brush lay between the taps, still covered in lather, and the lid hadn't been put back on a pot of hair-styling wax.

But none of this bothered her. It was his London pad, and he had been living in Warsaw for the past two years. What worried her was Borowski. She looked at the text again and then replied with a blank message, the agreed protocol. Moving fast, she removed the back of her phone and took out the SIM card, replacing it with another she kept in her purse. It had never been used before. She looked in again on Prentice as the phone rebooted, peering through a gap in the bathroom door. He seemed to stir, scratching himself before going back to sleep. Seconds later, a new message had appeared on the screen.

Monika stared at the words, barely able to believe what she was reading. Then she bent double over the lavatory and threw up.

65

'Tell me something,' Primakov said. 'What ever made you think you could trust them? After all they've done to you?'

'I put my faith in the Vicar,' Marchant said.

'A mistake your father never made.'

They were driving back towards Madurai in Primakov's car. A thick glass partition divided them from the front, where a Russian driver sat without expression. It was evident that he couldn't hear their conversation. Marchant wasn't surprised that Primakov had turned up at the airport. More worrying was his lack of concern that Dhar's mother was now in US custody. Marchant had told him the whole story: Fielding's assurances about Lakshmi Meena, how the CIA had agreed for Shushma to be taken to the UK. Primakov had been particularly interested in Fielding's role, asking Marchant to repeat exactly what he had said. Marchant had been happy to tell him. He no longer knew where his own loyalties lay, let alone Primakov's.

'Did you know that she was working at the temple?' Marchant asked.

'Of course.'

'Why didn't you do more to stop the Americans from taking her?'

'Like you, we had heard she was bound for Britain. I was also a little under strength. Valentin is in the Apollo hospital.'

Marchant didn't believe him. Moscow could have drawn on more resources to stop Shushma's departure. But for some reason they hadn't.

'Her son won't be happy,' Marchant said, trying to steer the conversation towards Dhar. The only thing he knew for certain was that he needed to see him, discuss their father man to man, brother to brother. Primakov had avoided referring directly to Dhar before, but it would be hard not to now.

'It will confirm his worst fears about the West,' Primakov said.

And then Marchant began to see things more clearly. Primakov hadn't flown to Madurai to prevent Shushma's exfiltration: he wanted to be sure that she was taken. It was the one act that could be guaranteed to get under Dhar's skin. Whatever the Russians had planned for him, it suited them if Dhar's blood was up.

'A son will do anything for his mother,' Marchant offered.

'Rage is important. It can persuade others to take you seriously. People who had their doubts.'

For the first time, Primakov looked at Marchant with something approaching knowingness in his moist eyes. Was it a sign at last? A part of Marchant no longer believed Fielding's reassurances about Primakov's loyalty to London. The Russian wouldn't give him anything because there was nothing to give. His brief was simply to keep the *jihadi* fires stoked in Dhar's belly, and to persuade Marchant to help his half-brother. There was no hidden agenda, no resurrection of old family ties, no belated clemency for his father. But somewhere inside him, Marchant still hoped he was wrong.

'Are you angry, too?' Primakov asked.

'Wouldn't you be? I promised Shushma I'd look after her, only to see her renditioned in front of me by James fucking Spiro.'

Even as Marchant spat out the expletive, a sickening feeling had started to spread: a realisation that he had been manipulated, that actions he thought were his own had actually been controlled by others. *Rage is important. It can persuade others to take you seriously. People who had their doubts.* He was the one raging now, against Fielding, Meena, Spiro, the West. And it would be music to Moscow's ears.

He closed his eyes. Christ, Fielding could be a cold bastard.

66

Even Marcus Fielding, working late, was surprised by the swiftness of Moscow Centre's response. GCHQ's sub-station at Bude in Cornwall had intercepted a call from Primakov to Vasilli Grushko, the London *Rezident*, within half an hour of Lakshmi Meena's departure from a remote airfield outside Madurai. Fielding played the recording again. Primakov spoke first, then Grushko.

'*He has been humiliated, which is always a good moment to strike.*'

'*And by his own side. Fielding is more heartless than I gave him credit for.*'

'*I can only assume that he wanted to win favour with Langley. By giving them Salim Dhar's mother, MI6 has gone some way to restoring a relationship they cannot live without for ever.*'

'*Where is Marchant now?*'

'*I dropped him off at a village. There was a wedding. He wanted some time on his own.*'

'*And has he agreed to help us?*'

'*Of course.*'

'*Then there is no time to waste. He must meet Dhar.*'

Fielding sat back, poured himself a glass of Lebanese wine and turned on a Bach cantata. It was a rare moment of triumph. Oleg, asleep in the corner, looked up briefly, sensing the change in mood.

There was no longer any talk of dangles, no equivocation in Grushko's voice. Fielding's only headache was Marchant. It hadn't been an easy decision to call on Spiro's services, let alone Lakshmi Meena's, but it was the only way to provoke Marchant. He wouldn't want to talk to his Chief, not for a while, which was why he had sent Prentice to pick him up from the airport, take him out for a meal in town, suck some venom from his wounded pride.

Fielding had told Prentice only the bare essentials of the operation to lift Dhar's mother. He wouldn't have expected to be given any detail. Need-to-know was a way of life for both of them. Prentice was unaware of Marchant's ongoing attempt to be recruited by Primakov, given that it was linked to the Russian's highly classified past. All he knew was that there had been a change of plan in Madurai, and that Marchant would be upset.

'We had to screw him,' Fielding had explained. 'You know how it is.'

Marchant would be astute enough to work out what had happened, why Fielding had been forced to intervene, pull the strings, but he would still be angry. He could let off steam with Prentice, have a moan about means and ends and Machiavellian bosses.

After he had calmed down, Fielding would have one last talk with him. Then he would be on his own, free to go off the rails, not turn up for work, drink too much. Marchant had form when it came to falling apart. In the months before he had left for Marrakech he had been a mess. And the Russians would lap it up, reassured that he was ready to be turned. Only then would it be time for him to meet Dhar. He owed it to Marchant to prepare him properly, let him genuinely feel what it was like to hate the West. Dhar would detect a false note at a thousand yards.

It was as he poured himself a second glass of wine that another encrypted audio file from GCHQ dropped into his inbox.

67

Marchant had asked Primakov to drop him off in the centre of Kanadukathan, about ten minutes from the airfield. It was a small village, and Marchant would have described it as poor if it hadn't been for the vast deserted mansions that dominated the dusty lanes. Meena had talked about them in Madurai. They were the ancestral homes of the Chettiars, a once-wealthy community of money-lenders, merchants and jewellery dealers who had fallen on hard times since the end of the Raj. Used now for storing dowry gifts, the mansions only came alive for family weddings, when the Chettiar diaspora would descend from around the world and fill the pillared courtyards with music and laughter.

Marchant strolled around the village square. The ground was covered in a confetti of paper and cardboard, the remains of exploded firecrackers. He could hear a wedding party in the distance, and wondered if one of Meena's cousins really was getting married. He had seen the celebrations from a distance on the way out to the airfield. It didn't matter either way, but he wanted to know. The world of lies and legends had lost its appeal after the scene with Spiro, and he needed to be reassured by something tangible, real.

He thought again about what had happened with Dhar's mother. It was clearer now, painfully clear. Fielding hadn't trusted him to betray, didn't think he had it in him to persuade the Russians of his treachery. So he had given Marchant a helping hand, asked Spiro to humiliate him in front of Primakov. The American wouldn't have needed much persuading.

'Are you angry enough to meet your brother?' Primakov had asked as he stepped out of the car. Did the Russian suspect what game Fielding was playing? That Marchant's rage had been conceived five thousand miles away in Legoland?

'I'd like to see him, yes,' Marchant had said.

'And he'd like to see you. But first I want you to do something for me. For Russia. Then we will get you out of Britain.'

Marchant walked around the corner towards the mansion where the wedding was taking place. A crowd had spilled out onto the road beneath loops of bunting that had been strung between tangled telegraph poles. Two women were walking towards him, arm in arm, their bright carmine saris illuminating the dusk. The one on the left reminded him of Meena, the same lambent eyes, the subtle sashay of hips. A stray pie dog lingered in the shadows.

'Can you help me?' Marchant asked her, ignoring the field agent's normal caveats. He was drawing attention to himself in a place where he was already a curiosity.

'We'll try,' she said, masking a giggle with her hand.

'I had a friend who was meant to be here today.' He nodded at the house behind them. 'Over from the States. Lakshmi Meena. You don't happen to know her, do you?'

'Sure. She's my friend's cousin. It's such a shame. Lakshmi was meant to be here, but she got held up in Madurai.'

'Thank you,' Marchant said. He felt stronger already, as if the world had been veering off its axis and was now spinning true again. He realised, as he walked on, how much he wanted to believe in Meena, believe that she wasn't another Leila. He was no longer sure he could face a life of trusting no one. Meena was beautiful, there was no point denying it, but it was his sympathy rather than his love that she kept asking of him. She had claimed that she had tried to stop Aziz in Morocco, then admitted that she could have done more. The appearance of Spiro at the airfield appeared to have pained her, but she had still boarded the flight.

He stopped, and turned back to the square, where he had seen a taxi waiting, and thought about Primakov's request. He was certain it was a test. If he was caught, the consequences would be serious. Should he run it past Fielding? Or was he now expected to play the traitor's game alone?

68

Monika had always thought she would be able to do it herself, that she owed it to her brother, but she couldn't. She hoped he would understand. She had the money in cash, £20,000 withdrawn from an emergency AW fund in London that was meant to be used for bribing disillusioned SVR agents.

As she stood outside a snooker hall in Haringey, north London, waiting for her contact to arrive, she wondered if she had any energy left to hide her tracks, to invent a cover story for the money. To begin with, she had resigned herself to being caught. She had imagined standing over him, waiting calmly for the police to arrive, but she couldn't do that either. Her survival instincts, honed in the field, were too strong. So she had contracted out her revenge instead.

She was spoilt for choice in London, but had settled on a Turkish gang with a proven record and an obsession with forensics. They had never been caught, and they asked for more when she told them the West End venue.

'It's very public.'

'Good. I want everyone to know.'

General Borowski would certainly know, but at least this way there was a chance of protecting herself afterwards, providing the political will was there. She was in his hands now.

69

Dhar listened in silence as Primakov told him about his mother's rendition. He knew that anger was a weakness, but it took all of his strength to remain calm and listen. The only outward sign of distress was a twitch in his lower left eyelid.

'This Spiro is the bane of many brothers' lives,' Dhar said. He was sitting upright, his hands flat on the table in front of him, on either side of a glass of water. They were talking in the hangar at Kotlas. Outside, it was raining again, rattling the metal roof.

'He was the one who waterboarded Daniel Marchant.'

Dhar tried not to think where the Americans would take his mother, how she would cope.

Reaching for the glass of water, he watched Primakov walk over to the window and look outside. Sergei was right. There was something about the Russian – other than the mix of cologne and garlic – that made Dhar wary. But he had no option but to work with him. He had come straight from seeing Marchant in India.

'If it's any consolation, your British half-brother is distraught,' Primakov said, turning back to face him. 'He gave your mother his personal word that she would be taken to London. If Spiro hadn't been armed, Marchant would have killed him.'

'He is ready to help us, then?' Dhar asked, happy to move the conversation away from his mother.

'Marchant could forgive the West once. But now, following your mother's rendition, he is struggling to call Britain his home.'

Dhar flinched again at the mention of his mother. He closed his eyes, trying to calm the twitch, control the body with the mind.

'We need to be sure,' he said, raising a reluctant hand to steady his eyelid. It was too much. 'Rendition' and 'mother' were words he never wanted to hear together again. 'After all that happened to Marchant before, he still went back to work for the infidel.'

'He wants to meet you. I have told him everything about your father, how I recruited him in Delhi, his twenty years of service to Moscow.'

'How did he react?'

'Like you, I think he suspected already. There was relief in his eyes. Let us see. He must pass one final test before he joins us.'

70

'I thought I should drive to Heathrow, pick Daniel up,' Ian Denton said, standing in front of Marcus Fielding's desk. Fielding was lying on the floor behind it, partly out of sight, trying to relax after another back spasm. 'He must be pretty cut up after what happened in Madurai.'

'It's OK,' Fielding said. 'I've just sent Prentice. With orders to get Marchant drunk. Look out for him when he's back in the office, though. He'll have no desire to talk to me.'

Fielding was touched by Denton's concern. Despite his cold-blooded demeanour, he had a warm heart. And he had always taken an interest in Marchant's welfare.

'Of course.' Denton paused. 'Is everything all right with Daniel?'

'As much as it ever is with him,' Fielding said. He wanted to confide more in his deputy, but he couldn't. Denton's own deep suspicion of the Americans had brought him close to Marchant in recent months, but Fielding knew that the plan to help Marchant defect must remain known only to himself.

'I'll leave it to Prentice, then,' Denton said. 'And look forward to signing off his exorbitant expenses.'

Fielding sometimes wished his deputy would unbutton a little, let things go, but he could never remember an occasion when Denton had got drunk. After he had left, Fielding unzipped the second encrypted audio file from GCHQ and listened, reading the covering note from his opposite number at Cheltenham. Grushko again, this time talking to an unnamed colleague in Moscow Centre. It had been recorded a few hours earlier.

'I still have my doubts.'

'About Marchant?'

'About everyone. Marchant, Comrade Primakov.'

'The Muslim is keen to see his brother.'

'I just think we should use him.'

'Argo?'

'That's what he's there for, isn't it? Moments like these.'

'It's a risk. Warsaw is on to him.'

'They get on well. Marchant will confide in Argo if he's genuinely upset. He should try to meet him at the airport when he arrives back in Britain.'

The recording ended suddenly. 'Argo' was an unusual choice, nostalgic. It was the codename the KGB had assigned to Ernest Hemingway in the 1940s. Fielding tried to linger on the historical detail, delay the realisation, the rising nausea, but it was impossible. In one awful moment, he had traced the line of succession, identified the inheritor. He reached for the phone, too heavy in his hand, and dialled General Borowski, head of Agencja Wywiadu, Poland's foreign intelligence agency, at his home on the outskirts of Warsaw.

71

'Come on, Daniel. That's what we do. We use people.'

Marchant hadn't been pleased to see Prentice waiting for him at arrivals. It was a sight that was starting to annoy him, particularly as this time Prentice explained that he had been sent as a peace envoy by Fielding. But he was an old family friend, someone he had always found it easy to confide in. His offer of alcohol was welcome, too. Marchant had been drinking on the plane, and was happy to keep going. A bender loomed. Prentice had driven him into central London, and they were now sitting at an outside table at Bentley's Oyster Bar in Swallow Street, off Piccadilly. It was one of Prentice's favourite restaurants.

'Are you using Monika?' Marchant asked, a smile softening the question's harsh undercurrent. Something about their relationship was still bugging him, and he was sure it wasn't jealousy.

'You've got a thing for her, haven't you?' Prentice washed an oyster down with a deep draft of Guinness. 'I can see why. She's a great lay.'

'I'm sorry, Marcus, we should have informed you of our suspicions.'

Usually, Fielding's conversations with General Borowski were upbeat. He was an old-school spy who liked to be taken to the

257

Traveller's Club for a sharpener whenever he came to London. Now, as they talked, Fielding felt only numbness. There was always the chance in his line of work that the man sitting at the next desk was praying to a different god, but it had still come as an almighty shock. Was this how the happily married felt when they discovered their partner had been cheating all along?

'How long have you known?' Fielding asked, trying not to think back, recalibrate the past, reassess the future.

'We never knew exactly, but the worry has been there for several months. At first, we thought it was someone else.'

'Who?'

'Come on, Marcus. You know there's little point in our game of causing offence unnecessarily. We have the right man now. That's all that matters.'

'And you're confident the codename matches?'

'We picked up "Argo" in an intercept last month.'

Fielding closed his eyes. For the first time in years, he felt he wanted to weep. 'You really should have pooled it. The damage could be irreducible. Ongoing operations jeopardised, entire networks blown.'

'I'm sorry, truly.' Borowski paused. 'There's something else. We put someone onto him as soon as he became our main suspect. Monika is one of our best agents – you may remember she helped Daniel Marchant earlier last year – but I'm worried. Argo has not only betrayed our country, he has caused the death of several colleagues, most recently her brother. She's taken it very personally.'

Marchant ordered another Guinness, his smile now slack with alcohol. Prentice liked to provoke him, and the only response was to join battle.

'I'm surprised you can still eat seafood, after what happened with the sushi at the gallery,' Marchant said.

'It wasn't the food, it was the wine,' Prentice replied.

'And there was I thinking you had a strong head. One glass of red and you were arse over tit.' Marchant paused, thinking back to the evening at the Cork Street gallery. He hadn't seen Prentice since he had collapsed in the corner. It had been unlike him. 'Monika was good to me in Poland, that's all. I wouldn't want her to get hurt.'

'She's a big girl, Dan.'

'Maybe she's using you.'

Prentice looked at Marchant for a moment, his gaze cutting through their drunken banter. Marchant was in no doubt that one of them was using the other. He just wasn't sure why.

'I'm a father figure. She lost hers when she was young. We're in the same business, we lie and cheat for the same noble causes.' Prentice shucked another oyster open with a knife. 'Where's the harm?'

CCTV cameras never pointed exactly where you wanted them, but Fielding could see enough from the intercepted live relay in his office to know that both men were drunk, relaxed, laughing. It couldn't be worse. The reason he had sent Prentice was to re-assure Marchant, give him an opportunity to whinge about MI6 and its methods. And that was exactly what the two of them appeared to be doing. He could only blame himself. They were good friends, even closer after Prentice had rescued Marchant from the CIA's waterboarders in Poland.

Fielding had to move fast. Moscow would be listening to their man, live-streaming every word. It was essential that Marchant played the right music, said nothing that undermined the genuine anger he had displayed in Madurai. If he revealed that it had been fabricated in order to convince the Russians, they would never go near him again. As far as Moscow was concerned, Marchant was ready to defect, not comparing drunken notes with a colleague about an unscrupulous boss. Fielding reached for his mobile phone.

'Talking of lying,' Marchant continued, 'you've known Fielding a lot longer than me. Has he ever double-crossed you?'

'First, he's using you, now it's double-crossing,' Prentice said. 'What mortal sin did our Vicar actually commit?'

Marchant knew Prentice had been told the basics about his trip to India, that he was there to bring back Salim Dhar's mother, but it was still an unusual question to ask another officer. Both of them were steeped in MI6's strict culture of compartmentalisation, Prentice more than anyone. He was one of MI6's longest serving field men, an old friend of his father's and one of Fielding's allies. He should have known better. Marchant decided to keep things general.

'Fielding told me I was to bring the target home, but that was never the plan. She was always heading further west.'

'And our cousins couldn't have renditioned her without your help?'

'That's about it.'

'A premier-league stitch-up. But it's unlike Fielding. Lakshmi Meena?'

'Way over her head.' Marchant suddenly felt protective. He was sure it hadn't been her plan. 'Spiro.'

'What an arsehole. You don't seem too cut up about it all. Fielding said you'd be out the door.'

'Did he?'

Marchant tried to gauge where the conversation was heading, what he could reveal. He wanted to confide in Prentice, confess

260

to him that he had failed to play the traitor. But he knew he couldn't. Prentice had been told nothing of Primakov's past, or of Marchant's efforts to be recruited by him. There was something else bothering him too, a distant nagging that he had learned not to ignore.

'Let's face it,' Prentice continued. 'It wouldn't be the first time you were on the outside.'

But Marchant wasn't listening any more. His phone had buzzed in his pocket, and he glanced at the text. It was from Fielding, and it consisted of only one word: 'Resign.'

He put the phone away and looked at Prentice, smirking. 'Lakshmi Meena. She wants to buy me a peace drink too.'

'Will you accept?'

'I'm not sure.' Marchant sat back, trying to look relaxed as he glanced around the bar. *Resign.* He assumed Moscow must be listening. 'You know, perhaps Fielding's right. I'm finished with all this. I've had enough. I hear what you say, but I'm not prepared to be a part of what happened in India. I gave Dhar's mother my word, for what it's worth. Now Spiro will kill her.'

A moment later, an Italian motorbike was beside their table on the pavement. Marchant had heard its accelerating engine, but assumed it was heading up Piccadilly, not coming down Swallow Street behind him. The next few seconds seemed to slow down, but he knew afterwards that they had passed with the speed of a professional job. There were two people on the bike, both wearing black leathers and helmets with tinted glass. The one on the pillion raised a silenced, long-barrelled revolver and fired twice at Prentice before the bike roared away, narrowly missing a group of pedestrians walking up from Piccadilly.

Marchant had instinctively turned his back as the shots were fired, lifting his legs and arms to protect himself. When he looked up, he saw a woman standing ten feet away, a hand to her mouth.

After what seemed an eternity, she began to scream, a terrible, almost inhuman cry. He turned to look at Prentice, slumped in the metal chair opposite him, his eyes more startled than pained. He had been shot twice in the forehead, two neat entrance wounds beginning to weep thick red tears.

72

'It's a bloody mess,' Fielding said, walking through the graveyard of the small Norman church at Coombe Manor. 'Officially, we're mourning the passing of one of the Service's finest officers. Unofficially, we're burying a traitor.'

Marchant looked out on the idyllic English setting, down the valley across fields dusted with poppies. It was the sort of pastoral scene his father had loved: rolling hills dotted with small pubs where eighteenth-century cartoons hung on deep red walls and cool slate floors offered respite from the somnolent heat of summer. At the far end of the valley the land rose steeply to Coombe Gibbet, where a group of cyclists was silhouetted against the blue skyline.

The secluded setting was on the borders of west Berkshire, in a green pocket of Albion that was thick with retired ambassadors and politicians. Many of them had turned out today, their dark suits jarring in the July sunshine as they gathered around the grave. Prentice's younger brother, who worked in the City and lived in the hamlet, had helped to carry the coffin, which was now being lowered into the ground.

'The Polish evidence is strong?' Marchant asked as the two of them dropped back from the main group.

'Incontrovertible. It's just a pity she took matters into her own hands. A debrief would have been helpful.'

Fielding nodded at a small gathering of people under the trees, at the far end of the graveyard. Monika was flanked by two bulky men in suits, one of whom was handcuffed to her. Marchant hadn't seen her inside the church, and assumed that she had just arrived. He would talk to her later, when his own feelings had settled. Prentice was dead, unable to justify himself, explain why he had crossed the divide. He couldn't forgive Monika for that, for ending the treachery but not the confusion. She had denied them all an answer, a taste of the forbidden fruits of defection.

He caught up with Fielding, who was heading over towards Ian Denton, a lean presence in the shade. Marchant knew that the deputy's attendance at the funeral was purely for appearances' sake. Most people assumed he had only turned up to make sure Prentice was dead. Denton had been sympathetic to Marchant, though, acknowledging that he had lost a close friend.

It was more complicated for Fielding. The news of Prentice's betrayal had aged him. Late nights at the Foreign Office defending his officers had left him gaunt and withdrawn. It wasn't just the security implications, it was the personal humiliation. Everyone knew that in Prentice he had finally found someone he could trust. He had dropped his guard. The D-Notice committee had done what it could to limit the media fallout, while Fielding had called in personal favours with security correspondents, but there was little disguising that the Service was reeling. A High Court injunction was out of the question, as national security was not at risk. Just MI6's reputation. I/OPS had set to work planting exaggerated press stories of Prentice's gambling habits, but the damage had been done.

'The one mercy is that Warsaw's not going public,' Fielding said. 'They can't afford to. Hiring gangland hitmen isn't part of the AW's charter. Hugo was in debt. He liked to gamble, owed bad people money. End of story.'

Marchant knew that Prentice had often rolled the dice. Even in death, his cover story was based on truth.

'Were our own networks compromised?'

'We're still checking. Did you manage to tell Prentice that you were resigning?'

Marchant thought back again to the restaurant, a scene his mind was keen to erase. He had relived the details too many times already for the police and MI6's own counter-intelligence officers: the unusual Benelli TNT motorbike, the silence before the screams, as if no one could quite believe what they had seen.

'It was the last thing I said before he was shot.'

'Then there's hope that the Russians still believe in you.'

'You're sure they were listening?'

'Moscow asked Argo to sound you out when you arrived back at the airport. And I bloody sent him.' Fielding shook his head and walked on. 'I'm sorry about Madurai and Spiro, but for a time they had their doubts.'

'And now they don't?'

'Let's hope not.'

'Where is she now? The mother.'

Fielding paused before answering. 'You tell me.'

Marchant stared at him and then turned away. He knew what he was meant to say. 'Bagram.'

The very name made him flinch. The airbase's notorious theatre internment facility was not for the faint-hearted. Up to five hundred enemy combatants could be housed there at any one time. Marchant was sure Shushma was safe, in a secure location somewhere in Britain, not at Bagram, but Fielding wasn't prepared to break the spell, not yet. It was a reminder of what lay ahead, the mindset he needed to adopt if he was to convince Salim Dhar of his treachery.

'And still with Spiro,' Fielding added. 'Don't resign just yet.

You'll be of more use to them in the Service. Dissemble, rebel, fall apart. Remember how you felt in India, how you feel now. They'll be watching.'

Marchant deeply resented the way he was being handled, but no doubt that was the point. It wasn't the time to challenge the Vicar about tactics, his lack of faith in him.

'They've asked me to do something,' Marchant said. 'A final test before they exfiltrate me.'

'Then make sure you pass it. I can't help any more. You're on your own now.'

Fielding was about to move to join the main group in the churchyard, but he hesitated, knowing there was something else that Marchant wanted to ask. They both knew what it was. The wider implications of Prentice's treachery stretched like poison ivy back into the Service's past as well as out across Europe's network of agents.

'Hugo was like family,' Marchant said, watching a red kite wheel in the sky above the church. He felt his eyes begin to moisten, and turned away from the bright sun. 'My father trusted him.' *Trusted a traitor. If Prentice could betray his country, then so could my father, his oldest friend.*

'I know. Use it. Embrace your worst fears. They may be the only thing to keep you alive when you meet Dhar.'

73

Primakov's test had sounded relatively straightforward at the time. He had asked Marchant to knock out Britain's early-warning radar system on the north-west coast for two minutes. Within that narrow window, two MiG-35 Russian fighters would penetrate British airspace, travelling just below the speed of sound until they were over land. Then they would turn around and head back towards Russia, leaving Britain's airspace before the radar was up and running again.

After Marchant had made some discreet enquiries, the reality seemed much more complex. The radar network was overseen by the Air Surveillance and Control Systems Force Command (ASACS) at RAF Boulmer in Alnwick, which was stood up in 2006 in belated response to the terrorist threats highlighted by 9/11. The Control and Reporting Centre, located in a reinforced bunker at ASACS, monitored the airspace around the UK, and was responsible for providing tactical control of the Tornado F3 and Typhoon F2 jets that were scrambled whenever the skies over Britain were violated.

The planes were part of the RAF's Quick Reaction Alert Force, and were based at Leuchars (covering the north) and Coningsby (the south). They had been particularly busy in recent years, shadowing the increasing number of Russian bombers that flew into the UK's Air Defence Identification Zone, a sensitive area just outside Britain's airspace.

There was only one man who could help Marchant, and he was sitting opposite him now in a corner of the Beehive pub in Montpelier, Cheltenham. Paul Myers liked his beer. He liked talking about Leila, too. Marchant gave him both, endless pints of Battledown Premium and stories of Leila in her early days at the Fort, and despised himself for it. Despite her betrayal, Myers had never managed to get over her, or dismiss the fantasy that she had once fancied him.

'She used to talk about you often,' Marchant said. Myers was clumsy enough when he was sober, but he looked even more vulnerable and awkward when he was drunk. Perhaps it was because he liked to remove his thick glasses after a few beers, exposing his clammy face to the world.

'Did she really? That's great. What did she say?'

'That you were a good listener.'

'They always say that. Particularly when they're pouring their hearts out about other men.'

'And if she hadn't met me, then maybe . . . '

'Honestly?'

'Be careful what you wish for. You'd be the one feeling betrayed now.'

'I do anyway. She betrayed us all, Dan.'

Had she? Marchant was always less sure when he was drunk. Alcohol could be very forgiving. For the first round, he had tried to sip at his beer, let Myers do the boozing, but it was no good. He had been drinking heavily ever since Prentice had been killed. There was no need to lay it on for the Russians, who were meant to be watching him for signs of disaffection. Besides, pretending to get drunk was not a skill he possessed. The KGB had become famous for it during the Cold War. His father had once told him

268

a story about the *Rezident* in Calcutta, who appeared to get lashed on vodka with his contacts, trading on Russia's reputation for hard drinking, then be spotted sober as a judge half an hour later. Barely a drop had passed his lips.

'Listen, bit of a turf war going on at the moment,' Marchant said, anxious to change the subject. 'I need your help.'

'New government, new rules. Fire away.'

Marchant knew that relations between Fielding and his opposite number at GCHQ, where Myers worked, had not been great in recent weeks, ever since Myers had pulled his rabbit out of the hat at the Joint Intelligence Committee. GCHQ was much more friendly with the Americans than MI6, and it had felt embarrassed by Myers's role in Spiro's humiliation. Myers was still meant to be on secondment to MI6, but had been ordered home.

'We need to put the wind up the National Security Council. The coalition has been throwing its weight around.'

'We?'

'Fielding. Armstrong. Listen, a couple of Russian fighters will be tipping their wings off the Outer Hebrides next Tuesday. Usual operation. Into our Air Defence Identification Zone, fly along the borders of UK airspace for a while. Only this time we want them to get a bit closer. Smell the whisky.'

'Nice one,' Myers said, his eyes lighting up. 'MiG-29s?' Marchant knew that he liked his planes, and thought the idea might tickle him. Myers was an active member of a remote-control flying club in Cheltenham.

'35s.'

Myers let out a loud whistle of approval, as if a naked blonde had just walked past. He had no self-awareness, Marchant thought, looking around the pub.

'No one's going to get hurt,' he continued, 'just a few politicians' noses put out of joint. Any ideas how we do it?'

'Build a massive wind turbine off Saxa Vord.'

'Why?'

'They're degrading our air-defence capabilities. It's quite a worry. Apparently, they create a confused and cluttered radar picture. Too much noise. Above, behind, around the turbines – you're invisible.'

Myers lived and breathed this stuff, Marchant thought.

'I'm not sure we've got time for that.'

'They're upgrading the system soon, anyway. No, what you need to do is take out a couple of remote radar heads. Saxa Vord, Benbecula, maybe Buchan. Depends where they're flying in.'

'We can't really "take out" anything. This is meant to be low-key, deniable. I was thinking of a cyber attack, untraceable.'

'The radar housing's reinforced anyway.'

Marchant tried not to be impatient, but Myers had an annoying habit of suggesting seemingly credible options, only to point out their flaws.

'Thinking about it, your best option is to target the Tactical Data Links, either the communication system between the radar heads and the Control and Report Centre at Alnwick, or between Alnwick and the Combined Air Operations Centre at High Wycombe.'

'Which would you suggest?'

'The second one. The inter-site networks are fully encrypted, but they still use an old 1950s NATO point-to-point system called Link 1 for sending the RAP from Alnwick to High Wycombe.'

'The RAP?'

Myers always seemed puzzled when others didn't understand what he was talking about, which was most of the time. And he used more bloody acronyms than the military, Marchant thought. 'Recognised Air Picture. It's a real-time 3D digital display, based on primary and secondary radar traces, showing what's in the skies over Britain and evaluating contacts against specific threat parameters.'

'And this vital part of our national defence is transmitted using sixty-year-old technology?'

'The Americans have been trying to get NATO to upgrade it for years. Link 1 does the job. It's a digital data link, but it's not crypto-secure. As it hasn't been encrypted, it would technically be possible to corrupt the air-surveillance data before it reached High Wycombe.'

'So the order to scramble the Typhoons might never be issued.'

'In theory, yes. At least, the order could be delayed. Only High Wycombe can send up the jets, and they like to have the full picture.'

'Could you do it? Get into Link 1 and delay the message to High Wycombe? The Russians will be out of there in two minutes. We don't need long.'

74

Salim Dhar pulled back the stick and put the SU-25 into an unrestricted climb. He felt in control, stomach tensed, ready to absorb the G-forces. For the first time, he had taken off on his own, without any help from Sergei, who was in the instructor's seat behind him. He wasn't one to lavish praise, but even the Bird had been impressed. The speed with which everything happened would still take some getting used to, but Sergei had drilled into him the constant need to think ahead.

All that remained now was for Dhar to release his ordnance onto the firing range that lay 20,000 feet below. According to Sergei, only the best jet pilots were able to fly solo and drop bombs accurately at the same time. It required precision flying and a rare ability to focus on specific parameters – height, speed and pitch – in order to get inside the 'basket'. The SU-25 had eleven hardpoints that could carry a total of almost 10,000 pounds of explosive. There were two rails for air-to-air missiles, and the capacity for a range of cluster and laser-guided bombs, two of which his plane had been loaded with before take-off.

Dhar felt for the weapon-select switch. It was on the stick, along with the trim, trigger and sight marker slew controls. Laser engage was on the throttle, along with the airbrake, radio and flaps control. He was finally beginning to know his way around the cockpit. From the moment he had first sat in it, he knew that the plane's myriad dials and switches represented order, not chaos, that each one served a specific purpose. He liked that. All his life he had been guided by the desire to impose discipline on himself and on the world around him. It was his mother who had taught him the importance of daily routine: prayers, ablutions, exercise, meditation.

Sergei had worked hard with him on the simulated targeting system for the laser-guided bombs, or LGBs, and he felt confident as he reduced power to level off at 25,000 feet and settled back. For the next few minutes, until they reached the target zone, the plane would fly with minimal input from him.

He was less happy with Primakov. It was never going to be an easy relationship with the SVR. In return for his protection, Dhar had agreed to strike at a target in Britain that was mutually important to him and to the Russians. It wasn't a martyr operation, but it was beginning to feel like one. There wasn't enough detail about his exit strategy. In Delhi, his escape route had been planned meticulously, from the waiting rickshaw to the goods carrier that took him over the Pakistan border.

Whenever he raised his concerns with Primakov, the Russian reminded him of the risks Moscow was taking by shielding him. Without the SVR's help, he would be dead. It was hard to disagree. The global scale of the CIA's manhunt had taken Dhar by surprise. It had also upset him. Drone strikes were killing hundreds of brothers. Using six kidnapped Marines as a decoy had bought him time, and the taste of revenge, but he knew he had been close to being caught on several occasions. Primakov reassured him that the SVR would help after the attack, but the truth was that he would be on his own again, on the run.

'Do you know what your final combat payload will be?' Sergei asked over the intercom as they approached the target zone. Dhar moved the gunsight onto a column of rusting tanks.

'A pair of Vympel R-73s,' he replied. He was sure that he would be able to deploy Russia's most advanced air-to-air missiles after endless sessions on the simulator. Besides, if all went to plan, the enemy would be unarmed and unprepared. And he would only need one of them.

'Watch your trim on the approach. What about LGBs?'

They will kill you after this is over, Dhar thought, easing the stick to the left, so there was no harm in telling him. But for the moment he said nothing.

'Engage the target now,' Sergei ordered, frustrated by Dhar's reticence.

Dhar released the bombs. The aircraft seemed to jump before, climbing, he rolled away to the left.

'Two thousand-pound laser-guided bombs,' he finally said, almost to himself. 'One of them is a radiological dispersal device.'

Sergei didn't say anything for a few seconds, as if he was allowing time for both of them to acknowledge the implications of what had just been said. 'That's a lot of collateral.'

Dhar couldn't disagree. A thousand-pound radioactive dirty bomb would cause widespread panic, fear and chaos. There would also be multiple civilian casualties. Not at first, but when the caesium-137 began to interact with human muscle tissue, the radiation dose would substantially increase the risk of cancer. If decontamination proved difficult, entire areas would have to be abandoned for years, if not decades, as the wind and rain spread the radioactive dust into the soil and the water supply. Were the British people innocent? He would have said yes a year ago. But something had changed since the discovery of his father's allegiance to Russia. Britain and its people were no longer off limits.

Dhar looked down at a rising plume of smoke below him, and thought again about what lay ahead.

'Target destroyed,' Sergei said. 'And no collateral.'

75

Myers had taken every possible precaution when he phoned Fielding. The GPS chip in his SIM card had been disabled, making its location harder to trace. It also incorporated triangulation scramble technology, first seen by GCHQ's technicians in a handset seized in Peshawar's Qissa Khwani Bazaar. By altering the broadcast power, it confused network operators about the handset's proximity to base-station masts.

He didn't want anyone to know that he was phoning MI6, least of all Marchant, who he felt he was betraying by making the call. It wasn't that he doubted Marchant's story. He knew there was an unspoken pact amongst the intelligence services whenever a new government arrived. Chiefs would stick together, wary of their new political masters as they established themselves. But his request to embarrass the National Security Council by allowing Britain's airspace to be breached made Myers uneasy. Marchant was on the warpath, which meant fat arses like his own had to be covered.

Myers looked around his untidy bedroom in Cheltenham as he waited to be connected: an empty pizza box on his unmade bed, dirty clothes on the floor, a half-built remote-control plane on top of an open wardrobe, and the bank of computer screens. He knew that some of what was on the hard drives should have stayed within the circular confines of the Doughnut, but at least he hadn't left his office laptop on a train. At the last count, thirty-five had been lost by GCHQ staff.

Myers justified his own software breaches on the grounds that he liked to work late, often through the night. And 99 per cent of the work he did on his home network was in the interests of the taxpayer and national security. Just not this particular request. He switched the phone to the other hand while he wiped the sweat off his palm. He never liked calling Fielding.

'This is starting to become a habit,' Fielding said. 'I trust the line is secure.'

'Untraceable. I'm sorry to ring you again, but I thought you should know.' Slow down, he told himself.

'Know what?'

'Daniel Marchant came to see me yesterday. He's asked me to do something, said it was your –'

Myers looked at the phone. Fielding had cut him off.

76

'I was performing a manoeuvre we call the "Pugachev cobra". The nose comes up like a snake and the plane almost stops in mid-air.' Sergei put down his glass and lifted his hand from flat up to ninety degrees, as if a venomous head was rearing. 'It is a Russian speciality, useful in combat, too. Hard to see coming. Pull a cobra, your attacker overshoots and suddenly you're on their six o'clock. My instructor at aviation school, Viktor Georgievich Pugachev, was the first. For many years, we were doing this in SU-27s, much to the embarrassment of our American friends. They can do it now in an F-22, but in other Western jets this manoeuvre is not possible.'

'And it went wrong?' Dhar asked, sipping at a mug of warm water. They were sitting in the hangar at Kotlas, the regular guards standing outside. The Bird had burst into song, talking more than he had ever done before. Vodka had loosened his tongue; or perhaps he had finally accepted that he was a man condemned to die. Apart from the alcohol, Dhar was enjoying his company. He had grown fond of Sergei in the past few weeks, liked the fact that his respect had to be earned. Their conversation tonight seemed to be a reward.

'Terribly wrong. We Russians like to push it to the limit at air shows. Give the people some value for their money for a change.

I was attempting the hardest, a flat cobra – it is easier in a climb – and I was entering too fast. I passed out for a few seconds – almost 15G. In order to perform the manoeuvre, first we must disable the angle-of-attack limiter, to allow the nose to pitch upwards. But this also disables the G-Force limiter. When I regained consciousness, it was too late. I tried to turn away from the crowd, but –'

Sergei stopped and blinked.

'And twenty-three people died?'

'Including seven children. I was sentenced to fifteen years, so was my co-pilot and two of the air show's officials.' Sergei paused. 'I don't understand your beliefs, and I don't expect you to understand mine. All I know is that you are at war, fighting your global *jihad*, and Russia has many enemies in the world. Sometimes our battles are the same. It's not worth my life to know any more. My orders are to train you for an operation that might help to restore the world order. But please, if you can spare the lives of twenty-three civilians, then do it. For me, for the Bird.'

77

Marchant didn't know how many twitchers would make the journey to the Isle of Lewis, but he knew that a Steller's eider was an extremely rare visitor to the Hebrides. The sea duck bred in eastern Siberia and Alaska, and had only been spotted a few times in Britain in recent years. A solitary drake had stayed off South Uist from 1972 to 1984, while another loner had summered at roughly the same time in Orkney. There would be some twitchers who would not make the journey, wary that it might be another hoax. In 2009, a golfer claimed to have spotted one in Anglesey, prompting a rush to Wales, but it turned out that the photo posted on the Internet was a reverse image of a bird that had been snapped in Finland.

Myers had been understandably nervous about interfering with the RAF's Tactical Data Links, but he had been far more excited about hacking into a birdwatching website and sending out a false alert. Earlier that day, thousands of twitchers and birders had received messages on their mobile phones and pagers telling them that a Steller's eider had been spotted off the coast near Stornoway and was 'showing well'.

All Marchant had to do now was monitor the blogs and chat-rooms. He had left Legoland early, and was sitting in an Internet café near Victoria Station, waiting for the first comments to be posted. The photos would follow, uploaded by twitchers who had spotted a very different flying visitor from Russia. At least, that was the plan.

By Marchant's calculation, the two MiG-35s would be entering the UK's Air Defence Identification Zone in thirty seconds. The Remote Radar Heads at Benbecula and Saxa Vord would already have picked them up, and the Norwegian air force would have tracked and shadowed their progress across the North Sea, alerting NATO allies along their projected flightpath. The order to scramble Typhoons from RAF Leuchars would only be given when the planes entered Britain's ADIZ – and if the Recognised Air Picture ever reached Air Command at High Wycombe, something that Marchant hoped Myers was about to prevent.

He looked at his watch again, and then his mobile rang. It was Myers, unbearably nervous, calling from an unknown mobile number.

'It's done,' he said. 'You've got two minutes.'

78

Thirty thousand feet above a roiling sea, two MiG-35s turned sharply to the south, their cockpits winking in the evening sun. As they began their descent towards the waves far below, both pilots knew that they were taking an unprecedented gamble, but they had been assured their presence would not attract the usual RAF escort. So far they had been left alone, apart from requests for identification from commercial air-traffic control on the 'guard' frequency, which they routinely ignored, a brief visit from two Norwegian F-16s, and a mid-air rendezvous with an Ilyushin IL-78 refuelling tanker.

At 1,500 feet they levelled out and took another, far graver risk. Within the next five seconds they would be entering Britain's national air space, where they could be legitimately shot down. They set a course for Stornoway on the Isle of Lewis, twelve nautical miles away. Then, after wishing each other luck, both pilots hit their afterburners and accelerated to Mach 1.

In Alnwick, on the other side of the country, the Aerospace Battle Manager on duty at RAF Boulmer froze as he watched the two primary traces on his radar. The Russians were ten miles off the north-west coast, and closing. He had already rung through to Air Command at High Wycombe when the planes first entered the UK's ADIZ, picked up by the radar head at Benbecula off North Uist, but his was a lone voice. The Russians weren't showing up on Air Command's real-time Recognised Air Picture for the sector. On his word, High Wycombe had brought two Typhoon crews at RAF Leuchars to cockpit readiness, but they were reluctant to scramble them until they had more concrete data.

'The skies above the Outer Hebrides are showing clear,' his opposite number had insisted.

Clear? He smacked the side of his radar screen in frustration. What the hell was going on? A terrorist strike? Two pilots trying to defect? It didn't make any sense. He was used to long-range Russian bombers – most recently a TU160 Blackjack – keeping him busy on their eleven-hour flights around the Arctic. Usually, they would head for the North Pole and then hang a left just outside the Scandie's ADIZ radar coverage and head down between Greenland and Iceland, skirting Britain's ADIZ.

Both sides knew the game. The Russian pilots liked to test the range of Britain's radars at Saxa Vord, Benbecula and Buchan, waiting for a response, which would often be intentionally delayed to confuse them. Moscow was also keen to measure the Quick Reaction Alert Force's response, and the RAF was happy for the practice, shaving a few seconds off every time. There was no real animosity. (On one infamous occasion, an RAF pilot had held up a Page 3 girl in the cockpit, prompting his Russian counterpart to moon from a window of his bomber in response.)

But this time was different.

79

'Any sight of the Sibe?' a birder in a bobble hat asked no one in particular. The men, more than fifty of them, and a handful of women, were standing in the evening light on a cliff in Stornoway, looking down across Broad Bay, where a group of seabirds were riding on the water. Some of the birders were using digiscopes mounted on tripods, others were looking through telescopes. All had binoculars – Zeiss, Swarovksi, Leica, Opticron. Marchant had given a precise grid reference of where the bird had last been seen, knowing that the modern twitcher's armoury also included hand-held GPS units.

'Not a squawk,' someone else said. 'Time to dip out. They're all common eiders.'

'And no sign of the stringer who phoned in the sighting.'

'I saw someone earlier with a nine iron.'

'The closest we're going to get to a Steller is in the pub. Anyone coming?'

'Hold on,' an older man said, adjusting his binoculars.

'What are you seeing?'

'Christ. To the right of the big rock, two o'clock.'

As one, the group of birders raised their magnified gazes out to sea.

'What the –'

Three seconds later, the two MiG-35s swept in low over their heads, forcing the group to duck and cover their ears. A couple of them remained upright, taking photos as the planes disappeared into the distance.

'No sign of any Steller's eiders, but we've just been buzzed by another Sibe – a brace of MiG-35s!! Beautiful-looking birds, particularly in supersonic flight. Take a butcher's at the photos below if you don't believe me.'

Marchant read the chatroom message, smiled and sat back, glancing around the Internet café in Victoria. On his walk over from Vauxhall he had been aware of a tail, possibly two, but he had no desire to shake them off. He thought at first that they were Russian, but then began to think they were American: the dispatch cyclist, the woman at the back of the 436 bendy bus, a tourist taking photos on the north towpath. Either way, they were too thorough to be Moroccan, and it would have taken hours to lose them. Besides, their presence was reassuring, evidence he was attracting attention, arousing suspicion.

He wasn't sure if it was the Bombardier he had drunk at the Morpeth Arms on the way, or a sense of professional satisfaction, but he felt a wave of happiness pass through him as he stared at the photograph on the computer screen. It was a good one, visual proof that he had done what had been asked of him. He was tempted to intervene, but he knew that he should let the web take its own viral course. The pilots would already have reported back, and Primakov would be relieved that he had passed his final test.

Then he thought again about the doubters in Moscow. According to Fielding, Primakov's superiors would be analysing his every move. If they had been listening in on his last fateful meeting with Prentice, they would know he was about to resign. But had they heard? And was that enough? An MI6 agent on the

284

eve of defection would be keen to embarrass the Service as much as possible. Marchant didn't know how or when Primakov intended to exfiltrate him, just that it would happen quickly. Primakov had promised a heads-up if he could manage it. Marchant realised how impatient he had become, how keen he was to meet with Dhar, talk about their father. The waiting game had gone on long enough.

He sat forward, copied the image of the MiGs and attached it to an email. Then he sent it to as many news desks as he could remember from his brief stint with I/OPS, writing 'MiG-35s over Scotland' in the subject box. He wasn't as careful as he would normally be on the Internet, but that was the point. He wanted to force Primakov's hand, get himself out of the country as soon as possible. Dhar wouldn't wait for him for ever.

After he was done, he glanced at his watch. Lakshmi had asked him on a date. The invitation bore all the hallmarks of a trap, but he had to go. He hadn't seen her since the Madurai débâcle. He just hoped nobody would get hurt.

80

Fielding stood at the window of his office and looked towards Westminster. A tugboat was towing a string of refuse barges downriver. He knew it was a gamble, but he couldn't afford anyone to suspect that Marchant's actions, whatever he was up to, had been sanctioned by him. If the Russians detected Fielding's touch on the tiller, however light, they would never let Marchant meet Dhar. And that remained the most important thing. Fielding was convinced that only Marchant could stop the *jihad* that was soon to be unleashed on Britain.

He had wanted to talk to Myers more, discover what he had been asked to do, just as he had wanted to ask Marchant about the test that Primakov had set him. But he couldn't. He didn't trust himself. If Marchant or Myers had told him, he feared a part of him would have demanded action: a visceral response honed over thirty-five years of public duty. That was what he did, why he had signed up. There was also the very real possibility that there might be other Hugo Prentices in the Service, listening in, reporting back to Moscow.

Instead, he had put his faith in Marchant, trusted him to defect responsibly and in isolation. He wasn't sure why he trusted anyone any more. He had relied on Prentice too much since Stephen Marchant's departure and death. In some ways, his old friend had been a hopeless choice of ally. Prentice had never been interested in fighting Foreign Office battles or playing Legoland politics. But it was what he represented that had appealed to Fielding: an old-fashioned field man who had repeatedly turned down promotion in favour of gathering intelligence. Prentice had been immune to legal guidelines on human rights, tedious departmental circulars on personal-development needs, blue-sky meetings and resource planning. Mistresses had appealed more than marriage, rented digs more than mortgages. He had just wanted to get on with his job. Nothing more, nothing less. Except that it hadn't been as simple as that.

'Ian for you,' Ann Norman said over the intercom.

The next moment, Ian Denton was standing in the middle of Fielding's office, looking a new man.

'Good news and bad news,' his deputy said, louder than usual. 'All our old SovBloc networks appear to be intact. Out of some perverse sense of loyalty, Prentice only seems to have burned Polish agents.'

Everyone knew that Denton had never liked Prentice.

'He did it for the money, Ian, not to skewer us,' he said, unsure why he was defending Prentice. But Denton's triumphant tone was irritating. He preferred his deputy when he was bitter and quiet.

'Does that make it any better?'

'Less personal. The bad news?' Fielding knew it would be Marchant. His line manager had filed a formal complaint about him earlier in the day, citing poor hours and a disruptive attitude. HR had added a note on his file asking if Marchant was drinking again. All was going to plan.

'We're getting word of a major security incident in the Outer Hebrides. The JIC is being convened, and we're being blamed. Oh yes, and Spiro's back.'

81

'Your brother has excelled himself,' Primakov said, walking around the bare hangar at Kotlas that had been Dhar's home for the past month. 'Do you not want for any more comforts?'

'I have all that I need,' Dhar said dispassionately. He was sitting at a bare wooden table, a copy of the Koran open in front of him. The austerity made Primakov crave a drink, a nip of whisky, but he had learned not to offend Dhar on the few occasions they had been alone together.

'He has proved that it is too easy to penetrate British airspace. You will have no problems.'

'Won't they be more alert now?'

'If Marchant can knock out the system once, it can be done again.'

'When is he arriving?'

'We will lift him tonight. The Americans are closing in on him.'

'And you are sure?'

'Sure?'

'About Daniel Marchant.'

Sometimes, Primakov found Dhar's stare too chilling. He looked away, out of the window, steeling himself, then turned back to face him, hands clutched tightly behind his back.

'Your brother is ready.'

82

In normal circumstances, Fielding would have objected to the presence of James Spiro at the Joint Intelligence Committee table, but their relationship was now one of delicate expedience. Spiro had been useful in Madurai, unknowingly helping to build up Marchant's credentials for defection. In return, Fielding had agreed with the DCIA to drop British opposition to Spiro's rehabilitation. He had been suspended from his position as head of Clandestine, Europe, but was now back at his desk at the US Embassy in Grosvenor Square.

Everyone knew Spiro had messed up over the drone strike, but the truth was that the CIA needed people like him, and they didn't have anyone to replace him with. What Spiro didn't know, as he addressed the meeting in tones of barely disguised vindication, was that he was still dancing to Fielding's tune.

'I'm sorry to do this to you again, Marcus, but Daniel Marchant has got a lot of questions to answer.' Fielding had to admire Spiro's resilience. A few weeks earlier, he had been sitting at the same spot at the table, his career in tatters, listening to Paul Myers humiliate him.

'Are you saying that Marchant in some way facilitated the breach of airspace?' the chairman of the JIC, Sir David Chadwick, said, looking across at Fielding.

' "Facilitated" is one way of putting it,' said Spiro. 'It wouldn't surprise me if he was standing on the shores of Stornoway with a couple of paddles and a fluorescent jacket, instructing the MiGs where to taxi.'

A chuckle rippled through Sir David's jowls, then he checked himself when he realised that no one else was laughing. He was an odious chairman, Fielding thought, obsequious in the extreme, always looking to see where the real power lay. Not so long ago, Spiro had been trying to frame him in a child-porn sting. Now he was cosying up to the Americans again.

'These are serious allegations,' Fielding said. 'Sorry to sound so old-school, but do we have any evidence?'

'I appreciate that this is the last thing you need, after the Prentice affair,' Spiro said, hoping to pile on the public embarrassment. Although he owed his own rehabilitation to Fielding, he couldn't resist the moment. There was too much history between the two of them, their respective organisations. 'One Soviet mole could be construed as careless. But two . . .'

'The evidence, please,' Sir David said, convincing no one with his attempt at neutrality.

'Where do we start?' Spiro asked, shuffling some papers and photos in front of him. 'The covert meeting with Nikolai Primakov in central London?' He waved a couple of photos in the air, one of Marchant entering Goodman's restaurant, the other of Primakov.

' "Covert" might be pushing it,' Fielding said. 'I seem to remember the dinner – sanctioned by me – took place at a well-known Russian restaurant in the middle of Mayfair. We were listening.'

'So were we,' said Spiro, 'until the Russians jammed the entire area. Must have been quite an important meeting. Then we have Madurai, south India. After we took Dhar's mother off your hands,

290

Marchant hitched a ride back into town with – guess who? – one Nikolai Primakov.'

He waved another surveillance photo in the air. 'I'm not sure I want to ask why Marchant's meetings with Primakov, former director of K Branch, KGB and now high-ranking member of the SVR, were sanctioned by MI6, so let's not go into that here. It kind of brings back bad memories when you discover Primakov had been good friends with Marchant's father. Of more interest to today's meeting is what Marchant was doing in an Internet café yesterday – after knocking off work early and dropping in for a warm beer or three at his favourite pub – forwarding photos of the MIG-35s to various national newspapers.'

Another sheaf of documents was waved in the air, this time press cuttings, as a murmur went around the room. Fielding was conscious that all eyes were on him now, but he had read the cuts in the car into work, smiled at the quotes from the twitchers. He was a bit of a birder himself, when he had the time, although these days he was reduced to spotting oystercatchers on the bank of the Thames below his office window.

'He used an anonymous Gmail account,' continued Spiro, 'but our people at Fort Meade narrowed the IP address down to three Internet cafés in Victoria. They needn't have bothered. All emails leaving that particular café go out with marketing headers and footers – unless you switch them off, which Marchant failed to do. I don't know how much evidence you need, Marcus, but we have photos of him entering the café five minutes before the anonymous emails were sent out.'

Fielding didn't reply. Instead, he was thinking of Marchant, the intentional trail he was leaving. Primakov must be close to exfiltrating him. According to the UK Border Agency, the Russian had left on a flight to Moscow earlier in the day, which Fielding took as a good sign. Marchant had been smart to attract the attention of the Americans: it was the easiest way to reassure Moscow Centre that it had the right man, that he was ready to defect, keen to meet Dhar. But it was a risk if the Americans got to him first. He hoped Marchant had his timing right.

'Marcus?'

'Let's bring him in,' Fielding said. He had no choice. He must be seen to be hard on Marchant.

'I kinda hoped you'd say that,' said Spiro. 'He's with Lakshmi Meena as we speak. Having yet another drink. She's ready when we are. I just thought that, you know, in the interests of resetting our special relationship, I should inform you first.'

Spiro looked around the table. His eye was caught by Harriet Armstrong.

'Would you like us to handle Marchant?' she asked. Fielding turned away. It was an unusual offer, a blatant challenge to MI6 that had all the hallmarks of their old turf wars. She was also reaching out to Spiro, a man she had once admired before she had fallen out of love with America. Fielding knew that she had felt increasingly sidelined by Six, but he was still surprised by the move.

'That's kind of you, Harriet,' Spiro said. 'And unexpected. I appreciate it. But I think, if it's OK with the assembled, this has now been upgraded to a NATO Air Policing Area 1 issue. And as such, we'd like to take care of it.'

83

Marchant knew his defences would drop if he had any more alcohol. Meena was looking more beautiful than he could remember, wearing the same embroidered Indian *salwar* that she had worn in Madurai. Her body language then had been diffident, hard to read. Tonight she was radiant, the mirrorwork on her neckline reflecting the candlelight, lightening her whole demeanour. He just wished they were meeting in different circumstances, where they could be true to themselves rather than to their employers' agendas. The last time he had felt like this was when he had said goodbye to Monika at the Frederick Chopin airport in Warsaw, hoping that she would step out of her cover and into his life.

'My mother used to read me a new tale every night,' Meena was saying as they sat at the small bar in Andrew Edmunds, a restaurant in Lexington Street. Her mask was slipping too. Marchant stuck to his script, trying to stay sober behind the miasma of Scotch. Soon they would be moving from the bar to the cramped dining area, where the lines of sight were less good. In his current position he had a clear view of the main entrance and the door to the kitchen. Tonight he needed to see everyone who came in or out.

'After each story, I would ask if Scheherazade had done enough, if King Shahryar would spare her,' Meena continued. 'I was more worried about her dying than anything else. And each time, the King let her live for another night. I was so relieved.'

'And this all took place in Reston? In between trips to the mall?'

Marchant had eaten a meal in Reston once, as part of a visit to the CIA's headquarters down the road, in the days before the Agency had become too suspicious to allow him on campus. All he could remember was the piazza at the Reston Town Center, an open-air mall that had boasted Chipotle, Potbelly Sandwich Works and Clyde's, where he had been taken for lunch by a gym-buffed field agent who swore by its steaks. It was strange to think of Meena living in such a sterile suburb in Virginia.

'Our home was a little corner of India. At least, my bedroom was. Wall hangings, incense, my own *pooja* cupboard. Mom didn't want me to forget.'

Marchant signalled to the barman for another drink.

'I don't want to sound like your mom, but haven't you had enough?'

She was right. Marchant was at the very edge of what he could consume and still be able to react quickly when it happened. There were only a few more hours, maybe less, of playing the drunk. A coded text from Primakov had told him it would be sometime tonight. It wouldn't be pretty. The American presence had made sure of that. He looked again around the small, candlelit room, scanning the punters. Someone had followed him to the restaurant, but he was confident that they were still outside.

'I don't blame you for Madurai,' he said. 'You had your orders.'

'That didn't make it any easier.'

He wanted to ask if Shushma was OK, but he knew he couldn't. It was better that he could still entertain the possibility that she was with Spiro. The thought of her in CIA custody, the genuine anger the thought stirred, was central to his imminent defection. It might even save his life when he finally met Dhar.

'I'm going away,' he said quietly. 'I've had enough.'

'Of me?'

Marchant managed a smirk. 'Of the West.'

'Was that why you helped to give the MiG breach so much publicity?'

He struggled to conceal his surprise.

'I don't know what you're talking about.'

'Dan, we met here tonight because I've got orders to bring you in.'

'Spiro's?'

'With the Vicar's blessing.'

Marchant paused, weighing up the situation. He was pushing it to the limit, and hoped that Primakov would move soon. Meena knew how to look after herself, but he was still concerned for her. And for the first time he felt that she was being straight with him. He wished he could reciprocate, but he knew that he couldn't, not yet.

'Are you going to ask me to come quietly?' he asked.

'No. I'm not going to do anything.'

'Nothing?'

'I just want you to tell me what's really going on.'

'You know I can't do that.'

'If you did, then maybe I'd know how best to help you.'

Marchant studied her eyes, calculating the implications. She was speaking too freely to be wired, which made him believe her. 'You really mean that, don't you?'

'I want to do one worthwhile thing while I'm still with the Agency, and I'm not sure bringing in a drunken MI6 agent with a penchant for rare Russian seabirds is what I had in mind.'

'The Steller's eider breeds in Alaska, too, you know.'

'Spiro's fallen for it, hasn't he?' Meena said, turning the wineglass in her hand. 'He's seen you go off the rails, but he's forgotten to ask why. Well, I know what makes a British MI6 agent try to be recruited by the Russians. Because he knows they have someone he desperately wants to meet. Fielding knows it too, which is why he asked Spiro and me to take Dhar's mother away. You hated the West for that, didn't you? And it made the Russians love you even more. That helicopter in Morocco – I know now that it was Russian. You were right all along. Tell me what I need to do, Dan. You're the only person who can stop Dhar.'

Marchant hesitated before speaking. 'How many people have you got outside?'

'Two vehicles, six people.'

'Do you know any of them?'

'Some, yes.'

'Good friends of yours?'

'Decent colleagues.'

'Walk out into the street and tell them I'm leaving in five. Then go home. All of you.'

'Why?'

'Because I don't want anyone to get hurt.'

But he already knew it was too late. He heard the car before he saw it, a black Audi pulling up outside. Two men wearing balaclavas got out from the back and ran into the restaurant while a third stood by the front passenger door, a handgun aimed into the dark street.

'Don't touch her!' Marchant shouted, as several diners screamed. The men grabbed him by both arms and frogmarched him out of the restaurant, barking orders at each other and at the diners, and waving a gun at Meena. The men were Russian, and it wasn't subtle, just as he had predicted. A moment later, the shooting started. The third man fired down Lexington Street towards Shaftesbury Avenue, where a black SUV had stopped at a diagonal, blocking the road. As Marchant was bundled into the back of the car, he looked back at the restaurant. The front window had been shot out, and the noise of the screaming diners was sickening. There was no sign of Meena.

84

'It just makes us look like such a bunch of bloody fools,' Harriet Armstrong said, declining Fielding's offer of a chair in his office. 'I've got Counter Terrorism Command demanding answers, and Jim Spiro can barely speak.'

A quiet American, Fielding thought. He almost felt sorry for Armstrong, but her recent *rapprochement* with Spiro had extinguished any sympathy he might have had for her situation. Besides, there was very little he could say to mollify her. MI5 *was* a bunch of fools.

'Much as I'd like to say that this was Marchant's work, the facts are these,' he said, steepling his fingers under his chin and sitting back. 'One of my agents has been seized on the streets of London by what we think were officers of the SVR –'

'Come on, we *know* they were.'

'– and I have urged the Prime Minister to protest in the strongest terms to the Russian Ambassador. Meanwhile, Six's stations around the world are on heightened alert, and I hope that the same can be said for Britain's ports, railways and airfields.'

'What's going on here, Marcus? Primakov was once one of ours.'

'A fact that only a very few people are privy to.' The last thing he needed was Armstrong spilling state secrets to Spiro.

'I thought Marchant was being sent to see if Primakov could be ours again.'

'He was. But I should remind you that certain senior figures in the SVR – Vasilli Grushko, for example – were opposed to Primakov's London posting from the start. They didn't completely trust him. It's no coincidence that Primakov left the country in a hurry this morning, and my guess is that seizing Marchant is the SVR's consolation prize. Marchant will be interrogated about Primakov, who will no doubt shortly be charged with betraying the motherland.'

Armstrong looked at him, weighing up what he said. She wasn't convinced.

'You don't appear to be too concerned that one of your officers has just been taken by a hostile country.'

'It's not the first time, and I doubt it will be the last.'

'America is not our enemy,' Armstrong said, walking to the door.

'It was when you and I were in India, fighting for what we believed in. Why are we suddenly being nice to Spiro again?'

Armstrong paused by the door. 'Because we've got no option, have we?'

Fielding knew she was right. Britain needed America. 'I'll let you know as soon as we hear word of Marchant,' he said. 'We're doing everything we can to find him.'

He watched her leave. As with the best lies, there was a strong element of truth in what he had told her. Grushko had long had his doubts about Primakov, but he must have overcome them to sanction the operation in Soho. Such a brazen act on the streets of London could not have gone ahead without the consent of the SVR's local *Rezident*. Which meant that Marchant was in. He had passed all the tests, and would soon be with Salim Dhar. Fielding just hoped that Dhar would believe in him too.

85

An alert officer at UK Passport Control at Heathrow had picked up Primakov's hurried exit, but they had failed to spot Vasilli Grushko, who had also left Britain earlier in the day, travelling with false documents on a flight to Moscow. He was now standing in the hangar at Kotlas with Primakov and Marchant.

'Welcome to Russia,' Grushko said, looking out at the rain on the runway. He was a short, wiry man with rimless glasses and sallow skin, in stark contrast to Primakov's rubicund presence. 'Is it your first time?' There was no warmth in his voice, nothing excessive about him at all, just a cold matter-of-factness that made Marchant wary.

'Officially or unofficially?' Marchant replied. His head was hurting from the alcohol of the night before, and the journey in an Illyushin cargo plane from Heathrow to Moscow, which he had spent curled up in a container. He had then been flown by an Antonov military transporter to Kotlas.

'You must be tired after your flight,' Primakov suggested, filling the awkward silence. 'If it's any consolation, my Aeroflot flight was no more comfortable. Your brother is out flying at the moment. Sleep now, and you will be ready to meet him.'

'Just one thing,' Marchant said. 'Was the American woman hurt? In the restaurant?'

'I am surprised by your concern,' Primakov said, glancing at Grushko, his superior, who remained impassive.

'She will shortly be leaving the Agency,' Marchant added. 'Disillusioned, like me.'

'She is in hospital, a gunshot wound to the arm,' Grushko said. 'Our men were authorised to kill her if necessary, but she did not resist, and for some reason you asked for her to be spared.'

'But she'll be OK?' Marchant asked, thinking back to the chaotic scene, his shout to protect Meena.

'She's fine,' Primakov said. 'She should be grateful for the injury. Her superiors are already a little surprised that she did not do more to stop you being taken. We will leave you now. You did well with the MiGs. Your brother was impressed. We all were.'

Primakov turned to Grushko, hoping for some supportive words, but none came.

'Do not step outside,' Grushko warned. 'The guards have orders to shoot.'

Marchant had passed two armed guards standing by the side entrance to the hangar when he had arrived. After Grushko and Primakov had gone, he looked around the empty space. Some camouflage nets had been hung on one wall, otherwise there was little to soften the oppressive concrete surfaces. So this was where the world's most wanted terrorist had been hiding, in a draughty hangar, surrounded by rain-soaked woodlands in a remote corner of a Russian military airfield in the Arkhangelsk oblast.

He turned away from the large doors, and saw a curtained-off area at the far end of the building. He assumed it was where Dhar lived. A mattress and some bedding had been put in the opposite corner for Marchant, along with a towel, a bar of unwrapped soap and a change of clothes. It wasn't exactly a defecting hero's welcome.

After washing in a bucket of lukewarm water that had been

301

left by the side entrance, Marchant looked again at Dhar's corner. Checking the door, he walked over and pulled back the curtain. There was a mattress and bedding on the floor, with a small wooden cargo crate beside it for a bedside table. A copy of the Koran lay shut, a letter inside it acting as a bookmark.

He recognised the handwriting at once. Glancing at the door again, he picked up the Koran and slid the letter out. The paper was creased, and looked well read. It was from his father, written in the same hand and in exactly the same words as the one Primakov had given to him. For a moment, he wondered if it was a forgery, but he was sure it was his father's hand.

To Salim, the son I never knew

If you are reading this, it must mean that you have finally met Nikolai Ivanovich Primakov. I will not try to guess at what path led you to him, only to offer reassurance that I have trodden a similar one before you. You are old enough, of course, to make your own judgements in life, but in the case of Nikolai, I merely wish to assist you, because other influences will be in play. He is, first and foremost, a friend, and you can trust him as if he was a member of our family.

He put the letter back in the Koran, which he placed back on the crate. In front of him, pinned to an old pilots' briefing board on the wall, were several photos. One was of a group of *jihadis* at a training camp, possibly in Kashmir. Another was of a young Salim Dhar sitting in what looked like the cockpit of a crashed Russian jet. The background scenery suggested it was in Afghanistan. Then he saw a photo of himself, taken with a long lens. He was outside Legoland, on the street opposite the main entrance, peering into the window of the motorbike showroom that he used to frequent in his lunch breaks.

'I used to ride an old Honda in Afghanistan,' a voice said behind him. Marchant spun round to see a man standing by the curtain, wearing a flying suit and holding a helmet in one hand. It was Salim Dhar.

86

Myers had drunk one too many Battledown Premiums at the Beehive and was struggling to slot the key into the lock of his Montepelier flat in Cheltenham. It was sometimes stiff, but tonight he wondered if he had got the wrong door. He looked up at the front windows to reassure himself, and then tried again. The door opened and he fell into the hall, gathering up the post that was on the doormat: the latest issue of *Fly RC*, a magazine for remote-control plane enthusiasts, and a takeaway pizza flier.

At the back of his addled mind he wondered if the lock was stiff because it had been tampered with, but he dismissed the thought. He had become paranoid since carrying out Daniel Marchant's request, seeing people on street corners, lurking behind curtains. As far as he could tell, no one had managed to establish a cause for the temporary delay in the Recognised Air Picture data at RAF Boulmer, let alone follow it out of the Tactical Data networks to Cheltenham. He had covered his tracks carefully, and he couldn't deny that the result had been spectacular. Whatever Marchant was up to, he was doing it with style. A pair of MiG-35s over bloody Scotland!

He tore open the magazine as he stumbled into the kitchen, idly flicking through the pages. A sport-scale park flyer of the Russian jet would be entertaining down at the recreation ground, but he couldn't find one listed. It might also attract unnecessary attention to himself, given the furore over the breach of airspace. Relations had plummeted between London and the Kremlin in the twenty-four hours since the incident. They weren't helped by the subsequent kidnapping of an MI6 officer on the streets of Soho.

For a moment, when he first heard the news at work, Myers had thought it might be Marchant, but his old friend was too streetwise to be picked up by the SVR in central London. He didn't dare ring him to check. Myers was nervous about making any calls after his brief chat with Fielding. Besides, Marchant was clearly up to something big, and he didn't want to be further implicated. He had already done too much.

After taking a leak that seemed to last for ever – he almost fell asleep as he stood swaying at the bowl – Myers headed for his bedroom. He knew he should drink some water, but he wanted to check his emails, maybe surf a few porn sites before crashing. He always kept the door to his bedroom locked because of the computers inside, but as he fumbled for the key fob in his pocket, he saw that the door was ajar. The sobering effect was instant. His brain cleared as an adrenaline rush ripped through his body, making his legs feel so heavy that they almost buckled.

He stood there for a few seconds, listening for a noise, pressing his heels into the carpet to stop his legs shaking, but there was only silence, broken by the noise of a solitary car passing outside. He took a deep breath, pushed open the door, and walked in.

'Don't say a word,' a voice said from the darkness. A moment later, Myers felt the cold metal of a barrel against the racing pulse in his temple.

87

'I became too fond of this in Morocco,' Dhar said, pouring out two glasses of mint tea. 'It is my one other luxury.' He had already offered Marchant some dried apricots from a paper bag on the floor between them. He was sitting cross-legged, his posture upright. He had changed out of his flying suit and was now wearing a long white *dishdasha* of the sort that Marchant had seen in Marrakech and a matching *kufi* skullcap. His austere appearance was reflected in the formality of their conversation. There was a stiffness to proceedings that was making Marchant tense. He was also struggling to sit comfortably on the ground. His crossed legs were cramping up, forcing him to rock forwards. He knew it made him look nervous.

'How long were you in Morocco for?' Marchant asked, taking the hot glass by the rim. 'Did you go there straight after Delhi?' He was hoping to slip into small talk, but knew at once that it was the wrong question to ask a man on the run.

'Please,' Dhar said. 'Let us talk first of family. My journey is of no concern. All that matters is that we are once again reunited.'

Dhar had hugged him when they first met in southern India. This time there had been no such warmth. Marchant had been caught snooping around his possessions, which didn't help, but there was also a different tension in the air: a pressing sense of expectation. Fielding had warned him that he would be killed if Dhar suspected anything. *Embrace your worst fears. They may be the only thing to keep you alive when you meet Dhar.*

'Dad wrote me a similar letter,' Marchant said, nodding at the Koran on the crate.

'Dad,' Dhar repeated, mocking the word. 'Father. Papa. Pop.' He reached forward and took another apricot. 'All those years I never knew him, never knew he was waging the same wars against the *kuffar*. It must be harder for you. Coming to the crusade so late. In some ways, I am closer to him than you ever were, even though I met him only once.'

Marchant could feel himself bridling inside, but he remembered why he was here, why Dhar had wanted to see him. They were the sons of a traitor, united in family treachery.

'It's true,' Marchant said. 'The man I thought I knew was someone else.'

'And it wasn't a shock? Primakov said you were relieved.'

'It was like finding the missing piece of a jigsaw. After the way I was treated by the Americans –'

'The waterboarding.'

'Yeah, after being nearly drowned at a CIA black site in Poland, I was beginning to wonder, you know, about our great Western values. When Primakov told me about Dad, my life began to make sense.'

'Brother, come here,' Dhar said, beckoning Marchant to stand. Both men rose, and hugged each other long and hard. Marchant was expecting it to feel awkward, but it wasn't. He hadn't been embraced by his own flesh and blood since his father had died. And as he held Dhar, breathing in the faint aroma of apricots, he wondered if this was what it would have been like to hug Sebastian if he had survived into adulthood. He had told Dhar all about his twin when they had met before, explained how his death had cast such a long shadow over his life, but, for the first time in years, Marchant no longer felt like an only child. When they let go of each other, both men's eyes were moist.

'My life made sense, too,' Dhar said. 'Can you imagine how hard it was for me when I first discovered that my father was the head of an infidel intelligence agency?'

Dhar managed a laugh in between wiping his eyes with the sleeve of his *dishdasha*. Marchant smiled, too, as they sat back down on the floor. It was a rare moment in a spy's life. Marchant had crossed over, immersed himself in a role like a seasoned actor, forgotten that he was playing a part. But no sooner had the spell been cast than it was broken. All the old fears came tumbling down around him again. Why had he found it so easy to celebrate his father's treachery?

'After he had been to see me in Kerala, the clouds began to clear,' Dhar continued. 'At first, I was confused by the visit, some of the things he said, but when I met Primakov and he told me everything – the nature of the American intelligence our blessed father had once passed to Moscow – it was like being reborn.'

'I'm sorry about your mother,' Marchant said, trying to steer the conversation onto safer territory. He had been genuinely angry about what had happened in Madurai, regardless if it had been fabricated by Fielding, and knew he could talk about it with conviction. He wasn't sure how much longer he could listen to Dhar extolling their father's treason.

'I'm sorry too. This man Spiro . . .'

'I promised your mother I would look after her. I feel I failed her, and you.'

'*Inshallah*, the time will come when such things will not happen again.'

'The deal was that we would bring her back to Britain, keep her away from the Americans. I gave her my personal undertaking that she would be safe. I can never forgive myself for what happened. I let her down, Salim. She trusted me, against her better judgement. I persuaded –'

'Enough.' Dhar held up a hand, as if he was halting traffic. Had Marchant pushed it too far? Dhar was angry, his equanimity disturbed by talk of his mother. He moved his raised hand to his eye as he turned to look out of the window.

'Do you trust Primakov?' Dhar asked, changing the subject.

'I don't know him well, but I respect our father's judgement. You read the letter. "Trust him as if he was a member of our family." '

'Grushko, the Russian who came today, has his doubts.'

'Grushko doesn't trust anyone. I think he even doubts me.'

Dhar turned to look at him with an intensity that Marchant had never seen in anyone before. In a certain light, his brown Indian irises shone as black as onyx.

'So do I.'

'I don't blame you. It doesn't look that convincing on paper, does it? MI6 agent bonds with *jihadi* half-brother.' Marchant was keen to lighten the mood, but Dhar wasn't smiling.

'What I am struggling to understand is why you returned to your old job in London. After all that had happened. The waterboarding in Poland, the way the Americans treated our father. How could you continue to be a part of that?'

'Because I wanted to meet you again. Remaining in MI6 was the only way. I wanted to come sooner, but the Americans wouldn't allow it.'

'The Americans,' Dhar repeated, smirking. 'You could have travelled on your own.'

'I thought I'd be more useful to you if I still had a job with MI6.'

'Such a Western way of looking at things. The job more

309

important than the person. You're family. You got my text? *Yalla natsaalh ehna akhwaan. Let's make good for we are brothers.* It was sent more than a year ago.'

'I got it. It was impossible to come sooner without losing my job. I couldn't have helped you – arranged for the MiGs to fly over Scotland – if I was on the outside, on the run again.'

'Tell me one thing. Your return to MI6, after Delhi, was before you discovered our father had been working for the Russians.'

Dhar's probing was beginning to worry Marchant. He was right. He had gone back to his desk in Legoland with his head held high, proud of his father's innocence rather than celebrating his guilt.

'There was a time when I believed in Britain, I can't deny that. Just as there was a time when our father believed in his country too. But the doubts were growing when I returned to MI6. About what I was doing, why I was doing it. I'm sure you've sometimes questioned what you do too.'

Dhar didn't respond.

'And those doubts became something stronger when Primakov showed up in London with the letter,' Marchant continued.

'We are blessed to have had such a brave father.'

Dhar smiled, and Marchant thought he was through the worst of it. But he wasn't.

'There is only one problem. Grushko is convinced that Primakov is lying.'

Dhar leaned over to his bed and took a pistol from under the pillow. He brushed the handle with his sleeve, then cocked it with the assurance of someone familiar with firearms. 'And if Primakov is not telling the truth, then neither are you.'

88

'How did you know I was involved?' Myers asked, sitting at the bank of computers. There had been two Russians waiting for him in his bedroom, one tall, the second one shorter with rimless glasses. The tall one had frisked him, while the other did the talking, although he wasn't one for idle chatter. It took Myers a few minutes to be sure of his identity. It was Vasilli Grushko, London *Rezident* of the SVR. He had seen his photograph at work, intercepted occasional calls.

'We have been following your friend Daniel Marchant for some time now,' Grushko said.

'Was it him who was taken? In London?'

Myers tried to prevent his left leg from shaking, but it was impossible. Instead, he bounced it up and down as if the movement was voluntary. At least they had stopped pointing the gun at his head. After frisking him, the weapons had been put away, but Myers was still all over the place, too many possible scenarios unfolding in his mind. The computers had already been turned on when he entered the bedroom. Had they hacked into GCHQ using his passwords? If they knew about his role with the MiGs, who had they told? Who else knew? He was just glad that he had gone to the bathroom when he first arrived, otherwise he would be pissing himself now.

'Your concern is almost touching. He is fine. Unharmed.'

'What do you want from me?'

'He came to see you. At the Beehive pub near here. Marchant chose the location well, because it was busy, but we think you were talking about the MiGs. Now that we have discovered you bring your work home' – Grushko nodded towards the bank of computers – 'we know for certain that it was you who helped him.'

'What do you want from me? Please. There was no harm. Nobody died. It was good publicity for Russia, your air force. Bloody lousy for ours. Air defences like a sieve.'

'It is quite simple. We want you to help him again.'

89

Dhar held the cocked gun to Primakov's head. The Russian had entered the hangar full of his usual bonhomie, and had not seen him standing behind the door. Dhar closed it and pushed Primakov into the middle of the building, where Marchant was standing beside a wooden chair, holding a rope in his hand. Marchant felt like a guilty executioner. It was as if Dhar had put their own relationship on hold while he sorted out Primakov. He had asked Marchant to help him interrogate the Russian, a process that Marchant assumed he himself would be subjected to later.

'Salim, this is unexpected,' Primakov said, nodding at Marchant, who looked away. Whatever else Primakov was, he was dignified, and the next few minutes would be demeaning. Marchant felt a mix of shame and nausea. After Dhar had shown him the gun, they had both slept, but Marchant's sleep had been fitful. He had woken at dawn full of dread, envying Dhar, who was praying calmly on a mat in the middle of the hangar.

'Is it really?' Dhar asked. 'Grushko says you have been under suspicion for many years.'

'A small price to pay for knowing your father so well. May I sit down?'

Dhar kicked the wooden chair towards Primakov, the scraping sound echoing in the hangar. The SU-25 jet that Dhar had flown the day before had been wheeled in through the main entrance overnight, and was now parked at the end of the hangar, the doors closed behind it. Marchant had noted that it was a two-seater, used for training. Apart from the plane, resting up like a vast squatting insect, the hangar was empty.

Dhar nodded at Marchant, who grabbed Primakov's arms and bound his hands tightly behind his back. He tried to do it painlessly, but he was aware of Dhar's eyes on him. Primakov's breathing had become heavier, rasping like a Siberian miner's. Marchant could smell the cologne, mixed now with the strong scent of sweat. If Primakov was going to give him a sign, something to reassure him about his father, it would have to be soon. Time was running out for all of them.

'Grushko is on his way back to Britain,' Dhar said as Marchant finished tying Primakov's wrists to the back of the chair. 'He would rather you were dead, but I wanted to ask a few questions first.'

'About your father?' Primakov was working hard to keep his voice steady, but it was fraying with fear.

'Grushko does not believe that you recruited Stephen Marchant.'

'What does he believe?'

'He accuses my father, our blessed father' – a glance up at Marchant, who remained behind Primakov, to one side – 'of having recruited you. I don't want to believe Grushko, but he is a meticulous man. He has been going through old KGB archives, file by file. Our father gave you intelligence about the Americans, it is true, but Grushko says that with hindsight much of this information was not as important as it seemed at the time.'

Marchant closed his eyes. It was the first time he had heard anyone on the Russian side question his father's worth as a double agent. But any relief he felt was short-lived. If Dhar decided that his father was not a traitor after all, he would come to the same conclusion about him, too. It was down to Primakov now, balanced on a high wire. He had to reassure two sons about their father, one hoping to hear of his loyalty, the other of his treachery.

'Comrade Grushko will find whatever he wants to find in the archive to support his case,' Primakov said, treading carefully. 'The files are endless, and so is his jealousy. Your father was a priceless signing. At the time, I was fêted by the Director of the KGB, hailed as a hero. Within months, I was awarded the Order of Lenin. I could do no wrong. I admit that on some occasions the intelligence was gold, at others it was dust. But I knew your father better than many – and all I can say is that he detested America to the day he died. Whether that makes him or me guilty of treason, I leave to others.'

Marchant looked down at Primakov. His chest was heaving, his voice beginning to crack under the strain. One wrong word and Marchant's cover would be blown, but he still needed something.

'Salim, Daniel' – a cock of the head towards Marchant – 'I don't know why you have suddenly decided to listen to Comrade Grushko, but before you give him too much time, there is something you should both know.' A pause as he gathered himself. More rasping. 'My instructions were quite clear: I was asked to bring you two together. A rising *jihadi* and an ambitious MI6 officer. Now that I have done my job, I may rest peacefully.'

'And whose instructions were they?' Dhar asked, walking up to Primakov. Marchant could hear his suspicion, his mounting anger. Primakov was wobbling on the wire. This was the moment, the sign Marchant had been waiting for.

Primakov paused. 'Your father's. He had witnessed the birth of Islamic terror, watched it grow in strength, knew that one day it would pose the greatest threat of all – to everyone: Britain, America, Russia.'

With no warning, Dhar whipped the pistol across Primakov's face.

'You are lying!' he shouted. Marchant had never heard him raise his voice before. 'It was Moscow Centre that asked you to bring us together.'

A trickle of blood was dripping from Primakov's mouth.

'So it was Moscow Centre,' he said finally, with the air of a condemned man. 'But at my suggestion, and your father's wish.'

'A lying *kuffar*,' Dhar muttered, walking over to the window.

'Salim, your father had always followed your progress from the other side of the world, but when there was a chance to meet you in person, he took it, knowing there might be some common ground between you.' Primakov was talking with difficulty, his cut lips bleeding, distorting his words. 'And of course he had another son, Daniel, carving out a career in intelligence in the West, despite the best efforts of the CIA. There was some common ground there, too, between all three of you. On the last occasion I saw him, your father made me promise to bring the two of you together when the time was right. He said you would both know what to do. That time has now come.'

Dhar walked past Primakov and stood with his face inches from Marchant's. The smell of apricots was strong and sour now.

'Do you want to, or shall I?' he asked, holding out the gun. 'We cannot let him continue to insult our father in this way.'

Marchant's heart was racing. He knew it was a test, one final challenge. If Dhar suspected Primakov, he suspected him too, but for the moment it appeared that Dhar wanted to believe in his father, his half-brother – his family.

'I saw something in our father's eye when I met him,' Dhar continued, now looking down at Primakov. 'And do you know what it was? Approval. Anything to stop the American crusade: MI6 officers passing US secrets to Moscow, *jihadists* shooting the President in the name of Allah. And now that he has gone, it is left to you and me.'

316

He turned back to Marchant, who hesitated for a moment, looking at the gun that was still in Dhar's outstretched hand. Suddenly he saw Dhar as a child, desperately seeking a father's endorsement, something he had never been given in his childhood. If his real father hadn't been a traitor to the West, Dhar would be left with nothing. Dhar had to believe in his father's treachery, dismiss Primakov's talk of another agenda. In his mind, Moscow Centre had brought Dhar and Marchant together for one simple reason: they were both their father's sons.

Marchant listened to the sound of Primakov's wheezing, the loudest noise in the hangar. The Russian had finally told him the truth, knowing that he would pay for it with his life. He had avoided any admission that he was working for the British – that would have implicated Marchant, too. Instead, he had told Marchant that his father had wanted him to meet Dhar, explore their common ground. That was enough. And Marchant knew now exactly what he had to do.

'Let me,' he said, taking the gun.

90

'I shouldn't be here, but I wanted to thank you in person,' Fielding said, standing at the foot of Lakshmi Meena's hospital bed. One arm was heavily bandaged and she had bruising below her left eye, but she seemed in reasonable spirits.

'For what?'

'For letting them take Daniel. It must have gone against everything you were taught at the Farm. I brought you these.'

He waved the bunch of full-headed Ecuadorian roses he was holding, and put them on the windowsill. He had also brought a box of honey mangoes from Pakistan.

'Thank you. I wasn't armed. There were at least four of them. In the circumstances, I had no choice but to protect myself. Have a seat.'

She gestured at a chair, but Fielding remained standing.

'Is that what you told Spiro?' he asked.

'It took a while for him to accept that they weren't your people.'

'We haven't had to resort to kidnapping our own officers on the streets of London. Not yet.'

'I don't suppose you're going to tell me what Dan's up to.'

He hesitated. 'All I can say is that you were right to trust him. I'm sorry about your arm.'

'You're asking a lot of him. To stop Salim Dhar on his own.'

Fielding glanced towards the door at the mention of Dhar's name. Through the frosted glass panel, he could see the profile of an armed policeman standing guard outside. He wanted to tell Meena that Marchant's orders weren't just to stop Dhar, but to turn him as well, but he couldn't. The stakes were too high. If Marchant could persuade Dhar to work for the West, it was not something Britain would ever be able to share with any of its allies, least of all America, whose President Dhar had come so close to killing.

'No one else can,' Fielding said, moving towards the door. 'It's family business.'

91

'Please place a flower on my daughter's grave,' Primakov whispered, leaning forward, his whole body shaking now. 'And may your father forgive you.'

Marchant wanted to look away as he fired. It took all his strength to pull the trigger, leaving him with no will to watch. But he knew Dhar was scrutinising his every move. Primakov's head lurched forward as if in a final drunken bow, and then he fell to the floor.

As the sound of the single shot faded in the echoing spaces of the hangar, Marchant prayed for the first time in years. He tried to tell himself that Primakov would have been executed by Grushko or Dhar if it hadn't been by him, but it didn't make it any easier. He had never killed anyone in cold blood before. Primakov deserved better. He had been one of his father's oldest friends, a courageous man who had carried out his wishes to the last. He hoped to God his death was worth it.

Dhar looked on impassively, then took the gun from Marchant without a word and walked over to his living area.

'Our father told us to trust him as if he was family,' Marchant called after him, feeling the need to explain himself as he tried not to stare at Primakov's slumped figure. A pool of blood had formed around his disfigured head, dust floating on its surface like a fine skein of flotsam.

'He made an error of judgement,' Dhar said. 'Primakov had other interests.'

'Like stopping the global *jihad*?' Marchant asked, regaining some of his composure. He needed to reassure himself that Dhar had moved on, no longer suspected him. 'He must have known you wouldn't like what he said.'

'Primakov was working to his own agenda. There are many within the SVR who are at war with Islam. He was trying to turn you against me, suggesting that our father had somehow sent you here from beyond the grave to halt my work.'

'Was he anti-Russian, too?' Marchant asked, thinking that was exactly what their father had done. His question was a risk, but he needed to know what Dhar thought.

Dhar fixed Marchant with his eyes, now shining blacker than ever. 'No. I do not believe Primakov was a British agent, if that's what you are asking. Grushko was simply trying to frame him. As Primakov said, there were people in Moscow Centre who were jealous of him when he recruited our father. His signing was quite a coup.'

Marchant couldn't ask for more. Dhar not only still believed that Primakov was working for Moscow, he was also sure that their father had been too. Primakov had chosen his words carefully. Thanks to him, Marchant was now safe, free from suspicion. He looked again at Primakov's body, remembering his final wish.

It was the first time Marchant had heard that Primakov had a daughter. He would make enquiries when all of this was over, find out where she was buried and put flowers on her grave. It was the least he could do. *And may your father forgive you.*

'Now I must prepare to fly,' Dhar said.

'Where are you going?' Marchant asked as casually as he could, glancing at the aircraft at the end of the hangar. From the moment Primakov had requested him to help with the MiG-35s' incursion,

Marchant had assumed that Dhar's plans involved an airborne attack of some sort. All he had to do now was persuade him to take him along.

'To the land of our father,' Dhar said, patting him on his shoulder.

'Then let me come with you,' Marchant said instinctively. It was the only chance he had of stopping Dhar. 'We still have so much to discuss. And I know the country well.' He managed a light laugh. 'I could show you the sights.'

Dhar paused for a moment, smiling to himself as he seemed to consider Marchant's offer. There was something Dhar wasn't telling him that made Marchant think that he had a chance. 'That is true. And it is a long flight. Have you flown in a jet before?'

'Only a Provost. But I have a strong stomach.' Marchant was thinking fast now, improvising. The last time they had met, Dhar had abandoned him on a hillside in south India when he left to shoot the US President. Marchant wasn't going to let him get away again. He had to be in the cockpit with him, find out what the target was, get a message to Fielding.

'You know they won't allow another Russian jet to enter UK airspace,' Marchant continued. 'I might be able to help, talk to traffic control. It could buy us a crucial few minutes before we're shot down.'

'Grushko has already taken care of that. He's with your friend Myers in Cheltenham now.'

92

'As far as we know, the facts are these,' Harriet Armstrong said, addressing a meeting of COBRA in the government's underground Crisis Management Centre. MI5, MI6, GCHQ, the Joint Intelligence Group, the Joint Terrorism Analysis Centre, the Defence Intelligence Staff and Special Branch were all represented by their heads, a measure of the gathering's importance (number twos or threes were usually sent). The Prime Minister was chairing the meeting, flanked by the Home Secretary and the Foreign Secretary. The Chief of Defence Staff was also in attendance, along with the Chief of the Air Staff.

'There are a number of possible domestic targets over the coming forty-eight hours, which we'll come to in a moment. In the meantime, Cheltenham' – a nod to GCHQ's director, sitting on Armstrong's left – 'has picked up a raised level of chatter, but I think Marcus will be able to enlighten us further on Dhar's possible intentions.'

The handover was brusque rather than warm. At an earlier meeting in Armstrong's office, Fielding had persuaded her not to go into any details about Marchant's attempt to recruit Nikolai Primakov. She had agreed, but it was clear she still resented Fielding for excluding her from other operational details.

'Thank you, Harriet,' Fielding said. 'I'll keep this short. We believe Dhar was taken from Morocco last month by the Russians, who have offered him protection in return for a shared stake in a state-sponsored act of proxy terrorism. What that act is, we're not sure, but it appears that Dhar has put aside a previous reluctance to strike against UK targets.'

'What about Daniel Marchant's kidnapping by the SVR?' asked the head of JTAC, looking across at Armstrong for support. 'I assume there's a connection.'

'We're not certain it was the SVR,' Fielding interjected.

All eyes turned to Armstrong, who paused before answering, keeping her own eyes down as she shuffled some papers. A Russian operation on the streets of London was her beat. 'Preliminary reports have established that the kidnappers were Russian, but we can't be sure they were SVR. D Branch is still working on it.'

Surprised by her support, Fielding tried to acknowledge Armstrong, but she didn't look up. He had expected her to confirm the SVR's involvement, make life more difficult for him.

'In answer to your question,' Fielding said, 'Marchant, one of our most gifted field officers, has been on Salim Dhar's trail for a number of months. After the terrorist attack on the London Marathon, he wanted to travel to Morocco, where he had good reason to believe that Dhar was in hiding, possibly being shielded by the Moroccan Islamic Combatant Group in the Atlas Mountains. Unfortunately, the Americans insisted that he stayed in Britain. It was a deeply frustrating time for all of us. After a year, we got our way and dispatched him to Marrakech. He was closing in on Dhar when he was exfiltrated by the Russians in an unmarked Mi-8 helicopter. He returned to London and was establishing Dhar's location through an SVR contact when he himself was seized.'

'What are the Russians saying?' the director of GCHQ asked.

'They're denying everything,' the Foreign Secretary replied, glancing at the Prime Minister. 'But it seems that Dhar had become too hot for Tehran, and Moscow took him on. We've protested formally about Marchant's disappearance and enquired through back channels about Dhar.'

'Just as the Russians denied that two of their MiG-35s were over Scotland,' the Prime Minister said. The incursion had made his coalition and its armed forces the laughing stock of NATO, giving him no option but to accept his Defence Secretary's resignation. The MiGs had turned around and were halfway across the North Sea before the Typhoons were even airborne.

'We're working on the assumption that the violation of UK airspace is in some way connected with Dhar,' Fielding continued. He knew it for a fact, of course, but he could never reveal that Marchant, one of his own agents, had facilitated the incursion in order to meet Dhar. Or that Paul Myers at GCHQ had also been involved. The breach had been put down to a cyber attack by Moscow, one of many in recent months.

'Which is why this weekend's RIAT, the Royal International Air Tattoo at Fairford, is top of our list,' Armstrong said. 'We've also got a Test match at Lord's against Pakistan, which could be a target, given Dhar's connections, and WOMAD, the world music festival in Wiltshire, which is less of a security worry, although I gather there was a bit of a disturbance in the Qawwali tent last year.'

The faint murmur of laughter released some of the tension in the room. Armstrong enjoyed being centre stage, Fielding thought. Not everyone appreciated her stabs at humour, or her Johnsonian memos on poor grammar. In another life, she would have been headmistress of a public school. The subcontinent had knocked some of the pomposity out of her manner, but not quite enough.

'The good news is that Fairford is already a secure site,' she continued, 'with a perimeter fence protected by the Americans.'

'The bad news?' the Prime Minister asked. Armstrong looked across at the director of the Defence Intelligence Staff.

'Washington is using the air show to showboat a big arms deal with Tbilisi,' he said, taking over from Armstrong. 'They're currently equipping the Georgian air force with C130 cargo planes to replace their ageing fleet of Antonovs. The US has also agreed to lease them F-16 fighter jets to replace their SU-25s, most of which were shot down by the Russians in the 2008 South Ossetia war.'

'An arms deal that Moscow is obviously far from happy about,' the Foreign Secretary said.

'Given the MiG débâcle, shouldn't we have our Typhoons and Tornados airborne all weekend?' the Prime Minister asked. 'Over Lord's, Gloucestershire and Wiltshire?'

'If only that were possible,' the Chief of the Defence Staff said.

'How long's the show?' the PM continued, ignoring the jibe. The RAF was locked in acrimonious discussions with the coalition about cuts to Britain's fighter-jet capability.

'Seven and a half hours of flying time.'

'Do what you can,' the PM said, looking at his watch.

'The US base commander at Fairford is an old friend,' the Chief of the Defence Staff said. 'I'll speak to him. Personally, I think it's highly unlikely the Russians would try anything, particularly on a weekend when there's so much hardware on the runway. The F-22 Raptor will be in town. The violation of our airspace, while deeply regrettable, was a one-off, a distraction. A Test match against Pakistan at the home of cricket is a far more probable target.'

'I agree,' Ian Denton said. There was a newfound confidence in his voice that surprised Fielding, who was sitting next to him. 'RIAT's the largest military air show in Europe. It's an American-run base, and security is always very tight. The Test at Lord's strikes me as a more likely target.'

Denton might be right – perhaps the MiGs were just a distraction – but Fielding doubted it. He'd been weighing up the possible options ever since Armstrong had alerted him to the air show. Marchant had been asked to help with the MiGs, an involvement that nobody else around the COBRA table knew about. Now he had been taken to join Dhar, wherever he was. In Fairford, with its American hosts and Georgian guests, Dhar and the Russians had found a mutual target.

93

'You are only carrying two Vympel and two LGBs, so we've loaded you up with four 1,500-litre drop tanks, two under each wing,' Sergei said over the r/t to Dhar, who was in the rear cockpit of the SU-25, where the instructor normally sat. It was raised a little, giving him a good view of Marchant, who was strapped into the seat ahead, listening in on the conversation. The avionics and weapons suites were identical in both cockpits – full dual control – but Sergei had disabled them in the front.

Marchant had met Sergei only briefly. Dhar spoke warmly of him, but the Russian had shunned eye contact as he had inspected the plane's undercarriage in the hangar. Afterwards, when he handed Marchant an ill-fitting flying suit and helmet, he had again avoided his gaze. There was a haunted look about him, Marchant had thought.

'Distance to target is 2,875 kilometres,' Dhar said, reading from a sheet of waypoints in the clear-panel leg pocket of his flying suit. 'And the *Grach* has a ferry range of approximately 2,500 kilometres. "Do the math," as our American idiots like to say.'

'The extra fuel and a good tailwind should get you there,' said Sergei.

Should? Marchant could have done without the mordant banter. He closed his eyes and tried to picture what lay ahead. Dhar had finally agreed to let him fly with him. Marchant wasn't sure if it was a reflection of how much he trusted or distrusted him. Either way, it had bought him precious time in which to work out what to do.

'We can be martyrs together,' Dhar had joked, making no mention of a return journey.

Earlier, Dhar had revealed their route – north into the Barents Sea, south-west down the coast of Norway into the North Sea, and then west into UK airspace – but there had been no talk of the target. Whatever it was, timing was evidently crucial. Dhar had checked and double-checked windspeeds on the journey, going through the waypoint ETAs several times with Sergei.

Marchant had already clocked the two missiles on the wings' hard points. Air-to-air suggested that Dhar expected airborne company, but why not a full complement? And now Sergei had mentioned two laser-guided bombs for a ground target. It was a tailor-made suite of weapons. But for what?

Marchant glanced around the cramped cockpit at the array of dials. The Jet Provost he had once flown in had been privately owned by an ex-RAF friend of his father. Taking off from Kemble airfield, near the family home in Tarlton in the Cotswolds, had felt like rising into the sky on rails: surprisingly smooth and steady. He suspected the SU-25 would be a rougher ride.

As the plane began to roll forward, Marchant peered through the mist at the godforsaken scenery. Dhar had taxied to the far end of the main runway. A light drizzle was falling. All Marchant could see was pine trees. The control tower was a long way off, barely visible in the murky distance. Halfway down the runway on the right were two MiG-29s. He guessed that they must be on permanent standby, like the Typhoons at RAF Leuchars and Coningsby that would be scrambled if Dhar showed up on the radar. Then he noticed the armed guards, dotted about on the periphery of the trees, out of sight of any US reconnaissance satellites. He had only spotted the two guards outside the hangar door before. Security had been ramped up for their departure.

Marchant thought again about Primakov, the sharp intake of breath just before he fired, as if the Russian was bracing himself. After the shooting, Dhar had not wanted to talk, preferring instead to spend time on his own behind the curtain. Marchant assumed that he was praying, not for the Russian's soul but for a successful *jihad*. As far as Marchant could tell, no one else seemed to be running the show or telling Dhar what to do. He was very much his own man, ignoring the guards and talking only with Sergei before climbing into the cockpit. There was a quiet confidence about Dhar, a self-assurance that gave him an air of authority.

'Comrade Marchant?' It was Sergei's voice on the r/t.

'Yes?' Marchant said, taken by surprise.

'Talk to comrade Dhar about collateral. He will understand.'

Marchant was about to ask for an explanation, but Sergei had already signed off.

'Did you get any of that?' he asked Dhar over the intercom.

'We can talk more later. Our flying time is more than three hours. Now we must prepare for take-off.'

94

Paul Myers had given up trying to make conversation with the Russians. They had sat motionless in his room throughout the night, waking him with a prod at first light. He had stumbled out of bed, forgetting that his hands were still tied, and they had accompanied him to the bathroom, where he managed his ablutions with difficulty.

It was only when they sat him down in front of the computers that he persuaded them to untie his wrists. If it had been a working day, he would have been missed by now, as he liked to work the early shifts at GCHQ in the summer, getting in at 7 a.m., sometimes earlier. It gave him longer in the park afterwards to fly his model planes. But today was a Saturday, and no one would miss him. He had made a loose arrangement to meet a couple of colleagues in the pub in the evening, but otherwise his diary was free, as it was most of the time.

The Russians wanted him to do exactly what he had done for Marchant: delay High Wycombe's real-time Recognised Air Picture feed. He had already told them that it would be hard to repeat the trick, but the Ministry of Defence's IT experts, many of whom he knew, had yet to trace the source or cause of the Link 1 breach.

Of more concern to Myers was what Marchant and Fielding would want him to do. Marchant was clearly party to the planned second violation of UK airspace. Would he want Myers to help him, or to stop him? His instinct told him to let the Russians run with it, whatever they were planning.

Nursing a hangover, he logged in to his GCHQ account and prepared once again to tamper with the Tactical Data Links that were meant to keep the skies above Britain safe.

'All I need is a start time,' he said, looking at his watch. 'I can't delay the RAP for long. A few minutes at most.'

'This time we need a little longer,' Grushko said.

95

The morning had dawned bright and clear in the Cotswolds, and the ground staff at RAF Fairford were already busy laying out the tables and chairs in the private enclosure towards the eastern end of the runway. It was a big day for the base, and General Glen Rogers, head of the United States Air Forces in Europe, was taking his run around the airfield early, before the VIPs began to arrive. The USAF would shortly be pulling out of Fairford, leaving it as a standby facility that could be reactivated at short notice for the use of B-2 Spirit stealth bombers and U2s.

All the usual merchandise stands were present. Jogging at a steady pace, Rogers passed the Breitling Owners' Club, a dogtag stamping stall for wannabe GIs, and a stand that would later be selling Vulcan memorabilia. Now that was a plane he wished he had flown. This weekend, though, was all about modern military hardware, and in particular the global export market for the F-16 Fighting Falcon, one of America's finest fourth-generation jet fighters, otherwise known as the Viper.

The delegation from Georgia had spent the night on the base, drinking too much of their own Kakhetian wine in the officers' mess, but he couldn't blame them. Today marked the official beginning of a new era for the Georgian air force. Six F-16Ds had already been delivered to Alekseevka Military Airbase, but the deal between Washington and Tbilisi would be formally signed off in the private enclosure. To mark the occasion, the F-22 Raptor, a plane that was strictly not for export, would make its debut at Fairford with a breathtaking display of fifth-generation manoeuvrability.

Rogers used to fly jets himself in the mid-1980s, briefly serving with the Thunderbirds F-16 display team, and he was particularly looking forward to the Raptor show. Today's pilot, Major Max Brandon, would demonstrate its vast air superiority over an old Russian SU-25 'Frogfoot', the current mainstay of Georgia's air force, in a mock-up of a Cold War dogfight that promised to be one of the highlights of the weekend.

The only blot on the Gloucestershire landscape was the arrival of Jim Spiro, the CIA's Head of Clandestine Europe. He had turned up in the middle of the dinner with the Georgians, wanting an urgent talk about a perceived security threat that was making the Brits jumpy. (Fairford always made the Brits nervous. A few years earlier, a B52 had flown in low over the runway as part of the display, only for the pilot to be told by ATC that he had got the wrong airfield. So much for precision bombing.) Rogers had not met Spiro before, and he hoped their paths would never cross again. Marines had that sort of effect on him, particularly ex ones who had featured in the infamous CIA torture memos.

If the Agency had its way, the contract with the Georgians would be signed in a reinforced bunker five hundred feet underground, and there would be no Royal International Air Tattoo at all. He had told Spiro to relax and enjoy the day, reminding him that it did much to reinforce the special relationship between Britain and America. That was the problem with the spooks – they saw threats everywhere.

96

Fielding had agreed with Armstrong that it was too much of a security risk for both of them to travel to Fairford, so she had stayed behind in London to liaise with COBRA, which was now sitting around the clock. The air show remained the most likely target, and Fielding needed to be there, even though he knew it could be dangerous. He also wanted to get out of London, away from the endless meetings, and clear his head. Ian Denton had offered to mind the shop in his absence – a little too keenly, Fielding thought afterwards.

Just outside the airfield's perimeter fence, he asked his Special Branch driver to pull into a lay-by, where several plane-spotters had parked up in camper vans, ready to watch the display without paying. Marchant had Fielding's personal number, and he still hoped that he might call him, give him some warning, however late, of Dhar's murderous intentions.

If the threat was airborne, it would involve a repeat of the earlier breach of British airspace. Had Marchant asked Myers to help him out a second time? So far, Fielding had resisted talking to him about Marchant's earlier request. The risk of being monitored by the Russians was too high. He assumed Myers must have hacked into Britain's early-warning radar network, allowing the MiG-35s to fly over Scotland unchallenged. Now he needed to know for sure if Myers was involved again. He dialled his mobile number.

Twenty miles away in Cheltenham, Myers watched his handset vibrate on the desk next to the keyboard. He looked at his Russian minders.

'Answer it,' Grushko said, waving his gun at him. 'And let us listen.'

Myers picked up the handset and switched it to speaker phone. The number was unknown, and he assumed it was someone from GCHQ. Colleagues often called him at the weekend with technical queries. He would remind them about GCHQ's internal IT support unit, and then do what he could to help.

'Paul Myers,' he said, as casually as possible.

Fielding detected the tension in his voice at once.

'It's Marcus Fielding. Is everything OK?'

'Fine, all fine,' Myers said, swapping the phone to his other hand and glancing at Grushko. Fielding always made his palms sweat. The added presence of the Russians was almost too much.

'Is it convenient to talk?' Fielding asked. Grushko nodded. 'I wanted to ask you about –'

'Could you hold on a moment?' Myers pressed the privacy button and turned to Grushko. 'He's going to suspect something. I'm sorry, I'm trying to act normally but this guy always makes me nervous. And he just knows when someone's lying. It's his job.'

'Then keep it brief. Does the Chief of MI6 ring you often?'

'Yes, no, I mean . . . I was seconded to Six for a few months, I worked directly for him.'

'He is an important man,' Grushko said, waving his gun at the handset. 'Talk to him.'

'Sorry,' Myers said, speaking to Fielding again. 'There was someone at the door.'

'Are you at home?' Fielding asked. He had expected him to be at work. If he was about to help the Russians again, he would be preparing to do it now. He sounded even more nervous than usual, under duress. Fielding couldn't risk asking what Marchant had requested him to do, but he still needed to give his call some purpose, a reason for Myers to be rung by a security Chief, in case he was being monitored.

'Yeah, got the weekend off.'

'I wanted to ask you about Daniel Marchant.'

Myers glanced up at Grushko, who leaned in towards him, listening intently.

'Dan? Is there any news? Was he definitely the one who was taken in London?'

'Yes. I was wondering when you saw him last, if he'd discussed anything out of the ordinary with you.'

'Is he OK?'

'We don't know. How did he seem when you last met him?'

Myers thought back to the pub, when Marchant had asked him about the MiGs. He glanced up at Grushko, who shook his head. Why did Fielding suddenly want to know? Last time they spoke he had hung up on him.

'Fine. I don't remember anything unusual. We drank too much beer and talked a lot about Leila.'

'We're working on the theory that he might have defected rather than been taken.'

'Defected? Dan?' Myers had never been good with people, but one thing in life he was certain of was Daniel Marchant's loyalty. He was about to say as much to Fielding when he saw that Grushko had sat back and was more relaxed. Myers had no idea what game Fielding was playing, but he did know when to keep his mouth shut.

'I'm afraid so,' Fielding replied. 'Listen, if you do remember anything, give me a call, will you?'

'Sure.'

In the lay-by outside Fairford, Fielding put down his phone. His rash impulse to find out more had nearly jeopardised everything. Myers was evidently about to repeat whatever he had done before for the Russians, and it sounded as if he was being babysat. If they were listening, he hoped he had said enough to confirm Marchant's defection story.

Myers placed the phone back on his desk. 'I can't believe it,' he said, as if to himself. 'Daniel Marchant defecting?'

'Is it really such a big leap for him to make?' Grushko asked. 'I am only surprised that he did not come across earlier, given the way he has been treated.'

Myers checked himself. He wanted to clear Marchant's name, tell the Russians how much his friend loved his country, but he had to shut up. Whatever was going on, Fielding and Marchant were in it together, and he didn't want to do or say anything that might compromise them. Marchant's defection had to be a cover story, otherwise Myers might as well pack his bags and emigrate.

'We have ten minutes before they reach the edge of the UK's Air Defence Identification Zone,' Grushko said, looking at his watch. 'Are you ready?'

97

The American Raptor took off before the Russian SU-25, accelerating down the runway to the thumping soundtrack of 'I Don't Want to Stop', by Ozzy Osbourne. It lifted off the ground and flew past the private enclosure at twenty feet, before pulling up into a vertical climb that had the crowds gasping. A pugnacious American had taken over the commentary box, his wild WWF style of delivery in stark contrast to the clipped tones of the ex-RAF pilot who had introduced the earlier aircraft.

'Ladies and gentlemen, I present the most feared combat aircraft in the world, the fifth-generation F-22 Raptor,' the commentator said, rolling out the Rs. 'This awesome aircraft enjoys superiority in every conceivable dogfight scenario. It has no rivals. There is no battlefield that the Raptor cannot dominate. There is no battlefield that the Raptor *will* not dominate. Designed without compromise to sweep our skies of all threats, keeping the peace through strength.'

The Georgian delegation had been joined by a posse of US military top brass and senior executives from the global arms industry. Acting against the CIA's advice, the US Secretary of Defense had also flown in to join the celebrations. Not everyone was pleased to see him, as he had halted future production of the $155-million Raptor, but his presence was a sign of the strategic importance of the Georgian deal.

After the Raptor came the SU-25, taking off without a sound-track and eliciting barely disguised disdain from the American commentator.

'Ladies and gentleman, a plane from another era, a mudfighter from the past, a relic of the Cold War, the SU-25, known without affection in the West as the Frogfoot. In a moment, the two planes will pass from left to right along the display line, where the quantum difference in technology will be plain for all to see.'

'Frogfoot One, time for your farewell tour,' Major Bandon, the American pilot, announced over the r/t as both planes banked at the far end of the runway.

'Copy that, Raptor One,' the young Georgian pilot replied, peeling away. The plan was to put the Raptor through its paces, while the SU-25 took a sanctioned tour of southern Britain before returning for the mock dogfight. 'Good luck.'

'Thank you, Frogfoot. Only sorry you won't be here to see the fun and games.'

'Doing anything special while I'm away? To please our generals?'

'A few tail slides, paddle turns and muscle climbs, the usual. Maybe a power loop or two. If you take your time, I might even pull a Pugachev cobra at the finish. There's been too much talk in your neck of the woods that we Americans can't get it up.'

'Dream on, Raptor One. Out.'

'And go to hell,' the American said to himself as he watched the SU-25 head off to the east. He knew the pilot was from Georgia, one of America's new allies, but the plane was Russian, and old habits died hard.

98

Marchant no longer thought that he had a strong stomach. He had been sick shortly after take-off, when Dhar over-corrected a sudden lurch to the right and put the plane into a 3-G turn. For a painful few seconds, in which he had nearly blacked out, he had wondered if they might not get further than Finland, but he was starting to relax as they flew low and fast over the North Sea towards the east coast of Britain. It was the speed of their progress that he found the most disorientating. At first, it had felt as if he was being dragged along behind the aircraft, like a waterskier. Dhar had told him to look far ahead, to anticipate. Marchant was impressed by how much Sergei must have taught him. He was flying well, untroubled by the G-forces. His only concern appeared to be their ETA.

'You're a natural,' Marchant said over the intercom.

'Another two weeks of training and you wouldn't have been sick, but there was not enough time,' Dhar replied.

'What's the big rush?' Marchant asked. Dhar had synchronised watches before they left, and had regularly asked him to call out the minutes and seconds.

'There is an important air show today. At a place called Fairford. It only happens once a year. I don't think they would have delayed it while I improved my flying skills.'

341

'Are we topping the bill?' Marchant asked, calculating the implications. He knew the air show well, having been taken there by his father when he was a child. Red Arrows and Airfix models, candyfloss and Concorde. Fairford held less happy memories, too. It was where he had flown from with a hood over his head and shackles on his feet, when the Americans had renditioned him to a black site in Poland. But his first thought now was of the number of people on the ground. Tens of thousands of potential casualties.

'That's one way of putting it.'

'Sergei mentioned collateral.'

'I know.'

'What did he mean?'

There was a long pause. Marchant adjusted his helmet and oxygen mask, thinking that contact had perhaps been lost.

'One of our LGBs is a dirty bomb.'

Marchant felt sick. It was only a few feet away from him. He thought of the contamination on the ground, the years of cleaning up. A thousand-pound dirty bomb exploding in the middle of a packed crowd would kill hundreds, but many more would fall ill afterwards from radiation sickness. And no terrorist had ever deployed one before. It had become the Holy Grail, not so much for the number of people it killed as for its propaganda value. The problem was its difficulty to assemble, unless you could tap into the caesium resources of a country like Russia.

'And Sergei didn't approve?'

Another silence.

'My mother loved Britain. For a long while I never knew why. Now I know her loyalties were misplaced. Our father's heart beat for another country. One day I will tell her. Despite Iraq, despite Afghanistan, I never hated Britain in the same way that I detest America. Perhaps I was blind, but it gave shelter to many brothers. Now it has become a legitimate target.'

342

'Its people or its politicians?'

Dhar said nothing. Marchant wished he could see his face, gauge his mood from his eyes. It was hard to tell from his voice alone, particularly over the plane's intercom, but something had shifted. Hairline cracks were appearing. Should Marchant tell him now about their father and Primakov? He instinctively glanced around the cockpit, above and to the sides, checking for threats. Marchant felt vulnerable with his back to Dhar, but there was nothing his half-brother could do except listen. He couldn't kill Marchant, physically throw him out of the plane, unless he could operate both ejector seats.

'Vasilli Grushko was right to be suspicious of Primakov,' Marchant said over the intercom, taking the risk. He would tell it to him straight, give the bare facts. 'What he found in the KGB archives was true. Primakov used to work for MI6. Our father signed him up in Delhi more than thirty years ago. In order for him to recruit Primakov, our father let himself be recruited by the Russians. It was a risk, and once or twice he handed over more than he should have, more than Primakov was giving to London. But he never once betrayed Britain. All the intel was about America.'

There was another long silence. Again Marchant began to think the intercom was faulty, and adjusted his helmet. He felt so defenceless with his back to Dhar.

'How do you know this?' Dhar eventually said, almost in a whisper.

'I've seen the file. Moscow Centre thought it had the Chief of MI6 on its books, when in fact Primakov was working for us. He was, right up until the moment he died.'

Marchant closed his eyes, imagining Dhar's face behind him. He had to keep it together, not let Primakov's death choke him up.

'Until the moment you shot him,' Dhar said.

'I'm my father's son, Salim. I've never stopped working for MI6, or believing in Britain. My defection was hollow, nothing more than an elaborate charade, a way of meeting you, my brother.'

'Is there no truth in your Western life? Is everything lies?' The aircraft rocked in a pocket of turbulence.

'Our father disliked America. There was nothing false about that. If the CIA had ever found out what he was telling the Russians about them, he would have been arrested and tried for treason, if they didn't torture him to death first. I dislike America too. I mistrust its military foreign policy, its corporate and cultural power, its fundamental values, the way it's started to define what it means to be human. But our father loved Britain with a passion, just as I do. Your mother wasn't misguided. She was right. And she isn't in the hands of the CIA. She's safe, in Britain. I give you my word, just as I gave it to her.'

Marchant was bluffing now, but he was confident that Shushma hadn't been with Spiro for long in Madurai, that it had just been a ruse by Fielding to get him into the right mental place. And Lakshmi wouldn't have allowed any harm to come to Shushma, he was sure of that. Despite everything, he realised how much he had come to trust her.

'So you lied to me about my mother too,' Dhar said.

'I had no choice. Unlike you. What is our exact target? Why the dirty bomb, the air-to-air missiles?'

'Do you know why I agreed to bring you along today?'

'Tell me.'

'Because I discovered that Fairford is close to Tarlton, where our father lived, where you grew up with your other brother. I wanted you to show me the village as we flew over, point out the house. It is 18.5 kilometres due west of the airfield.'

Marchant was taken aback by the way Dhar's mind worked. Everything was thought out, had a reason. For a moment, his task seemed hopeless, but he had to turn around the *jihadi* juggernaut.

'I can still show you. Tarlton's a beautiful place. We used to play in the orchard, Sebbie and me, throw apples into the long grass behind our father's back, pretend the rustling sound was approaching tigers. He was always fooled – at least, he said he was. Do you know what his wishes were? Why he asked Primakov to bring you and me together? He wanted you to work for MI6. He didn't expect you to change your views on America – he shared many of them himself, as I do. It's what unites all three of us. He just hoped to explore some common ground. Find out what each side wants from the other. We need a back channel into the global *jihad*, just as you need one with the West. It's what our father most wanted, Salim.'

After another long pause, Dhar eventually spoke. 'I'll be of no use to anybody if I don't go through with this today. The *jihadi* who almost shot the US President, who almost –'

'Almost what? Tell me the precise target.'

But before Dhar could speak, a deafening noise above the cockpit made Marchant duck. He turned around and saw a jet fighter disappearing into the distance.

'What the hell was that?' Marchant asked.

'Another SU-25. From the Georgian air force. And only thirty seconds late. *Inshallah*, our time has come.'

99

The Aerospace Battle Manager on duty at RAF Boulmer had been tracking the solitary Russian jet for some time now, ever since the Finns and Noggies had flagged up a warning. It was heading from the north-east directly towards the UK's ADIZ at 600 mph, and was running out of time to alter course. In a few minutes it would be flying over the Humber estuary. Of equal interest was another trace heading towards the coast in exactly the opposite direction. He had run a check on its assigned squawk transponder code, and it appeared to be an authorised aircraft flying out of the Royal International Air Tattoo at Fairford. It was north of its permitted flyzone, but what concerned him more was that it was on a near-collision course with the incoming jet.

He had been off-duty when his colleague had cocked up over the MiG-35s, but everyone at RAF Boulmer had been dragged over the coals afterwards. So he didn't hesitate to call up Air Command at High Wycombe and recommend that two Typhoons be scrambled from RAF Coningsby to intercept, identify and report. Their reaction made him break out into a cold sweat. There were no incoming or outgoing military jets showing up on Air Command's Recognised Air Picture for the region.

*   *   *

The crowd at Fairford was loving the Raptor display, particularly in the main hospitality marquee, where the Georgian delegation was now drunk on the spectacle as well as their wine. Each manoeuvre was accompanied by a thumping soundtrack: 'Saturday Night's All Right for Fighting', by Nickelback, for the high-speed pass; 'Come Back Around', by Feeder, for the J-turn.

'Major Brandon will now utilise the awesome vector thrust of the twin engines to literally rip the aircraft through the vertical and back to a level flight,' the commentator continued. 'Ladies and gentlemen, I give you the power loop.'

The mood was no less ebullient in the static display behind the Georgians. A child in a pram wearing big red headphones arched his back and clapped with joy as the plane made another fly-by in a weapons-bay pass. An American crew in their flying suits was perched on the wings of a Lancer B1 Bomber that had flown in overnight from Texas. They were enjoying the sunshine, heads rocking to the music as they admired their compatriot's performance.

'Supercruise speed?' one of them asked.

'1.7,' another replied, shielding his eyes from the sun as he tracked the plane into the distance. 'He's yanking and banking the hell out of it today.'

The commentator came over the loudspeaker system again as the Raptor turned sharply at the western end of the runway.

'The pilot will be experiencing something approaching 9G as this fine fifth-generation fighter sweeps through a flat 360,' he said. 'On his return to the display line, Major Brandon will perform a slow high-alpha pass at 120 knots, then hit the afterburner and accelerate into a near-vertical climb to 10,000 feet in a manoeuvre we proudly call the "muscle climb". After that he will be rejoined by the SU-25 Frogfoot, which should be heading back towards the airfield from the east any time now – providing it hasn't run out of gas.'

*　　*　　*

Fielding rang through to Armstrong as he watched the Raptor climb vertically into the sky at the end of the runway. He remembered seeing the Vulcan do something similar in the 1970s.

'Can you hear me? It's Marcus. Any news?' Armstrong was sitting at the COBRA table in the underground crisis-management centre, monitoring developments.

'Air Command has just given the order to scramble two Typhoons from Coningsby,' she said. 'There's been a similar systems error with the Recognised Air Picture. They're not taking any chances this time. It seems a rogue Russian jet is heading your way fast.'

'It's Dhar,' Fielding said quietly.

'A ground sighting in the Midlands suggests it's a two-seater.'

'Dhar and Daniel Marchant.'

'I hope to God you know what you're doing, Marcus. The Typhoons have orders to shoot it down.'

The Aerospace Battle Manager at RAF Boulmer was relieved that the two Typhoons had been scrambled, but he was still dealing with the most stressful day of his professional life. The Russian jet was now deep inside British airspace, flying fast and low towards southern England, but what had happened to the outgoing Georgian aircraft? It seemed to have vanished moments after it had passed the Russian one, just off the coast. What was more, the incoming Russian jet was broadcasting exactly the same transponder squawk code as the one that had disappeared off his screens.

He put an emergency call through to the coastguard, informing them that a plane had gone down ten miles off the coast of Grimsby, and then he rang Air Command again.

Major Brandon glanced down at the crowds as he flew over them in a dedication pass. After banking, he looked across the airfield towards the east. Frogfoot One had enjoyed its farewell tour of the British countryside and would shortly be rejoining the air show for the finale, a dogfight that would leave no one in any doubt about the superiority of the Raptor. He didn't really know why the Georgian pilot was bothering to show up again for a humiliating few minutes. It was just a shame that he was only carrying dummy weapons today. Two clicks over the r/t alerted him to someone else on frequency, and he saw a familiar shape closing from the east at his altitude.

'Welcome back, Frogfoot One. You've missed quite a party. Give me thirty more seconds before I'm on your six o'clock. I'm about to pull that Pugachev cobra we were talking about. One final treat to keep your generals sweet.'

Dhar heard the American, but chose to remain silent, just giving two more taps on the PTT switch to signal his assent. He was confident that everyone – the crowds, air-traffic control and the American pilot – would assume that his aircraft was the same one that had left the air show twenty minutes earlier. After all, SU-25s weren't a common sight over the Cotswolds. To look at, it was identical – except that the weapons slung beneath its wings were not dummies. A few moments ago, he had held a brief conversation with the control tower at RAF Fairford. The exchange had passed without suspicion, their warm welcome back confirming that the switch of squawk codes had been successful. Dhar had never met the brave Georgian pilot who had been recruited by the SVR. All he knew was that he had orders to ditch his plane and eject after passing him over the North Sea.

'Frogfoot One, do you copy me?' The American said. 'I'm proceeding east to west along the display line, with all due respect to Viktor Pugachev. Watch and learn, Frogfoot.'

Dhar could see the Raptor in the far distance now, rearing its nose as it seemed to almost stall, exposing its underbelly. He flicked the weapons select switch on the stick, just as he had done countless times on the simulator with Sergei. Only this time it was for real. The Vympel under his left wing was a heat-seeking air-to-air missile that travelled at two and a half times the speed of sound. It was packed with a 7.25-kilogram warhead and had a maximum range of twenty-nine kilometres. Dhar was less than two kilometres away now, and closing. Minimum engagement range was three hundred metres. He looked across at the American aircraft, using his helmet-mounted sighting system to designate the target. And then he fired.

Marchant thought they had been hit when the missile scorched away from under the plane's left wing. Then he realised what was going on.

'Jesus, Salim, what are you doing?'

'Exploring the common ground.'

100

At first, the crowd assumed that the missile streaking across the sky was all part of the spectacular show, and a cheer went up. Major Brandon was less ecstatic. His heart missed a beat when an alarm in his cockpit warned that an incoming missile had locked on to the infra-red heat of his F-22's exhaust. His first thought was that the aircraft's flat vector nozzles were meant to disguise the heat. His second thought, honed in hours of training, was to deploy his Chemring flares, but he wasn't carrying any because their use had been banned by the air show's organisers. The last thought he ever had was that he was a sitting duck, nose stuck in the air and travelling at a hundred knots.

'Frogfoot One?' he said, a moment before the missile found its target, embedding itself deep within the left engine and then tearing it apart.

Dhar took the plane on a long sweeping arc away from the airfield, glancing down to his right at the plume of smoke rising from the runway.

'Now we drop our first bomb.'

'Salim, we've got to stop this!' Marchant shouted. 'We're going to be shot down any minute. Every fighter in southern Britain will have been scrambled.'

'Frogfoot One, please identify yourself,' a voice from the control tower demanded on the military emergency frequency. Dhar flicked off the radio. He could see the flames of the Raptor now, the wreckage on the runway, as he continued to bank around to the east. He thought of Sergei, the photos he had shown him of his own crash, the carnage as his MiG had skidded through the crowds, carving families apart. The Raptor had broken up over the runway, causing little collateral damage. But Dhar knew that what he was about to do now would not be so precise. The hospitality marquees were to the left of the runway, just before the control tower. The American military had assembled *en masse* in the largest tent, entertaining their Georgian counterparts. Enemies didn't get more legitimate.

'Tell me the target,' Marchant said, desperate to engage Dhar. The aircraft had levelled out now, and was about to begin a low approach from the east.

'The Georgian government is converting their country into a Christian one, turning their back on our Muslim brothers to appease America.'

'Are they here? The Georgians?'

'In the marquee next to the control tower. Here to buy F-16s from the Americans.'

So that was why they had flown to Fairford. There was a logic to Dhar, a rationale, however dark, that demanded Marchant's respect, if not his understanding. He knew that neither the SVR nor Georgia's Muslim population was keen on the country's realignment with America. Had Dhar done enough already in the eyes of other *jihadis* to cool the relationship? Marchant looked down through the canopy. The SU-25's cockpit visibility was not great, but he could make out a row of stalls, packed with people, immediately behind the hospitality marquees.

'Don't do it, Salim. It's too crowded. Too many innocent lives will be lost.'

Marchant knew he had to keep talking, try to sow seeds of doubt. Despite his self-assurance, Dhar would be questioning his own actions. Marchant had read enough intelligence reports from Guantanamo. Even the hardest *jihadis* deliberated about the legitimacy of targets, wrestled with how to determine the innocent.

'The dirty bomb is not for now,' Dhar said, flicking the weapons select switch on the stick. He opted for the conventional LGB and locked onto the marquee with his gunsight, letting the Klyon laser range-finder retain the target as he approached. Then he closed his eyes and thought again about his father. Deep down, below the layers of prayer and wishful thinking, he knew that Marchant had spoken the truth. It had been too much to hope for the Chief of MI6 to betray the West. At least, in his father's anti-American stance, there had been some evidence of their shared blood. Stephen Marchant would have approved of the swaggering Raptor's destruction, the silencing of the hysterical commentator and the incessant rock music.

'This is not what our father would have wanted,' Marchant said, scanning the skies. 'You've made your point, given America a bloody nose, screwed the arms deal. Now let's get out of here.'

Dhar was determined to release the bomb as the plane flew fast along the display line. He had rehearsed it so many times on the simulator in Kotlas and above the ranges of Archangel with Sergei. *Please, if you can spare the lives of twenty-three civilians, then do it. For me, for the Bird.* Innocent lives would be lost, but the military target was legitimate. Generals, Georgian and American, chests blooming with medal ribbons, plotting their next assault on the Muslim world.

But as he looked down at the marquee, his mind surging with thoughts of Sergei, his father, Daniel, he pulled up at the last moment into a steep climb, the G-forces pushing him back into

353

his seat as if in reprimand for the destruction he had been about to unleash.

'If I am to retain any credibility,' Dhar said quietly, as he levelled out at one thousand feet and turned towards the north-west, 'I must go through with my final target.'

101

Fielding had watched with horror from the lay-by as the Raptor was engulfed in a fireball and fell from the sky. His thoughts were with the pilot, but he was also trying to calculate the damage to Britain's relationship with America should it ever be known that Daniel Marchant, a serving MI6 officer, was with Salim Dhar in the cockpit of the other jet, as he now suspected was the case.

He had to redo those calculations as he saw the SU-25 turn and begin a second approach. If Dhar attacked the marquee where the American Secretary of Defense was holding court with the Georgians, Fielding knew his career was over. But as the aircraft drew close to its target, he began to sense that his faith in Daniel Marchant had not been misplaced. Dhar was leaving it very late to strike at the marquee. Had Marchant talked him out of it?

His phone rang as the aircraft passed low over the control tower and pulled into a steep climb. It was Harriet Armstrong.

'Is it true? Dhar's just taken out an American fighter jet?'

'It's true.'

'And Marchant's with him?'

'Yes, he is.'

'Jesus, Marcus, what the hell do I tell COBRA? And the Americans?'

'Tell them that Marchant's just saved the life of the US Secretary

355

of Defense, as well as a tent full of American and Georgian top brass.'

He hung up as he watched the SU-25 disappear into the distance, wondering why Dhar was now heading north-west towards Cheltenham.

The Russians had left Paul Myers shortly after he had begun to corrupt the Recognised Air Picture. He didn't know how many jets would attempt to violate the UK's airspace while its defences were compromised, or what their mission was. All he knew was that Daniel Marchant was involved in some way.

'I suggest you keep the window open for as long as you can,' Grushko had said, just before he departed with his colleague. 'Unless you want your friend Daniel Marchant to be shot out of the sky.'

Myers was suspicious that they weren't remaining with him. It was true that he didn't want to do anything that might put Marchant in more danger than he was in already. Again he tried to think what Marchant would want, and decided to interfere with the Recognised Air Picture for as long as he could. But the Russians had been in an unseemly hurry to leave.

'Have you lived in Cheltenham long?' Grushko had asked just before he left.

'Ten years, maybe longer.'

'It's strange. The poorer parts remind me of Chernobyl, where I grew up. Before the accident, of course.'

After twenty minutes of delaying and corrupting the RAP, Myers had left his flat and driven to work. He wasn't due in until Monday, but the experience of being held hostage in his own home had left him feeling shaken and vulnerable. He also needed a change of scene after being cooped up in his airless bedroom for twelve hours. GCHQ was bright and airy and, as the director often reminded staff, one of the most secure work environments in the country. He would walk the Street, buy some food and sit out on the grassy knoll in the sunny central enclosure. Then he would ring Fielding back and tell him what had happened, although he suspected that the Vicar already knew.

'Just so you know,' Armstrong said, back on the phone to Fielding, who had ordered his driver to head at speed for Cheltenham, 'there are now six jets closing in on Dhar with orders to shoot him down. I've stressed to the Chief of Defence Staff that an officer of MI6 is also on board, but he has been deemed expendable. In your absence, Ian Denton has signed off on it. I'm sorry.'

'I'd be grateful if you could pass on my objections to COBRA,' Fielding said. Denton's decision surprised him. His deputy should have rung him first. 'Salim Dhar doesn't do things by halves. He didn't try to assassinate the American Ambassador in Delhi, he pointed his rifle at the President. He thinks big. Before we take out the jet, it's worth considering the payload it might be carrying. There's a chance Dhar's armed with a nuclear weapon, or possibly a dirty bomb, which would rather spoil the Gloucestershire countryside if we shoot him down. The Russians are behind this, remember. The difficulty of sourcing radioactive isotopes isn't a factor here.'

'Are you saying we should just hold fire and watch while a state-sponsored terrorist flies around Britain attacking targets at will?'

'Of course I'm bloody not. But we need to establish contact with Marchant first, before we risk triggering a major nuclear incident.'

102

'There it is,' Marchant said, looking down at the circular silver roof of GCHQ, shimmering like an urban crop circle on the outskirts of Cheltenham. Its grassy centre was surrounded by the ring of the main building and, further out, radials of parked cars. The town was to the east, and the M5 to the west. It had taken two minutes to fly the twenty miles from Fairford. For a moment, Marchant thought the building would make an excellent substitute for Wimbledon's Centre Court.

'So this is the place that has led the global hunt for me and many of my brothers,' Dhar said. 'It is smaller than I thought.'

Marchant was thinking fast now, measuring opportunities against risks. His priority was to persuade Dhar not to drop a dirty bomb on a densely populated area. But it was also evident that Dhar was willing to consider working for MI6. This was a hope that Marchant had held onto ever since he had first met Dhar in India more than a year ago, when he had found out they were half-brothers. It was why he had travelled to Morocco, chased leads into the High Atlas, flown to Madurai and faked his defection to Russia. And it was why Nikolai Primakov had died in a draughty hangar in Kotlas. He owed it to his father's old friend to turn Dhar.

The risks of running him would be considerable, not least the problem of London's relationship with Washington, which would want his head more than ever after the attack at Fairford. Dhar would never stop waging his war against America. If he did choose to share information with Britain, spare the land of his father from the full wrath of his *jihad*, the rest of the world must never know.

But would Dhar's stock have risen after taking out the US Air Force's pride and joy at an air show? It was brave and spectacular, in a *Top Gun* sort of way, but not exactly another 9/11. If Dhar was to be an effective British asset, he would have to do more. Which was why Marchant was desperately trying to think through the implications of an attack on GCHQ.

A dirty bomb dropped into the middle of the doughnut would partially disable the facility for months, if not years, and would be a massive propaganda victory for *jihadis* everywhere. Air filters and life-support systems in the underground computer halls were designed to ensure that basic services continued in the event of a surface nuclear attack, but the disruption to the offices above ground would still be considerable. Caesium was particularly difficult to clean off metal surfaces such as the building's aluminium roof.

Then there was the population of Cheltenham to consider. It was too late to evacuate the town, even if it was possible. The panic as people fled after an attack would cause chaos as well as deaths; and then there would be those who died later from radiation-induced cancer.

'A conventional thousand-pound bomb would do it,' Marchant said. It seemed that it had been Dhar's plan to drop the standard LGB on Fairford and the dirty bomb on Cheltenham: one for the SVR, one for himself, both sides happy. Marchant had talked him out of the first; now he had to do the same with GCHQ.

'Do what?'

'Give you front-page headlines around the world and destroy much of the building.'

'But I hate this place, and the people who work there,' Dhar said, banking the plane around to the south. 'They are the foot-soldiers of Echelon. Do you know how it feels to be hunted day and night, searching the skies for satellites and drones, not knowing if you can breathe at night for fear of being heard?'

'You tricked them easily enough about your location in North Waziristan,' Marchant said. He was surprised to hear Dhar namecheck Echelon, the Western computer network that sorted and analysed captured signals traffic. The hunted had finally found the hunter.

'That was the fools at Fort Meade. They are easier to shake off. The people down there have been on my tail for years. I will never have a better opportunity.'

'We'll be shot out of the sky any second now, trust me. But if they know we've got a dirty bomb on board, they might just think twice before firing.' Marchant paused. 'Drop the conventional bomb on GCHQ.'

Dhar seemed to hesitate, long enough to give Marchant encourage-ment. It was so frustrating to be sitting in front of him and not face-to-face. A conventional bomb was the lesser of two evils. Marchant knew that the GCHQ building had been built to with-stand a plane crashing into its roof. The glass was bombproof, too. With a bit of luck, a thousand pounds of explosive dropped into the central garden would cause only minimal damage. Again, it was about finding common ground.

Dhar would get his headlines, and it might buy them some time to escape, although the SVR's exit strategy did not inspire confidence. The plan was to head south-west after Cheltenham and eject in the Bristol Channel, where Dhar would be picked up by a Russian-manned trawler. Marchant would have to make his own way in the water.

'I need to use the radio, tell traffic control we're carrying a dirty bomb,' Marchant said, but he was interrupted by an alarm signal in both cockpits. The aircraft's internal and external fuel tanks were almost empty. 'And I need to ring my friend at GCHQ, get everyone to move away from the windows.'

'No warnings.'

Before Marchant could argue, Dhar had banked again and was flying straight towards the building.

'I need to call traffic control,' Marchant insisted.

'Afterwards,' Dhar said, as he locked his gunsight onto the grassy heart of GCHQ.

103

Paul Myers heard the jet overhead, and thought its engine sounded different from the Typhoons and Tornados that were a regular sight in the skies above Gloucestershire. He glanced up as he walked past the smokers' pagoda and headed back into the main building, but the sky was bright and he couldn't see anything. Besides, he was still hungry, and he needed to buy something else to eat from Ritazza.

A moment later, he was lifted up and thrown through the open door with enormous force. His crumpled body landed in a heap on the smooth tiles of the Street as the sound of broken glass cascaded behind him and thoughts of Chernobyl faded from his mind.

Marchant didn't know until later whether the bomb dropped on GCHQ was conventional or radioactive. Events moved fast after Dhar banked the aircraft towards the Bristol Channel. Amid the noise of the fuel alarm, Marchant persuaded him to switch the r/t back on, and a warning came over the emergency military frequency almost immediately that their aircraft was about to be shot down.

'We have a dirty bomb on board!' Marchant barked back in reply, looking around frantically as he tried to spot the RAF jets that he assumed must be approaching. He hoped to God he was right. Even if Dhar had already released it, the threat might save their lives. 'Repeat, we are carrying a thousand-pound radioactive dispersal device.'

The pilots of the two Typhoons closing in on the SU-25 from the west heard Marchant's words. Surprised by the English accent, they referred upwards to Air Command for confirmation that they had permission to destroy the aircraft. They added that the SU-25 was losing speed and altitude, and appeared to be about to ditch in the Bristol Channel. After a brief pause, during which Air Command consulted COBRA, the order came back to hold fire. Marcus Fielding had finally managed to get through to the Chief of the Defence Staff.

In the event, there was no need for the Typhoons to deploy their missiles. Dhar had been battling to keep the aircraft airborne, and it had now become a lost cause. He had managed to reach the Bristol Channel, but they were a mile short of the planned rendezvous with the Russian trawler.

'Prepare to eject,' Dhar said calmly. Marchant realised that his ejection seat was controlled by Dhar. He could have removed him from the plane at any time. It gave him hope that Cheltenham had been spared too.

'I promise I'll take care of your mother,' Marchant said, as he closed his eyes and braced himself.

104

'Are you telling me that Daniel Marchant should be regarded as a hero?' Jim Spiro said incredulously, looking around the table. The Joint Intelligence Committee was at full strength, with senior intelligence officials from Canada, Australia, New Zealand, Britain and America in attendance.

'Salim Dhar was on a mission to Britain to destroy three targets,' Fielding began. 'The F-22 Raptor because it was a symbol of American military might; the delegation of Georgian and US military personnel as a thank-you to the Russians for protecting him; and GCHQ as part of his own personal crusade.'

'And he achieved two of the three,' said Spiro. 'Remind me why exactly we should be thanking Marchant?' He nodded towards the director of GCHQ on his left. 'I'm not sure Cheltenham will be putting a photo of him in their hall of fame. If any halls are still standing.'

Fielding had hoped he could let Spiro down gently, as relations with America had to continue, but it was hard to resist giving him a bumpy landing.

'We believe Dhar was carrying two air-to-air missiles, and two thousand-pound laser-guided bombs. One of them was packed with radioactive caesium-137. I don't need to remind anyone here of the devastation that would have been caused by a dirty bomb dropped either on the crowd at Fairford or on a town the size of Cheltenham. I've just come back from a debriefing with Marchant, and he confirmed that it was always Dhar's intention to drop the dirty bomb on GCHQ – a personal *bête noire* of his. As we all know, the thousand-pound bomb that struck the building was, thankfully, a conventional one, and there was only minimal structural damage and one life lost.'

'How can we be sure the bomb he didn't drop was dirty?' Spiro asked.

'Royal Navy divers have found wreckage of the SU-25 in the Bristol Channel, and are in the process of stabilising the unexploded ordnance. They've confirmed the presence of caesium-137. We're lucky it wasn't detonated by the impact of the crash.'

'So why did Dhar bother to drop anything?' the director of GCHQ asked. 'He'd clearly had a change of heart.'

'Marchant talked him out of the dirty option, but failed to persuade him to abandon the whole idea,' Fielding replied. He had to be careful what he said at this point. It was fair to say that Marchant might have been able to prevent the conventional attack too, but had been mindful of Dhar's *jihadi* credentials. A discredited Dhar would have been of no use to anyone. Nobody in the room, not even Harriet Armstrong, knew that Dhar had finally been turned, and had the potential to be the biggest asset MI6 had ever run.

'So what you're saying is that Dhar only achieved one of his original three targets,' Armstrong said, seemingly supportive.

'Correct. And for that we must thank Daniel Marchant.'

'It's all very well you guys patting each other on the back,' Spiro said. 'I've got to explain to Washington why the most advanced jet fighter ever built was taken out by a lousy lump of old Russian hardware, flown by the world's most-wanted *jihadi* and a rogue MI6 agent.'

'You can tell them that if it hadn't been for the presence of an MI6 agent in the cockpit – and, for the record, Daniel Marchant is no rogue – the damage would have been incalculably worse.'

'There's only one thing that's going to make my President happy, and that's the scalp of Salim Dhar. Are we any closer to knowing how he disappeared?'

'The helicopter that found Marchant reported nobody else in the water. The entire area continues to be searched as we speak, but so far it's as if Dhar never existed.'

Fielding was lying, of course. He had no choice. According to Marchant's debrief, the SVR had arranged for a trawler to be in the area. It had taken it a few minutes to find Dhar, as the plane had fallen short of the agreed ejection zone, but by the time the search-and-rescue helicopter had arrived, Dhar was on the trawler and heading out towards the Irish Sea.

105

Marchant still had a sore back from the Zvezda ejection seat, but otherwise he felt fine as he waited in one of the debriefing rooms for Fielding to return for a second visit. At Marchant's request, the helicopter had taken him to the Fort, MI6's training facility at Gosport, after picking him up from the Bristol Channel. The pilot had initially objected, but it was eventually agreed after some calls had been put through to Whitehall. Marchant had been given a physical check-up, then allowed to rest in one of the old rooms overlooking the sea, where he had studied as a new recruit with Leila.

As Marchant had explained to Fielding, he had thought Dhar was dead when he first spotted him in the water, a hundred yards away. He had released himself from his parachute and swum over to him, dreading what he might find. A dead Dhar suited America, but not Britain. But Dhar was fine, if a little groggy. Marchant had doubted whether the trawler would show up, but a forty-foot vessel registered to St Ives was soon approaching from the south-west.

'For a few moments, I thought I was going to drown,' Dhar had said.

'I know the feeling,' Marchant had replied. When he had first hit the sea and water had filled his nostrils, memories of being waterboarded had come flooding back.

'You know I cannot take you with me,' Dhar said.

'I'm not sure I'm invited,' Marchant replied, glancing at the approaching trawler. They were both shivering, speaking slowly as they trod water. 'Thanks, by the way.'

'For what?'

'For letting me come along. And for not destroying Cheltenham. Will the Russians be happy to see you?'

'No. Georgia's drunken generals will still try to impress America. But it is time for me to move on. Islam is sometimes useful to Russia, but mostly it is a threat.'

'And you never did get to see Tarlton.'

'Next time, perhaps.'

'How will you make contact? The storytellers of Marrakech?'

Dhar smiled at Marchant. 'You know me too well. My taxi is here.'

Marchant swam away as the trawler drew near. He wanted to be at a safe distance in case the SVR had already concluded that he wasn't such a committed defector after all.

'Our father, he would have approved,' Marchant called out, hoping that Dhar could still hear him. 'Family business.'

Now, as he heard someone approaching the debriefing room at Gosport, Marchant was certain that he had turned Dhar. Last time, after India, he had hoped in vain.

It was Fielding who knocked and appeared in the doorway.

'I've brought someone along to see you,' he said, slipping away as Lakshmi Meena entered the room.

'Is your arm OK?' Marchant asked as they embraced. Her wrist was in plaster, and her hug was not quite as warm as his.

'I'm fine. How about you? I went by your flat, brought you some clean clothes.'

'Thanks. Was the door open?' They both smiled. Then she kissed him gently on the lips.

'I found this, too. It had been delivered. I thought it might be important. The rest of your post was just bills.'

She held up a padded envelope, addressed to him in unfamiliar handwriting. Marchant looked at it, then put it on a table to one side.

'How's Spiro?'

'Mad at me for not preventing your so-called defection.'

'Even though I stopped him killing your Defense Secretary and his generals?'

'You still took down a $155-million Raptor. The media lapped that up.'

'I hope they're keeping me out of it.'

'It's been agreed by London and Washington to airbrush you from the story. It was getting kind of hard to explain.'

'But it was a two-seater plane.'

'The media are reporting a bold strike at the West by Salim Dhar and a *jihadi* brother.'

'Half right, at least about the brother.'

'You did well to stop him. I don't suppose you have any idea where he is now?'

'Is that you asking, or Spiro?'

'Most of the Western world.'

Marchant hoped that one day he would be able to tell her that Dhar had been turned, that Britain now had an asset at the heart of the global *jihad*.

'Is his mother safe? Shushma?' At least he could talk to Lakshmi about her.

'She's fine. Spiro handed her over to MI6 when we landed back at Brize Norton. That was always the deal with Fielding. He wants a word with you on his own, by the way. I'll get him.'

'Will you stay after that? Please?'

'Is a graduate of the Farm allowed to stay at the Fort?'

'I'm sure it could be arranged, in the interests of a special relationship.'

Two minutes later, Fielding and Marchant had stepped outside the debriefing room, leaving Lakshmi on her own, and were walking along the perimeter fence that overlooked the sea. A warm wind blew in off the water, lifting strands of Fielding's thinning hair. It was greyer than Marchant remembered.

'You did well,' Fielding said. 'It was a tough call to make about GCHQ, but the right one. Dhar's value has soared on the international *jihadi* markets. The chatrooms were ecstatic after his attempt on the President's life in Delhi. This time they're beside themselves. They never thought someone could strike at the heart of Western intelligence.'

'I gather there were some casualties.'

'I wanted to talk to you about that. While the government's been playing down the damage, our stations abroad are exaggerating it to the foreign media. Well-placed sources are talking about cover-ups, crucial computer networks down for months, morale at GCHQ at an all-time low.'

'And the truth?'

'One death, thirty injuries. Minimal structural damage. But I'm afraid Paul Myers took quite a hit.'

'Is he OK?'

'Conscious, a little confused. He should make a full recovery. He'd been in the central garden, but he was hungry, and was on his way back inside to get something to eat when the bomb struck.'

'Saved by a doughnut.'

They both laughed and walked on, watching the wind whip off the tops of the waves.

'And you're confident that Dhar is ours?' Fielding eventually asked.

'This time I am. We found some common ground.'

'Coastguard located a drifting trawler just off the coast, by the way. Three dead Russians on board, no sign of Dhar.'

Marchant thought back to the sight of Dhar bobbing in the water. Even then, half drowned and semi-conscious, he had been full of confidence.

'If this proves successful, we have your father to thank,' Fielding continued. 'You know we couldn't have done it without him. A long time ago, he realised where the world was heading, and saw in his two sons a possible solution.'

'The old man made some mistakes along the way.'

'Did he?'

'Trusting Hugo Prentice.'

'We all did that.'

'The silly thing is, I miss Hugo, despite everything he did.'

'*For while the treason I detest, the traitor still I love.* Lakshmi's waiting for you. Enjoy your evening. I have a meeting back in London with Denton. If I was a more suspicious man, I might think he was after my job.'

106

Marchant couldn't sleep that night. It wasn't that the Fort's beds were more uncomfortable than he had remembered, or because he was sharing his with Lakshmi. They had made love after dinner in the room in a way that had restored his faith in women. In some ways it had been cathartic to sleep with Lakshmi in the place where he had first done so with Leila, the woman who had so wholly deceived him.

Lakshmi had told him stories of her childhood, and he had opened up about his father and Sebastian in a way he hadn't done for years. The only person he didn't talk about was Dhar.

Now, as he lay there listening to the sea wind rattling the Fort's old leaded windows, his hand on Lakshmi's sleeping thigh, he remembered the package she had brought from his flat. He slipped out of bed, careful not to wake her, and unwrapped it by the moonlight of the window.

His hands turned cold when he saw what was inside. It was the sketch of the nude that had been for sale in Cork Street, number 14, the one that had been used as a signal by Nikolai Primakov. Someone had stuck half a red sticker onto the corner of the glass, like the one that had once denoted that it was under offer and that the meeting with Primakov was on.

Marchant glanced across at Lakshmi, then turned the picture over.

There was some writing on the back giving the gallery details, the price and the artist. He inspected it more closely, and saw that the brown adhesive tape had been slit open and resealed down one side. He reached across for a knife from their dinner, the remains of which had not been cleared from the room, and cut the backing open. Inside was a letter. He slid it out and read.

By the time you read this I will be drinking Bruichladdich and eating grain-fed Nebraskan steak at the great Goodman's in the sky. I suspect there will be no other way to bring you and Salim together. Have no regrets. I don't. Your father was a good man who had faith in both of his remaining sons to do the right thing. He had faith in me too, and I hope I have had the courage to repay it. He saw the future, and in his sons he saw a way forward, an opportunity to stop the conflict. It is up to you now.

What I have to tell you today, as I prepare to leave London for the last time to meet you at Kotlas, is something that I wanted to say in person, but the risks were always too high when we met in London. Moscow Centre has an MI6 asset who helped the SVR expose and eliminate a network of agents in Poland. His codename was Argo, a nostalgic name in the SVR, as it was once used for Ernest Hemingway.

The Polish thought that Argo was Hugo Prentice, a very good friend of your father, and I believe a close confidant of yours. He was shot dead on the orders of the AW, or at least of one of its agents. Hugo Prentice was not Argo.

That mistake was a tragedy, destroying his reputation and damaging your father's. The real Argo is Ian Denton, deputy Chief of MI6. The SVR asked Denton to meet you at the airport on your return from India, but Fielding, by chance, had

*already sent Prentice. Go carefully. Denton's treachery is
destined to extend much further than Poland.*

Marchant put the letter down. His first thought was to ring
Fielding, but there was no knowing if the line was secure. He
went over to the door and checked that it was locked. Then he
walked to the window and glanced around. It was a full harvest
moon, and its reflection stretched out across the water from
the horizon. No one was about, and he knew the Fort was
secure, but old instincts had kicked in. If Denton was working
for Moscow, then no one was safe from the Russians, least of
all him. He had tricked the SVR into a false defection, and
sabotaged Dhar's Russian-sponsored attack on the Georgian
generals.

He put the letter back in its hiding place behind the nude
sketch, and climbed into bed. Suddenly he felt exhausted, more
tired than he had felt for years. Lakshmi was stirring. Marchant
lay there, thinking of Prentice and Primakov, friends of his father,
both of them now dead. Then he turned and hugged Lakshmi,
linking a leg over hers.

'Is everything OK?' she whispered, half asleep.

But he didn't answer. He didn't want to lie any more, not to
her. Instead, he held her head gently between both hands and
kissed her warm lips. Eventually, after they had made love again,
he sat up in bed.

'There's something I need to tell you,' he said, thinking of Dhar,
the burden of running him on his own. He could tell her now.
She wasn't like Leila. Hadn't Fielding said she could be trusted?
Then he thought of Denton, the threat he presented. He could tell
her about him, too, confide his fears. He wasn't sure he could cope
with the loneliness of deceit any more, the isolation of espionage.
He craved companionship, the truth of honest love.

'What is it?' Lakshmi asked. Marchant paused, looking at her lying naked in the moonlight. Then he spoke.

'There was once a king called Shahryar, whose wife was unfaithful to him. He executed her, and from then on he believed that all women were the same, until finally he met a virgin called Scheherazade, who told a thousand and one stories to save her own life.'

'And did he trust her?'

'He did.'

Lakshmi looked at Marchant for a moment, her eyes moistening. 'Was that all you wanted to tell me?'

'That's all.'

ACKNOWLEDGEMENTS

Many thanks to my panel of pilots, Steve Allan, Peter Shellswell, Peter Goodman, Jerry Milsom and Mike Wright. To Andy Tailby for sharing his knowledge of UAVs. To Rob and Mags Hunter, Marilyn Heilman and David Stevenson, who read early proofs. To Jane Bayley at Naturally Morocco and Said Ahmoume, who drove me over the Tizi'n'Test pass in the Atlas mountains, where this story began. To Giuseppe Zara in Sardinia. To Johnnie and all the staff at Visalam in Chettinad, south India. To Mike Strefford for his insights into mobile-phone security. To Ollie Madden and Kevin McCormick at Warner Brothers, and Steve Gaghan. To Sylvie Rabineau at Rabineau Wachter Sanford & Harris. To my agent, Claire Paterson, and Rebecca Folland, Kirsty Gordon and Tim Glister at Janklow & Nesbit. To Patrick Janson-Smith and Laura Deacon at Blue Door, and to my editor, Robert Lacey and Andy Armitage.

I am also grateful to Andrew Stock, Andrea Stock, Stewart and Dinah McLennan, Giles and Karen Whittell, Christina Lamb, Nick Wilkinson, Rob Fern, Justin Morshead, Ann Scott, C. Sujit Chandrakumar, Neil Taylor, Wendy Lewis, Charlotte Doherty, Jessica Kelly, Len Heath, Hayley, Sheri, Andrew and Deki at Karmi Farm, the three Saras and Susan, Chandar Bahadur, and Abdou id Salah. There are other people who have helped with this book but wish to remain anonymous. They know who they are and that I am indebted to them.

Finally, a big thank you to my children, Felix, Maya and Jago, and most of all to Hilary, my wife and muse. أنت قدري.